The Healer of Guildenwood

The Soultrekker Chronicles
Book One

Mary E. Calvert

WestBow Press
A DIVISION OF THOMAS NELSON
& ZONDERVAN

Copyright © 2016 Mary E. Calvert.

All rights reserved. No part of this book may be used or reproduced by any means, graphic, electronic, or mechanical, including photocopying, recording, taping or by any information storage retrieval system without the written permission of the author except in the case of brief quotations embodied in critical articles and reviews.

Scripture quotations are from The Holy Bible, English Standard Version® (ESV®), copyright © 2001 by Crossway, a publishing ministry of Good News Publishers. Used by permission. All rights reserved.

This is a work of fiction. All of the characters, names, incidents, organizations, and dialogue in this novel are either the products of the author's imagination or are used fictitiously.

Map by Mary E. Calvert.

Credit to Shutterstock for author supplied images.

WestBow Press books may be ordered through booksellers or by contacting:

WestBow Press
A Division of Thomas Nelson & Zondervan
1663 Liberty Drive
Bloomington, IN 47403
www.westbowpress.com
1 (866) 928-1240

Because of the dynamic nature of the Internet, any web addresses or links contained in this book may have changed since publication and may no longer be valid. The views expressed in this work are solely those of the author and do not necessarily reflect the views of the publisher, and the publisher hereby disclaims any responsibility for them.

Any people depicted in stock imagery provided by Thinkstock are models, and such images are being used for illustrative purposes only. Certain stock imagery © Thinkstock.

ISBN: 978-1-5127-5158-1 (sc)
ISBN: 978-1-5127-5159-8 (hc)
ISBN: 978-1-5127-5157-4 (e)

Library of Congress Control Number: 2016912529

Print information available on the last page.

WestBow Press rev. date: 09/07/2016

*Dedicated to the memory of my parents,
Earl and Margaret,
who shined the Light on me for over forty years.*

ACKNOWLEDGEMENTS

A huge "thank you" to my editorial "dream team," Marjorie Vawter of The Writer's Tool Editing and Azalea Dabill of Dynamos Press, for your guidance, your encouragement, and for pushing me to make this story the best that it could be. This could not have happened without you.

For my friends and extended family, too numerous to mention, thank you for your encouragement over the many years I talked about "my trilogy" ad nauseam. I'm sure there were moments you thought I was delusional, but I appreciate your indulgence. I'm glad to *finally* be able to share what has been in my head for so long.

To those willing to take the time to read my story and give their stamp of approval, Chrysandra Brunson and Brad Strait, I so appreciate your endorsements!

I am forever grateful to my family for putting up with mounting laundry, late meals, and dusty furniture so that I could get those spurts of inspiration onto my computer's hard drive. Maybe now, Rob, I can learn to iron your shirts the way you like them.

And lastly, I am thankful to God, for taking this young girl's imaginary play world in the basement of her childhood home and helping me transform it into what I still affectionately call "Bensor."

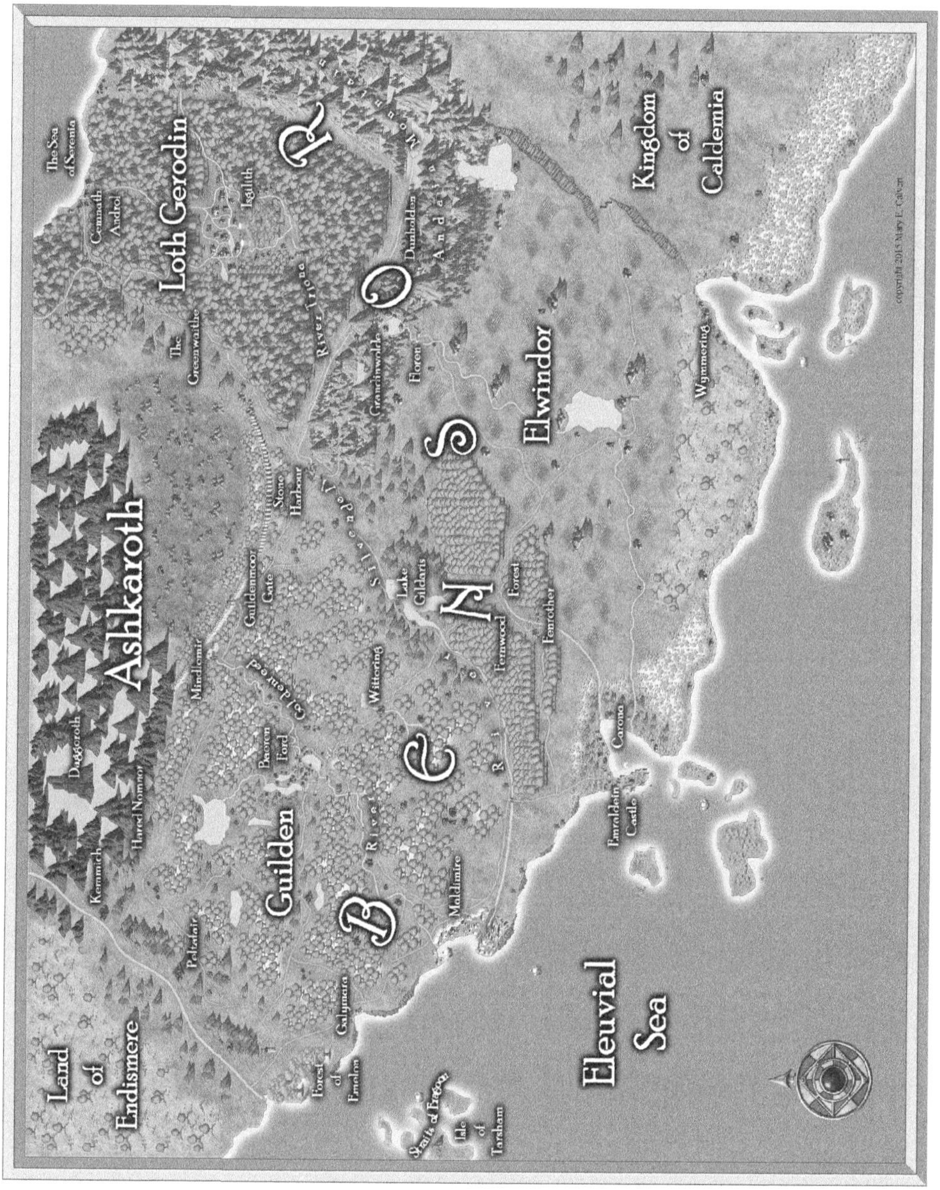
Land of Endismere
Ashkaroth
Loth Gerodin
The Sea of Serenia
The Greenwaithe
Guilden
Elwindor
Kingdom of Caldemia
Eleuvial Sea
Kemmich
Duggoroth
Hared Nomnor
Mindlomir
Guildenmoor Gate
Stone Harbour
River Triona
Dunholden
Floren
Lake Gildarts
Fernwood Forest
Fenrother
Wittering
Baeren Ford
Maldimire
Forest of Emelon
Isle of Tarsham
Emraldein Castle
Carona

For we know that the whole creation has been groaning together in the pains of childbirth until now. And not only the creation, but we ourselves, who have the firstfruits of the Spirit, groan inwardly as we wait eagerly for adoption as sons, the redemption of our bodies.
Romans 8:22–23 ESV

PROLOGUE

December 21

So, there I was, trying my best to live life as a normal adolescent, not making waves and certainly not drawing any unwanted attention to myself. My major concerns could be summed up as follows: making good grades, getting into a good college, and trying to snag a date to prom who did not look, act, or smell like a Neanderthal.

With graduation only six months away, the finish line was in sight. I had almost managed to survive high school without doing anything too bizarre . . . but nothing extraordinary ever happens to people who are not a little weird. And over the course of one night, I became the Queen of Weird.

Waking one morning in late December to find myself, not in my nice, warm bed, but sprinting barefoot through the woods in ankle-deep snow, wearing nothing but a thin nightgown was, without a doubt, bizarre. The biting cold sent a shockwave through my body, yet onward I raced, ignoring the pain and the cold that seared through my awkward flesh.

"Allynon!" I cried out frantically at the silent, ghostly trees emerging through the fuzzy gray dawn.

The path ahead twisted under branches that reached down as if to grab me. Yet nothing would hinder my flight, not even the brambles that clawed at my legs as I passed. I cried out in pain. Still I raced through the quiet, snow-covered landscape, vaguely aware that I was being followed. My heart pounded inside my ears, and the frigid air I sucked in burned my lungs.

"Allynon!" I yelled once more, stumbling when I spied a man with long, dark hair on the path a little ahead. He stood there serenely under the trees with arm outstretched as if he had been waiting for me. Tall and wearing a cloak of brown, the features of his face appeared blurred. But if only I could reach him, I knew I would be safe.

It was the last I saw of him before I hit the ground, sending a cloud of snow in every direction. What foul spell had been cast on me that I had become so slow and clumsy? I looked up in time to see a deer on the pathway where the man had been standing. It startled at my frenetic behavior and bolted through the trees.

Behind me, I could hear footsteps and the sound of voices. I rose to my feet and took off once more, reaching behind me to check for my bow and quiver only to grasp vainly at the air. Desperately, I grabbed for my sword and found it missing as well. Whoever was pursuing me, I could not outrun them for long, barefoot as I was. Nor could I hide without my tracks betraying me. My only hope was to engage them in hand-to-hand combat.

I pivoted my body and planted my numb feet into the snow, fists poised to strike a blow. "Halt! Make yourself known lest you wish to know my wrath!" I felt vulnerable and poorly equipped to defend myself, but I hoped my forceful words would be enough to give pause to my pursuers.

"Margaret Ann!"

Margaret Ann. The sound of that name rang with familiarity, like putting on an old, forgotten pair of shoes and discovering that they still fit perfectly.

Two people emerged on the path from the direction I had come. A middle-aged man and woman, both dressed in robes and wearing shoes not the least bit suitable for wintry conditions. I tensed as they approached, yet their manner was not threatening. On the contrary, they stared as though frightened of *me.*

I saw the man's slightly graying hair and the way the woman's wiry spectacles sat astride her distinctively bony nose. Recognition set in, and I felt my muscles relax as I stared at them, hardly believing my eyes.

"Mother! Father! How many long ages have passed since last I saw you?" I ran to them, falling into their arms as tears of joy streamed down my face. "How I have missed you!"

"But, honey, you just saw us last night." My father's voice was rough.

"Last night," I repeated as if in a trance. Had it really only been eight hours or so? It seemed like ages ago.

My father touched me on my hand. "Don't you remember the Christmas dance at the community center? How Brent Jamison virtually ignored you all evening? How you came home early?"

The look on my face must have been blank. "Father, what day is it?" I asked at last.

"Why, Saturday, December twenty-first."

The winter solstice.

My heart still pounded as if I had yet to convince myself I was in no danger. I glanced at the lofty, bone-like boughs above that disappeared into the pale gray sky beyond. "Where are we?"

Father rubbed the back of his neck. "I was letting Sidney in from his morning walk when you came bursting out the basement door and went running across the lawn and into the woods."

"Margaret Ann, you're not one to walk in your sleep," my mother commented, still trying to catch her breath. "But you looked as if you were in a trance. Did you have a bad dream?"

Dream? *This* was the dream.

I searched my memory. Faint visions flickered there, all disappearing before I found anything to latch onto. "It would seem my dreams *were* plagued, but as is their nature, they have fallen beyond the precipice of conscious memory."

"And you were shouting. But the words you spoke . . . it was garbled, like you were talking in a different language."

"And you kept saying something about Alcoholics Anonymous," my mother interrupted. "Alanon, to be exact."

At the mere mention of that word, tears welled in my eyes once more, and I trembled with an overwhelming sense of sorrow that came from nowhere. I fumbled for my handkerchief, but it wasn't to be found.

"*What* in the world is the matter?"

"Oh, Father, I know not!"

"You don't sound at all like yourself."

"Come on," my mother urged. "It's freezing out here, and we'll all catch our death in this cold."

"But I must find him!" I insisted.

"*Him?*" I could hear the distress in my mother's voice even as my father's brow contorted into a frown. "*Who* in the world are you talking about?"

Shivering, I glanced behind me at the spot where the man had been, but we were all alone. My father removed his robe and placed it around my shoulders before they led me back down the path through the trees, where I saw a brick house sitting in an open area on the edge of the woods. Hastily we walked across the frozen lawn, entering the structure through a door in the back that had been left slightly ajar.

"I hope this sleepwalking doesn't become a habit," my father murmured as he held the door open for me.

It seemed we were in some sort of cellar, though in the darkness I saw no wine casks or sacks filled with provisions for the winter. "Would that there was a lantern, but none I see."

My father reached around me and flipped a switch on the wall. Immediately the area was bathed in light, illuminating the perplexity written all over his face. "Welcome to the twenty-first century," he said with a nervous chuckle. "Maybe you should think about joining us here." He was trying to make light of the situation, but I knew he found me baffling.

Confused, I stared a moment at the source of the light on the ceiling above then made my way up a flight of stairs, holding tightly to the banister all the way as my legs shook clumsily. At the top, I entered a small but inviting parlor of sorts, filled with a settee and chair covered in the most ample upholstery I had ever seen.

My mother directed me to the settee. My knee collided awkwardly with a table that sat before it, causing me to wince in pain. I fell onto the settee, sinking into the soft, plush cushion where she wrapped me in a blanket. She then reached over to a box on the table in front of the settee and gave to me the piece of paper she drew from it—or was it a finely woven cloth? The texture was neither. I gripped it in my fingers for a few moments before raising it to my face. It absorbed my tears better than the finest handkerchief, and I felt comforted.

My mother crossed her arms, eyeing me warily and, seeing that I had calmed, joined my father in what appeared to be the kitchen, based on the table that sat in its midst. No hearth or kettle I saw. There, they kept looking at me every few moments and muttering to each other words I could not make out. I gave my head two swift shakes, wondering if the cold had somehow affected my hearing.

As warmth returned to my limbs, I stared at my surroundings, at once so familiar and yet so foreign. I heard an odd gurgling sound coming from the kitchen, and in a few moments the area was permeated with a pungent, yet strangely comforting aroma that enticed me from my spot on the settee.

"You need some hot food in your stomach," Mother said when I approached. "Er, how about some oatmeal?"

I nodded uncertainly as I stared at the kitchen cupboards. My father blew his nose, and I wondered if he had a cold.

My mother went to the cupboard, pulled out a paper pouch, and handed it to me. I knew nothing but to stare at it in puzzlement. What was this? "There's milk in the refrigerator," she said, handing me a bowl.

"And the oatmeal?"

"Why, it's in the pouch." A strange expression rested on her face, like she was stumped.

I tore into the pouch, sending a spray of brownish powder flying all over the kitchen counter. "Pray forgive my awkward manner," I apologized, feeling the blood rise to my face.

"Maybe I'd better take care of it," Mother muttered, carefully tearing open another pouch and pouring the brown flakes into the bowl. She then added milk poured from an oddly shaped, slightly transparent vessel and mixed it with the dry, flaky bits. "Why don't you heat it in the microwave?"

I'm certain my face showed nothing but confusion, until I followed my mother's gaze to the box-like contraption sitting on the counter. Taking the bowl, I walked over and stood there for a minute, studying the thing intently, not exactly certain what to do next. Slowly I lifted my finger to a button and pushed. The door sprang open, and I jumped, slopping the contents of the bowl down the front of my nightgown. Dismayed, I let out a faint shriek.

My father dropped the thick stack of paper he'd been gazing at on the table. "Honey, what's going on? Something isn't right."

"Of that I am most certain, Father. Your manner of speech is quaint, but do you not think it rather, er, coarse?"

"*My* manner of speech . . . ? And what is this 'father' business? You've never referred to me like that before." His alarm sharpened his voice, but I was sure he wasn't angry. "Is this some sort of joke, I hope?"

I could feel my lip begin to quiver as a hot tear fell down my cheek. I stepped closer to the table, brushing at the sticky goo on the front of my nightgown. "No, Father, I swear it is not so!"

"Then what has happened to my daughter?" he demanded. "Why did you go darting off into the snow in your bare feet? And why do you sound like you've just stepped out of the Middle Ages?"

"And you seem to be having a hard time remembering things, simple things," my mother added.

"It's that Brent character, isn't it? He really upset you last night, didn't he?" It took a lot to get my father angry, but I could detect a glimmer of agitation in his eyes. "I ought to have a word with that young man."

I reached out to touch his arm. "Please, it matters not in the least. Hardly does the name 'Brent' hold any meaning for me, no matter what may have come to pass prior to this day. I am quite certain it is at present nothing to me."

"William, whatever it is, I'm sure it will pass." I know she wanted to be hopeful, but Mother's quivering voice gave away her true feelings.

Father sighed, sinking back into his chair. "Let's hope so. With the Christmas season upon us and me with a cold right before I have to deliver a sermon tomorrow, I don't need anything else to worry about."

"Slippery elm."

They stared at me with their heads cocked to the side. "I beg your pardon?" my father said.

"The bark of slippery elm is restorative to those suffering from respiratory conditions," I explained. "I could go into the woods and attempt to find such a tree. Although, 'twould take several hours to soak and grind into powder."

He shivered slightly. "I'm not too keen on ingesting tree bark."

"Indeed. Perhaps you would be more inclined to ingest hyssop tea, which would have the same effect. Of course, I would also recommend a steaming bath in lavender, and perhaps I could prepare a balm of thyme to relieve your congestion."

Mother stared at me, openmouthed. "I didn't know you'd been studying medicinal herbs."

Had I? Another memory stirred but vanished before I could latch hold of it. "Nor did I."

My father scratched his head. "Tell me, what should I do about my athlete's foot?"

I didn't hesitate. "Mix garlic in a jar with calendula petals, comfrey root, and vinegar. Store the mixture in a dark place for a fortnight, and then prepare a tincture for the affected area."

I could see mother eyeing me suspiciously from the corner of her eye. "There's something about you. You seem somehow older, more knowing." She suddenly gasped. "You've been with a man!"

An image of the man in the forest flashed through my mind, only to vanish before I could grab hold of it. My reticence, it seemed, must have upset my father, for I saw the veins bulging in his neck. "Nay! It is not so!" Certainly I would remember something like *that*.

But it was too late. "That would explain it." Hardly had I ever seen my father so angry. But then again, he had always been very protective of me, especially after we lost my brother. "Not only did that Brent Jamison violate her body, but he messed up her mind as well."

"'Tis not true!" I protested, and then fell silent for a moment as another thought popped into my head. "Regina Elaine Lord!"

"You mean Reggie?"

"She will verify my account."

"Thank goodness you remember *something*."

"Speaking of Reggie, you are in no mental condition to go horseback riding with her this morning." My mother's countenance left no room for argument. "You'll have to let her know that you won't be joining her."

"Then send for her immediately!" The words tumbled from my mouth with an air of command.

"Er, why not just give her a call?" my father said, handing me a sleek black object small enough that I could hold it in my hand. I gasped when I saw an image spring to life on its shiny surface, the image of two miniature versions of my parents staring back at me. And with them was a young woman who looked vaguely familiar—until I realized that the young woman was . . . me. It was so mesmerizing I could hardly take my eyes off it.

I suppose it was obvious I had no clue what to do. With a sigh, my father took the thing back and magically conjured something akin to vibrant, gleaming star stones with a slight touch of his finger. "Here," he said as he placed it back in my hand with a perplexed huff. I marvelled at the object in my hand. It was enchanting. And then I heard a voice coming from within!

"Hello?"

I knew that star stones could sing, but I had never known them to speak. Tears of joy and wonder flowed from my eyes. "Greetings! How honored am I that you should speak!" I exclaimed emotionally, practically trembling with excitement. My father's face twisted as he guided my hand to place the thing next to my ear.

"Margaret Ann, is that you?"

"Er, yes," I replied tentatively. "And who might you be?"

"Didn't you just call me? It's Reggie!"

My heart sank as it occurred to me what I had already suspected—I had come to a frustratingly familiar, cold, dark place that seemed completely devoid of anything magical. "Er, Regina Elaine Lord?"

"Yep, that's me. Why so formal?"

Was I? Had I not spoken normally? Not exactly certain how to respond, I chose to remain silent.

"You coming over soon?"

"It grieves me that I shall be unable to accompany you this morning as we had apparently agreed upon hitherto."

"What?" The voice on the other end sounded more than a little concerned. "Did you just step off the *Mayflower*?" Mayflower? Why would one step on a flower? I decided to ignore that statement, too. "Perchance could you verify to my parents that I have as yet not been violated in body? They seem misinformed concerning my virtue."

"*What* are you talking about?"

"My virtue. It seems my parents believe some present difficulties I am experiencing have arisen from a lack thereof."

"Oh, you mean *that*?" I could hear Reggie chuckling on the other end. "M.A., you're as pure as the driven snow. In fact, I can count on one hand the number of boys you've ever kissed."

"Then I am absolved."

"What has happened to you? I mean, you were perfectly normal when I saw you last night." There was a pause at the other end. "Well, on the other hand, you *were* acting a little odd yesterday."

What could that mean? I searched my memory but had little recollection of the previous day. "Do forgive my eccentricities."

"Actually, I think it's kinda cool . . . that is, in a weird sort of way."

Cool? Weird? "I must admit that I've not been myself, though for what reason I know not."

"Say no more!" Reggie exclaimed. "I'm coming right over."

I stared at the now-silent speaking box until I noticed my parents sitting at the breakfast table, glancing at me uncertainly.

My mother turned her gaze to the view outside the kitchen window. "Er, looks like it's starting to snow again." She stood to peer closer, her lips pursed with annoyance. "And it looks like the rabbits are back."

My father followed her gaze. "There will be a lot more by this summer, and all of them devouring our garden."

Ah, a chance to be helpful, to get their minds off my seeming affliction. "Might we have a bow and arrow? I could kill them, skin them, and have them roasting in the fireplace straightaway."

Immediately my mother turned from the window and stared. "Margaret Ann, you're scaring me!"

Feeling the tears well in my eyes once more, I left the kitchen and headed up to my room, tripping on the stairs as I went. Why was I so clumsy? At the top of the staircase, I turned and strained to hear my parents' conversation. Why was it so difficult to hear?

"Peg, what were you thinking?" I could barely make out my father's words. "I know you are very intuitive, but you should know Margaret Ann better than to accuse her of something like *that*."

"William, there's something different about our daughter, and I don't mean the sleepwalking or the way she talks or how clumsy she has become. There's something about her that reminds me of the immigrant kids I work with at the shelter—like someone who has witnessed too much for her tender years. It's . . . it's like she became a woman overnight, *literally* overnight."

"Well, I surely would like to know who she was going to meet in the woods at the break of dawn," Dad added.

"Right! And what on earth does he have to do with Alcoholics Anonymous?"

Silence. "Maybe she's having some sort of delayed grief reaction." My father's voice cracked.

"But that was five years ago, and she's been through counseling. Isn't that why she took up martial arts, because our therapist said she needed an outlet for her grief after . . . after Will died? And up until this morning, I thought it had worked."

"No, this seems to be something different," my father said, no doubt staring into space while rubbing his chin pensively as he often did whenever he felt perplexed. "Well, I'm going to get to the bottom of it."

I heard the sound of my father's footsteps across the wood floor in the kitchen, and I shrank back against the wall.

"What are you doing?"

"Looking for a good therapist." Next came a curious clicking sound that lasted for several seconds. "Ah . . . Dr. Susan Renfroe . . . specializing in trauma, depression, and memory retrieval."

"But, William, do you really think she needs psychotherapy?"

"If this *phase* doesn't go away by the time school starts back in January, then it'll be like throwing her to the lions. You know how kids are. Besides, don't you want to know why she's acting so strangely?"

I could bear this talk no longer! Indignantly, I turned and continued up the staircase when I had the sudden urge to relieve myself. Bother! I would no doubt have to venture outside to the privy as this quaint cottage would certainly have no indoor plumbing. Then I passed by a small, narrow room where I spied a porcelain-like bowl on a stool and knew exactly its function. And I had to admit that the perfectly wound roll of cloth-like paper that sat next to the chair was quite satisfactory. Even the manner of disposal, once I discovered the magic lever, was not the least barbaric.

As I turned to leave, I froze when I spied myself in a looking glass. Because it wasn't me. Only it was me, with bluish eyes, matted, shoulder-length brown hair that had streaks of blond throughout, and what was this? An ugly red bump on the tip of my chin? Why, I had become a . . . a teenager!

Oh, the cruelty!

Unable to bear the sight of myself a moment longer, I hurried back into my room and shut the door, tears streaming down my face. On my disheveled bed lay our Pomeranian, Sidney, curled up and looking like a big ball of fur. It felt so good to see him and to bury my face in his soft fur, for it also seemed ages since I had done either.

"Oh, Sidney, they think I've gone mad," I sniffled. "And what's more . . . I think perhaps they're right!" For a long moment I gazed upon my bedchamber. The furnishings did not look familiar—the books, the desk, the bed—as if I didn't really belong here.

Then my gaze landed upon a picture of my grandmother, and I remembered the gift she had given me on my sixteenth birthday—an antique amethyst ring with a square purple stone surrounded by two small diamonds on either side. On the inside of the ornate band was engraved my grandmother's nickname, known only to the family, as was the date of her birth. I'd vowed never to remove it from my finger. And I hadn't. It was the last thing I had seen when I turned out my bedside lamp the night before.

But it was gone.

Frantically, I shot up and tore the bedsheets off my bed, sending Sidney scrambling to the floor to escape the carnage. I searched high and low for a long while, but still the ring was nowhere.

Surrendering at last to the apparent fruitlessness of my search, I collapsed upon my bed once more, tears welling at this latest mystery and the fear that I had indeed gone completely stark raving mad.

"Get a hold of yourself, Ar . . . Margaret Ann," I chastised, attempting to rationalize this whole situation. "Nay, *I* am acting perfectly normal. It is everything else that is amiss."

For an instant, a deep longing ached in my heart for someone, or perhaps something. Why couldn't I remember? And why did this void in my memory feel all too familiar, as though this was not the first time I had felt such disorientation? As I clutched a pillow between my arms, I suddenly felt very, very alone.

Had I known then what I know now—that this type of amnesia is just one of the pesky side effects of getting my soul ripped from my body—well, perhaps I would have been spared the fear that I had lost my mind, at least. But it would have done nothing to diminish the aloneness of being a soultrekker.

A *soultrekker*? you ask. Well, we are quite a rare breed. In fact, I know of only one other, but certainly there are more. And so I shall tell the tale of my adventures as one whose soul has left its body to travel to worlds unknown for a time . . . and for a purpose greater than I could have ever imagined.

And perhaps, for any other soultrekker out there who chances upon my account, you will know that you are not alone.

CHAPTER 1

June, six months later, when memories of the day before my weirdness started came flooding back

---

A "therapeutic impasse," she called it. Six months into therapy and Dr. Susan still could find no explanation for my "eccentricities." Only two things were certain: a) I was not psychotic, and b) I was not suffering from multiple personalities. Despite my sudden formality and refined mannerisms, my overall personality had remained intact. And Reggie had seen to it that I was learning once more to be a "normal" teenager (whatever that means).

However, there were moments when my mind would drift off during our sessions together, as if some part of my subconscious was longing for . . . something. And a tinge of sadness always seemed to accompany the longing.

The previous six months had been a challenge, especially having to endure the whispers and laughter of my peers as I walked through the corridors at school. It felt so foreign to be laughed at, the source of derision . . . especially to ears that seemed to be ringing with echoes of praise and adoration.

And then there were those unexplainable moments, like when I went on a family outing to one of those Renaissance-style fairs and decided to try my luck, for the first time it would seem, with bow and arrow. It felt so natural to hold the bow in my hands, to nock the arrow between my fingers and to let it fly, watching as it pierced the center of the target with deadly precision. I'd not felt so exhilarated in a long while. My parents, well, their mouths were agape, especially as I let more arrows fly one after another, each coming within an inch of the center.

There I sat in the waiting room of Dr. Susan's office, pondering the strangeness of the previous six months and questioning for the thousandth time what had brought on such oddity. Nervously I wondered what the next couple of hours would uncover, if anything. The start of college was little more than two months away. Traditional therapy had failed—desperate measures were called for. And that meant Dr. Susan would be inducing me into a "relaxed state of consciousness" as she called it, something that would hopefully help those buried memories of the night of December twentieth surface more readily.

Not that there hadn't been some breakthroughs along the way. Why, just the week before, memories of the day preceding the morning I awoke in my altered "state" had come flooding back to me. And I must admit, I was not exactly forthcoming with Dr. Susan concerning *all* that I remembered, or she would have perhaps reconsidered her assessment that I was not psychotic. For it was on that day that I heard the "voice," albeit for the first and the last time.

It all began that morning in Advanced Composition. It was the last day of school before Christmas vacation, and we were taking a break from our studies for a little refreshment of popcorn and cookies. I was sitting there minding my own business and listening to Mr. Byrd casually question us about our plans for the following year when I heard a voice, a female voice. She said, *"I've been watching you for a long time, Margaret Ann."* It was a cheerful sound, one that reminded me of windchimes ringing in a gentle breeze. Nothing scary—and yet it terrified me.

I jerked around and eyed the young man sitting in the far corner of the classroom—Mark Malkovich. Certainly *he* would have every reason to want to see me squirm. Why, it had only been the previous day that I had come upon him terrorizing poor, geeky Harvey Gustafson in the parking lot after school. All it took was the reminder of how I had belted him with one of my Tae Kwon Do moves only weeks before for him to slither away, coward that he was. Apparently, he had not been aware of my martial arts black belt or of my disdain for groping hands. Or of my overactive sense of justice for the weak and nerdy. Yet there Mark sat with his head on his desk, snake-like eyes closed as drool ran down his cheek, collecting on a notebook that lay beneath.

So perhaps Mark Malkovich was innocent—this time. But there was more than one suspect in Advanced Comp who would've liked me to believe I'd lost my mind and was hearing voices.

I glanced across at Blair Bassett, my archnemesis since junior high, who was sitting with her gaze turned upward in a state of perpetual boredom.

"Did you say something?" I whispered.

Blair simply curled her upper lip as if she smelled something putrid. "Hearing things, Margaret Ann? Maybe you should go see a psychiatrist."

"And what are Miss Shepherd's plans for next year?" Mr. Byrd questioned, saving me from having to come up with some witty retort.

"Um . . . well," I stammered, trying desperately to collect my thoughts. "I'm trying to decide between Allerton and Glenhaven."

"Accepted at both?"

"Yes, sir."
"Scholarships?"
"Um-hmm."
"And what course of study do you intend to pursue?"
"Psychology."

Mr. Byrd peered at me over a pair of reading glasses that sat precariously on the tip of his nose. "And what do you intend to do with *that*?"

I liked Mr. Byrd, so I didn't mind so much this bantering back and forth. "Well, I want to figure out what makes people tick and then fix it when they're broken."

"Ah, youthful idealism." Mr. Byrd chuckled as he took a slurp from his ever-present coffee mug. "You all want to change the world."

"And you will, my love." I bolted upright in my seat and froze, hardly daring to look around. There it was again—ghost, hallucination, someone playing a cruel joke—take your pick!

Grimacing, I shook my head and glanced at the speaker on the wall. Ah, perhaps there was a problem with the intercom system. But if that were the case, then why did no one else hear what I heard?

Suddenly, a kernel of popcorn landed on my shoulder and cascaded down into my lap, and I nearly jumped out of my skin. I turned around and was relieved to see the culprit sitting there with eyes glued to the ceiling, fingers twiddling feverishly—a dead giveaway—Harvey Gustafson, himself. He had been enamored of me since the eighth grade. Ahh, Harvey, of course! Mystery solved! But really, this sort of behavior was just a tad creepy, even for him.

My first inclination was annoyance, but then I felt the features of my face soften as I saw him pining away like a puppy dog. I could not bear to shatter his ego so close to Christmas with no opportunity to make amends until January.

"My Christmas present, Harv?" I gave him a patronizing smile. *"Really,* you shouldn't have."

Harvey guffawed annoyingly, like a pig on No-Doze, as the color rose in his cheeks. If only he were Brent Jamison. Alas, he was not, and encouraging Harvey was something I had to nip in the bud right away.

But as gently as possible. I could never allow myself to be unkind to one so frustratingly naive, or to hardly anyone else for that matter.

"Such purity of heart is rare."

"Okay! Who said that?" I blurted.

Everyone in Mr. Byrd's class turned to stare at me as if I had just grown a second head.

"Are you all right, Margaret Ann?" Mr. Byrd asked.

"Just losing my mind is all." I laughed weakly, shrinking down into my seat in hopes of disappearing altogether.

As if to save me from greater humiliation, the bell rang, and I could only hope that my outburst would be forgotten by January. Quickly I gathered my belongings and darted to my final class of the day.

An hour later, with nostrils still burning of rubbing alcohol from the mannequin I had just saved in my CPR class, I slammed my locker shut, glad that for the previous hour I had not experienced anything at all supernatural.

"It's party time!" a voice called from behind. For a moment I was startled and then realized that *this* voice was all too familiar . . . and real.

I turned to see Reggie standing behind me, her signature blond hair tousled about her face. Such blond hair couldn't be natural, but she swore it didn't come from a bottle. "*Hola, amiga!*"

"You have *got* to give me a ride home today," Reggie pleaded. "If I have to listen to another belching contest by those middle-school morons all the way home, then you'll have to visit me in prison, because I won't be responsible for my actions."

"No problem. I'm going in that direction anyway. It's my week to volunteer at Fair Haven."

"What a lifesaver!" Reggie exclaimed. "I owe my freedom to you."

The two of us followed the stampede toward the front doors of the high school.

"Don't look now, Margaret Ann, but I see Brent up ahead and he's looking right at you."

My knees immediately turned to the consistency of Jell-O. Nervously I flipped my hair out of my face, all the while trying to keep my eyes fixated on anything but the object of my affection. Feigning a deep conversation with Reggie, my heart pounded the closer we came to where he leaned against a locker.

"Hi, Margaret Ann," Brent greeted cheerfully as he moved in to walk beside me. He could be so friendly at times, yet so shy. The paradox was often quite perplexing.

"Oh, hi, Brent," I replied, trying to not appear overly eager. "Are you so-o-o ready for a break?"

"Of course! No Mr. Casey's calculus for two weeks is enough to celebrate!" he said, flashing me a boyish grin framed by a tangle of wavy dark hair that fell daringly to just below his jawline—a regular maverick. It was enough to make a girl swoon. "Hey, you goin' to the Christmas dance tonight at the community center?"

I paused for a moment. It was good for a woman to be a little mysterious. "Well, probably."

"Cool! Save me a dance?"

"If you're lucky!" I teased.

"Great. See ya then." And with that, he walked away.

My face was burning as I turned to Reggie, who looked not at all pleased.

"So what am I, chopped liver?" she complained.

"He looked nervous," I rationalized. "It's like he likes me, but he can't seem to work up the nerve to ask me out on a date. What's up with that?"

"Maybe he's extremely shy. Or a slow mover. Maybe he's afraid of rejection," Reggie offered. "Wait, I know . . . maybe he's afraid of an inquisition by the Reverend Shepherd."

"Well, I'm getting tired of waiting!" I sighed. "Someday I hope to meet a man who knows he wants me, someone who would go to the ends of the earth to be by my side." Someone who actually possessed a backbone.

"Well, you probably won't find a man like that in this town."

"Scores of men will fall at your feet, but be wary, my child, until you find the one whose heart is true."

There it was again! Glancing over my shoulder, I practically bolted out to the parking lot.

"Margaret Ann, wait!" Reggie called as she struggled to keep up. "What's gotten into you?"

"Nothing," I snapped. "Nothing at all."

Up ahead, Blair Bassett and two other cheerleader-types loitered around a red sports car, a cloud of smoke swirling above their heads. The ringleader stared at the two of us with a pained expression that made her look as if she were experiencing bad gas. "Watch out, here comes Miss Goody Two-Shoes and her sidekick," she said, loud enough for us to hear. "On the way to the loony bin, where you belong?"

"Does Blair Bassett really think we care what she does with her lungs?" Reggie muttered.

I remained quiet, ignoring her sneers. It wasn't always easy to live in such a small town and to be known by everyone as the daughter of Reverend William Shepherd. It seemed there were those who regarded me with suspicion, believing that I somehow had the power to call down fire and brimstone on those I came upon doing something they shouldn't. And then there were some who were downright mean about it. All I wanted was to be treated like everyone else, to blend in.

"Well, aren't you going to say anything back?" Reggie protested.

I shrugged. "Why should I feed into her petty little game?"

There were certain battles I knew weren't worth fighting. And there were some that were. And, frankly, I wasn't in the mood. All I wanted was to get away from school and those blasted voices as fast as I could.

I drove the old family sedan out of the high school parking lot and rambled down the road before nearing the train tracks that ran straight through downtown. The clanging of bells signaled an approaching train.

"Darn it!" I exclaimed, looking at the clock on the dashboard. "Stupid 3:20 train! If I'd only been two minutes earlier!"

"I know how we can pass the time," Reggie offered while unzipping her backpack. After a moment of fumbling around, she retrieved a newspaper she had stuck between two notebooks. "I snagged the entertainment section from the newspaper in the library."

"Um, isn't that called 'stealing'?"

"I call it 'borrowing,' thank you," Reggie retorted. "Anyway, I thought we could read our horoscopes, you know, and see what the future holds."

"A bunch of rubbish!" I groaned. "But, hey, I'll humor you."

"Yeah, I know, astrological mumbo jumbo," she mumbled as she thumbed through the pages. "Ah, here we are . . . hey, here's mine . . . 'Choose your investments wisely. There is opportunity to achieve financial security.'"

I couldn't help but snicker. "Some fortune, for someone who hasn't even had a real job yet."

"Laugh if you will, but this is serious stuff." Reggie's voice was full of indignation. "Hey, you're a Gemini, right?"

"Just barely. I'd be a Cancer had I been born one day later."

"I know, I know . . . how you were born on summer's eve . . . how romantic. You sound like a feminine hygiene commercial," Reggie muttered sardonically. "Hey, check this out—'Your life will soon change in a very unexpected and extraordinary way.' Hmm, I wonder what that could mean?"

"Right," I said, my voice dripping with sarcasm. "Like the stars can *really* determine my destiny."

The last of the train slipped past the railroad-crossing gate.

"In your case, Margaret Ann, beyond your wildest dreams."

"Who are you?" I yelled. Where *was* that voice coming from?

"*What* is the matter?" Reggie had one hand on the passenger door handle. "You're scaring me!"

Scaring her? She wasn't the one hearing voices.

A horn from the line of cars behind us sounded, and I saw that the crossing gate had gone up. I floored the gas pedal, jarring the car as it raced over the tracks.

"Sorry, I'm just a little freaked out," I murmured. How could I tell anyone, even my best friend, that I'd been hearing voices all day? That I'd apparently developed a sudden case of schizophrenia?

"Why?"

"Never mind. It's nothing." But it *was* something. And I wished desperately that someone else could hear the voice, too. But then all that would prove was that there were two of us going crazy, not just one—me.

Saying very little other than a few "Yeahs" and "Uh-huhs" during the remainder of the ride, I couldn't shake my thoughts as I pulled into Reggie's driveway.

"Are you still going to give me a ride to the dance tonight?" Reggie looked uncertain as she climbed out of the car.

"Yes, I'll be here at seven thirty," I promised. That is, barring a nervous breakdown.

As I drove away, all the pent-up confusion of the day came tumbling out. "I am Margaret Ann Shepherd, born seventeen and a half years ago, and I am not, repeat, *not* crazy!"

Turning up the radio to ward off any other unwanted commentary from THE VOICE, I sang at the top of my lungs until I reached the Fair Haven Nursing Home where I volunteered every other Friday afternoon. And I must admit that memory of my time there remains sketchy to this day. However, certain images stand out in my mind of that particular visit. Like, being handed a Santa hat by the nursing home director as she told me I was going to play Santa's elf for the residents' Christmas party that afternoon. I remember asking if she had any pointy ears to go along with the hat, to which she replied, "Not to be the kind of elf that you're going to be." We were both joking, but now such banter strikes me as extremely ironic.

The other moment that stands out in my memory of my visit to Fair Haven was slipping away from the party for a while to visit with Mrs. Tudor in her room. Now, I know I shouldn't have had a favorite resident, but Mrs. Tudor with her bright pink lipstick and feisty spirit had always touched my heart. She had been one of the few people who did not think me absolutely mad after my weirdness began. In fact, she thought my manner of speech rather delightful!

"How you have changed from the shy girl who used to come to the home," Mrs. Tudor said, taking my hand in hers before it was time for me to leave that afternoon. "What a strong young woman you have become, a young woman who has brought life to me during your visits . . . a young woman destined for greatness."

"Thank you, Mrs. Tudor," I whispered with tears in my eyes, truly humbled to hear such comforting words after all the strange events of the day.

But no sooner did I begin to feel comforted when the "voice" had to put in its two cents, and I heard it say something like, *"The heart of a ruler is the heart of a healer."* What could that possibly mean?

I gulped suddenly to stifle a scream. "Did . . . did you hear that?"

Mrs. Tudor looked a bit confused. "No, but then my hearing is not what it used to be."

"I'm sure it's nothing . . . nothing at all." I gave the elderly woman a weak smile and then turned hurriedly toward the door. "Merry Christmas, Mrs. Tudor. See you in two weeks."

I quickened my pace toward the front entrance where the director was filling out paperwork at the nurses' station. She looked up as I approached. "Did you have a nice visit with Mrs. Tudor?"

"Enlightening as always," I quipped as I hurried past.

"Merry Christmas to you, Margaret Ann."

"Yes, you too." By now I was halfway out the front door.

"And tell Reverend Shepherd I'll have one of my pecan pies waiting for him when he drops by next week," she called.

"Thanks, I'll tell him," I yelled over my shoulder.

I pulled my jacket close against the evening chill and climbed into my car. The sun of this world had already slid down behind the foothills, stark naked trees looming black against the red backdrop.

I turned the key in the ignition and backed out of the parking place, mumbling to myself. "Okay, hallucination . . . ghost . . . whoever you are, would you *please* stop picking on me? You don't even make sense," I pleaded. "I mean, really, 'The heart of a ruler is the heart of a healer.' What's that supposed to mean? And 'Scores of men will fall at my feet to profess their love'? Well, I kinda like that idea, but . . . wait! What am I saying? A hallucination giving me advice on love? This is insane!"

With that I floored the gas, and within ten minutes I pulled into my driveway, all without further commentary from my imaginary "friend."

The next thing I remembered was dinner. My mother was dishing out Chinese food from a cardboard container when I entered the kitchen.

"So, how was your last day of school for two weeks?"

"A little weird, but okay." How could I possibly tell her I'd been experiencing hallucinations all day? At my feet Sidney danced around, quivering with anticipation until I scooped him up into my arms.

"Honey, could you help your mom tomorrow?" my dad chimed in from the refrigerator.

I placed Sidney on the floor so I could help set the table, and I'm sure my expression turned to one of disappointment. "Well, Dad, Reggie and I had talked about going horseback riding tomorrow at her uncle's farm."

"Horseback riding, now that's something I haven't done for a while," my mom said. "Maybe one of these days I can tag along?"

"Sure. That would be cool, I guess."

"My daughter, the closet adventurer." Dad chuckled. "Just like her mother."

"But with your grandparents arriving in a few days, I need your help to wrap presents tomorrow night while your father and I are at the Kelley's annual Christmas party."

"But, Mom, I may have other plans." I still hoped that a romantic encounter with Brent at the dance later that evening would finally result in a request for a date.

"What other plans?"

"Well . . ."

"Still hanging on to the notion that this Brent character is going to show you some attention?" my father piped in. "If he were half a man, he'd stop leading you on."

"Bill, he's only a boy."

"Young lady," he continued, much to my dismay, "you need to stop wasting your time pining away for someone who can't seem to make up his mind what he wants. He's not worthy of you, my dear."

"But, Dad, if you only knew how nice he really is," I contended, beginning to feel the blood rush to my face.

"They raised you as I would have."

"And you just *have* to put in *your* two cents, don't you!" I blurted out, eyes searching the ceiling above.

Both my parents looked up from what they were doing in astonishment.

"No, no, not *you*!" I exclaimed. "I'm just . . . I'm just . . . being hormonal." Dad wouldn't want to touch that one with a ten-foot pole.

"C'mon, dinner's getting cold," Mom said as she placed a carton of steamed rice on the table. "I'm sorry, but between the Garden Club Christmas luncheon and the grocery shopping, I didn't have time to make dinner. So, I hope you like moo goo gai pan."

"That's cool." My voice was shaky.

We sat down to dinner at the kitchen table where one chair stood empty and silent, a cruel reminder of its past occupant. My mind raced back to that day over five years before. I had been so angry at my big brother over something so miniscule that I had no memory of it as later events unfolded. The last words I spoke to him as he walked out the door to go swimming at the lake were ones of hatred. Little did I know that he would slip into a diabetic insulin shock and drown before I had the chance to tell him how sorry I was and that he was the best brother I could ever imagine. How I had suffered as the echo of my hateful words stung in my memory, and how I had wished a thousand times that I could have been there to rescue him.

It was the reason my parents had put me in martial arts lessons to begin with, after our therapist had encouraged them to find a way to help me release my pent-up feelings of grief and guilt. And it was altogether surprising how much emotion I discovered needed to be released . . . and how tough I could be when I wanted.

Over the years I had accepted that my brother's death was not my fault, but sometimes the sting of my last words to him still throbbed. I sighed as I

Mary E. Calvert

took my last bite of moo goo gai pan, wishing Will was still around to confide in about the "voices." Pensively I pushed myself away from the table. "I'd better go and get ready for the dance."

"Don't forget your fortune cookie," my father said, tossing one through the air in my direction. "You look like you could use a laugh."

Catching it, I tore off the crinkly paper and broke open the crumbly shell, pulling out the tiny piece of paper inside. For a moment I stood there in stunned silence, hardly believing my eyes. "Your life will soon change in a very unexpected and extraordinary way." It was the exact same fortune as the horoscope Reggie had read to me earlier! Normally I put absolutely no stock in horoscopes, fortune cookies, or anything else superstitious, but this was a little too coincidental. "Looks like the joke's on me!" I muttered, reading it again just to make sure I was seeing it correctly.

"What is it?" mom asked.

"Nothing, really," I muttered, stuffing the fortune in the pocket of my jeans. "Or maybe someone's trying to tell me something." With that, I disappeared through the kitchen door and upstairs to the bathroom, where I pushed all my uncomfortable feelings aside to fret over the zit that was threatening to make an appearance on my chin.

The next few hours of my life remain lost to conscious memory. I can only recall the aftermath of that unpleasant evening and the consolation of having a friend like Reggie.

It was a quarter after eleven, much too early to leave the dance. Feeling down and dejected, I pulled into Reggie's driveway. Both of us had ranted all the way home about the way Blair Bassett had flirted shamelessly with Brent the whole evening. She knew what she was doing, and Brent being the spineless wimp that he was walked right into her snare.

Before she got out of the car, Reggie's tone became serious. "Brent doesn't know what he's missing out on if he lets Blair sink her claws into him. You're one of the nicest people I know. Blair doesn't even come close to you when it comes to what's inside."

"Thanks, Reg," I said, deeply touched. "That makes me feel better. No less crazy after the day I've had, but better. Besides, there are worlds beyond this small town. Remember, next year we start college."

"Yeah, just think of all those college men." Reggie sighed.

"The operative word here being 'men.'"

"So, you'll be over tomorrow morning?"

"Bright and early."

"Great! Uncle Pete's expecting us by ten," Reggie said as she started to get out of the car.

"Can't wait. I'm ready for a good long ride through the woods."

"All rightee. See ya!" Reggie exclaimed as she slammed the car door shut.

I backed out of the driveway. The clock on the dashboard read 11:30, and I was beginning to feel sleepy. My foot pressed harder on the accelerator as I twisted my way out to the main road through town. The full weight of the evening's disappointment washed over me like a deluge at that moment, the sting of unrequited love still fresh. But had it truly been love? Probably not. No tears threatened to surface. The momentary frustration would soon disappear, perhaps even by the morning.

If nothing else, it had kept my mind off the day's weirdness, at least for a few hours. There had been no other strange occurrences since dinner. Maybe it was all over.

It was 11:43 when I pulled into my driveway. I turned off the ignition and stepped into the silent, cold stillness of the night. Pulling my jacket close, I could see my breath in the light glowing from the front porch lamps.

"Come now, my love, and begin the task that you will be born to do."

I spun around and scanned the darkness of my front yard warily. Nothing stirred but some orphaned leaves blown about by a sudden gust of wind.

"Little ghost, you must be terribly confused. I've already been born, thank you!" I murmured, fumbling hurriedly at the front door to turn the key in the lock. Once inside I bolted the door shut and stood there panting for a moment.

From the den, I could see a light shining, and I could hear the sound of Gershwin coming from within. My father was a premiere connoisseur of music, and some of my earliest memories were of sitting at his feet as he listened to anything from Bach's oratorios to Frank Sinatra and Tony Bennett. The music was enough to calm my spirit for the moment.

I walked into the family room to find my father sitting in his leather recliner scribbling notes on a legal pad. Sidney had managed to settle into the crevice between Dad and the arm of the chair and only raised his head and gave an obligatory tail wag before settling back to sleep.

"Hi, sweetheart," my father greeted, looking up from his notes as I entered. "Are you alright? You look like you've seen a ghost."

"I'm okay . . . just cold."

"How was the dance?"

"It was all right," I replied. "Dad, you didn't have to wait up for me."

"Not a problem. I have to do a little work on Sunday's sermon anyway."

I took a seat on the edge of the coffee table beside his chair.

"You look disappointed."

"Dad, how do you always know what I'm feeling?"

"It's not that difficult, my sensitive girl. You've always worn your emotions on your sleeve."

I sighed. "Um, Dad, I hate to admit it, but you were right about Brent. Looks like he's under Blair Bassett's evil spell, too," I lamented. "He practically ignored me all evening!"

"Blair Bassett, huh? You know, popularity comes and goes, but no one can ever take your integrity unless you let them," Dad sympathized, giving me a pat on my arm. "Don't worry, my sweet girl, you'll find your niche someday . . . and a man who will treat you as the jewel you are."

Without warning, Dad gave a violent sneeze into the Kleenex he'd been holding in his hand. "I'm afraid I'm catching a cold."

"Then take a Tylenol and go to bed," I offered.

"I still have a little work left, but you'd better get yourself upstairs if you're going riding early tomorrow."

I stood and headed for the stairs. Suddenly I turned around and kissed my father on the forehead, an act driven by the bewildering sense that I would not see him again for a very long time. "I love you, Dad."

"Love you too, honey. Stay warm tonight. I hear there's snow moving in."

As I walked quietly past my parents' bedroom, that same wave of loneliness crashed into consciousness once more, and I had the sudden urge to look upon my mother's face. Carefully I peered into the darkened room where Mom stirred at the sound of the creaking door.

"Are you home already?" came her voice from the darkness.

"I'm sorry. I didn't mean to wake you. I . . . I just wanted to say good night."

"I can never fall asleep until I know you're home safely anyway," she reassured. "How was the dance?"

"Disappointing, but I don't feel like talking about it. It's been a long day and I'm tired."

"Then go get a good night's sleep, sweetheart."

"Good night, Mom."

I walked into my room and closed the door behind me as I pondered the strange occurrences of the day. "Must be hormones," I rationalized wearily as I peeled off my clothing and slipped into a flannel gown. I nestled under my warm down comforter and picked up the copy of Byron that sat on my bedside table. I flipped the pages and read my favorite poem:

> "She walks in beauty, like the night
> Of cloudless climes and starry skies;

And all that's best of dark and bright
Meet in her aspect and her eyes . . ."[1]

Weariness soon tugged at my eyelids, and then came the last odd occurrence of my very strange day, though it did not seem odd at the time. I reached over with my right hand to turn out the lamp beside my bed, and the last object my eyes fixed upon was the amethyst ring my grandmother had given me on my sixteenth birthday—the same ring that had shown up missing the following morning when my oddity began. With everything else I was experiencing, the ring was the least of my concerns at the time. And though I searched my room from top to bottom at least a dozen times in the following weeks, it was nowhere to be found.

But back to the night in question. I sank under my covers, pondering the strange events of the day, when I began to consider an explanation for the voice and even the cryptic message in the fortune cookie and horoscope that terrified me most of all. Perhaps it had been God speaking to me all that time, like I was some kind of modern-day Moses or Saint Paul.

Yet I had always imagined God's voice to be masculine or at the very least gender-neutral—not decidedly feminine. And I know it wasn't exactly a burning bush, but a *fortune cookie. Really?*

I cleared my throat and whispered. "Um . . . God . . . are you trying to tell me something? Okay . . . I'm ready. What do you want from me?"

I waited breathlessly in the darkness. Silence, except for an occasional gust of wind through the branches of the tree outside my window.

Then I heard something, but this time it was not from a voice that I could hear with my ears. Instead it came from an overwhelming feeling deep within, a strong sense that I was not to be afraid. That I was loved with a love that nothing, no height nor depth, not even the expanse of an infinite universe could ever separate me from.

I closed my eyes and sighed, enjoying the reassuring glow. And mistakenly, I went to sleep believing I would wake up in the morning and everything would be back to normal.

Yet there I sat, six months later, waiting nervously for a therapy session that would hopefully explain why everything was definitely *not* normal.

---

[1] Byron, Lord George Gordon. "She Walks in Beauty." *Byron: Complete Poetical Works*. Ed. Frederick Page. Oxford: Oxford University Press, 1970. 77. Print.

CHAPTER 2

Dr. Susan

"Margaret Ann . . . Margaret Ann, Dr. Renfroe will see you now." The receptionist's voice roused me from my thoughts.

I glanced nervously at my mother, who had accompanied me to my session. She was still on the same page of her book she'd been reading ten minutes before when I glanced over her shoulder. I'm certain she was as nervous as I, wondering what would possibly come of today's memory induction.

"Hello, Margaret Ann," Dr. Susan greeted warmly as I entered her office. She looked up from the papers on her desk and caught her breath when she first regarded me. I bowed my head, ever so slightly, in response.

"Why do you stare at me so?" I found that she often did, with that same curious expression on her face.

"I haven't been able to put my finger on it before now, but there's something about you that appears, well . . . regal."

Regal? I said nothing in response.

"I hope you had a good birthday this weekend."

"Eighteen years old," I remarked pensively. "No longer a girl but not yet a woman, or so it would seem."

"And do you still consider yourself a 'girl'?"

"Strangely, no. I feel ages older, though I know not why," I explained. Immediately that familiar wave of sadness washed over me and then was gone before I knew it. "Please, if you will forgive me, I must admit that these pleasantries are but a nerve-wracking necessity when I stand at the brink of possible enlightenment, either for good or for ill."

"Yes, I can certainly understand why you would be feeling anxious today," Dr. Susan acknowledged, "but I want you to try and relax. I've told you all about the process of memory retrieval; there is no mystery behind it and nothing at all to be afraid of."

"With the exception of what I may discover."

"Yet you have the power to stop the session at any time if you feel too upset to continue. And keep in mind that you will only experience memories, however real they may seem."

"*If* there is anything to remember."

"Yes, well, our hope is that you will recall *something* from the night in question. But before we begin, I'd like to find out if there is anything else you've remembered, since last week's session, about the events leading up to the night of December twentieth."

"There are indeed two items which may be of consequence that I have been averse to sharing with you previously. The first I believed had nothing to do with me per se, yet I now believe it bears revealing."

"The only way that I can help you is if you tell me all," Dr. Susan said reassuringly.

"I have spoken to you of Blair Bassett."

"You said several months ago that she had been giving you a hard time since your, er, difficulties arose."

"She had been relentless in her mockery . . . that is, until . . ."

"Until what?"

"It was March seventeenth of this year, St. Patrick's Day, when a rather odd event happened that made her abandon the foolish impudence that came at my expense. It was on that day that she walked into the school cafeteria and, upon seeing me, mocked me in front of everyone. 'Forsooth, do my eyes deceive me, or is it Margaret Ann Shepherd? How goeth it with m'lady today?'

"I continued to sit there calmly, eating my sandwich, until I spied the silly green lei I wore around my neck to keep from getting pinched, and all at once I imagined Blair Bassett as green-faced as a leprechaun. The image in my head was so vivid 'twas all I could do to keep from laughing out loud." I couldn't help but chuckle at the memory. "Then, the most amazing phenomenon occurred . . ."

I stopped speaking for dramatic effect when I saw Dr. Susan leaning in toward me. "Yes?" she prodded.

"Her hair turned green! Green, I tell you! From the roots to the tips of her hair, a wave of bright green spread throughout her tresses like paint spilling down a canvas. And what is more, her voice changed to sound as one who had inhaled helium. All of the students who were there at the time, as well as several teachers, can verify my account."

Dr. Susan, who typically did a very good job hiding her own emotions, had difficulty concealing her stunned expression. "I had heard of some sort of strange happening over at the high school around that time, but I had no idea you were involved," Dr. Susan admitted. "How do you explain what happened?"

"It remains a mystery," I said, shaking my head. "Perhaps my nemesis's numerous hair-dying jobs finally caught up with her. And it is possible that her voice change was the result of a sudden onset of a rare form of laryngitis. It did eventually return to normal, but there remained a green tint in her hair as recently as graduation. Many even laughed as she walked across the stage to receive her diploma—I actually felt pity for her."

"My goodness!"

"However, the incident turned out to be a most fortuitous event for me as Blair somehow had the idea that I was responsible for her changed state and avoided me like the plague from then on. Although, between you and me, I had nothing to do with it. I mean, how could I have? I am no conjuror of magic."

But the truth was, there had been *other* strange, unexplainable occurrences those past months, like objects around me moving of their own free will during moments when my emotions were intense and having a clear sense when Sidney was hungry or thirsty or had a belly ache, as though I could read his thoughts.

Dr. Susan sat in her chair in silence. She must have been more than a little perplexed as to what to say.

"In fact, there are others who believe as such, and they are careful not to offend," I sighed. "Though I hear their whisperings behind my back, and it does make for a rather lonely existence."

"And yet your friend Reggie has remained by your side."

"Regina Elaine Lord," I said pensively, "a true friend if ever there was one."

"She's been there for you throughout your ordeal, hasn't she?"

"Yes. She came directly over on the morning of December twenty-first, for she knew something must be terribly wrong for me to cancel our riding engagement. She said that I appeared quite dazed, as if not exactly sure of my whereabouts. I know I gave her quite a fright."

"You mentioned there were *two* things you wanted to tell me," Dr. Susan said, glancing at the clock.

"Indeed." I shifted my weight uncomfortably and cleared my throat, trying to get up the nerve to divulge the secret I knew needed to be disclosed. Slowly, I lifted my eyes to meet those of my therapist. "I was reticent to mention this last week, as I did not want you to think me mad. But I can assure you that such phenomena had never happened to me before December twentieth and that such has not happened since."

Dr. Susan's eyes grew wide with anticipation.

"It was on that day that I heard a voice. Distinctly kind and feminine it was, and I remember having heard it all along throughout that day."

"What did it say?" Dr. Susan asked, visibly struggling to control the emotion in her voice.

"Something about 'beginning a task.' And also that I needed to find a man whose heart is true, and something about a ruler's heart being that of a healer, and something about it, whatever *it* is, having watched me for a long time. I must say it was most disconcerting at the very least."

"That *must* have been frightening," Dr. Susan said, her eyes expressing deep concern. "And you say that this was the only experience you have had like that one?"

"Indeed it was. And I know what you must be thinking, but I am not one to hallucinate. Nor have I ever taken any drugs—though Reggie and I did sneak into her parents' liquor cabinet once for a glass of sherry—but more than a year had passed in the interim."

"To what did you attribute the, er 'voices'?"

"Voice," I corrected. "To any number of explanations, but none seemed to hold true."

"Is there anything else you have since remembered that may be helpful?" Dr. Susan asked.

"Nothing."

"And you still haven't found your lost ring?"

I shook my head.

Dr. Susan sat back in her chair with a thoughtful expression upon her face. "You *did* have quite a remarkable day on the twentieth of December. Unfortunately, however, it only deepens the mystery of why you woke up the next morning in the state you were in."

I nodded in agreement, fighting to hold back the tears that threatened to erupt. Suddenly I leaned forward in my seat and looked straight at my therapist, my heart pleading for help. "Pray unlock the secrets hidden deep within, that I may know the source of my affliction."

Dr. Susan, with her warmest, most reassuring smile, leaned over and gave me a pat on the knee. "That is my goal. From there, well, we'll see. But rest assured that I will be here for you."

"I knew I could trust you," I said. "I've known it from the moment I stepped into your office—I could see it in your eyes."

The seasoned therapist smiled gently. "Well now, shall we begin?"

I nodded and took a deep breath.

"Are you comfortable? Do you need anything?"

"No, thank you," I replied. "I'm well."

"Very well, then, let us begin. You're my last session of the day, so we'll take as long as we need," she explained. "First of all, I want you to relax on the couch and close your eyes."

I willed myself to release the tension I felt in my stomach, and I could feel my muscles relax as I sank into the soft, cushiony couch.

"Now I want you to concentrate on my voice and only my voice. I will be counting backward from ten to one, and by then you will be completely relaxed and focused." Dr. Susan drew out the words in her most soothing tone of voice. "Ten . . . nine . . . empty your mind of all distractions . . . eight . . . seven . . . you are totally safe—nothing can harm you here . . . six . . . five . . . breathe deeply, in . . . and out . . . four . . . three . . . you are almost totally relaxed now . . . two . . . one."

I was vaguely aware that my head had gradually drooped onto my chest and that my breathing had slowed dramatically. "Margaret Ann, if you hear my voice, I want you to raise your right index finger."

Slowly, shakily, I lifted the index finger of my right hand into the air.

"Now, Margaret Ann, I want your mind to go back six months, to the night of December twentieth. You returned home from a party at the community center and have gone to bed . . ."

My face twitched a bit.

"Tell me what you remember."

"I have really weird dreams," I began, "that make me toss and turn. I wake up tangled in my bed sheets . . . pillows are scattered around the bed . . . I look at the clock . . . it's three minutes after two o'clock. I try to fall back asleep, but it's very hard."

"Why can't you fall back asleep?"

"There's a bright light outside . . . must be a streetlight or a passing car . . . but it's *so* bright. . . . Wait, there's no streetlight in front of our house, and I don't hear any car going by. That's really weird . . . I open my eyes again . . . the light has moved! It's . . . right outside my window now . . ."

At this point I had no awareness of being inside Dr. Susan's office. In my mind, I had returned to my bedroom and to the wee hours of December twenty-first. "It's . . . it's coming inside my room, this ball of yellow light . . . I can't stop it . . . I want to scream . . . I try to scream, but I can't. I can't even feel my throat," I exclaimed, choking back my terror.

"It's okay, Margaret Ann, you can go on."

"Aliens! I'm being abducted! This can't be happening to me." I could feel hot tears emerge from under my closed eyelids, and then my breathing slowed. "But no . . . this thing . . . this presence . . . not an alien . . . so beautiful . . . pure, fluid light in the shape of a woman's face. Whoa! This is so weird . . . it seems to be smiling at me . . . and now it's speaking with that same, tinkling voice I've heard all day . . ."

"What does it tell you, Margaret Ann?"

It took a few moments before I could reply. "That it's going to be okay. That I'll only be away for a little while," I answered. "I tell it that I don't want to go, but it says that I have been chosen. Once again I try to scream, but my throat feels nonexistent. I feel so strange . . . weightless . . . I can't even feel my body, and yet I'm moving toward the yellow glow . . . it's calling me to it . . . it is so beautiful . . . I . . . I can't resist," I said dreamily. "All my books, my trophies, my desk, fade into darkness . . ." I gasped.

"What is it?"

"I see myself, lying motionless there on my bed. I'm hovering right above myself looking down . . . I must be dead . . . but how?" I wondered out loud, feeling more curious than alarmed. "I'm rising now . . . the roof of my house . . . there it is below me. I see my darkened neighborhood . . . there's a light on in the house across the street . . . now I see our town . . . and a huge dark area that must be the lake where . . . where . . . now I see mountain ranges and white peaks shining in the moonlight . . . and continents. I'm so far from home now . . . the earth is slipping away beneath me . . . I travel up a long, long shaft of light . . . like a tunnel through the night sky . . . stars are hurling past at astonishing speed . . . I must be dreaming, a really weird, realistic dream."

I fell silent and squinted my eyes as if trying to see something far in the distance. "I see a huge yellow ball of light far ahead of me . . . I seem to be going toward it. . . . It's still so very far away. . . . Where am I going? How long have I been dead now?

"I get closer to the light. . . . It takes forever to get there. . . . I hear what sounds like a heartbeat—its pulsating draws me in . . . I am surrounded by a sea of yellow light . . . it totally engulfs me . . . but wait . . . there is something else here . . . it's a small gray dot, but it's coming closer to me . . . or I come closer to it . . . it's, it's . . . why, it looks like a woman, the silhouette of a woman shrouded under a thin gray veil. If I get any closer I'll wake her . . . wait, I *am* getting closer, but she's still asleep . . . wait, wait . . . where did she go?"

As I sat there on Dr. Susan's couch, I had the hazy sensation that I was stretching my body, like someone waking up in the morning. "I feel whole again, like I can move of my own free will, and yet . . . it's as though I am waking from a very deep sleep. I . . . feel . . . so . . . groggy . . . and I hear something . . . a woman's voice. . . . That same mysterious voice I've been hearing, and it seems to go on for ages . . . so tender and loving. The words are foreign, but somehow I know their meaning . . . I feel so warm, such love . . . it surrounds me . . . I don't want to leave this place."

At this point, there was no awareness of anything beyond that of my memory. Anything that occurred within the context of Dr. Susan's office, all the questions she posed for the remainder of our time together were but a sidenote to what I experienced in my head. As far as I was concerned, I was back in that light and nothing but her occasional questions or comments existed outside of it.

"The light shines brilliantly, and then everything goes dark, like someone's turned out the light," I continued. "Minutes, days, or even years pass, I don't know."

Then from somewhere quite far away, I heard the faint voice of my therapist. "What"—the voice cracked—"um, what happened then?"

There was another moment of silence that seemingly lasted forever, that is, until I heard the echo of my old voice from someplace far off. "Then . . . it was then that I was born."

CHAPTER 3

"The late afternoon sun shining through the treetops . . . a warm breeze gently rustling the greenery of early summer. The sound of birds singing. Something moving below . . . A horse. A big, white horse . . . Dear God, where am I? What's happening to me?"

"Wha . . . what happened then?" Dr. Susan gasped.

The sound of men laughing. Columns and a huge gate. Two gray towers rising above on either side.

I must be going crazy! This can't be real!

A group of men clad in old-fashioned garb stood in the distance, each with a huge broadsword by his side. They were talking amongst themselves and paid no mind to me.

Just then the white horse on which I sat shifted its weight and turned to eye me with one of its deep brown orbs. It seemed to care not at all that I had suddenly appeared on its back, and it stood placidly as if in obedience.

I seemed to be in the middle of a courtyard before a huge, tightly shut gate. The two towers rose above the gate on either side and a semicircle of columns, about fourteen in all, each standing about fifteen feet from each other, spanned the courtyard from the bottom of one tower to the other. Beyond the tower and columns a large wall stretched out on either side of the gate into dense forest that lay beyond. The place struck me as quite pretty, with the columns seeming to serve no other function than decoration. But the men who stood nearby did not appear to be celestial beings, and with their stern faces the overall mood of the place seemed not at all heavenly.

Should I approach them and declare my presence or quietly attempt to slip away? As three more guards drew near on horseback from the only road that led from the gate, I decided to take my chances with diplomacy.

"Tell me, are any of you Saint Peter?" I called out, recognizing nothing in the sound of my own voice.

The men jerked their heads in my direction. Their eyes grew wide and their mouths flew open as they regarded me for the first time. Their conversation forgotten, the five guards on foot walked toward me as if in a trance, and the other three on horseback approached me from the other side. I was surrounded, with no chance of escape.

However, I seemed to be in no immediate danger. There was no malevolence about them, only a look of awe.

"Why are you staring at me? Is something wrong?" My hand went to my throat. Why did my voice sound so much lower than expected? And why was I suddenly in the presence of Robin Hood and his band of merry men? *Wrong? Everything* was wrong.

"Forgive us, miss, but we've not seen yer kind 'ere for ages." I glanced at the man who had spoken. While most of the others sported hair that fell well below their shoulders and beards that were in various stages of untidiness, his face was clean-shaven, and his light brown hair, tinged with blond streaks from the sun, fell to just above his collar. And there was a thoughtful look of wonder in his eyes.

"Aye, 'tis an omen for good, that it is," said another, whose long gray hair lay in a single braid down his back.

"Or for ill," said yet another, whose scraggly eyebrows lowered with suspicion.

"Tell us, 'ave ye news from the northern forest?" one of the mounted guards asked in an excited whisper.

"The northern forest?" I repeated. All of this was so confusing. "Am I not in heaven?"

"As close to heaven as ye kin get in this world, I'd say," said the man who had first spoken to me, the well-groomed one with the light-brown hair. "Do ye not know where ye be?"

Tears threatened to erupt as I shook my head.

"Why, ye are at the Guildenmoor Gate in the country o' Bensor," he said.

"This has got to be a mistake!" I wailed. "How will I ever get back to where I came from?"

"And exactly where *do* ye hail from and who might ye be?" questioned the guard who thought my presence a bad omen, his voice tense with apprehension.

I tried desperately to search my memory, but nothing surfaced. "I . . . can't seem to remember. I only know that it's very far away."

"Ye didna come from th' other side o' that gate o'er there?" he said, pointing behind us.

I glanced back at the huge, tightly shut portal. "No, I don't believe so."

At that word, the entire group of guards murmured amongst themselves in a disagreeable sort of way that made me feel very uncomfortable . . . and slightly at peril.

"They kin be verra sly, they kin," said the one with the scraggly eyebrows.

"Aye, we mustn't let down our guard," said another, a man of slight build who looked as though a stiff wind could knock him over.

I was growing more and more distressed by the second, and it must have shown on my face. The well-groomed guard with the kind eyes gave me one glance and called up to one of the turrets. "Sentinel!" No response. "I say, sentinel!" he called again.

High above, the top of a metal helmet was barely visible over the edge of the wall. A second guard with a quiver full of arrows hanging on his back emerged and shook the wearer of the helmet. The napping sentinel, roused to action, peered down with his comrade over the high wall onto the scene below.

"'As anyone come through the gate today?"

"Not a soul. Gate's been shut tight since noon," the more alert guard answered.

"Just as I thought," the well-groomed man said, and he looked up at me, his manner visibly relaxed as a smile spread across his lips. "Nay, no creature so fair could come from beyond that gate, and though I've seen but a few elves in me life, no fairer nor nobler people there are. Ye are an elf, are ye not?"

"An elf?" Was this some sort of joke?

"Aye, surely ye are one yerself."

I stared at him blankly. Then, from somewhere deep inside the corridors of my memory, I recalled someone once telling me as much. Slowly, almost dreamily, I nodded my head. "Yes, I suppose I am," I said weakly. "Please, I'm very tired and apparently very lost."

"Aye, miss. 'Tis 'ard to think straight when the body's weary. What ye need's a place to rest yer 'ead," piped in one of the guards who had not spoken before that moment. There was a big, toothless grin on his face, which was turning a deeper shade of red by the second.

An older guard who stood nearby slapped him on the side of his head. "An' I suppose ye think ye'd be the one to provide such a place."

"Aye! What's wrong with bein' chivalrous?"

"I'll wager chivalry 'as nothin' to do with it."

"*I'll* take 'er!" Everyone grew silent as the man with the kind eyes stepped forward. "But, mind ye, I'll not 'ave anythin' spoil me leave. So, miss, ye'll need to keep a low profile, as it were."

I nodded dutifully, not at all sure I wanted to go anywhere with anyone. Certainly I had stepped through some sort of portal that transported me back in time, and I dared not wander too far from it and the opportunity to get back to the place where I belonged as I certainly didn't belong in "Bensor."

"A small inn lies west what should suit ye fine," he continued. "Me duty 'ere is finished for a time, and I'd be honored to take ye there. For ye see, 'tis not safe for a woman to travel alone so close to nightfall, 'specially close as we are to the Gate."

"Frondamein!" came a gruff voice from a row of dilapidated guardhouses that stood on the edge of the columns.

"Quick, 'tis Festius!" he exclaimed hurriedly. "The boss don't take kindly to yer type. Ye must 'ide yerself." With that he turned and walked rapidly toward the row of houses.

Without a word, two of the three guards on horseback maneuvered around to block the sight of me from whoever was exiting the old building. One of them motioned with his hands that I should place something over my head. Hardly had I noticed before that I was wearing a hooded cape . . . and a long dress. What in the world was I doing wearing a long dress while riding a horse? And for that matter, why was I on a horse to begin with? And where on earth was Bensor? And what was wrong with my voice?

I pulled the hood of my cape over my head but managed a quick glance at the approaching man with the gruff voice and the strange name—Festius. He was dressed in the same garb as the other men—tunic, leggings, boots, sword—but he was dressed in all gray. He held an open bottle in one hand and a small pouch in the other as he walked toward the man who was to be my traveling companion.

"Be gone with ye now, but retairn ere the crescent moon," Festius said with a hint of menace in his voice as he handed over the pouch. My companion and apparent protector pulled open the string and glanced inside, surveying the contents that clanked when he gave them a quick jingle.

"Aye, ere the crescent moon." Bitterness virtually dripped from his voice.

The man in gray turned to stare at the group of guards. "What ye be starin' at? Get back to yer posts!" he yelled before stamping back to the guardhouse.

The well-groomed man walked over and untied a waiting brown mare that had been tied to a post. The other guards dispersed like a pack of whipped dogs. The suspicious guard strode over to my soon-to-be companion and whispered, "If it's all the same, ye'd best be wary." He must have thought he was speaking quietly, but I could easily hear every word.

"Aye," my companion nodded in response as he mounted his horse. He rode over to the place where I waited.

"Shall we begin our journey?" he said.

"Yes, but . . . first, could you do me a favor and give me a pinch?"

"Pinch a lady! Ma'am, I dunna know that I could . . ." The guard's face turned a deep shade of crimson.

"Please," I said, "here, on my arm."

I stretched out my arm in his direction, and with a look of great hesitation he reached out and pinched me on the forearm, causing me to wince at the slight sting. "I guess I'm *not* dreaming," I gulped, feeling quite shaken.

"Er, afore we begin, allow me to introduce meself," he said with an uncertain smile. "Me name's Frondamein, Frondamein o' Baeren Ford."

I managed a weak smile in return. It seemed they all had strange names. "And my name is Mar . . . Ar . . ." My eyes darted upward for a moment, as if trying to retrieve something important from memory. "Ar . . . wyn. My name is Arwyn," I said, surprising myself as the words came tumbling from my lips. What? That couldn't be right! Yet . . . somehow it was.

"Pleased to make yer acquaintance, Miss Arwyn," Frondamein said as he clicked his tongue. "On, Haseloth!"

"But . . . but," I stammered, trying desperately to memorize every detail of my surroundings. Perhaps, if I could make my way back here, I could find the doorway that led home. Yes, that's what I would do—I would have my companion bring me back to the Gate the following day. I would find the portal that led through the time warp, or whatever it was, and poof! I'd be home! Or so I hoped.

"Come," he urged. "Close as we are to the Gate, we mustn't be caught out on the road come nightfall."

And what was the whole mystery surrounding "the Gate," anyway? What sinister thing lay on the other side? And why, if it were indeed so menacing, was a handful of ragamuffin soldiers there to guard it?

With great hesitation, I snapped the reins lightly against my horse's back. Dutifully, the placid creature fell in beside the brown mare . . . as if it knew exactly what I wanted it to do.

But what I really wanted was for it to take me back home.

CHAPTER 4

"My companion seems nice enough. I guess I should trust him—I don't have a choice. Besides, none of this is really *happening anyway. If I believed for one minute that it was, I would probably . . . well, I don't know what I would do. But it would probably involve a lot of screaming."*

My head was swimming as we passed through the row of columns that lay on the edge of the courtyard. There was nothing at all normal about the situation in which I found myself. People didn't just step back in time, no matter what the storybooks said, and I knew there had to be some logical explanation for my predicament.

But perhaps even more alarming was the fact that I remembered virtually nothing that had happened prior to my appearance at the Gate, as if my previous existence was like a dream teetering on a precipice, threatening to vanish altogether from conscious memory. I only remembered enough to know that things were completely wrong.

"Ah, Miss Arwyn, 'tis good to be on the road again and a-headin' for 'ome." Frondamein said, breaking the silence.

Miss Arwyn? Who was he talking to? Oh, right . . . me. I felt his gaze but remained quiet. My eyes darted everywhere, as if I half expected the trees to reach out and grab me.

"I'll ne'er forget the fairst time I saw an elf. A wee lad I was when I came upon 'im a-sittin' under an apple tree in me da's orchard. All cloaked in white, me thought I'd seen an angel . . ."

We had been traveling a short distance to the south, at least what I imagined to be a southerly direction based on the position of the setting sun. All at once the road we were on intersected with another that ran in an east-west direction. Taking the turn to the right, Frondamein led the way along a westerly course that followed a meandering stream. A warm breeze blew upon my face, and the trees were clothed in a sea of green leaves, all of which struck me as quite abnormal for what to my mind should have been wintertime. And the fresh, sweet fragrance of the forest reminded me more of the spring.

For a time, Frondamein's voice murmured on as he related the story of his first elvish encounter and then years later when a noble-looking elf who was accompanied by two elven maidens with crowns of flowers in their long, flowing hair passed through his village on the way to some important business elsewhere.

"'Ow elegant and graceful they were, like kings and queens, and they showed such kindness to us poor townsfolk."

I could tell that he looked at me for some sort of reaction, but I wasn't feeling very sociable. It had been at least a quarter of an hour since we had left the Gate, and I hadn't spoken two words since.

I felt so . . . weird. I touched my face, trying to find any semblance of familiarity there. None. Then my fingers of my free hand moved to the back of my head, where I grabbed a handful of thick hair and pulled it around for examination. How lengthy it had become and how dark the rich brown color looked in the light. How long had this ordeal lasted, anyway? From the corner of my eye I could see Frondamein glancing at me with a peculiar look on his face as though I were the strangest creature he had ever seen.

I glanced far up the road in the direction we were heading, where two approaching riders caught my gaze. Even at that distance, I could tell that they were no ordinary men, and my eyes grew wide as I looked to Frondamein for some kind of reassurance.

Upon seeing my reaction, he squinted his eyes as he gazed up the road, but it was still several moments before he saw the source of my distress.

"Miss Arwyn, ye'd best don yer hood and remain quiet." He swallowed hard. "Gargalocs dunna take kindly to Bensorians, 'specially elves. But ye musn't wairry, for I'll protect ye if there be trouble."

What in the world was a Gargaloc? I wondered, as I placed my hood over my head.

I saw the blood drain from Frondamein's face. Whatever such creatures were, they must be terribly frightening. I dug my heels into my stirrups and bit my lip, bracing for whatever peril lay ahead.

As the two riders approached, I could barely suppress a faint gasp when I observed their large, hulking bodies. Coarse hair, which grew in abundance from their arms and backs, protruded from under the edges of their tunics. Their hands and feet appeared grotesquely large, almost inhuman, and their noses were turned upward, looking more like pigs' snouts than anything else.

Their slightly slanted eyes stared menacingly, or perhaps curiously, at me as they passed. I forced myself to look away and avoid their gaze. Beside me, my traveling partner's body had become rigid, and I could see his hand move to the hilt of his sword.

In a moment, the two riders passed by without incident. I looked over at Frondamein, whose expression had turned to relief.

"And what exactly were those!" I demanded when they were out of earshot.

To my great surprise, Frondamein merely looked at me and chuckled. "Why, ye're no more a spy than Haseloth 'ere," he said. "Nay, I see naught but goodness when I look in yer eyes."

"And someone who's pretty freaked out right about now," I said, realizing my blunder as the words came tumbling out of my mouth. Surely he would understand my meaning by the grimace on my face.

"Aye. The sight of a Gargaloc isna a pretty one."

"What's a . . . Gargaloc?"

"A bunch o' half-breeds, the nasty, detestable spawn of Ashkaroth's mountain hags," Frondamein replied, a note of bitterness tinging his words. "But I hate to speak o' such unpleasantness in the presence of a lady." He remained quiet for a moment, which I suspected was an unusual occurrence.

"So, Mr., uh, Frondamein, sir, are you from around here?" I asked, stifling the urge to start screaming madly. So much had happened so fast, and everything I had ever known and loved had been jerked out from under me with no explanation whatsoever. It was enough to drive anyone mad, but I knew I'd better hold myself together until the time when I could go and have a nervous breakdown all by myself.

"Nay. Me home's a day's ride south o' here, in a town called Baeren Ford. 'Tis where me wife and I have a small place. I'll be headin' there tomorrow, as I do every time there's a new moon."

"Listen, I don't mean to be nosey, but why work so far from home?"

His eyes focused on the center of my face, at my nose, and again that quizzical expression reappeared. "'Tis not by choice, Miss Arwyn," Frondamein said with a twisted smile. "'Ad I not been 'commissioned' to do guard duty at the Guildenmoor Gate by the powers that be, I'd still be at work on me family farm. The soil's where me 'eart is."

"Can't you quit and go home?" I asked, forcing myself to engage in this conversation so as not to appear completely aloof. I would deal with my situation later, that is, if I didn't wake up soon. I was not thoroughly convinced that I wasn't dreaming.

Frondamein glanced over his shoulder. We were totally alone.

"Would that I could retairn to the life I loved so, 'specially now that Loralon is with child," Frondamein said.

"Loralon is your wife?"

"Aye, that she is, and as darlin' a thin' as e'er there was," he replied. "I wairry for 'er so down in Baeren Ford all by 'erself with me so far away. But alas, Draigon would 'ave me thrown in Dungard were I to leave me post."

"And who exactly is Draigon?"

"Ye've not haird o' the 'great' Draigon?" Frondamein said with a smirk on his face. He glanced around again and lowered his voice. "We must be wary, Miss Arwyn. 'Is spies are everywhere, and Ashkaroth's but a stone's throw away."

From what I could tell, we were out in the middle of nowhere. Yet judging by our recent encounter, I was glad to be in the company of a cautious companion.

Leaning toward me in his saddle, Frondamein spoke in a lowered voice. "Draigon is the self-proclaimed ruler o' Bensor, but the wairst of it is, methinks 'e's in the sairvice o' Dar Magreth."

"And who is Dar . . . whatever you said?" I asked. This was all becoming much too complicated.

"Dar Magreth, the queen, or should I say the witch of Ashkaroth, the country what lies just beyond the Gate. Lives in a dark tower in the mountains to the north, she does. But if ye ask me, I'd say Dar Magreth is an evil bein', a spirit not o' flesh and blood as you and I. Wears a long black robe, or so I've haird, and a mask what looks like a great cat to 'ide 'er face from the light o' the sun. 'Tis said a kiss from 'er lips kin turn whate'er they touch cold as stone!"

"You have *got* to be kidding!" Frondamein shot another confused glance my way. "I mean, that's quite . . . unusual."

"Aye, legends do have a way o' becomin' larger than life. After all, few mortals 'ave e'er seen Dar Magreth, least not in recent years." Frondamein shrugged. "Not that th' opinion of a farmer counts for much, but I believe she 'as only ill will toward Bensor and is quietly invadin' our country with 'er army o' Gargalocs."

"You mean, those, er, *people*, we saw back there?"

"Aye."

"And being a guard at the Gate, you probably know when they come and go."

"Quite right, Miss Arwyn, more so at least than th' average Bensorian."

"So, why do you think Draigon secretly works for the evil sorceress?"

"Now, Miss Arwyn, I'm but a simpleminded farmer, but I'll tell ye what I've seen wi' me own two eyes—Gargalocs comin' and goin' as they please and no one says a waird. 'Ow they're all a-gettin' in is more than I kin see, for they're not all of 'em comin' through the Gate. Yet no Bensorian kin pass the borders o' Bensor without sufferin' a grand inquisition—and only then for the pairpose o' trade. 'Tis like we're prisoners in our own country."

"But you oversee who enters and leaves the country."

"'Tis only a formality," Frondamein said. "Me presence there makes no difference but to give me fellow Bensorians peace o' mind. Little do they know me main duty is to keep 'em from leavin'." He kept his gaze on his horse's mane, and his brow darkened into a scowl.

"In the days o' me youth, I remember a much different Bensor." He sighed. "'Twas in the last days o' th' Eldaran Council, before Draigon seduced the spineless lords with 'is trickery." Frondamein shook his head. "But I'm gettin' ahead o' meself. If ye'll humor me a moment, Miss Arwyn, let me go back a few years. For ye see, rumor 'as it Draigon was orphaned as a child, abandoned by 'is parents to the streets o' Maldimire. Kin ye imagine doin' such a thin' to a child? E'en Draigon desairved 'is parents. Then perhaps 'e'd not 'ave turned out so foul."

I settled into my saddle, suspecting a long story ahead.

"Nonetheless, 'e was taken in by the wife o' one of the lords, who was 'imself a stern man who 'ad little fondness for children," Frondamein continued. "E'en so, 'e took it upon 'imself to train the boy in 'is footsteps. Draigon eventually came of age and, with pairsuasion from 'is adoptive father, was given a seat on the council. 'Twas but a few years later that 'e started makin' trouble, convincin' the weak-minded mortals on the council that the elf lords were bent on usurpin' the rule of Bensor for themselves. But, as rumor 'as it, 'is hatred of elves 'ad more to do with 'im bein' rejected by an elven lass."

"But I thought you suspect that he is in the service of Dar . . . Dar . . . you know, the elven witch?"

"Aye, but no doubt he'd cozy up t' anyone, if 'twould be in 'is best interest."

As interesting as his story was, it had little to do with me. After all, what had I to do with the intrigues of an obscure country I'd never heard of before? Still, I thought it best to give him the courtesy of my attention, as kind as he was, despite the urgency of my present circumstances.

"'Twas the beginnin' of troubled times, it was. A witch hunt o' sorts ensued, and for a time elves were regarded with suspicion, some e'en imprisoned for bein' elvish. 'Tis no wonder they all abandoned the forests in the south and moved to the shelter o' Loth Gerodin. None were left on the council, and 'twas only a matter o' time the dwarf lords were banished as well, as Draigon 'ad led the mortal lords to believe 'em an inferior people. And so, with only corrupt and elderly mortals left to rule Bensor, I believe 'e quietly murdered 'em all 'til 'e was th' only one left."

"The dude needs to get a life!"

"Beggin' yer pardon, miss?" I looked over and saw that Frondamein's face was scrunched up all funny as he eyed me.

"Er, what I mean is, sounds like he needs a good therapist . . . that is," I explained hurriedly. "Um, so he's making a mess of everything?"

"Aye, that 'e is. Ye see, Miss Arwyn, Bensor is a country of unmatchable beauty, known especially for its enchantin' forests. In fact, the name Bensor comes from the elvish waird *bensofauf,* or *tree.*"

I looked at my surroundings and had to admit that Frondamein was at least right about the forests. The road upon which we traveled twisted under a high green ceiling that was alive with the sounds of birds coming in to roost for the evening and the largest butterflies I'd ever seen alighting on the branches above. Even the forest floor was carpeted with spongy moss and cool patches of ivy that clung to the tree trunks in long, kingly capes draped to the ground.

"What a pity so many trees 'ave been cut down and sold to Ashkaroth, but what Askaroth does with 'em I know not. Draigon says the money's used for 'improvements,'" Frondamein sneered. "Improvements, hmph! The only thin' improvin' is the money in 'is own coffers.

"Why, he's made the dwarves in the Andains into slaves, forcin' 'em to wairk without givin' 'em their fair share o' the gold and jewels they mine. E'en the poor farmin' folk o' Guilden and Elwindor are subject to Draigon's whims when it comes to payin' taxes. 'Tis e'en been rumored that if a family canna pay 'e'll 'ave innocent people, e'en children, 'eld for ransom until someone comes up with the money. Some ne'er do."

"That's terrible!" Now he had my attention. The confusion of my strange situation was replaced by a growing sense of injustice.

"Aye, that it is, Miss Arwyn," Frondamein agreed. "We canna e'en dance and sing songs t' Omni anymore at our circles, and . . ."

"Circles?"

"Aye, the places we once went to pay homage to Omni . . ."

My face must have been blank.

"Ye know, the good and all-powerful Giver and Sustainer o' life."

That somehow rang a bell.

"And our schools . . . 'e closed 'em. Says school takes away from a hard day's work, 'e does, but I for one want me child to grow up readin' and a-writin'."

"Of course!"

"We're in a time of uneasy peace 'ere in Bensor, and I fear the wairst is yet to come," Frondamein continued. "All th' elves 'ave long since left their ancestral 'omes and sought refuge far from Draigon's presence in Maldimire. Draigon 'ates 'em, 'e does, for they 'ave special powers and are a harder people to control than us mortals, who tend to be a bit too complacent, if ye ask me. The elves' presence in the south is sorely missed. Ye are the fairst I've seen in Guildenwood for years."

I marveled at his words and was about to correct his impression of me but thought better of it as the man so obviously respected my supposed kind. I only hoped it wouldn't eventually get me into trouble.

"Ah, to return to the Bensor o' me youth. In those days e'en a young lass could travel alone. Now I hear more and more o' Bensorians ambushed and robbed by Gargalocs runnin' amok in our country. E'en the capitol city o' Maldimire, once a jewel in Bensor's crown, 'as been corrupted by the filth of Ashkaroth. And Draigon sits back in 'is palace and allows 'em to destroy it all."

Frondamein sighed and had a faraway look in his eyes. "As a boy I loved to go with me da to Maldimire's markets, where people came from all o'er the world to trade their wares. 'Twas but a fortnight ago when last I was there, and saddened I was to see what was once so beautiful so neglected by those who care not for it, nor this country."

"Frondamein," I interrupted, "what's being done to stop Draigon?" My future in this place, if any, was looking quite dim. The hope of somehow finding my way home was the only thing that helped me cling to my sanity.

"Miss Arwyn, we Bensorians are verra peaceful, simpleminded. Our hearts are in the soil and by the hearth, not in the comin's and goin's o' Draigon and Ashkaroth. A simple life, for mortals at least, is what we long for; and 'tis this, I fear, 'twill be our undoin'."

"Surely someone could stand up against him," I said, a bit perturbed that this Draigon was getting away with so much.

"'Tis true I know more than th' average Bensorian, yet I am but one farmer. What kin I do?" Frondamein shrugged. "Th' elves 'ave the means and p'rhaps the numbers to stand up against Draigon, and support an uprisin' they'd do if need be. But cut off from the rest o' Bensor they are becomin', which is no doubt Draigon's desire."

I remained silent for a moment as I pondered the man's words. My prospects here were appearing grimmer by the moment.

"So is there any hope?" I said at last.

Frondamein hesitated a moment before he spoke. "Aye . . . though I musn't speak o' hi . . . that is, o' such thin's . . . not now." His voice trailed off, and he glanced at me sidelong, a hint of doubt clouding his eyes. I decided it was best not to press the issue.

As the light of the sinking sun faded to the west, signs of civilization appeared along the road. We passed a small but hospitable-looking cottage where a man had climbed to patch his roof with a bundle of river reeds as his wife directed their placement from below. She was the first female I had seen since my arrival, and I could not help but stare at the woman's style of dress. It appeared rather drab compared to the elegant, brightly colored blue gown that I wore.

Several more such cottages came into view, where mouth-watering aromas of roasting meat poured forth through open windows as women worked busily inside preparing evening meals. Outside, men sat smoking pipes on their front door steps while children played at their feet, and hopeful cats and dogs lingered about front lawns waiting for a morsel thrown in their direction. Such a peaceful scene made Frondamein's dismal portrait of this land difficult to believe, and I wondered if perhaps my companion weren't a bit of a gloomy chap. I hoped this to be the case, despite the fact that his overall demeanor appeared quite pleasant.

We came to a junction with a large signpost sitting right in the middle of the road, the words *Maldimire* etched into the marker pointing toward the south and *Mindlemir* on the one pointing in the opposite direction. Frondamein turned north and led the way along a good-sized river.

As we approached a picturesque stone bridge, three boys with fishing poles dangling into the water below looked up and saw us coming. Upon seeing me, they dropped their poles with a shriek and went running off ahead of us into the village. "An elf! An elf's a-comin'!" they yelled with excitement.

Please! The last thing I needed was a lot of unwanted attention.

Not long after crossing over the bridge, we passed under a stone archway overgrown with honeysuckle and into the heart of the village. On either side of the road sat quaint cottages and some two-story stone buildings. Colorful signs hanging out front advertised services within. Carpenters, smiths, tanners, and bakers were but a few of the trades lining the main street through town.

And everywhere, people were coming out into the street to see what had caused the commotion. They stared with mouths agape as Frondamein and I passed, and I could hear their whispers.

"Isna that Frondamein o' Baeren Ford she's with?"

"'Tis a strange thin' indeed."

"Portends well, I'd say."

How surreal everything was, as if I had stepped into a restored village from ancient times where all the actors were going about their roles as if nothing were the matter. I still had no clue as to where I was or why I was there, and I kept waiting for someone to come out from backstage to tell me this had all been some very elaborate practical joke.

CHAPTER 5

"I know it's a rather bold move, to up and invite myself to move in, but desperate times call for desperate measures."

"It sounds like you feel at the end of your rope." My therapist's voice broke into my memory, and the normal, modern-sounding voice I found somewhat comforting.

"What else am I to do? I'm all alone in this place, and who knows if there are others as decent as he?"

Merchants busily packed up their leftovers from the day's market as we approached the village square. Chickens and an occasional goat roamed through the wide village streets, and through occasional gaps in the stone buildings, I could see that the village lay on the edge of a lake.

My presence was causing quite a stir, but for what reason I couldn't guess. It only fed into my growing sense of bewilderment.

Passing through the town square, men and women were setting up tables and stringing lanterns along ropes that dangled between buildings above the marketplace. A festive atmosphere hovered in the air.

"Today's the Eve o' Summer," Frondamein explained. "Tomorrow there'll be celebratin' across Bensor as summer and the year 2501 begin. Folks'll come for miles to take part in the festivities and the feastin'."

"Twenty-five hundred and one," I repeated to myself. If it was New Year's and about to be summer, Bensor must be somewhere in the southern half of the world, I reasoned, trying feverishly to make some sense out of this impossible mystery. I couldn't seem to remember what year it was, but that number seemed way off.

"Ah, here we are, Miss Arwyn, th' Old Oak Inn," Frondamein said. He led the way into a courtyard in front of a charming-looking old building covered three-quarters up the walls with ivy. An ancient oak tree with branches spiraling into the heavens stood to the left of the front door. Two oil lanterns on either side of the door had already been lit as the light of day waned, creating a rather friendly welcome.

An adolescent boy sat on the front step, chewing on a piece of straw. "Good evenin', Durkin," Frondamein said. "'Ave ye any rooms this eve for two weary travelers?"

The stable boy looked up at me and bolted from his spot on the steps, shaking the dirt from his trousers. "Oh, aye. We've not 'ad much business o' late, e'en with the festival tomorrow 'n all," the boy said, keeping his eyes on me. He suddenly remembered the piece of straw protruding from his teeth and quickly threw it aside, looking away as his face glowed a brilliant shade of red.

"Well, would ye then be so kind as to see our hairses to the stable?" Frondamein said with an amused smile.

"Aye." Durkin took the reins from Frondemein.

Frondamein helped me to the ground. As I turned to face him, I let out a short gasp upon having to look slightly downward to meet his gaze, for he was himself not wanting when it came to height. For a moment the whole world seemed to spin and my legs felt as though they would buckle underneath me. I reached to steady myself against the horse as I rubbed my brow with my hand.

"Miss Arwyn, are ye feelin' poorly?" Frondamein said, his brow furrowed with concern.

"Just a bit dizzy," I replied, attempting to smile.

"What ye need is a full belly and a peaceful night's sleep 'n ye'll be good as new," he offered.

The thought of food suddenly made me aware of how famished I really was. A steak and potato with a side salad and perhaps a piece of chocolate pie would hit the spot fine. And milk.

The young stable boy grabbed both horses by the reins and led them away as Frondamein and I headed for the front door of the inn. Walking suddenly felt an unnatural feat as my legs wobbled.

It was then that an impossible thought first tickled deep within the corridors of my mind, a thought that I quickly dismissed as completely preposterous.

"Miss." Durkin spoke across the front lawn. "Ye forgot yer pouch." The boy reached up to the back of the white horse and untied a brown leather knapsack I'd not seen. Durkin brought the retrieved knapsack over and handed it to me, still blushing. I stared blankly at the mysterious package, managing to emit a faint "thank you."

Frondamein made a gesture toward the front door of the inn. As he politely held open the wooden door, I was forced to bend my neck slightly so that my head would clear the doorway.

"Ye elves, ye are a tall lot," Frondamein commented as we stepped inside a dimly lit hallway with a strong musty odor, the combination of pipe smoke and the smell of old timbered ceiling rafters. The scent evoked in me the pleasant comfort of safety.

At the end of the hallway was an opening into what appeared to be a large room where we could see a rotund man carrying platefuls of food in his hands. The man stopped for a moment at the door, squinting into the dim corridor.

"Be with ye shortly," he said as he carelessly set the plates down in front of several men who were laughing and gulping down mugs of ale. Someone made a comment that made the man laugh so that his booming voice echoed into the hallway. Holding his stomach as he continued to chuckle, he walked toward his latest customers.

"Ah! Frondamein, old chap, good to see ye," he said as he wiped his hands on a towel which hung from his apron.

"I hope you and yer kin are well," Frondamein greeted in return.

The man stopped, staring at me with a quizzical look on his face. "And could this be that wife ye've been tellin' me about?" he said, though the doubt in his voice was obvious.

"No, 'tis not me Loralon. This is Miss Arwyn. Appeared at the Gate this afternoon, she did, and is a-lookin' for a place to rest for the night," Frondamein said. "Miss Arwyn, this is Horrin Buckleskin."

"Nice to meet you," I said, extending my hand. Horrin Buckleskin stared at it blankly until he finally realized that I expected him to grab hold.

"At yer sairvice, miss," he said as I pumped his hand up and down.

A short, plump, but very hefty-looking woman wearing a long dress with a tight, low-cut bodice appeared in the door. A mass of braided golden hair encircled her head and her eyes twinkled. "Ah, I see we've more guests."

"Aye, Mrs. Buckleskin, that we do," Horrin replied. "Ye remember Mr. Frondamein?"

"Forget one of our best customers? Are ye daft, man?"

Horrin ignored his wife and continued. "And this is Miss Arwyn."

The innkeeper's wife walked boldly up to me and looked me over from head to toe. "'Ow lovely ye are. We've not seen yer kind in these parts for at least a year, p'rhaps longer. Now where exactly do ye hail from?"

"Er, Miss Arwyn is from a faraway land," Frondamein interrupted. "Showed up at the Gate this afternoon, she did."

Horrin rubbed his chin and eyed me suspiciously. "Say, she's not from..."

"Tch! Horrin, 'ow could ye think such a thin'?" his wife scolded. "Ye'll 'ave to excuse me 'usband, Miss Arwyn. I'm afraid 'e's dealt wi' more than 'is share of Ashkars these past few years, and they're not all of 'em the unsightly kind like them Gargalocs."

The innkeeper's face brightened. "I hope ye'll find it in yer heart to forgive me, Miss Arwyn. Ye're most welcome at me 'umble establishment."

The Healer of Guildenwood

"Thank you, Mr. Buckleskin," I said, forcing a smile.

"Enough o' the talkin'," Mrs. Buckleskin announced. "Now come 'n get yerselves a meal sure to fill yer stomach and put meat on yer bones."

"Aye, aye woman. Now back to the kitchen wi' ye," Horrin said as he sent his wife away with a slap on her all-too-ample rump.

Horrin gestured toward the back room where the men were eating. "Come now," he said. "Ye look ready for a feast!"

As I walked into the room a hush came over the table where the men sat as each of them stared at me until we sat down on the other side of the dining area. Though they didn't seem at all malicious, it was quite disconcerting to have my every move closely scrutinized.

Frondamein and I sat down across the table from each other on wooden benches. No decorations adorned the walls inside other than a large map hanging above our table. Candles on the tables and in the sconces on the walls had been lit, creating a cheery ambience as the light outside the room's large window quickly disappeared. Yet even in the fading light I could see the lake outside, its surface shimmering with an orange glow.

Though very old and quaint, it was also quite evident that the inn was clean. Mrs. Buckleskin obviously saw to it that no crumbs were left about to attract vermin.

"Frondamein, 'ow's that little wife o' yours?" Horrin Buckleskin said.

"Fine as kin be, and expectin' our fairst child in a few months." Frondamein beamed.

"Ah, congratulations, Mr. Frondamein. 'Tis always good to 'ear o' new Bensorians comin' into the world," Horrin said. "Say, ye're not afraid to leave yer Loralon alone in Baeren Ford bein' with child 'n all?"

"Aye, it frightens me, Horrin, but what else kin I do? Draigon would 'ave me thrown in Dungard were I to abandon me post for good, and I dare not move Loralon closer to the Guildenmoor Gate. 'Tis safer the farther she is from Ashkaroth. Things aren't as they once were."

"Ah, 'tis true, and what a pity," Horrin sighed. "If only *he* would come."

"Aye, we're all of us awaitin' *him*, but we canna sit around while our country falls down about our ears," Frondamein said, clearing his throat as he glanced at me.

His statement begged the question, who is this *he*? But I thought better of bringing it up, considering by Frondamein's body language that he felt wary about discussing *him*, whoever *he* was, in front of a complete stranger.

"Still, we are but two simpleminded men, Horrin. What do we know o' politics?" Frondamein added, eyes darting to the others in the room.

The innkeeper glanced at me. "Ye must forgive us, Miss Arwyn, for discussin' Bensorian business in the presence of a lady," he said.

"On the contrary," Frondamein whispered. "Miss Arwyn 'ere believes someone should start a rebellion, and I'd 'ave to agree. We Bensorians are much too slow to action."

Ugh! "Wait a minute now, Frondamein!" I protested, struggling to keep my voice down. "I don't want to be accused of starting trouble."

"Not to wairry! Draigon would give little importance to the wiles of a woman," Horrin said with a twinkle in his eyes. "But I'm forgettin' me job. What kin I get for ye this eve? We've roast mutton on the skewer," he suggested.

"Fine choice," Frondamein said. "And I'll 'ave a pint as well."

Horrin then turned to me. "I'll have what he's having," I said hesitantly. "I'm so hungry I could pig out!"

Both Horrin and Frondamein glanced at each other with raised eyebrows. "Miss Arwyn," the innkeeper said, "ne'er 'ave I haird that expression before, but I'm sorry to tell ye that we've no pork tonight. Still, I suppose I could trouble the butcher for a favor."

"Oh, please no," I said, feeling embarrassed, "I'm sure that the, er, mutton will be fine."

"Verra well then. And ye'd like a pint as well to wash it down with?"

A pint? "Well, I *would* like a tall glass of milk, that is, if you have any."

Horrin scratched his head. "Miss Arwyn, we've no way to keep it from spoilin' durin' the heat o' the day. Perhaps m'lady would care for some nice apple cider instead, eh?"

"All right," I agreed.

When the plump innkeeper disappeared through a door to the kitchen in the back of the room, I turned to Frondamein and found him staring at me with an air of awe. Although he seemed to be a young man, tiny lines crept across his brow and branched out from the corners of his eyes—signs of a merry heart or a mind full of care, perhaps both. It made him look all the wiser, and I guessed there was more to him than appeared on the surface. But for his burly physique, which must have come from years of hard labor on his family farm, a gentle countenance was evident in his bright blue eyes.

"It's a shame you can't be closer to your wife," I commented, feeling sympathetic. "You must be very concerned about her living all by herself."

"The townspeople are quite neighborly and see to it that she's well looked after," Frondamein said, his eyes downcast. "Yet I canna help but wairry. 'Twould be such a comfort for someone to be there who kin keep an eye on 'er when I'm away. But alas, I know o' no one. We've verra little family left."

I remained silent for a moment, pondering my own situation. Frondamein seemed a kind, thoughtful sort of man, and I imagined his wife would be the same. And seeing as I had no other options in this foreign place, I could barely keep my wild idea inside. "Maybe I could help," I said quietly, showing some restraint.

Frondamein looked up. "Ye'd stay with Loralon and watch o'er her?"

"Well, maybe for a while, for as long as I'm needed that is," I offered, feeling suddenly quite desperate. "But it doesn't sound like you can be too trusting of strangers, and I would certainly understand if you didn't accept my offer, but I . . ."

"Miss Arwyn, do ye know ye kin tell a lot from a pairson by lookin' in their eyes, things like whether they're honest and good?"

"Yes, I suppose so."

"'Tis a trick I discovered a long while ago. Nay, in yer eyes I see naught but gentleness and a kindly heart," he said with utmost sincerity, which he had given me no reason to doubt. "But an elf o' yer obvious greatness is willin' to live with a poor family in Baeren Ford?"

"I don't need to live with my kind right now," I bluffed, concealing my loneliness in this strange new world. One thing was for certain—I did not want to be left alone with all those heinous Gargalocs running around the place. Frondamein himself seemed to be not only kind, but protective as well, and I needed someone like him on my side.

I decided to trust my instincts, even if it meant going farther away from the Gate the next day. Better that than to be left alone with no one to turn to. I would find my way back to the Gate later.

"The work will not be easy and is ne'er done," Frondamein warned. "The life of a peasant is full o' hardship."

"I'm not afraid of hard work."

Frondamein's face beamed with delight. "Then 'tis settled, Miss Arwyn. Tomorrow we leave for Baeren Ford!"

Mrs. Buckleskin burst through the door with two steaming plates in her hands, Horrin following closely carrying two mugs.

"Ah, a feast fit for a king," Frondamein said as Mrs. Buckleskin placed our order on the table along with a loaf of bread.

I stared at the meal of mutton and potatoes before me, wishing for a side salad. As I took my first bite, I was surprised at how savory the meat was, flavored with unusual spices I couldn't identify. Both of the Buckleskins stood by expectantly. I took a sip of my cider and smiled. "Everything is wonderful."

Based on the smiles that spread across their faces, the innkeeper and his wife seemed genuinely delighted that I was pleased.

"And ye like our cider?" Mrs. Buckleskin asked. "'Tis 'omemade, ye know, like our ale. But our ale *is* a bit strong for a lady such as yerself."

"Me wife, however, kin down a gallon in the blink of an eye and still see to the cookin' and cleanin' at that," Horrin bragged.

Mrs. Buckleskin laughed heartily and jabbed her husband in the ribs, the white flesh of her ample bosom undulating with the motion.

Throughout our meal Frondamein described his beloved country of Bensor with help from the old map that hung on the wall above our table. Bensor itself was shaped roughly like a tilted boot, cut off above the ankle, with three distinct regions. I listened carefully as he talked about the wooded region of Guilden, where I had found myself that afternoon, with its rolling hills dotted with small farms and villages inhabited primarily by mortals. Then there was Elwindor, the region to the southeast, which had more wide-open spaces where larger herds of animals grazed and vineyards flourished in the warmer climate.

To the northeast lay Loth Gerodin Forest, "Bensor's Garden," and the most enchanting and mysterious place in all the land. Elves had made this region their refuge for many years as it lay far from the prying eyes of Maldimire, cut off from the rest of Bensor by the Andain Mountains. Many were the stories of arrogant adventurers who entered the dense forest without an elven guide, only to never be heard from again. In fact, all roads to the elven cities remained magically hidden and almost impossible for mortals to find.

Colonies of dwarves inhabited the majestic Andain mountain chain that ran from the north down into the center of Bensor. More persecuted by Draigon than any other Bensorian people, the dwarves now did hard labor in the mines that had been theirs for nearly two thousand years.

Through all three regions flowed the mighty River Silvendell, deep and wide enough to allow small vessels to sail as far north as Stone Harbour. The river cut a path through the southern part of Loth Gerodin and then past the western end of the Andains where it began its trek south, carving its way through a landscape dotted with vineyards and ancient bastions until it eventually emptied into the Eleuvial Sea at Maldimire. It was said of the river that it shimmered like silver when touched by the light of a full moon, and thus came its name.

I studied the map carefully, trying to find any feature on it that I could recognize. To my dismay, it looked totally unfamiliar.

I had already consumed half the loaf of bread, two servings of meat, three servings of potatoes, and I was on my third glass of cider. In all my memory I could not recall ever being so hungry, and Frondamein was amazed at the amount of food I had devoured.

"Looks as though ye've not seen the likes o' food for a while," he commented.

"Don't worry, I'm not usually so famished," I explained.

"'Tis good for a woman to have a hearty appetite," Horrin Buckleskin added as he set two pieces of blackberry pie on the table before us.

Our meal finished and both of us contentedly full, Frondamein pulled a pipe from a pocket in his tunic, from which he also brought forth a small pouch filled with tobacco. Still feeling as though I were in the midst of some lingering dream, I watched as he carefully stuffed the tobacco into his pipe and then lit it with a piece of straw he had set ablaze with one of the candles on the table. The smoke soon permeated the area with a pleasant aroma.

There had been a steady stream of people entering the inn since we sat down to eat, and nearly every table in the dining area was now full. From the corner of my eye I had watched them enter the room expectantly, until their eyes rested on Frondamein and me. It was as if half the town had abandoned dinner plans to come to the Old Oak Inn that evening in order to see the spectacle of me, the supposed elf, whatever *that* was. But all I could conjure were images of tiny little men with pointy little hats and beards. The one thing I was certain of was that I was an ordinary person like they. So what was all the fuss about?

With all the customers, Horrin was kept busy running to and fro with mugs of ale, all the while enjoying a dose of friendly bantering.

After a while, Frondmein let out a yawn. "Well, Miss Arwyn, where'er ye came from, I'm glad ye've chosen to make Bensor yer home and that ye'll be a-comin' to stay with me and me wife."

I managed to smile in response, but deep down I still held out the hope of somehow finding my way back to the place where I had come from. Back to the place where I could blend in. Back to the place where someone, surely, was wondering where I was by now, although for the life of me I couldn't remember who that would be.

"We shall leave for Baeren Ford airly on the morrow, for 'twill take us the better part o' the day to reach our destination, and I'm anxious to see me wife and know she's well," Frondamein said as he waved Horrin over to the table.

"If ye'll be so kind as to put the meal on me tab," Frondamein said as he gathered his belongings.

"Aye, that I'll do, Mr. Frondamein." Horrin then turned to me. "And, miss, I wish to beg yer pardon once more for airlier. With all the Gargalocs comin' and goin', we're all a bit ill at ease. They've e'en been so bold as to come into th' inn for a pint, but I draw the line at lettin' 'em sleep in our beds, brutes that they are."

"Well, yes, judging by their appearance, they must have an extra Y chromosome or perhaps some other genetic abnormality. At any rate, quite difficult to rehabilitate," I replied casually.

"An extra what?" Frondamein asked with raised brow.

And then I looked up at Horrin, who chuckled uncomfortably as he eyed Frondamein. "The wiles of a woman! No more mysterious creatures there be. Why, I understand less than 'alf o' what me own wife says!"

Polite as they were, I still suspected that they thought I was speaking some sort of "elvish" gibberish. I just *had* to remember that I had come to the backwoods.

"Come now, and I'll show ye to yer rooms," Horrin said and then turned to walk toward the hallway. I was about to follow him when I remembered the knapsack that had accompanied me on my journey that afternoon. Quickly I snatched it up before following Horrin and Frondamein out into the hall.

Horrin picked up a candle from a table in the entryway, for night had fallen and the light of the sun had long-since disappeared. He led the way up a narrow, rickety old staircase to the second floor where he turned down a corridor and entered a room that overlooked the lake. The three of us went inside the stark room where Horrin lit another candle sitting on a small table beside an old wooden bed. The only other piece of furniture was an old armoire that had seen better days.

"I've a very 'umble inn, Miss Arwyn, nothin' like what ye're most likely accustomed to. Still, 'twill be a place to rest yer head for the night."

"I'm sure it'll be fine," I replied, taking the key the innkeeper held out to me.

"I'll bid ye good night as well," Frondamein said. "If there be any trouble, I'm just down the hall."

"Heaven forbid!" Horrin exclaimed as the two men walked out of the room.

I locked the door behind them as their voices faded away down the corridor.

Standing in the middle of the floor, I felt even more alone than before. The candle that stood on the bedside table emitted enough light to somewhat dispel the gloom, but it did nothing to lighten my spirits.

I became aware of a weight in my hand and remembered the mysterious pouch. Sitting down on the bed, I eyed the bag for a moment and then cautiously untied its strap. Carefully I gave it a quick shake, halfway expecting some creature to come crawling out.

Holding my breath, I shook the bag's contents onto the bed, surprised when several garments came tumbling out. The first was a folksy-looking green gown of sorts with a short skirt that was slit up the front as though it were meant for riding, a rather immodest thing had it not been for the pair of brown leggings I found with it, no doubt to be worn underneath. There were also two leather riding boots and what appeared to be a long nightshirt.

The Healer of Guildenwood

After that, the bag seemed empty. Still, I gave it another shake. To my surprise, a small leather pouch fell out onto the bed. I untied the drawstrings and emptied the contents. Several small items clanked together loudly as they fell onto the quilt beside me. I scooped the objects up in my hand and examined them in the light of the candle.

Sixteen small circles of gold reflected the light of the nearby flame. I gasped at how weighty the small fortune felt in my hand, and how smooth the coins as I carefully placed each back into the pouch, which I immediately deposited back into the knapsack so I would be sure not to lose it.

Marveling at the contents of the knapsack, I wondered how they had come into my possession and if someone had intended for them to be mine. The clothing would never fit, for they had obviously been made for someone much taller than I. Still, there was no point in letting them wrinkle.

I grabbed the candle beside the bed and took it, along with the garments, over to the armoire. Expecting to find something on which to hang them, I opened the door to the armoire and was shocked to find a woman standing there! I gasped at the sight of her, yet I could tell that she was just as surprised to see me.

In an instant came an even more terrifying realization—I wasn't looking at another person at all! What I was staring at was my own reflection in a dingy mirror.

From deep in my belly, a cry threatened to erupt. Quickly I placed a hand over my mouth to stifle a scream.

Clothing forgotten in a pile on the floor, I raised a hand to touch my face, exploring my cheeks, nose, and lips that I parted to expose a row of perfect white teeth. I looked to be at least several years older, though no wrinkle or blemish etched the surface of my face.

My fingertips traveled down the length of my long neck, and I'm sure I must have blushed in the darkness when they found the fullness of a very womanly bosom. In fact, it was quite embarrassing to be touching another woman's breasts. I had to remind myself that those breasts were . . . mine.

I then grasped locks of dark brown hair in my hands, amazed at how its soft curls spiraled down to my waist. My eyes, the color of emeralds, revealed the shock with which I beheld my new image. Perhaps at any other time it would have pleased me, but at that moment I felt nothing but horror.

A long, belted blue dress adorned the, that is, *my* body. I lifted the skirt a few inches to expose two leather sandals and still further to see two long, slender legs underneath. How far away the floor suddenly felt, far enough that if I were to faint, I would certainly wake with a nasty headache!

I stared, unbelieving, into the mirror for several minutes. During the confusing events of the day, the fact that my body felt physically different was just one of the many mysteries swirling in my already-overwhelmed brain. Compared to everything else that had happened, the fact that my height, the length of my hair, and the sound of my voice seemed off-kilter had been but a minor nuisance tickling the back of my mind. Now, however, the full effect of this new form bombarded my awareness like a thunderous avalanche racing down a mountain.

For a moment the room spun and I felt as though I *would* faint. Forcing myself away from the mirror, I made my way to the edge of the bed and held my head between my legs as a wave of nausea hit. Feeling a breeze blow through my hair, I rushed over to the open window and leaned outside, partially expelling the contents of my stomach as tears ran down my face. The night air helped to ease the queasiness, yet a maelstrom of questions whirled through my mind to the point that I believed I had surely gone mad.

It was several moments before I finally moved to brush several long, curly tendrils of hair from my face. A light flashed across my hand, reflecting the light of the candle inside the room. Upon further examination, I was surprised to notice for the first time a very familiar looking gold ring with a single purple stone surrounded by two diamonds riding there. Somehow I knew that I had brought it from that *other* place, my only link to my previous existence, and though my memory of it was foggy, the sight of the ring was enough to give me some comfort.

Below my window, the inky blackness of the lake concealed the mysteries of its nocturnal dramas, yet up above the sky was blanketed with what looked to be a million tiny beacons.

"What in the world am I doing here?" I wondered out loud.

I gazed at the stars, yet they revealed nothing. Only the sound of the bullfrogs and an occasional hooting from an owl could be heard over the gentle breeze.

I turned toward the bed and laughed suddenly. Why was I getting so worked up? After all, I was certain I would awake in the morning and discover that this had all been a weird dream—a really weird dream.

A great weariness suddenly overtook me. Not even bothering to put on the nightshirt, I climbed onto the lumpy mattress. It was not long before I fell into a deep sleep.

CHAPTER 6

"Okay, so maybe I'm not dreaming," I said.

"Then how do you explain what has happened to you?" came a familiar voice from somewhere close by, one that gave me great comfort when I heard it.

"Maybe I'm in some kind of time warp, but really, I have no clue," I replied. "I only know that I have to do whatever I can to keep a low profile and try to figure out how to survive without the use of anything remotely modern."

Ah, music. What a relief! All I had to do was reach over, push a little button and go back to sleep. No more weirdness!

With my face still planted in my pillow, I reached over to the bedside table, fingers groping for the switch, when all they found was a bowl of tepid water. In a state of drowsy confusion, I lifted my head and rubbed the sleep from my eyes, squinting at the sunlight that spilled into the window and onto the foot of the bed. A host of noisy blue and yellow birds flitted from tree to tree outside, signaling the morning with a symphony of melodic calls. So that's what had awakened me!

In a rush of remembrance, the events of the day before came flooding back into consciousness. I bolted upright in bed, my heart racing as I quickly took in my surroundings by the light of day. Springing from the bed, I ran across the room to the armoire, gasping once more as the stranger emerged before me in the looking glass. I touched the unfamiliar face with unfamiliar hands, watching as its color drained away from my cheeks. Feeling weak and dizzy, I made my way back to the bed and sat down, clasping my arms tightly around my knees.

"Arwyn, you have got to get a hold of yourself," I chided. "And what's up with this 'Arwyn'? My name is . . . is . . . oh, if only I could remember," I said, grabbing a handful of hair with each fist and shaking my head in a fit of panic.

Suddenly I jumped to my feet and began marching around the room as if searching for an invisible foe. "All right! Whoever was responsible for sending me here, I want you to stop playing games with me!" I pleaded in a loud whisper. "You've made a *huge* mistake, and I *demand* that you send me back to where I came from!"

I gave a start when there came a sudden knock at the door. "Miss Arwyn, I know 'tis airly but Mr. Frondamein says ye'll need to be leavin' soon." It was Horrin Buckleskin.

"Tell him I'll be right down—" My voice cracked.

My clothing still lay in a heap on the floor. Gathering the knapsack, I stuffed them in, all the while muttering to myself. "I *have* to talk Frondamein into going back to the Gate. It may be a bit out of the way, but I'm sure he won't mind. I know I'll find the way home there—I simply must!"

Gathering my composure, I went to the ceramic washbasin beside the bed and splashed water onto my face. I still wore the dress I had been wearing the day before, only now it was wrinkled from having been slept in all night. I attempted to smooth it out a bit but with only a passing thought, for there were much more important matters at hand.

After carefully checking to make sure I'd not forgotten anything, especially the pouch of gold coins, I picked up my bag and opened the door into the quiet hallway. Hoping not to wake the other guests, although it seemed that Frondamein and I were the only ones, I tiptoed along the creaky floorboards to the stairwell and down to the room below where Frondamein greeted me with a cheerful smile.

"Good mornin' to ye, Miss Arwyn," he said. "Me apologies for the airliness o' the hour, but we'll need to get on the road now to make Baeren Ford by sundown."

"Er, okay," I replied, still hoping to find that portal leading back home. Why, I could be back within a couple of hours! "Besides, I'm sure I couldn't sleep another wink even if I tried."

Mrs. Buckleskin appeared in the kitchen door carrying a tray with two mugs of steaming hot tea, a cup of milk, and a loaf of bread. "Mind ye now, ye'll not be a-leavin' on an empty stomach if I have anythin' to say in the matter," she chirped. "And miss, here's that cup o' milk ye were askin' for last night. Come straight from the cow—dairymaid brought it afore sunrise, she did."

"Thank you very much," I replied as I thirstily accepted the offer. I took one sip of the milk and found it lukewarm. Still, it hit the spot. I quickly consumed the contents and asked for more. After two more mugs-full, I finally declared myself satisfied.

"My, I've seen naught but a newborn take such a likin' to milk as you, miss," Mrs. Buckleskin commented.

The hasty meal consumed, Frondamein and I made our way outside

The Healer of Guildenwood

where Durkin had the horses waiting. The redness returned to his face when I smiled at him in greeting. There was a time in the past when I would have responded more encouragingly to the handsome adolescent's attention, but now the thought of flirting with a boy his age seemed oddly repugnant. "Thank you for taking care of my horse," I said to him.

"'Tis a fine hairse ye've got there, mum," Durkin said as he nervously kicked at a stone on the ground.

For the first time I took a good, long look at the magnificent creature on which I had mysteriously found myself the day before. In the morning sun, his mane appeared the color of spun gold and his hide shimmered an unearthly, almost iridescent white.

With two dark eyes the steed stared at me with intelligent curiosity. As Frondamein busied himself with his horse's harness, I could not help but walk over and stroke its neck gingerly, and it seemed a silent connection passed between us as we gazed squarely into each other's eyes. He neighed gently, lifting his head into the air and bringing it down to rest upon my shoulder.

I could feel a tug at my heart. No, that would never do.

"That's a fine saddle as well," Durkin commented, breaking into my thoughts. "I've not seen it's like since the last time elves showed up in Mindlemir."

I eyed it for myself and could see that beautifully intricate designs looking something like vines weaving in and out and ending in circular patterns had been etched into the leather at the edge of the saddle.

Frondamein walked up to see the saddle for himself. "That's elven craftsmanship, all right. In all me days, I've not seen such skilled work on a saddle."

Horrin Buckleskin burst through the front door of the inn. "Off, are ye now? I see the boy 'as tended well to yer hairses," he said approvingly.

"Durkin's as good a stable boy as e'er there was," Frondamein replied.

"Aye, and it seems 'e's taken a fancy to a sairtain elven maiden." Horrin said under his breath, to which Frondamein smiled in response. They were the only two who found the comment at all humorous, for I could see the boy's face turn a deeper shade of red as he gave a loud cough and turned away.

"Mr. Buckleskin," I said as I rummaged through my knapsack, hoping to change the subject as quickly as possible. "You've been so nice to me." In a moment I found the object of my search and withdrew the small pouch containing the gold coins. I shook three of the coins into my hand and held them out to the innkeeper. "I don't know how much I owe for the room and the meals, but maybe this will cover it."

"Ah, 'tis much more than enough, Miss Arwyn. Do ye not know ye've a small fortune there?" Horrin said. "Besides, Mr. Frondamein 'as already seen to yer obligation."

I looked at Frondamein and smiled gratefully, and it was now the older man's turn to blush. With that, we mounted our horses.

"Oh, Horrin Buckleskin," the innkeeper muttered, "ye'd forget yer name every day were it not for yer wife yellin' it at ye a dozen times in as many hours." Raising his voice he turned to me, "Would ye be so kind as to wait for an old man to tend to 'is duties?" He turned toward the inn as Mrs. Buckleskin appeared at the door with a burlap sack in her hand.

"Ye'd 'ave our guests go 'ungry on the road, now wouldn't ye," she scolded.

"I was just on me way . . ."

"Tch! Ye'll 'ave to forgive me husband," Mrs. Buckleskin said as she handed the sack to the round-bellied man. "Here's a little somethin' for the road. Ye'll be gettin' 'ungry later."

Horrin Buckleskin obediently handed the sack to Frondamein with a wide grin on his face. "Keeps me in line, she does."

Frondamein returned the smile. "Much obliged, Horrin."

"Miss Arwyn, 'tis been a pleasure makin' yer acquaintance. We dunna see enough o' yer kind these days," the innkeeper said, his face beaming with sincerity.

"Ye'll stay 'ere now, if e'er ye retairn to Mindlemir," his wife added.

"I'd be glad to," I replied politely, though deep down I hoped to be home as soon as possible.

Mr. and Mrs. Buckleskin and Durkin all waved good-bye as we rode across the inn's courtyard and past the front gate, where I was surprised to find a throng of people lined up as if waiting for our departure. As we rode past they waved, wide-eyed, wishing us a safe journey.

"Do they do this for everyone who comes through town?" I asked Frondamein.

"I'd daresay not," he replied, and it seemed to me he sat a little taller in his saddle and a smug grin spread across his face—as if he were in a royal procession. As for me, I felt more like a circus sideshow.

Farther along, the main thoroughfare through town was beginning to fill with merrymakers preparing for the day's festivities, setting up their booths and bringing in food for the feast that would occur later. It was only a matter of minutes, however, before we passed under the archway that marked the entrance to the village and started heading south. At last we came to the road that led to the Guildenmoor Gate, and I slowed my horse to a stop. Frondamein rode a little farther before he noticed my reluctance to continue.

"Forget somethin', Miss Arwyn?"

"Well, I was wondering if we could perhaps . . . er . . . return to the Guildenmoor Gate," I stammered. "I believe I may have lost something there."

Frondamein scratched his head. "The Gate's far out o' the way. 'Twould put us after dark afore we arrived in Baeren Ford, and our hairses aren't likely to take kindly to such a long trip. 'Tis a long day for 'em as it is."

I looked down the road that headed east and realized my dilemma. Either I could return to the Guildenmoor Gate alone and search for the way home, thereby possibly never seeing Frondamein again and having no one else to turn to. Or I could accompany him to his village and then return later to the Gate when I was able.

There was really only one choice my prudent mind would allow. There were no guarantees in either direction, but at least by going with Frondamein I wouldn't be alone.

Hopes temporarily dashed, along with the optimistic mood that had gone with them, I prompted my horse straight down the road that led into the heart of Bensor and, I feared, farther away from any conscious memory of the world I had left behind.

The journey started well enough as the morning sun dispelled the thin, ghostly fog that blanketed the land during the night. Everywhere the world was abuzz with exuberance, for it was the first day of summer, and it seemed as though all nature was celebrating the birth of the new season.

Every now and then I caught glimpses of the River Goldenreed, which had left its headwaters behind in Mindlemir on its southerly trek to the sea. Through gently rolling forests and pastureland dotted with charming thatched-roof cottages it meandered, passing ancient stone fences laced with flowers of every color and variety. Wild deer, foxes, and rabbits bounded playfully in meadows where grazing sheep offered them little more than a glance. The sweet smell of honeysuckle permeated the air, and the coolness of early morning dissipated as the sun made its way higher in the sky. It was all picture-perfect, like I'd somehow strayed into a storybook, or painting of a countryside so innocent and pristine that it couldn't possibly exist in the real world.

Frondamein led the way through small, picturesque villages bustling with activity as people went about preparing for the new year's festivities that would begin early in the afternoon. Some were but tiny hamlets where perhaps a few dozen people lived while others were large enough for a central square. Wherever we went, whether in the villages or the countryside, the friendly Bensorians along the route waved to us as we passed, and everywhere I received the same curious gazes.

With every bend of the road, I had to remind myself not to be enchanted by it all, not to think of this land as the most beautiful place I had ever seen—at least the most charming place I could ever *remember* seeing. There could be no emotional attachment. Nothing that would make it difficult for me to make a break for the Gate when the opportunity presented itself. I didn't belong here.

Thankfully, Frondamein's talkative nature provided some respite for my anxiety. Hearing the stories of his boyhood in Guilden was enough of a diversion to keep my feverish thoughts tamed for the moment. And it wasn't a bad thing to learn about the people I would be living with for a while. I was intrigued to learn how Frondamein and his wife, Loralon, had known each other since they were "babes in their mothers' arms," had fallen in love in their youth and then were wed when they came of age.

Frondamein spoke sadly of his father, who had died several years earlier and left the family farm to him, his only son, and of his sister Maerta, who had long since settled in Galymara where her husband had found work as a fisherman in the bountiful waters that flanked Bensor's western coast. Years passed between visits, and Frondamein would have had almost no contact with her, were it not for his guard duty that sometimes led him to other parts of Guilden.

Following his father's death, Frondamein had been quite content to take over the family business until he was forced into the service of Draigon. When it became impossible for his new bride to run the farm on her own, he grudgingly sold his beloved family home near Baeren Ford and moved Loralon in with her one-hundred-twenty-year-old aunt Hedgepeth, who lived by herself on a small farm near the village. However, poor Hedgepeth caught ill and passed on about a year or so before, leaving the cottage to Loralon and Frondamein.

Although Frondamein worried that Loralon was there all alone, the villagers were quite neighborly. Many had known the two of them for years and were glad to look in on Loralon from time to time. And, as fortune would have it, the village of Baeren Ford was a reasonable day's journey from the Gate. So, altogether it was not the worst of situations, though it was certainly not ideal.

Frondamein reminded me of a pot simmering on a stove that had not quite reached the point of boiling. Despite his overall pleasant demeanor, I could tell that he harbored a great deal of bitterness by what had been taken from him and a fierce determination to keep what was still his. And when it came to his beloved Bensor, he felt helpless to stop its slow decay by those who cared nothing for it. However, with every mile we traveled closer to home and wife, the creases on his face melted away.

As for me, I was quiet for the most part and only responded with a few "uh-huhs" and "oh, that's very interestings." After all, there was little I could tell him as there was hardly anything I remembered about myself, like where I was from, who my parents were, my friends, what I did for a living... all those "normal" things that make for pleasant chitchat. I certainly didn't want to tell him what was *really* on my mind—that I had seemingly appeared in this place from out of nowhere, with no explanation whatsoever. He'd think I was completely insane. And maybe I was—after all, why else could I remember so little from my past?

As the mid-day temperature rose, we stopped along the riverbank to give the horses a break. While the horses drank their fill from the crystal-clear waters of the river, Frondamein and I dined on the apples, bread, and cheese provided by Mrs. Buckleskin. Beside us the lazy Goldenreed flowed swiftly in some places as it plunged over rocks and logs in its way, only to lull through deeper, quieter channels. Under the surface of the water the tall river grass for which the river was named undulated with the current and cast a sparkling golden hue when struck by the rays of the sun.

I watched distastefully as Frondamein walked over to the riverbank and dipped his hand into the water, drinking thirstily as he raised it to his lips. "You're not afraid of bacteria?" I asked.

"Bac... teria?" Frondamein said with a confused look on his face.

"You know... little things in water that make you sick."

"Been drinkin' it all me days, and it 'asn't killed me yet. In fact, they say a drink from the river'll add another year to yer life."

"And how old would that make you?"

"I expect I'll live to be about five hundred." Frondamein grinned. "Me grandfather lived to nearly one hundred and fifty. Rather old for a mortal."

"I'd say so! You must have mighty good genes in your family."

Frondamein eyed me questioningly. "Ye must forgive me as I'm not acquainted with elvish wairds, Miss Arwyn." He sat thoughtfully for a moment, picking at the crevices between his teeth with a piece of straw. "Ye elves, on the other hand, ye need not wairry about such, as ye know ye'll be livin' fore'er as 'tis, unless o' course ye meet with an enemy who's intent on yer blood," he said matter-of-factly, as if the issue of mortality and immortality was an accepted reality in the world of elves and humans.

I remained silent for a moment as I pondered Frondamein's words. Living to be hundreds of years old was hard enough to believe, much less the idea of living forever. I dismissed the thought as outrageous.

"Miss Arwyn." Frondamein's voice broke into my thoughts. "We'd best be a-leavin'. Me Loralon awaits."

Thirst getting the best of me, I stood up and marched over to the edge of the river and dipped my hand in. After a refreshing taste of the cold, clear water, I wiped my chin and noticed that Frondamein was staring at me inquisitively. "Thought ye were afraid o' the bac... whate'er it was ye said."

"If it will help me live longer, I suppose I can put up with a few intestinal problems."

The sun hovered above the horizon in the western sky when Frondamein announced at last that our destination was imminent. The anticipation of seeing for the first time the place I would reluctantly call home, at least for a little while, caused my stomach to churn unmercifully. That, and meeting the wife who would no doubt have the power to reject the whole notion of needing an "assistant."

Furthermore, we had been riding at a trot for the majority of the day (and me wearing a long dress, no less), and as smooth and easy as my horse had been to ride, my new body was beginning to suffer from a full day in the saddle. The thought of a hot bath and comfortable bed was foremost, but I didn't know if I could count on either.

On the last leg of the journey, the road curved through lush green meadows, and we were forced to stop for a few moments while a young shepherd guided a flock of scruffy sheep across the road on the way home for the evening. The river suddenly took a sharp turn toward the west and plunged down several feet into a great pool where it cut a narrow gorge through the terrain. An old stone bridge spanned the gorge, and on the other side we crested a hill and looked down upon a hospitable-looking village nestled comfortably in a lovely little valley. I nudged my horse to stop beside Frondamein, and together we gazed upon the scene as a warm orange glow settled above the land to the west.

"Miss Arwyn, our journey's done," Frondamein said quietly. "This is Baeren Ford. We're 'ome."

CHAPTER 7

"You must feel very relieved that this Lor . . . Lor . . ."
"Loralon," I replied absently.
"That Loralon is willing to let you stay for a while," Dr. Susan's voice droned on in the background of my mind.
"That's one hurdle out of the way. Only a thousand left."

———◆———

To our right, I could see the Goldenreed emerge through a cleft between two hills and roll along past an old mill until it emptied into a small lake in the middle of the valley. On the near side of the lake was a quaint village where several rows of stone buildings stood side by side, forming a square in their midst. In the middle of the square, a fountain spewed, and a large bell tower rose high above the goings-on down below.

Beyond the village on the other side of the lake, cottages dotted the hillside, each with boundaries that were clearly defined by stone fences. Almost every plot of land had its own vegetable garden and most had patches reserved solely for flowers, a necessity for nature-loving Bensorians, as Frondamein explained. On the far side of the valley, up beyond the village was the larger Lake Ellowyne that spilled over its southern boundary, creating a stream that rambled past a row of houses, eventually flowing into the smaller lake below.

But it was the ruins of an old fortress, long abandoned, on a hilltop overlooking the village that particularly moved me. A crumbling shell was all that remained. Its ominous walls stood sentinel over the quiet valley, a silent remnant of ages past. The pastel sky silhouetted gaping holes where once tall windows and gateways had been. As we rode down toward the village, my eyes were irresistibly drawn to the ancient bastion.

"'Tis Arnuin's Hold," Frondamein said, noticing my curiosity. "And that's a story what deserves tellin', but now's not the time nor the place, for wary we must be speakin' o' such thin's . . ." His voice trailed off in such a way that made me wonder what secrets the ancient ruins could possibly hold.

"What a sad, lonely place it is," I said, my heart moved by the majesty of the silent fortress towering above. "Still, there is something rather peaceful about it."

"'Tis nothin' more than a place for children to play now." Frondamein sighed as we passed beneath the ancient ramparts and down toward the town.

The road led through the village square and back over the Goldenreed above the place where it emptied into the lower lake. Weeping willows lazily caressed the surface of the still water as families of ducks and geese settled underneath for the night.

As the bell tower in the village square chimed the hour, we passed beneath the southern end of the fortress where a crowd had gathered under a small grove of apple trees. Lanterns of various shapes and sizes dangled from ropes strung between the trees and over tables set up for the feast celebrating the coming of summer. The sounds of laughter mingled with the sound of singing minstrels, and I could see Frondamein scanning the throng for his wife, but she was apparently nowhere to be seen for he kept pressing down the road.

As we passed, I could feel dozens of eyes upon me and could hear a wave of surprised chattering sweeping through the crowd in the wake of our appearance. How I wished we had arrived in town on a day when the whole village wasn't out! I glanced over at Frondamein and could see the smug smile had returned to his face.

Making our way through the center of the village to the hillside beyond, Frondamein led the way past another stone building at the lake's edge with a sign above the front door that read "Blue Willow." A man standing under the sign directed two burly men carrying a large cask of ale. As we approached, he squinted at us.

"Frondamein, old chap, is it you? I hardly recognized ye, what wi' the company ye're keepin,'" he said as he eyed me.

"Miss Arwyn, this is Padimus, proprietor of Baeren Ford's only tavern."

"Nice to meet you," I replied.

"A pleasure, miss," Padimus said as he gave me a large grin. "Tell me, what brings an elf such as yerself to these parts? Ye look as though ye're from the northern forest?"

Frondamein interrupted. "Miss Arwyn 'ails from a faraway land; a newcomer to Bensor, she is. Out o' the goodness of 'er 'eart she's kindly agreed to live in me 'ome and look after Loralon while I'm away at the Gate."

"Verra kind indeed," Padimus replied as he scratched his chin. "Now, speakin' o' yer Loralon, I saw 'er this morning on 'er way to market. Said she expected ye'd be comin' 'ome this eve."

"'Ow is she, Padimus?"

"Fine as a fox in a henhouse, and gettin' bigger every day, if ye know what I mean." The taverner grinned.

Frondamein returned the smile. "Well, we'd best be a-gettin' 'ome so I kin see 'er for meself."

"Aye, musn't keep 'er waitin' a moment longer," Padimus said. "Although, I've news for ye meself, if I kin trouble ye a moment longer."

"Aye," Frondamein said as he leaned down. The expression on his face turned serious.

"One o' them men come by the tavern two days ago, pokin' about as they usually do, askin' about any newcomers in town and the young men who've come of age," Padimus said in a lowered voice. "'Tis always the same. They stay for a day or two and ride about the village as if lookin' for someone and then they leave, not to be heard from for months."

Frondamein sighed. "Draigon's henchmen to be sure, but why they're so interested in the good folk o' Baeren Ford, I'll ne'er know."

"Not to wairry, Miss Arwyn," Padimus said. "When it comes to what goes on in the village, I'm like a mole in a hole—I see and 'ear nothin'."

"'Tis rather 'ard to believe, 'specially o' the town taverner," Frondamein said with a smirk.

"They'll 'ear naught from me, o' that ye kin be sure." Padimus smiled. "I've seen no elf for ages, and if they ask, I'll tell 'em ye're as mortal as the rest of us."

"Aye," Frondamein added. "In time, she'll blend in fine."

I smiled uncertainly, still not sure what this whole "elf" business was and why people made so much to-do about it.

As we made our way from the tavern, Padimus called after us. "Stop by while ye're in town, Frondamein. You too, Miss Arwyn."

We continued on along the lake where children played on the grassy banks, passing by several quaint cottages and over a bubbling brook that coursed from the hill down through the valley, emptying into the water below. On the other side of the brook was a pretty little thatched, white wattle and daub cottage with a garden and small pasture lying between it and the woods that lay on the edge of the village.

"'Ere we are, Miss Arwyn," Frondamein said, slowing in front of the small house. "'Ome at last."

A white picket fence lined with flowers and a profusion of weeds surrounded the front lawn, in the middle of which stood a quaint covered well. A gate that had become unhinged sat propped in a state of disrepair against a honeysuckle-covered arbor leading through the fence. The house was built into the side of a hill, upon which rose a giant old oak tree, its huge limbs sprawled out as if sheltering the little cottage beneath in its watchful care.

Frondamein and I rode past the end of the picket fence and up to the stable that adjoined the main house. On the other side of the stable was a good-sized but partially cultivated vegetable garden and behind that, a small field where a single cow grazed.

I eyed my new home carefully and was quite charmed with my initial impression despite its somewhat disheveled appearance. Upon seeing the small but cozy house, if there had been any doubt before, in my heart I knew that the inhabitants could only be good and kindly people.

Frondamein climbed from his horse and tied its reins to the fence and did the same with mine as I dismounted. I went to retrieve the knapsack from my horse's back as a woman with bright red hair braided down her back appeared at the front door of the cottage.

"Frondamein, love!" the woman exclaimed as she ran across the lawn and into her husband's arms. Frondamein picked her up off her feet and spun her around, kissing her eagerly.

"I've missed ye so, me darlin'. 'Ow's the little one?" Frondamein said, gently placing his wife back on the ground and patting her bulging belly.

"Beginnin' to move about so's I kin 'ardly get a good night's sleep for the kickin'. We're goin' to 'ave us a rowdy young'n, we are."

"And why are ye not at the festivities with all th' other townsfolk?"

"I knew ye were a-comin' 'ome this eve. Could feel it in me bones. Wanted ye all to meself, I did . . ." Loralon's voice trailed off as she looked up and for the first time saw me, the stranger, standing there.

"Loralon," Frondamein said, taking her by the hand and leading her over to the place where I waited. "This is Miss Arwyn. Traveled to Bensor from a faraway country, she did, and arrived yesterday by way o' the Guildenmoor Gate."

Loralon bowed her head slightly. "Welcome to our 'ome, 'umble though it is," she said uncertainly.

"You're all Frondamein talks about," I offered. "I feel like I know you already."

"Miss Arwyn's an elf, like the ones I've told ye about," Frondamein explained, barely able to contain his excitement.

Loralon's eyes grew wide with wonder. "An elf . . . in Baeren Ford? Ne'er did I think I'd see such a day!"

Frondamein seemed pleased that Loralon shared his enthusiasm, though I detected a hint of uncertainty in her voice. "Frondamein 'as told me much about yer kind, but I've not 'ad the good fortune to 'ave met an elf meself . . . until now. Tell me, what brings ye to these parts?"

"Er, Loralon, we've a matter to discuss," Frondamein said, as he took his wife by the arm. "Miss Arwyn, p'rhaps ye'd like to go inside 'n rest yerself. I know ye must be weary from our journey."

"Okay . . . I mean, all right," I said calmly, but deep inside my stomach churned away. If Loralon rejected me, I would be out on my own in a strange land. And certainly she had the right to do so. After all, what woman would allow another woman, especially a stranger, to come and live under the same roof?

Frondamein led me to the front door of the cottage and stepped inside.

"'Tis a rather 'umble dwellin', but 'tis 'ome nonetheless," he said.

"'Ad I known a guest was a-comin', I'd 'ave been better prepared," Loralon added. Out of the corner of my eye, I could see her give her husband a quick jab in the ribs.

"What a neat old house," I said as my eyes adjusted to the dim lighting.

"I try 'n keep it tidy," Loralon said.

"Oh, I meant that it's very nice."

"And not so old either," Frondamein added. "'Twas built only a dozen or so years ago."

I gazed at the interior of the cottage. On the other side of the room a warm fire glowed in the fireplace. A sumptuous aroma filled the room, presumably from whatever bubbled in the large black kettle that hung over the flames, and it mingled with the scent of lavender from the various bundles of dried flowers that hung from the rafters. Before the hearth a gray and white cat lazed on a large woven rug next to a rocking chair. Opposite the rocking chair next to the hearth there stood a spinning wheel surrounded by several baskets filled with wool dyed in a plethora of colors. Under the large window on the front of the house was a weaving loom where a partially completed cloth of intricate design lay.

The furniture in the cottage was sparse but adequate for a small family. In addition to the rocking chair, a cushioned settee sat along the far wall of the room, and on the near end of the room closest to the front door there stood a rectangular table surrounded by four chairs. In the corner, wooden bowls and pewter dishes were neatly displayed in a wooden cupboard.

Blessedly, the dirt floor of the cottage had been covered with wood slats, and although the floor looked uneven and, I suspected, subject to creaking, it was at least better than walking directly on the ground. Up above, various items such as brass pots, dried herbs, sacks of onions and potatoes, and smoked slabs of meat hung from exposed rafters and out of reach of any vermin that might be about. Opposite the front door, I peered down a narrow staircase into a cool underground pantry that had been dug into the side of the hill in back.

I glanced around the tidy cottage at the fresh flowers that had been placed in vases on the table. It was obvious that Loralon placed greater emphasis on maintaining the inside of the cottage than the outside. But with her condition being what it was, who could blame her? All the more need for an extra pair of hands to help out. How difficult could it be?

"You have a very cozy home," I said as I turned to the couple.

"Surely nothin' like the great elven cities ye must've lived in," Loralon said, although her eyes were unable to hide her pride upon hearing my praise. The petite woman, who seemed so young to be married and expecting a child, stared at me with a look of wonder. Her freckled face was pretty, and there was something about her bright brown eyes that spoke of a childlike innocence.

"Miss Arwyn, do 'ave a seat and rest yerself," Frondamein said. "Loralon and I will tend to the hairses."

I took a seat on the settee as Frondamein and Loralon stepped outside. The shadows on the front lawn had grown long as I watched the two walk toward the stable. I crept closer to the window and could make out the quizzical expression on Loralon's face. Although their voices were muffled, it surprised me that if I focused hard enough, I could hear even their whispers through the windowpane.

"And just what do ye think ye're doin', Mr. Frondamein, bringin' an elf of all creatures to our little house with not the slightest warnin'?" Loralon rebuked as she cautiously glanced over her shoulder toward the front door. "What's an elf got to do with us simple folk anyway? Doesna she know all 'er kind 'ave moved north?"

"Shhh." Frondamein put a finger to his wife's lips and glanced nervously toward the house. "Miss Arwyn 'ad traveled far and 'ad no place to stay when I met 'er yesterday. In fact, she seemed a bit lost."

"Me dear, kind Frondamein, always takin' pity on those in need."

"It wasna pity what prompted me deed," Frondamein said, stopping to untie my horse's rein. "Arwyn needs pity from no one. Nay, e'en when I met her I could tell she was someone extraordinary."

"Indeed . . . quite fetching she is." There was misgiving in Loralon's voice, and she lowered her gaze to the ground.

"Is she?" Frondamein placed his hand under her chin and guided her eyes to meet his as he smiled at her adoringly. "Barely 'ad I noticed, love, but not nearly so fetching as the woman I now 'old in me gaze."

Loralon smiled demurely and batted her eyelashes at her husband. "But why, pray tell, is she not with 'er people?"

Frondamein glanced toward the cottage again, and I quickly moved back into the shadows to not be caught eavesdropping. He and Loralon disappeared around the corner of the stable with the horses. I made my way silently to a door that looked as though it led into the stable and put my ear to it, easily hearing their whispers.

". . . Doesna seem too bent on goin' north for now . . . seems to be all alone in the wairld." There was a pause in the dialogue as I strained to listen. "Loralon, me darlin' love, I've asked Miss Arwyn to come live 'ere with us for a time."

Silence—that is, except for the pounding in my chest.

"'Ave ye lost what good sense Omni gave ye?" I heard Loralon finally exclaim. "We've barely enough to get by as it is!"

"But I wairry so about ye here all by yerself," Frondamein said. "'Specially wi' the way things are nowadays. Besides, the wairk's too much for one in such a delicate condition. Just look at this barn!" I could hear their voices getting louder and the sound of feet shuffling through hay.

"Will ye forgive me the mess?" Loralon apologized. "Tendin' the garden 'as taken all me time, and I've not 'ad a moment to tidy the barn. And I tire so easily these days."

"'Tis exactly why I asked Miss Arwyn to come. Likewise, the extra 'elp'll give ye all the more time for the sewin', which'll add to the money I bring in."

"She'd be willin' to come and live with two peasants in Baeren Ford? Surely she's grown accustomed to a much grander dwellin' than this."

"P'rhaps she was sent to us direct from Omni, and if so, then I'll not be the one to question it. For as long as she chooses to stay, I'll be grateful. A good and kindly woman she is, Loralon. I kin see it in 'er eyes."

"But where, pray tell, will she sleep?"

"I'll prepare the loft," Frondamein answered. "We've the extra bed from me da's farm."

"But the loft was to be for our child."

"The child'll sleep in our room until 'e's old enough to climb the ladder, and by then I'm sure Miss Arwyn will 'ave moved on," Frondamein said.

The silence that followed seemed to last an eternity. Loralon spoke at last. "Frondamein, love, ye know I trust ye. I'm yer wife, and I told ye I'd obey ye so long as ye'd ne'er raise a hand to me . . ."

"And that I'd ne'er do, love."

"If this is what ye intend for me to do, then obedient I'll be. But mind ye, I'll not take kindly to another woman a-thinkin' she kin move in and take o'er the place."

"Me darlin', ye'll always be the lady o' this house, and o' me heart," Frondamein said. There was silence for a moment, and I could only guess that the two were locked in a passionate embrace. "Ye'll let me know now if the arrangement's not workin' to yer likin'. 'Owever, I know ye'll get along famously."

I could feel the blood rush back into my face as I breathed a heavy, relieved sigh. Then came the sound of footsteps on the other side of the door into the stable. Hurriedly I turned and rushed back to the settee right before Loralon and Frondamein entered the room.

"Me 'usband tells me ye're to stay with us for a bit," Loralon said with a forced smile on her face.

"Well, yes, I would be very grateful," I said awkwardly as I stood and walked toward the couple. "I don't want to be a burden to you, but I promise to work hard and pull my own weight."

"I'll 'ave to admit it does get verra lonely when Frondamein's away. I'd be glad for the company," Loralon conceded.

"Y'all don't know how much I'd like the company too," I replied sincerely.

"What, pray tell, is a 'yawl'?" Frondamein asked curiously.

"You know, 'you all' . . . y'all," I attempted to explain. "Nevermind. It's an, er, elvish thing . . . I guess."

"Then 'tis settled," Frondamein said triumphantly, "and a feast we shall 'ave tonight to celebrate such a grand occasion!"

In a surprising move, Loralon approached me and, standing on her tiptoes, reached up to embrace me. Moved by the gesture, I gratefully accepted what had been the first affectionate overture I had received in this stranger-filled world.

"P'rhaps ye'd like to freshen up a bit afore supper," Loralon offered.

She led me through a door to the left of the fireplace and through a small bedchamber to yet another room at the back of the cottage that could only be described as a lavatory. In it was an actual ceramic tub raised above a cavity in the stone floor where the charred, ashy remains of some dirt-like substance lay dormant. An old-fashioned pump delivered water into the tub, from which a copper pipe emerged underneath to drain the leftovers down through the wall and outside into a waiting barrel, Loralon explained. Besides the tub, the only other item in the tiny room was a ceramic bowl and large water pitcher set atop a small table.

"We've the best in plumbin'." Frondamein beamed proudly. "Old Hedgepeth saw to it but two years afore she passed on."

"Aye," Loralon added, "did ye e'er 'ear o' such a thin'? No more bathin' in a barrel! Though, we still use the fire to heat the water, but the peat's what keeps it 'ot for the next pairson."

I thought the whole set-up rather primitive indeed, yet the alternative of bathing in a barrel made me grateful for the foresight of old Hedgepeth. I seemed to recall that the people who lived long ago in the place where I had come from were not as fond of bathing as it seemed Frondamein and Loralon were, and for their apparent regard for good hygiene I was also relieved. "But where is the . . . ?"

"Privy?" Loralon said. "Step this way." With that she opened a door on the north side of the room. A narrow stone path that had been cut into the hill in back and lined with a fence led a little ways behind the lavatory to a wooden outhouse.

"It's all, er, very nice," I commented, trying my best to maintain a pleasant smile. This would certainly take some getting used to.

The Healer of Guildenwood

Back inside the cottage, I discovered that the much more enticing aroma coming from the kettle on the fireplace was a beef stew with a few garden vegetables thrown in. I followed Loralon and Frondamein's lead and sopped up every morsel on my plate with a piece of freshly baked bread.

The conversation was a bit strained at first, with talk centering around Frondamein's Bensorian-turned-Draigon-lackey boss, Festius, and the man's disloyal, good-for-nothing ways. Still trying to make a good impression, I felt my continued acceptance was not a sure thing as Loralon kept shifting her gaze to me warily. But it was difficult to make a good impression when I dreaded any personal questions that had to do with my past, which remained a huge, vacant abyss in my mind.

Fortunately, as the darkness grew around the tiny cottage, the conversation focused on Frondamein and Loralon. Frondamein, the gentle-spirited and contemplative farmer, seemed to me more suited for carrying a book than a sword, or even a plow, for that matter. But for all the innocence and naïveté in Loralon's bright brown eyes, her fiery red hair perhaps hinted of a high-spirited woman, one with a tendency toward suspicion concerning anything new and different.

Then came the question I'd been dreading. "Frondamein tells me ye hail from a faraway land," she said with narrowed gaze. "Tell me, what's the name o' yer country?"

I paused for a moment to search my memory for any small thread to grasp onto. Loralon and Frondamein leaned in closer, waiting expectantly for a reply. Then from somewhere deep in the corridors of my mind, a name popped into consciousness. It was enough for the moment. "Ameri..." I began. "Ameri... go. Amerigo. Yes, that's it. It was named after a man... an explorer I believe."

"Ne'er 'eard of it," Frondamein said as he leaned back in his chair and took a puff from his pipe. "Tell me, is it east o' Caldemia or on the other side of Endismere?"

"Yes, that's right," I replied hastily. "It's a very small country, far out of the way." I shifted my gaze quickly in Loralon's direction to see her reaction. Loralon, however, was staring off into the distance and quietly repeating the name several times to herself. "Amerigo," she finally said out loud, looking at her husband in a most curious manner. "What a nice name, that. Do ye not agree, Frondamein?"

Frondamein stared at his wife in amazement, until a knowing smile came to his face. "Aye, it's got a rather nice ring to it, it does."

Not long after the contents of his pipe had disappeared into the rafters in a dreamy haze, Frondamein excused himself from the table and climbed the ladder into the loft, where he disappeared for a while. Loralon and I cleaned the remains of our meal to the sound of thuds and bumps coming from above.

Eventually I climbed the ladder myself and glanced around the loft where a bed and small bureau plus a few other odds and ends were crammed into the small space. A wooden chest blocked a small doorway that led from the loft into the hayloft above the stable, and I found Frondamein on the other side of the door.

"Are you pulling or pushing?" I called to Frondamein.

"Pullin'. This old trunk 'olds nothin' but farm tools, of which I doubt ye'll 'ave need for in yer bedroom. Thought I'd get it out o' the way so ye'd 'ave a tad more space. The loft's small enough as 'tis."

With me pushing and Frondamein pulling from the other end, we were eventually able to force the trunk into the hayloft. Without the blockage, I crawled halfway through the doorway and peered down from the ledge onto the horses standing below.

"I know yer room's a bit close to where we keep th' animals, but p'rhaps the stench willna be too strong, 'specially when the door's closed. I really should nail it shut and daub it with mud as we've no good need for it anyway."

Once Frondamein had placed the trunk in the corner of the hayloft, he crawled back through the doorway into my new quarters. Shutting the door behind him, he pulled the bureau around to block it. He then opened its top drawer and pulled out a blanket and some pillows. "'Tis all what's left from me family's farm," Frondamein explained. "Been sittin' up 'ere for ages, but I'm glad ye'll be puttin' it to good use, Miss Arwyn. I'm sorry we canna offer ye more."

"I'm just glad to have a roof over my head," I admitted. "How can I ever thank you for taking me in?"

"We've already discussed that, 'ave we not? Take care o' me sweet Loralon is all I ask."

I glanced around the tiny loft that was to be mine. Though the furniture was meager, the bed, bureau, and a modest bedside table fit quite snugly in the small space.

"Ye'll need a cloth to dust the fairniture and a curtain for privacy," Frondamein said. "Me Loralon kin make ye one in no time. She's the best seamstress in Baeren Ford."

"Yes, I noticed the spinning wheel and loom," I said. "I seem to remember seeing several like them in a museum one time."

"A museum?"

"It's a place where things that were used many years ago are displayed so that people can see how others once lived," I explained. Funny, the things I *did* remember.

Frondamein scratched his head. "I know the wheel and loom 'ave been 'round for a while, but ne'er did I know they'd 'old such fascination for folk."

"So, Loralon is quite the seamstress," I said in an attempt to change the subject.

"Aye, quite talented she is, which comes in 'andy when the money runs low. Plus it keeps 'er out o' trouble," Frondamein added with a mischievous gleam in his eye.

"I kin 'ear ye," Loralon said as she appeared at the bottom of the ladder. "Arwyn, pay no mind to me silly 'usband."

A wave of exhaustion suddenly came over me. Before I succumbed, I climbed down the ladder and walked out into the stable where the beautiful white horse stood placidly. A foul odor hovered in the air as flies buzzed about hay that had been lying there for several days. Frondamein had seen to it that the horses had received fresh water and hay after their long trip, but the stable was in overall disarray.

I stepped over to the gentle horse that showed no signs of fatigue from the day's journey and stroked its muzzle. Nearby the saddle that had ridden on its back had been carefully set astride the wooden barrier between the stalls. "How on earth did you come to me?" I whispered into his ear. "If only you could talk, what secrets would you tell? If only you could tell me what I'm doing here." I sighed. The horse looked in my eyes and neighed quietly. "I suppose you and I are meant to be together. So I guess I should give you a name." Suddenly, a word popped into my head, presumably from nowhere. "Avencloe? Is that your name?"

The majestic beast abruptly bobbed its head up down and whinnied as if in agreement. "I have no idea what it means, but you seem to like it." I placed a blanket over his back and gave him a quick pat. "Well, Avencloe, as long as you and I are together, we'll watch out for each other. All right?"

After Frondamein and Loralon had wished me a pleasant sleep, I climbed the ladder to the darkened loft, lit only by a single candle that sat on the small table beside my bed. I absentmindedly reached my hand to the wall and made an upward stroking motion with the knuckle of my forefinger. The loft remained shrouded in darkness. What a silly thing for me to do!

Then misjudging the distance between my head and the slanted ceiling, I straightened abruptly, causing my head to come into contact with one of the wooden beams above. I squinted and rubbed my brow, frustrated that my body did not always work as gracefully as I wanted it to. It was not the first time that day I had acted in a clumsy manner.

Carefully, I walked the few steps to the neatly made bed where my knapsack lay, retrieved the nightshirt inside, and slipped it on. I then climbed onto the rather lumpy mattress that was barely long enough for my unfamiliar, tall physique.

Once I blew out the candle, I could see out of the only window in the loft and upward into the starry night sky. As the night sounds of cicadas and croaking frogs began to lull me to sleep, I was shaken back into consciousness as my keen ears overheard the whispers of the two who shared a bed right below.

"Do ye really think she's an elf?" I could hear Loralon say. "She seems no different than you and me, as mortal as we are."

"What, my dear, did ye expect an elf to look like?"

"I dunna know. I've not been so privileged to 'ave seen one, but I always expected 'em to 'ave the pointed ears. I saw hers tonight at dinner, when she brushed 'er 'air out of 'er face, and they're the same as ours."

There was a moment of silence, as if Frondamein was pondering this new mystery. "Well, p'rhaps not all breeds 'ave em," he replied thoughtfully.

With every other physical change I had attended to, the thought of having pointed ears hadn't even crossed my mind. After all, up until the day before I had believed elves to be the stuff of fairy tales.

In the darkness of the loft, I quickly fingered the flesh under my mounds of hair and could detect nothing out of the ordinary there. Could this be a telltale sign of my true nature? Was I perhaps truly mortal and not an elf at all?

"I'll tell ye, Loralon, Miss Arwyn possesses that sairtain 'elvish quality.'"

"And what be that, I ask ye?"

Frondamein let out an indulgent sigh as if he were a patient teacher gently prodding a pupil. "Elves are sublime creatures, full o' beauty, grace, and elegance. They live in this world yet transcend it in their agelessness and lofty pursuits. Some are e'en said to 'ave special powers to communicate with the beasts o' the forest, to read the thoughts of others, and to command the forces o' nature. But, mind ye, Loralon, there are none more noble than they."

Wow, these people must be highly mistaken about me.

"You should be an elf, for all yer fancy talk." There was silence for a moment. "Frondamein, why are we humans not revered as they?"

"We are a more airthy, more practical, simpleminded people. We tend to be ruled by our passions, and unfortunately that makes us more inclined to temptation. We mortals fall somewhere in between elves and dwarves in the grand scheme o' thin's."

"But why must there be such an order? Are we not all the same in th' eyes of Omni?"

"Aye, but that's the way thin's are, me dear. But ye mustn't wairry yer pretty 'ead o'er such concerns. Aside from Draigon and 'is minions, we've all been able to live in peace for generations."

"And 'ow long will that last, pray tell? Ye've said yerself we all grow more mistrustful the longer we live apart."

"Our true ruler will change that when 'e arrives," Frondamein murmured.

"*If* he arrives."

"'E will, p'rhaps when we least expect it, but what I needs most right now is sleep."

There was a moment of silence, and then Loralon spoke once more. "Well, I still think she's mortal."

I lay in bed and stared at the thatched ceiling, only a few feet above, and pondered the conversation to which I had been privy. What had Frondamein meant about a *true ruler*? My thoughts raced back to the day before when I had asked him if there was any hope to be found in this land, and his response had been puzzling. Could this be that hope he had vaguely referred to?

Somehow, I would broach the subject with him again, when the time was right. Yet, I still held out some faint glimmer of hope that tomorrow I would at last wake up from this dream, back safe and sound in my own comfortable bed.

CHAPTER 8

"My position here is still quite shaky, and I haven't quite figured out how to use this new body. Frondamein and Loralon look at me sometimes like I have two heads or something."

My eyes opened the following morning, but the dream from which there was no awakening continued. Here I was, stuck in this time warp with no hope of finding a way out—at least not yet. I forced my feet onto the bare wooden floor of the loft, dreading to discover what bizarreness *this* day would bring.

As I put my clothing away in the bureau, I happened to find an old hairbrush in the bottom drawer. Glad for the chance to finally groom my long locks, I carefully brushed my hair in a way that would hide my ears, making a mental note to never wear a style that would expose them for what they were—or were not.

What would it hurt if people really believed that I was an elf, especially if it earned me a certain amount of respect? And if need be, I could play the ear card if I happened upon someone who didn't take as kindly to elves as the villagers. And if anyone asked me point-blank what I was . . . well, I'd think about that later.

I descended the ladder to find Loralon cracking eggs into a pan as Frondamein busily placed logs on the fire.

"Good mornin' to ye, Miss Arwyn," he greeted cheerfully.

"Hey! What's up?" I greeted back.

Loralon and Frondamein looked at each other in bewilderment. Suddenly, a smile crossed Frondamein's face. "Oh, a riddle is it? Hmmm, let's see . . . stars. No, must 'ave somethin' to do with hay."

"The hayloft," Loralon said warily.

"Why yes, you're absolutely right," I said sheepishly, grateful that yet another blunder had gone unnoticed.

"Arwyn, we've 'am for breakfast this mornin' and eggs fresh from the hen 'ouse," Loralon said as a slimy yellow yolk splattered into the frying pan.

The Healer of Guildenwood

"No, thank you," I replied. "I try to stay away from cholesterol."

Loralon and Frondamein both looked up from their work. "What is . . . cho-les-ter-ol?" Frondamein asked.

I pondered the question for a moment. "You know . . . I've forgotten," I said at last. "I believe I'll have some ham and eggs after all. And some milk, too."

"If the old cow'll cooperate, then ye'll 'ave as much milk as yer 'eart desires," Loralon said as the frying pan she was attending hissed and spewed above the fire.

After our hearty breakfast, complete with three mugs of milk, Frondamein took me, his novice farmhand, out to the garden as he pulled the old mule along behind. There he demonstrated the proper way to attach the mule's harness and plow, apologizing all the while for asking me to do such difficult manual labor. And although I wasn't thrilled about the prospect, I knew that Loralon would soon be in no condition for such work. My situation was still rather precarious, and learning anything that would add to my usefulness was also a matter of self-preservation.

However, mastering the art of plowing in such a primitive manner proved a difficult task. Keeping the plow in line and the mule from wandering off brought out ranting such as I had not uttered before in all my memory. "You must think you're something, taking advantage of the new girl," I muttered under my breath as the plow went veering off course behind the wayward mule. "But let me tell you, Mister, that when it comes to donkeys, you are actually the *worst*."

"Insultin' 'im willna get 'im to do as ye wish. Keepin' a firm hand on the reins will," Frondamein explained as he took hold of the reins. Completely exasperated, I gladly handed them over.

To my relief, attention soon turned to the stable, where Frondamein showed me how to sweep up the old straw and replace it with fresh for the horses and mule. The cow, on the other hand, generally stayed in the field behind the house. It grazed alongside a mischievous and very independent goat that sometimes had to be rescued when it climbed onto the roof from the hill in back.

Disappearing momentarily, Frondamein returned to the stable leading the brown and white cow with a rope and proceeded to show me how to properly milk the animal. The goat, on the other hand, was a bit more stubborn and refused to cooperate despite prodding and irritated murmuring from Frondamein.

Late in the morning as I threw grain onto the ground for the chickens that pecked and strutted underfoot, Loralon went about gathering the remaining eggs from the small henhouse.

"Tch! What a pest!" Loralon cried as she peered into one of the compartments. Reaching in almost nonchalantly, the petite young woman calmly pulled out a rather large snake by its tail. I let out a shriek upon seeing the hideous creature and how Loralon so boldly handled the thing. "'Tis only a snake. 'Twill do ye no harm."

"Aren't you afraid it may be poisonous?"

"A snake? Poisonous? Could there be such a thin'?"

"Where I come from there is," I said, shrinking away from the serpent that Loralon casually dangled a little too close for comfort. The helpless thing writhed about in the air trying to find an escape as Loralon held firmly to its tail.

"I suppose it could give a rather nasty bite, but 'armless it is, 'cept to mice in the garden, which is where it should be," Loralon said as she walked in that direction.

"If you say so," I said, wiping my brow.

"Er, Miss Arwyn," Frondamein said as he approached with a look of misgiving on his face. "Regretfully there's a lesson in farmin' what must be taught."

"Could it be any worse than plowing?"

"Dependin' on 'ow ye look at it," he said, leading me out to the field in back. "It's time ye learn about fertilizer . . ."

That afternoon as the hot sun beat down on the land, Frondamein, Loralon, and I worked in the garden pulling weeds and gathering vegetables in straw baskets. There in the garden neat rows of corn stalks and vines laden with tomatoes, cucumbers, squash, beans, and peas had sprung from the ground while lacy-looking greenery hovered above the surface, attesting to the turnips and carrots that grew below. I could not help but smile as Frondamein gently tended to the garden's growth like a father would care for a small child.

Throughout the day, townspeople had wandered past the cottage for a glimpse of me, the supposed elf, for news of my arrival had already spread through the village like wildfire. I tried to ignore all the attention and go about my instruction as though nothing was out of the ordinary, but I was beginning to feel like a freak of nature.

After dinner that evening, the three of us sat outside on the front lawn in wooden chairs as the light of the sun faded in the sky. Loralon sat snapping green beans as Frondamein smoked his pipe, a column of smoke spiraling up and disappearing into the evening air. It was all I could do to stay awake after my busy day. Again, I relished the idea of a hot bath but couldn't stomach the tremendous effort it would take for that to actually happen. Besides, I had hardly broken a sweat all day, and I wondered if perhaps elves didn't perspire.

"Th' Elwei, she is bright this eve," Frondamein commented as he took a puff from his pipe. He glanced over at me as if to see my reaction, but it was Loralon I noticed who shot him a look of warning.

Okay, I'd take the bait, if for no other reason but to try and stay awake a little longer. "So, what's the . . . ?"

"Elwei?" he responded, and then he leaned over toward me and whispered. "Do you see that star o'erhead? The yellow one?"

I glanced above and could see a bright yellow blaze, the first star that had yet appeared in the night sky. Something about it tickled a very faint memory, which immediately dissipated like Frondamein's pipe smoke in the evening breeze. I nodded.

"Do you remember askin' if there be any 'ope we Bensorians cling to in these unsairtain times?"

Now he piqued my interest. "Yes."

Frondamein gave a quick glance down the road in both directions, but there was no one to be seen, and then he glanced at Loralon. "Dunna fret, love. There's no pryin' ears about." Loralon merely huffed and went back to her snapping. "Ye see, Miss Arwyn, there are laws now against speakin' o' the Elwei."

"There are laws against speaking of a star?" This was so confusing, not to mention a tad crazy.

"Aye, and I could be sorely punished for doin' so. Still, no law could e'er erase what is written on the hearts of all Bensorians, for therein lies the hope o' Bensor." Fromdamein gave one more quick glance toward the road and then leaned in even closer. "Listen closely, Miss Arwyn, and I'll tell ye o' the prophecy . . ."

CHAPTER 9

"Though the story of the doomed lovers distracts me for a little while, the reality of my situation comes crashing back as I discover yet another mind-blowing piece of this bewildering puzzle."

As the lakeside came alive with the sounds of nocturnal creatures, Frondamein spun a tale of past ages when Omni, the All, created the world and placed in it the Firstborn of His children, the Eldred, forty-eight elves to rule the forests, forty-eight humans to rule the seas and the open places, and forty-eight dwarves to rule the places under the earth. To these Eldred, Omni gave mystical powers and lands to cultivate with beauty and goodness. It was from these one hundred and forty-four that all the peoples of the world descended.

Among the Eldred was an elven maiden named Elwei, and to her He gave the small land of Bensor. Elwei was said to have been a woman of astonishing beauty, fierce in strength and wild as the unicorn, passionate when it came to her beloved Bensor.

Elwei poured all her might into cultivating the garden of Bensor for her people to live in and love as she did. For over thirteen hundred years she labored in peace as the peoples of the world flourished. But her most cherished moments were the times when she walked with Omni Himself under the elderhelm trees of Loth Gerodin. It was during those times when she would say, "I think I should like creatures who are part man and part horse to inhabit my garden." And Omni would say, "Very well," for He loved Elwei and delighted in her delight. And that was how centaurs came to be. And Elwei said, "And I should like little people to live in the tree trunks and tend to the flowers and till the soil of the forest, and giants as strong as a mountain but as gentle as lambs to move the earth," and that is how gnomes and trolls came to be. And so it was for many a year until the land of Bensor had become a place of supreme beauty and rest.

But one day, Omni came to Elwei bearing sad tidings. "Something has gone terribly wrong in a far, faraway place," He said. "And like a pebble

The Healer of Guildenwood

dropped in a pond, the ripple that was begun ages ago has almost reached this far corner of My world, and when it does reach this fair place, nothing will be the same. My dear child, I cannot remain here with you as before. But do not be without hope, for a part of Me will remain ever present, and a day will come when the light will return, and your heir will be the one to bring it." That was the last Elwei saw of Him face-to-face.

And then all that Omni had predicted came true. A great shadow overtook the land, and though Elwei and many others remained faithful to the one Omni, there were those whose hearts turned to evil. And so it was with the elven maiden, Dar Magreth, who had been given the mountainous land north of Bensor for her own. Dar Magreth began to covet the land of Bensor, which she believed was superior to her own, and to resent Omni for having given it to Elwei. And, believing that Omni had abandoned Elwei, she plotted to take the land of Bensor for herself.

In the hope of usurping Elwei's influence among the peoples of Bensor, Dar Magreth started dabbling in the dark gifts and eventually became seduced by the Underlord, neglecting her own country. Once a land of beautiful green mountains with flowing waters that emptied out into dense forests and rolling meadows, Ashkaroth became a barren, windswept, colorless land.

Dar Magreth and her small band of followers unsuccessfully challenged Elwei's claim to the land of Bensor and were forced to retreat even farther into the mountains where she transformed Daggoroth, an ancient volcano eroded by the winds and rains of time, into a menacing bastion shrouded in a veil of darkness. It was there that she bred men with mountain hags to produce her army of Gargalocs.

In the meantime, two brothers, both noblemen, and the great-great-grandsons of one of the original Eldred, voyaged from the western country of Endara on a quest for adventure. Their journey led to Bensor, where one of the brothers, Arnuin, fell desperately in love with the beautiful Elwei. He vowed his eternal devotion to her and swore to join in her plight against the increasing threat from the north. The two were wed one starry spring night in the forest of Loth Gerodin. It was a marriage of elf and mortal, the beginnings of an alliance that would last for generations, though not through the line of Arnuin.

Arnuin's brother, Galibrant, also fell in love with an elven maiden of Loth Gerodin, and after the two were wed, they returned to Endara where he was crowned king following their father's death. Galibrant's line had produced many a good and noble ruler and continued to be strong and powerful to that day.

A tragic ending, however, befell the ill-fated Elwei and Arnuin. As Dar Magreth's forces grew more and more powerful, together they gathered a mighty army to hold back the increasing threat from Ashkaroth. Arnuin set forth to build several safe bastions throughout the land, including the fortress of Arnuin's Hold that now stood in ruins above the village of Baeren Ford. But his greatest achievement was a vast wall across the northern border of Bensor to keep it inaccessible to Dar Magreth and her troops.

After years of labor, the wall extended all the way from Hared Nomnor in the west and along the northern border of Guilden to the southern part of the Greenwaithe. As the wall neared completion, Dar Magreth had managed to gather an army for a surprise attack in an effort to establish a stronghold in Loth Gerodin Forest. Yet as Arnuin surveyed work on the wall, warned by spies of the army's approach, he sounded his golden trumpet and summoned elvish forces from all over Loth Gerodin to arms. With Dar Magreth's attack foiled, a bloodbath ensued on the Greenwaithe and those that remained of the Ashkar forces went limping back into the mountains, and Dar Magreth, caught off guard by the intensity of the Bensorian army's vengeance, barely escaped with her life. She retreated into the dark places of the Ashkaroth mountains and once again retreated into silence for many a year.

The victory, however, was not without cost for the forces of Elwei and Arnuin. After the fighting had stopped, as Arnuin surveyed the death toll on the field of battle, a stray arrow from out of nowhere struck and killed him. So moved was Omni by the intensity of Elwei's grief that it was said He reached down His hand one starry night and removed her from that world, though childless she was and without an heir. He transformed her into the most brilliant star in the Bensorian sky so that she could continue to watch over her beloved land from above.

With their leader dead and Elwei gone, work on the wall was eventually abandoned, leaving a vast section along the western part of Loth Gerodin incomplete. The grieving and leaderless land of Bensor was in a state of disorder until Galibrant, the brother of Arnuin, returned to Bensor by sea with an Endaran fleet after he learned of Arnuin's death. Galibrant restored order and created in Maldimire a council of lords that became known as the Endaran Council, established to lead Bensor in the absence of Elwei and Arnuin.

For several long centuries the Council consisted of just and honorable elves, mortals, and dwarf-lords, and for a while an uneasy peace fell upon the land. It was during this time—nearly five hundred years after Elwei had left the world—that Amiel appeared. Amiel was a powerful wizard who claimed to have fought alongside Elwei in the wars against Dar Magreth many generations before. His only evidence to this fact was the ancient and magical sword he bore, the Veritana, known in legend to have been wielded by Elwei. The hilt of the sword was inlaid with a famed but peculiar emerald, forged there by Elwei herself.

By this authority, Amiel foretold the coming of Bensor's true ruler, the heir of Elwei, who would awaken the light of the Veritana emerald, one who would wield the Sword without dying, for the light within the emerald could only be wielded by the one who already possessed it.

"But what could that mean?" I asked, "'The one who *already* possessed it?'"

Frondamein shook his head. "'Tis a mystery, that one is, the answer to which only Omni knows, or them what's no longer around . . . or p'rhaps the true ruler 'imself." Frondamein stopped speaking for a moment to refill his pipe. "As it was, Miss Arwyn," he continued after taking a couple of puffs, "we Bensorians wanted so for our true ruler to come that we built a wondrous castle by the sea in 'opes that such would hurry 'im to our shores. The castle of Emraldein was said to be our crownin' achievement, as all the peoples o' Bensor 'ad a hand in its makin'. It sits on an island at the mouth o' the Lower Silvendell, at the place where it spills into the Eleuvial. At one time, 'twas verra beautiful and surrounded by lush gardens o' strange and exotic plants. 'Tis e'en said a mystical spring bubbled up from the ground in the center o' the island and flowed into the sea."

"Cool!"

"Actually, 'tis quite warm there, for it lies in the southern part o' Bensor," Frondamein explained. "Now, none but the most foolish dare go near Emraldein or the town o' Carona what lies along the edge o' the bay surroundin' the island."

"Why did everyone desert such a place?" I asked.

Frondamein gave a quick glance toward the road and continued his story.

Shortly after the castle was completed, Dar Magreth made trouble in Bensor again. Her spies had apprised her of the wizard's prophecy, and all her will turned to keeping Bensor's true ruler from coming.

Ashkaroth's army had been secretly growing for years. Dar Magreth ordered that a fleet of ships be built and each quietly sailed, one by one, down the River Iona at the western border of Bensor and out into the sea. From there the army mustered on the deserted island of Casibar off the coast, making it a rallying place from which they attacked the castle. Not expecting a strike from the south, Amiel's unsuspecting forces were caught off guard. Although they fought bravely, the Bensorian army suffered many losses. Yet in one last effort, it succeeded in driving Dar Magreth's forces from the castle grounds, though it was said that the coastline surrounding the castle grounds flowed red from the blood of the fallen.

Despite the Bensorians' hard-won victory, Dar Magreth had one last surprise for the battered and dispersed army. In the hull of one of the ships was a beast so foul, so monstrous, that it could have only been spawned in the bowels of Daggoroth. With large black wings, it was something akin to a dragon, yet covered in black hair and possessing an ability to walk upright. With one final blow, the beast was unleashed to invade the castle grounds and drive out all the remaining Bensorians. Everyone fled the castle and the city of Carona. Even Amiel disappeared.

To that day the Sword awaited, having sat on the throne of Emraldein for ages as a challenge for the true ruler. Only the rightful heir to Bensor's throne would defeat the beast and take up the Sword without tasting death. As legend foretold, the golden horn of Arnuin would sound throughout Bensor when the Sword would be claimed, proclaiming to all that the true ruler had come.

For nearly two hundred years both Emraldein and Carona had been deserted, and still the beast guarded the gate so that none dared challenge the prophecy. There were tales from many a seafarer who had sailed by the castle of an ominous dark cloud that constantly hovered overhead, and from time to time they could hear the roar of the beast even far out at sea.

As the years went by and the glorious castle fell more and more into decay, even the Endaran council fell into decay as the lords died off and were replaced by the spineless and those subject to corruption. The final blow to their authority came only twenty-five years before, when Draigon obliterated them once and for all, seizing all power unto himself.

As Frondamein spoke, my rational mind grew more and more skeptical of his far-fetched story. Monsters and magical swords and people who turn into stars—such was the stuff of fairy tales. Frondamein seemed a sensible fellow, but perhaps he was a bit taken by the local lore.

"But, Frondamein," I interrupted, "do you really believe there is such a creature? And that there is such a thing as a Sword that brings death to all who touch it?"

"Aye, that I do," he replied solemnly, "and Draigon now sports a wooden leg to prove it. 'Tis why he's sometimes called 'Peg Leg.'" Frondamein chuckled. "A whole man 'e was afore 'e challenged the Sword a few years back. Did it under pressure from the people, 'e did. Rode up to the front door o' the castle, but 'e was too great a coward to go it alone. Nay, 'e was surrounded by a small army o' Bensorian men: innocent tanners, smiths, farmers, and the like, those 'e considered dispensable." Frondamein's tone suddenly became very quiet. "I was one o' the few who escaped."

I stared at Frondamein in amazement. "You were there?"

"Aye. Twas three years ago when one of 'is lieutenants 'ad come through me village lookin' to recruit strong men for the task. I'd just been wed to me sweet Loralon and was as 'appy as could be when I took me crops to market one day. There 'e saw me strength, for I was quite a strong chap from workin' 'ard on the farm, and 'e recruited me under threat o' bein' sent to Dungard were I to resist. 'Ardly 'ad I the time to go 'ome, gather me clothes, and kiss me wife good-bye afore I was off to Maldimire." Frondamein's voice cracked a bit, and I noticed that his hands started to shake.

"After a month o' trainin' in the art o' battle, Draigon considered 'is recruits ready. We set out airly one mornin' for Carona and arrived at the end o' the second day on the edge o' the desairted town. So dark and eerie it was, for sunlight barely kin penetrate the blanket o' clouds what hovers constantly o'erhead."

Even in the darkness of the front lawn, I could see the horror etched onto his pupils like stubborn cobwebs that refuse to be brushed away.

"We camped that night amongst the ruins o' some old courtyard, surrounded by the calls o' wild creatures in the nearby jungle. 'Twas as if the verra air, which hung still as a skeleton in the grave, knew that somethin' was about to 'appen.

"Airly the next mornin' we rode toward the castle, sairtain we were to meet with death on that verra day. I could e'en see the fear in Draigon's cold gray eyes, ordinarily so arrogant. Easily we rode through the front gate and onto the castle grounds with Draigon shielded in the middle of our band. The dark walls o' the castle rose silently above us. Suddenly there was a stirrin' in the air, and I smelled a most ghastly stench that made me feel as though I'd be ill."

Frondamein shuddered, and for a moment I thought the memory too frightening for him to continue. "Then we 'eard a most terrifyin' wail," he continued. "I'll not forget the sound of it if I live to be three 'undred. And then we saw it—a dark, winged shadow o'erhead. With wings like a bat and large enough to cloak a hairse, it came screamin' down afore us, standin' as a man on two 'airy legs but twice as tall, blockin' our way to the castle. Awful it was, a huge black thin', with fangs and razor-like claws. Blood it 'ad in its eyes, and a hunger for 'uman flesh.

"Draigon pressed onward, foolishly detairmined to validate 'is reign by claimin' the Sword. We fought 'ard with sword and arrow but were no match for the beast, whose unnatural power was not o' this wairld. All the trainin' forgotten, we desperately fought to stay alive. In all the chaos, I found meself scramblin' up the front steps o' the castle tryin' to find a place to hide. Then I noticed one o' Draigon's lieutenants, a brutal man by the name o' Salamar, disappear through an archway into the castle. I followed 'im into the darkness inside, and ye'll ne'er believe what I saw . . .'"

My eyes widened with anticipation.

"I'd haird all the legends afore, and ye could say I was a bit skeptical meself. But no more. I'm a believer, I am," Frondamein exclaimed, pounding his fist for emphasis. "For ye see, there in the darkness o' the throne room I watched as Salamar approached the throne, kickin' away the skeletons o' those poor souls who 'ad long since met their deaths at the Sword. What a fool 'e was!"

I realized that I was leaning forward, heart pounding as I listened to Frondamein's account. Surely I wasn't starting to actually *believe* this far-fetched tale. I mean, *really*!

"'E turned and saw me standin' there, and with a smirk o' triumph upon 'is face 'e placed 'is 'and upon the Sword's hilt. All of a sudden, 'is body twitched and turned, and 'e fell upon the floor in front o' the throne, writhin' in agony. I ran up to 'im as 'e was takin' 'is last breath, afraid to touch 'im for fear I'd meet wi' the Sword's power meself. But I'll not forget the look upon 'is face. Haunts me to this day, it does.

"As it was, I 'ad three choices. I could remain in the castle and wait for death to come or touch the Sword and be o'er and done with it all quick-like. Or I could attempt to escape and risk gettin' ripped apart by the beast."

Frondamein stopped talking for a moment and glanced over at Loralon, who was popping beans almost feverishly. His eyes softened as he looked at her. "For me dear Loralon's sake, I decided to take me chances on escape, so I ran outside the castle and found that most o' the company 'ad either fled or been devoured.

"Nearby I could 'ear an awful tearin' sound and someone screamin' in agony. I grabbed me hairse, which 'ad escaped beneath a covered terrace, and made me way toward the castle gates when I saw Draigon lyin' there on the ground, 'is left leg gnawed off below the knee. The bodies o' several men lay strewn about nearby. I was about to leave 'im for dead when 'e called to me, all pitiful."

"Now Miss Arwyn," he said, leaning in close to me,"I canna bear to see any creature in pain, e'en one so loathsome; so I quickly 'elped 'im onto the back o' me hairse, and we made for the front gates as fast as Haseloth could go. Me dear friend, Bartolmus, a tanner from Gildaris, was fleein' on 'is hairse when the beast swept down and lifted 'im 'igh from 'is saddle, no doubt makin' sport of 'im afore castin' 'im to the ground." Frondamein's brow furrowed, and he shook his head as if to remove the memory. "The few of us what were left met back at the camp and made ready to 'ead back to Maldimire, grateful to 'ave escaped with our lives.

"Draigon 'imself is lucky to be alive, were it not for us. And 'ad 'is quest succeeded and 'e 'ad made it to the throne, 'e would 'ave died for sairtain the moment 'e touched the Sword."

"It was stupid of him to think he could possibly be Bensor's true ruler to begin with," I commented, beginning to wonder if perhaps Frondamein's story was not as far-fetched as I had believed. He certainly seemed very lucid otherwise, not prone to hallucinations or embellishing.

"Aye. 'Twas no surprise that only a man honorable enough to be favored by Elwei—that which 'e is not—could 'ope to wield the Sword." Frondamein sighed. "Still, one would think such an ordeal would 'umble a man, but not so with Draigon. In fact, 'e's become all the more a tyrant and now 'as forbidden anyone to speak o' the Elwei or the Sword and 'as thrown into Dungard those who 'ave questioned 'is position.

"Soon after 'is quest failed, I believe, 'twas then that 'e sold 'imself to the Sorceress. Not that 'e wasna evil already, mind ye, but that's when methinks 'e aligned 'imself with the north because soon afterward them Gargalocs started pokin' about our country. I'd wager 'e thinks that with the 'elp o' Dar Magreth, e'en though she is 'erself a disgraced elf, he'd crush the true ruler when and if 'e appears."

Frondamein grew silent for a moment; then he turned to look at me and said in a rather perturbed tone, "And do ye think I got one 'thank ye' for fairst of all savin' the man's 'ide and then tendin' to 'is leg?" He shook his head. "No, not a one. The only 'thanks' I got was an order to pairform guard duty at the Gate. Now 'ow do ye like them apples?"

"Draigon sounds like a jer . . . that is, a tyrant," I sympathized. "But tell me, has anyone challenged the prophecy recently?" I asked curiously.

"Aye, from time to time there's waird from the south o' someone foolish enough to flairt with death. Many 'ave met their doom in their arrogant quest to become Bensor's true ruler. Most dunna e'en make it to th' outer walls o' the castle afore bein' slain by the beast. Others 'ave made it to the throne room only to meet their death th' instant they lay a finger on the Sword. Still others come not in sairch o' glory but for the castle's many treasures. None 'ave come out alive."

"And so the Sword still occupies its throne at Emraldein after all these years, and Bensor is still without its true ruler," I said, trying to keep everything straight in my mind.

"Aye, I'm afraid 'tis so," Frondamein said. "Many 'ave lost 'ope in the prophecy. Canna say I blame 'em. After all, Amiel's not been seen or 'eard from in 'undreds o' years. Still, Miss Arwyn, I'll not be one to lose faith. I only 'ope our true ruler'll come within me lifetime," Frondamein said with a faraway look in his eyes. "My, what I wouldna give to 'elp restore the gardens at Emraldein to their original glory, but I'm afraid 'tis but a dream."

"Nothin' but a bunch o' rot!"

Frondamein and I both looked up, surprised by the venom that came from the mouth of otherwise sweet Loralon.

"Dear, ye musn't lose 'ope . . ."

"Lose 'ope . . . in what, pray tell? An old fairy tale me da used to tell me when 'e tucked me in bed. 'Dunna ye wairry yer little red 'ead, Loralon, dear. The true ruler'll come and all will be well.' Well, I say we all need to stop believin' in ancient legends and take matters into our own 'ands!"

"And do what, pray tell?"

Loralon threw her hands in the air. "I dunna know . . . start a rebellion . . . though he'd likely kill anyone who tried," she muttered.

"Dear, losin' our 'ope's exactly what the enemy would 'ave us do, but without our 'ope, what are we?"

Loralon gave a huff and went back to shelling her beans, and afterwards an awkward silence prevailed. My brain was busy at work, trying to make sense of all I had heard, but I didn't know who was right, Frondamein or Loralon.

For what seemed a long while, no one said a word. I looked up in the night sky and saw the waxing sliver of the moon dangling silently above the treetops and noted how unusually large it appeared. "Look at how big the moon looks tonight," I finally said in an attempt to break the silence.

"Looks as it always does, and a constant reminder that me time at 'ome's runnin' out," Frondamein said bitterly.

"I'm sorry, I didn't mean to bring up a sore subject." It seemed the entire evening had been rife with sore subjects.

"'Tis all right, Miss Arwyn. It's just that there's but six days between the new moon and the crescent, the whole o' me leave, and I've but three days left afore I must retain. Too soon if ye ask me."

"Six days—why, that seems like a long time," I said as my brain busily began making calculations that did not add up to the way I understood the natural order of the world to be. "How long 'til the full moon?" I asked suddenly, on the verge of discovering yet another dimension to this whole dizzying mystery.

"Oh, twenty-four days. About 'alf a month."

Forty-eight days in a month? "And how many months in a year?" My voice was quivering.

"Why, eight o' course." Frondamein said as he and Loralon exchanged puzzled glances.

The Healer of Guildenwood

I remained silent for several moments, my mind frantically working to do the math. Why, that would mean there were almost four hundred days in a year! Four hundred revolutions on this planet's yearly trip around the sun!

I was glad that the darkness concealed the paleness of my skin as the blood drained from my face. "Where I come from we count time differently," I said weakly. "If you'll excuse me, I'm not feeling well. I believe I'll head on up to bed."

"As ye wish," Loralon replied.

I stood suddenly and had to brace myself on the back of my chair for fear I would faint.

"Feelin' poorly again, Miss Arwyn?" Frondamein asked.

"A little dizzy. I'll be fine," I said as I walked toward the front door of the cottage. "Goodnight."

Upstairs in the loft, the terrible possibility dawned on me that I was not even in the same world as before. How could this possibly be? What I had seen of Bensor so far appeared much like the place from which I had come, only an earlier version of it. It wasn't like there were leprechauns running around or winged horses and such—only talk of elves and magical swords and horrible beasts, and I still wasn't convinced that it all wasn't a case of imaginations gone wild.

My mind was again thrown into a confusing labyrinth of questions that led nowhere. For what seemed like hours I lay on my bed, slipping in and out of consciousness. But perhaps only several minutes had passed. Who could tell? In this topsy-turvy world, I certainly had little trust in my senses or anything I had previously accepted as reality.

My mind was a blur of images, from magical swords to winged beasts to epic battles and shining yellow stars. And interlaced with my subconscious wanderings, I seemed to hear fragments of a conversation. "Dizzy spells . . . cravin' for milk . . . clumsy . . . with child . . . 'usband dead . . . wandered the world in 'er grief . . . kin cause a pairson to act rather odd at that . . . 'tis why Omni saw fit to bring us together . . . well, p'rhaps."

And it was at some point that I fell into complete, blissful unconsciousness.

CHAPTER 10

I was still in an altered level of consciousness, but somewhere in the distance I could hear my old familiar voice rambling on. "I stick out like a sore thumb in this totally backward place. But now that I've saved a life . . . well, maybe they'll finally accept me . . . that is, until I can find my way back."

The next few days were much the same as the first, with work in the garden and care of the animals being top priority. It was a never-ending cycle of cleaning and tending and preparing, all without the conveniences I had taken for granted in my previous existence. The struggle to survive in this land forgotten by time made it difficult to focus on any loftier pursuits, and for the time being my main goal was simply to adjust to this new way of living. Focus on the bare necessities of life also helped to keep my mind off my predicament, at least for a while.

However, it seemed that Frondamein treated me more gingerly than before, encouraging me to stop and rest more often. And every once in a while I would catch him and Loralon looking at me and shaking their heads with the most pitiable expressions. Was I really that pathetic?

Much to Frondamein and Loralon's dismay, Frondamein's leave was nearing an end and it was the afternoon before he was to return to his post at the Guildenmoor Gate. All in all, the cottage had come to look a great deal more orderly. The garden and flowerbeds were no longer cluttered with unsightly weeds, and Frondamein had found the time to fix the gate leading onto the road.

As if to celebrate a job well done, the three of us abandoned our chores at the cottage and walked down the road to the Blue Willow for refreshment and to fraternize with the locals. Along the way we passed a group of young boys swimming in the lake, each taking turns swinging out over the water on a rope tied to an overhanging tree branch. I regarded them with envy, wishing I could join them rather than face the crowd at the tavern. Up until then, I had found safety in the confines of Frondamein's little home, having only to deal with the steady gaze of passers-by from the road. Facing a whole room full of curious villagers and the questions they could ask seemed much more daunting.

Inside the tavern, we entered a large room where dozens of people sat around tables drinking ale from large mugs, all listening to a strapping young man with dark hair, mustache, and a wily look in his eyes who was standing before a massive hearth with one foot perched on a chair. He gestured dramatically as his voice boomed with an air of haughtiness. The man continued speaking until he noticed that several in his audience had turned their attention elsewhere. He looked toward the back of the room and saw the three of us taking our seats at a round table. All eyes were then drawn to me, and a wave of excited whispers and murmurings swept over the crowd.

"And then they inquired 'bout the load in the back o' me wagon," the man continued in an even louder voice. "Well, good people o' Baeren Ford, I wasna about to let them filthy Gargalocs steal that fine wine ye count on me to bring back from Elwindor. So I jumped down from me wagon, sword in 'and, and I challenged the both of 'em at once." A gasp came from the crowd, which only encouraged the man to playact the encounter, using members of his audience to demonstrate the chain of events.

"Who is that man?" I whispered to Loralon.

"'Is name's Hamloc. Works for old Padimus 'ere in the tavern. 'E's considered by some the most eligible man in town."

"He *is* kinda good-looking in a rough sort of way, and by the looks of it those girls over there think so, too," I said as I observed several young maidens sitting close at hand, giggling with every wink he sent their way. "Still, he seems full of himself."

Hamloc went on with his story for a while, feeding off the crowd's awe. He described his harrowing ordeal with the Gargalocs in gory detail, explaining how he single-handedly fought the slow and dim-witted but very strong beasts to the death on a lonely road in western Elwindor so that he could bring the people of Baeren Ford their wine. Following the dramatic presentation, the people inside the tavern raised their mugs in salute to their hero as Padimus gave him a big slap on the back. The man grinned smugly as he met my gaze across the room.

"Who shall be the next to entertain us with a tale?" Padimus asked as he looked around the room. No one spoke up. "Miss Arwyn," he said as all eyes fixed upon me once more, "ye're a stanger to this land. P'rhaps ye'd be kind enough to share a tale from yer 'omeland."

"This is what we Bensorians do when we come to tavern," Frondamein explained. "We see who kin tell the best tale."

I knew I should have stayed back at the cottage. Drawing even more attention to myself was not exactly what I had wanted. "Groovy," I replied with a plastered smile, trying to appear enthusiastic.

Everyone in the room grew silent and stared at me with a collective look of confusion. Realizing my faux pas, I put my hand over my mouth as if I had belched.

"Must be an elvish word," I heard several whisper.

"Well," Padimus said, "do ye know a story or do ye not?"

I thought for a moment, searching my sketchy memory for something, anything I could retrieve from my prior life. Then a memory from somewhere tickled my consciousness. It was enough. "Yes, I do know one."

The crowd in the tavern shifted in their seats as they prepared to hear my tale. I glanced over at Hamloc and could see him standing silently, leaning against the hearth with a mug of ale in his hand.

"Once upon a time in the land of Kansas," I began, "there lived a girl named . . . Doris. No, that's not right. Her name was Dorothy." Why did the story of Dorothy and her adventures in Oz come to mind? Maybe because I was a fish out of water, too.

"Do-ro-thy . . . what kind o' name's that?" cried a voice from the sea of villagers.

"Quiet! An' let the lady tell 'er story," someone else said.

I cleared my throat nervously and continued, "One day, Dorothy made a wish to escape from what she considered to be a very dull life in Kansas when a great storm blew in that whisked her away to a magical land called Oz . . ." On and on I talked, spinning a tale as best as I could remember from the small shred of memory I clung to. It seemed to work for they all sat there breathlessly, hanging on my every word. "And so, Dorothy had learned that there really is 'no place like home.' . . . And that's the end."

I sat quietly, waiting for some kind of reaction from the listeners, but everyone sat in silence with blank looks upon their faces for what seemed like centuries.

"Whoever 'eard of a talkin' scarecrow," a man in the audience finally said, "or talkin' lions or monkeys what fly."

"Now wait a minute," an old woman chimed in, "there's many a story from Loth Gerodin of e'en stranger creatures. Anythin's possible," she said as she gave me a toothless grin.

"And Miss Arwyn, bein' an elf and all, I'm sure she's seen such creatures in Loth Gerodin," said another, younger man who, being slightly inebriated, stood up in the midst of the crowd and waved his mug carelessly in my direction. "Waird 'round the village is ye hail from the northern forest. Ye do hail from Loth Gerodin, do ye not?"

All eyes were again upon me. I wasn't going to get out of this so easily. "Well actually, I am from the country of . . ."

"Amerigo," Loralon said in my defense. "Arwyn's from the country of Amerigo."

"Ne'er haird of it," the young man said.

"'Tis a rather small country," Loralon continued.

Frondamein had been deep in thought, remaining very quiet throughout the entire interchange. His face suddenly brightened. "Bravo, Miss Arwyn!" he exclaimed. "Grand story. Bravo!" All eyes were now on Frondamein. "Whether there be such creatures as talkin' lions and the like, why, 'tis not the point at all. What matters is Dorothy 'ad no need o' the wizard as she 'ad all she needed from the verra beginnin'."

"Well yes, Frondamein, you're absolutely right," I said as the crowd nodded their heads in a sign of approval.

"Interestin' story, verra entertainin'," I could hear people say.

On the other side of the room, the man who had spoken earlier caught my eye and silently lifted his mug to me. His gaze I found disconcerting, and I quickly looked away.

"Thank ye, Miss Arwyn," Padimus yelled over the voices of his customers. "Kiril, such a fine story desairves a pint of ale on the 'ouse."

Suddenly a heavy-set young man with wavy light brown hair set a frothy mug on the table before me as he looked upon me with eyes full of sympathy. I wasn't sure exactly what I should do, but I found myself once more at the center of attention. Slowly I lifted the mug to my lips and took one gulp of the contents inside. As the bitter liquid burned my throat on the way down, my face contorted and I let out a long cough to the sound of stifled tittering amongst the crowd.

"P'rhaps me lady would prefer a glass o' wine instead?" Padimus offered.

"Oh, no thank you," I said. "What I'd really like is a glass of milk if you have it."

To that, the whole tavern erupted in unsuppressed laughter, and all I wanted to do was quietly melt in between the cracks in the floor like the wicked witch in my story.

"Not to wairry, Miss." Padimus grinned. "They're laughin' 'cause they know that e'en the milk served in me tavern's strong enough to put 'air on yer chest." The laughter grew even louder. "Now who'll be the next to spin a tale?"

"Beggin' yer pardon, Miss Arwyn, but there's no sense in lettin' a good pint of ale go to waste," Frondamein said as he slid the mug in his direction.

"I wouldna mind a swig meself," Loralon said.

"Oh, but you shouldn't, not in your condition. It could harm the baby," I urged.

"And I suppose ye should know, bein' in the same condition yerself," Loralon replied.

"What?" I exclaimed.

"Ye know, bein' with child 'n all."

"You mean, pregnant?" What would possess them to think such a thing?

"Aye!"

"I'm not pregnant!" I protested, more loudly than I'd intended. "Why, I'm not even married!"

An abrupt silence descended upon the tavern, and I realized everyone in the place had overheard my unexpected outburst. I could feel my face turning beet red when from outside the tavern my humiliation was interrupted by the sound of a woman screaming. In an instant, the tavern customers headed for the front door to investigate the source of the commotion. I followed behind and, as I made my way through the crowd, could hear the woman more clearly.

"Me son! Me poor son drowned!" she wailed.

Instinct took over, and in an instant I pushed through the crowd of onlookers until I saw a sobbing woman holding the lifeless body of a young boy I had seen earlier swimming in the lake. Not caring how it would look to the villagers, I rushed to the boy's side and tore him from his mother's arms.

"Are ye mad, woman?" the woman cried in alarm

"I'm trying to save his life," I responded, attempting to remain calm while working quickly to position the boy on the ground. I tilted the boy's head back and put my ear to his mouth as the crowd murmured behind me. "I must have quiet!" I demanded, surprising myself with the authority in my voice. No sign of breathing and no pulse.

Amidst the sound of gasps, I bent over the still body and clamped my mouth onto the boy's, forcing air into his lungs with two steady breaths while holding his nostrils shut. Somewhere in the recesses of my mind I saw myself in a different form, hovered over a pliable human imitation breathing forcefully into waxy lips that had been swabbed with a strong-smelling liquid. The object at the time was to impress an onlooker, apparently a person of authority, who hovered nearby while scribbling something onto a piece of paper. But now a life hung in the balance.

Yet even deeper still, I felt the groanings of an ancient, buried pain, as if my success would somehow put me on the path to my own redemption.

"Come on, breathe!" I urged as I pressed my palm against the boy's bare chest and pushed down forcefully several times.

There were some in the crowd who yelled disheartening comments in their alarm over my baffling behavior. Trying my best to ignore them, again I placed my lips on the boy's mouth and exhaled twice. The small chest expanded from the breath I forced inside. "Please breathe," I whispered as I began the pumping motion again. Another breath into the mouth and repeat the sequence again, I thought to myself.

Right as I was about to begin another set of compressions, a small geyser of water spewed from the boy's mouth as he sputtered and coughed. I could hear the crowd behind me gasp in disbelief as the boy's mother rushed to take him into her arms. "Me little child, snatched from death's door!" she cried, smothering the boy's forehead with kisses and holding him close to her bosom.

"It's a downright miracle!" one of the bystanders yelled.

Shaken and weak from the ordeal, I stood back as the crowd gathered around the boy. As I wiped my brow, something on the road caught my eye. There I saw a gnarled, bent-over old man with a long, gray beard sitting upon the back of an old donkey. He would have looked like any other old man but for the large black raven that rode upon his shoulder and the way his piercing eyes seemed to stare from under two bushy eyebrows directly into my soul. I met his gaze for several moments, intrigued by his watchfulness, but was forced to turn away when the mother of the young boy approached me.

"Ye saved me only son's life," she said with tears in her eyes. "'Ow kin I e'er repay ye?"

"There's really no need for that," I replied. The crowd that had been so disheartening only moments before now looked at me with wonder.

"Me name's Grendela. And this is me son, Newlyn," she said as a man carrying the still-dazed boy in his arms walked up next to her. "I'd be honored if ye'd come dine at me 'umble 'ome night after tomorrow. I'd 'ave ye o'er tomorrow, but seein's me 'usband'll be in the fields 'til late, I know he'd also want to thank ye himself."

I smiled and leaned over to embrace the woman. "I'd love to," I said. "I'm so glad Newlyn's okay. He should probably go home and get some rest now."

"Aye, that 'e'll do, miss, that 'e'll do," Grendela said, taking her son from the man's arms.

As the onlookers dispersed, each quietly filed past me with wide eyes filled with awe, some even nodding their heads respectfully. Loralon and Frondamein, who had observed the whole incident, exchanged perplexed looks. It was clear that they did not know what to make of me.

Once the crowd had thinned, my gaze returned to the spot where I had seen the peculiar old man. I glanced up and down the road, but he was nowhere in sight. Where he could possibly have disappeared to in such a short time was baffling.

As the sun made its exit in the western sky, Frondamein, Loralon, and I walked together back up the road, and I was glad to return to the peace and quiet of the cottage.

CHAPTER 11

"It's not that life is unbearable, although living in such primitive conditions when I'm accustomed to a faster pace of life is taking some getting used to. It's more the principle of the thing—people just don't switch bodies and pop into other worlds without warning. It goes against the laws of nature, not to mention it makes me a complete oddball."

"Your situation certainly is . . . unusual," Dr. Susan's voice commented.

"And what if . . . what if I never figure out who I used to be? What if I can never return to the life that's been stolen from me?"

"It seems you're afraid of losing your true identity, but you can't remember what that identity is." Just the kind of thing a therapist would say.

"It's like I'm a simmering pot, and I feel I'm about to reach my boiling point."

It was early the next morning when Frondamein left for his post at the Guildenmoor Gate, his short respite having come to an end. He grudgingly packed his belongings and saddled his horse as Loralon filled a burlap bag full of bread and cheeses. After bidding me farewell, Frondamein walked with his wife out to the road where the two embraced, and once again I found myself spying on them—only they were outside by the road and I was inside the sitting room, and even my bionic ears couldn't hear what they were saying. I could only guess they were talking about me. Yet by the look of Loralon's body language and the way she nodded her head submissively, it appeared I had been accepted—at least for the time being.

After one last embrace, Frondamein mounted his horse and rode off. For several minutes Loralon gazed up the road in the direction he traveled, waving to him one last time from afar before turning to come inside. She slowly walked toward the cottage, her eyes reddened from tears that refused to be confined a moment longer. Feeling helpless to take away her sadness, all I could do was offer a comforting shoulder as she entered the room.

Loralon wept quietly for several moments before she looked up at me and smiled. "Funny, though Frondamein's left, the 'ouse doesna seem so lonely as usual."

That afternoon, Loralon and I walked together to the marketplace, passing many going to and fro on the main road through the village. One man whom I recognized from the day before in the tavern tipped his hat and smiled as we approached. "Miss Loralon, Miss Arwyn, groovy day to ye."

"And a groovy day to ye as well," Loralon answered back.

Taken aback by the man's vocabulary, I could only muster a nod of greeting.

"Ye've made quite the impression, ye have," Loralon said quietly as she leaned closer to me.

"I would actually prefer to remain a bit more anonymous," I confided. "I feel out of place as it is."

"I suspect ye'll find anonymity a wee difficult in this village. But dunna wairry yerself," she added, "no one'll let on to th' enemy ye're 'ere."

What? I stopped dead in my tracks, but Loralon continued along greeting the neighbors cheerily so that I had to hurry to catch up.

When we arrived at the bustling market, merchants stood beside carts laden with fruits and vegetables, beckoning us to stop and examine their goods. "Get yer groovy cucumbers here," a woman with a shrill voice called out, "plucked from the vine this mornin'."

A rather large man in a bloodied tunic stood at the door of his butcher shop with a knife in one hand and a large slab of meat in the other. "Mutton, freshly slaughtered mutton," he bellowed above the noise of the crowd as he caught Loralon's eye. Confidently he walked over to us, pointing his knife at the piece of meat flapping in his hand. "What a groovy roast 'twould make, wouldna it, Miss Loralon, or p'rhaps Miss Arwyn would like a nice mutton stew."

I took a step back as he waved the shiny knife precariously in front of me, emphasizing every other syllable he said. And I crinkled my nose in distaste as several flies alighted like vultures on the red, oozing flesh.

"P'rhaps another day, Manyus," Loralon said as she started to walk away.

"Ah, but, Miss Loralon," the butcher said apologetically, "I'm forgetin' the debt I owe ye for the beautiful dress ye made me daughter on the occasion of 'er weddin'. I'd be pleased for ye to take this piece o' meat as partial payment for yer sairvices . . . or ye may come into me shop and pick out a larger one if ye like."

"That I'll do!" Loralon disappeared into the doorway of the butcher's shop for a few moments before returning with a burlap sack bulging with several slabs of beef. She gave me a sly look. "Worked for weeks on 'is silly daughter's dress, I did. The ghel kept changin' 'er mind and 'ad me work me poor fingers to the bone. It's goin' to take a lot more than mutton to pay that debt."

"Why, Loralon, what a keen businesswoman you are!" I said, quite impressed with my new friend's shrewdness.

We continued through the marketplace, at times stopping to purchase such items as flour, honey, and berries. The noisy market brimmed with the sounds of merchants announcing enticing bargains as children ran among the carts, laughing gleefully as they played their made-up games. Through the middle of the crowd came a man prodding a covered pushcart, selling dozens of brass and copper pots and pans that clanked loudly together as they swayed back and forth from the awning.

As I followed Loralon's lead in the market, I observed her friendly haggling with the persistent merchants and began to pick up the subtle nuances of bartering, which appeared to be a ritual that intensified the bonds of neighborliness and compromise amongst the villagers. Furthermore, I was beginning to learn Bensor's system of currency, and as my mind thought back to the bag of gold I had found in my possession several days before, I came to realize that I owned a small fortune, the origin of which was still unknown.

"Ye'll need more suitable clothes for life in the village than the ones ye have," Loralon commented. She had examined my two garments and determined that neither were really suitable for everyday life. "P'rhaps we'll stop at the dyer's shop to find ye some material."

I followed obediently as Loralon led the way to one of the many shops on the village square and stepped inside.

"Good afternoon, Loralon . . . Arwyn," the dyer's wife greeted cheerfully. News of my presence in the town had undoubtedly reached the ear of every villager by then. Remembering the rather unusual names of so many who already seemed to know who I was promised to be a rather daunting proposition and one that could lead to many embarrassing situations.

"Good afternoon, Feyla. It seems Arwyn's in need o' more suitable clothin' for work at the cottage," Loralon explained. "That which she 'as is much too fine for farmwork."

"'Tis a shame we canna always dress in the finery, but I suppose it makes no difference to the chickens and the cows what ye wear, now does it?" Feyla said as I smiled at the friendly shopkeeper. With that she led me over to a table where several rolls of fabric lay. "I'm afraid we've not much to choose from. The fine elvish silks and laces are 'ard to come by these days 'n the next finest fabrics are to be found no closer than the markets o' Maldimire," apologized Feyla, who was herself cloaked in a very attractive gown of green with red, yellow, and purple birds meticulously embroidered around the neckline. "Still, we've some rather nice wools and linens—and in several colors at that."

"I'm sure they'll be fine," I said, fingering the rather uninspiring fabrics dubiously.

"We'll need a good bit—to fit yer tall frame that is," Loralon commented.

"And full enough so that I can easily ride my horse."

"A pity more women dunna wear the leggings o' men. 'Twould make ridin' all th' easier," Feyla said.

"Arwyn does 'ave a ridin' gown, and leggings what go with it," Loralon explained.

"'Tis no surprise," said the dyer's wife. "Waird 'as it they're popular with th' elvish women, isna that true, Arwyn?"

"Why yes, they are," I said, quickly looking away. It had always been difficult for me to bluff, much less tell an outright lie. "Er, what exactly would you recommend for me?"

"The green wool would suit ye fine as it matches yer eyes," Feyla suggested. "And p'rhaps a bit o' the lavender as well with the white linen to go underneath."

"Sounds good to me."

"We'll need yer measurements, though," Feyla said as she retrieved a measuring tape and a pair of shears from a drawer beneath the table. For several minutes the dyer's wife worked to take my measurements and then carefully cut off the required yards from the rolls that lay on the table, all the while chatting about her husband's need to make a trip to Maldimire in order to purchase more material for the shop. "And would ye believe, waird 'as it there's now a shop in Maldimire where ye kin walk right in 'n purchase from the shelves a gown what's already been made."

"'Ow could such a dress fit proper, what with no measurements taken aforehand?" Loralon sniffed. "Garments should be made with the wearer in mind."

"Aye, I'd 'ave t' agree with ye on that one," Feyla said. "Speakin o' which, Loralon, I saved a last bit o' silk for meself and was 'opin ye'd make me a new dress." The shopkeeper walked over to a cupboard in the corner of the room and opened one of its drawers, retrieving a long piece of cobalt-blue fabric.

"'Ow nice it is, Feyla," Loralon replied, running her fingers along the fabric, "and what a handsome job yer 'usband did on the dye. 'Twill be a fine dress indeed! But I'll need to see to Arwyn's new clothes fairst, ye understand."

"Aye, but I'd be most appreciative if ye'd see to me measurements now?"

Loralon looked at me. "Well, we've no more shoppin' to tend to. Would ye care to wait for me, Arwyn?"

"Actually, I believe I'll head on home with our groceries and begin supper."

"Groceries?" Loralon said as she raised an eyebrow.

"One of them elvish words, no doubt," the dyer's wife suggested.

"Yes, you know me, always forgetting to stop speaking elvish," I bluffed. "Well, I must be going."

I gathered the neatly folded fabric under one arm and picked up the straw basket that held our other purchases.

"Ye'll start to peel the potatoes?"

"I'll be glad to," I replied.

"What a dear ye are," Loralon said.

"Nice to meet you, Feyla," I said as I headed for the front door of the shop.

"And ye as well," Feyla replied.

As the door closed behind me, I realized that I had forgotten the key to the cottage. I turned but stopped short at the shop door as I overheard the two women talking about me on the other side.

"So what's it really like to 'ave an elf about the house?"

"Same as any other woman," Loralon said. "Frondamein insists she's an elf, but I sense a high-spirited mortal woman 'idin' behind that composure that doesna speak o' the elvish restraint. But then again, I'd not met an elf afore the likes of Arwyn, which makes me opinion count for little."

"P'rhaps ye're right," Feyla said. "But I'd say she does 'ave the elf in 'er all right. Now, if ye'd see to me measurements."

I almost turned the doorknob into the shop when I remembered that Loralon hadn't locked the cottage door to begin with, something that seemed a common practice among the villagers. This seemed a bit foolhardy, or perhaps I had been too conditioned to caution.

I turned and walked away; but the present overheard conversation, in addition to the one Loralon and Frondamein had in bed several evenings before, made me all the more confused as to my true nature. I pondered this mystery as I headed back through the market and up the road to the cottage.

Along the way I passed the Blue Willow on my left. It was still too early in the day for there to be much business at the tavern, but the crowd was due to arrive as soon as the sun began its westward descent. From the corner of my eye, I detected a shadowy figure in the tavern's doorway as I passed by, and it was not long before I heard footsteps approaching from behind.

"'Twas some feat ye performed yesterday," a masculine voice boomed. "Ye have the whole town talkin'."

I spun around to see the dark-haired, burly man from the tavern walking up beside me. His blue eyes stared piercingly as a faint, mischievous smile appeared on his lips. "I don't believe we've been introduced," I said.

"Hamloc, at yer sairvice," the man said, bowing low as he took my free hand and gave it a kiss. The sensation of his prickly mustache on my skin made me cringe. "Now what's such a pretty thin' as yerself doin' in this small town?"

The Healer of Guildenwood

"Bensor is a free country, isn't it?" I answered with an air of insolence, though in all my memory I could not recall ever having spoken so curtly to an adult before. Surprised by my sudden rudeness, which Hamloc apparently ignored, I turned to continue on my way. Hamloc followed along, though he offered no help with my packages.

"Found the elvish life dull, did ye, with all that readin' and music? Lookin' for a little excitement among us mortals?" Hamloc said as he gave me a sly smile.

"I'm finding life here actually rather quiet," I replied.

"'Tis true ye'll find no excitement 'ere," Hamloc said with an almost resentful sound to his voice. "'Owever, 'tis not as safe 'ere for a pretty young thin' as once it was. Ye need a strong man to protect ye from those nasty Gargalocs. And seein' as I'm the only man in town brave enough for the task, ye'll be glad to know I'm right down the road when ye need me," he said, giving me a wink.

"Thank you for your kind offer. However, I'm quite capable of taking care of myself," I said, trying hard to maintain a facade of politeness.

Hamloc let out a patronizing laugh. "Ye elves and your manner o' speech. Ye dunna talk like ye're from around these parts."

"That's because I'm not, if you haven't figured that out already," I muttered under my breath.

"Still, I must say I find it verra, verra appealin'," Hamloc said as his gaze moved from my face down to my waist. Could he have been more obvious?

I could feel the blood rising in my cheeks and was glad to arrive at the front gate of the cottage. "Excuse me, Mr. Hamloc, but I have to go make dinner," I said as I opened the front gate and walked toward the door.

"And ye'll call if ye catch any Gargalocs a-sneakin' about."

Was this guy for real? "I'll drop what I'm doing and call out your name if I see any dare to enter this town."

"Ye'll be callin' on me soon enough," I heard him say as I disappeared into the house.

Later that evening I told Loralon about my encounter with Hamloc—another reason I wanted to go home and stop attracting unwanted attention. "He gives me the creeps," I observed.

Loralon remained silent, and I noticed that her face was all scrunched up as she stared at me. "Where are these *creeps* he gave ye?"

I shook my head, frustrated that I was always seemed to be putting my foot in my mouth. "No! What I mean is, he's too macho for his own good."

"*Macho?*" she repeated.

"Hmm." How could I explain myself in terms she would understand? "He thinks he's God's . . . that is, *Omni's* gift to women."

A smile crept across Loralon's lips. "*Macho*, eh?" She started to titter, and then her tittering turned into full-blown laughter, and we both laughed so hard that tears ran down our faces.

From that moment on, I started to look upon Loralon differently, for in that moment, I found in her a glimmer of someone familiar and comforting—someone I had known long before. If only I could remember who.

As the summer days grew warmer, Loralon and I arose before the sun to finish the hard labor outdoors before the heat of the day set in. During the afternoons while Loralon worked on my new clothing in the cool interior of the cottage, I took to exploring, at first remaining close to the village. I discovered a faster path across the lake by way of two bridges that converged on a small island where the lake narrowed at its southern end. A toothless old bridgekeepr and his wife lived on the island in a stone house that hung precariously over the water, and each were prone to delaying anyone who passed for a bit of village gossip. To someone like me who desired anonymity, they were a bit too nosey, and I found myself waiting until I saw no one about before hurrying across to the opposite shore.

Avencloe and I then took to going on long runs across sprawling green fields and exploring the woodlands as far as the shores of Lake Ellowyne above the village, each day venturing farther and farther afield, working up the courage to return to the Gate. After all, it would be a long journey on my own, and I didn't relish the idea of going it alone.

In the depths of the forests that surrounded the village, I discovered an abundance of woodland creatures. There were the usual squirrels, raccoons, and deer; then there were a few small mammals unlike any I'd ever seen before. But still, I spied nothing too outlandish. It was my awareness of them that was heightened—the fact that, when I concentrated, I could practically hear a chipmunk breathing in the branches above my head. And the flowers, with colors that exploded on the forest's green palette, filled my nostrils with a sweet bouquet mingled with the earthy scent of the forest floor. There was always something new to see, some new path to be explored.

But by far the thing that made my explorations most exhilarating was Avencloe, who ran tirelessly like the wind, urged on by a seeming inner drive. The majestic horse jumped streams and fences in such a smooth and graceful manner that I felt as though I were riding on the wings of an eagle. In fact, there were times I closed my eyes and could have sworn we were flying, and indeed our passage was enough to make the leaves and the grass quake from the force of the wind it created. As we streaked across the high meadow in a fury, I could look down into the village below and see people stop and stare. Even if they thought me reckless, I didn't care. All that mattered was that, for a few blissful moments, I was virtually oblivious to everything but the sound of the rushing wind as it whipped through my hair.

My daily rides became the greatest joy in my life, and although I consciously resisted forming any emotional attachment to anything in my new life, I could not help but fall in love with the beautiful surroundings of Baeren Ford, and I felt no fear the more I explored. But above all, a bond of trust and love was growing between Avencloe and me that I could hardly deny.

I was also becoming quite fond of Loralon and knew with every passing day it would be more difficult for me to find the will to return to the Guildenmoor Gate, especially when there were no guarantees that my quest there would be successful. Yet memory of my previous life remained sketchy at best, and I feared it would soon be erased from my mind altogether.

Late one afternoon as I returned to the village following a long gallop through the meadow, I found myself gazing up at the sad ruins of the fortress that stood silently above the village. Seeing how the sunlight pierced through the gaping holes in the walls of the battlement, casting a golden hue inward, I became mesmerized by the austere beauty of the place. Rather than turning toward home, I rode on an overgrown pathway past imposing walls of the fortress that had been leveled to half their original height. Farther up the hill, a high parapet connected two huge turrets, sentinels of its mysterious past.

Compelled onward by an irresistible urge, I rode through the remains of what was once a large gate and into the middle of a vast labyrinth of crumbling gray walls. The path where noblemen once walked was now only trod by flocks of sheep and children who failed to heed their mothers' warnings about the supposed ghosts that haunted the castle. But on that afternoon the fortress remained silent save for sporadic gusts of warm air whistling through the numerous fissures in the walls.

I came to a large rectangular structure with each of its four walls still intact. There I dismounted and walked through a large archway into the center of the crumbling building. The roof of the structure had long-since collapsed, leaving the interior exposed to all the elements. Rays of sunlight shone through the many arched openings high in the walls, casting patterns of light and dark upon the grassy floor beneath. I heard a cooing noise above and looked upward toward the blue sky in time to see several pigeons return to their roosts in high crevices for the evening.

In the very center of the great room stood a perfectly round circle of stone, worn down by the weather but nevertheless intact. I ran my fingers along runes that had been carefully carved onto the top of the circle, wishing that I could read the unfamiliar script. Then my eyes were drawn upward to a mosaic on the wall that depicted a very noble-looking man and beautiful woman with long, dark hair standing side by side. The lower portion of the picture had crumbled, leaving an uneven line across the waists of the two people who stood silent and frozen forever in the wall. I stared at the strong and majestic faces captured in the mosaic, despite the primitive nature of the art, and had the sudden urge to weep.

For several moments I stood with eyes closed, enjoying the warm sunlight as it beamed down upon my face from above when suddenly I had the distinct feeling that I was not alone. Quickly I turned to see the figure of a man standing in the shadows. As he stepped out into the sunlight, I could see that it was the old man who had been watching me from the road several days before.

For a long moment, we regarded each other silently. At last he spoke, seemingly to himself. "'From the shadow of Arnuin's Hold,'" he said mysteriously, his eyes holding the same piercing quality as before. "Welcome, Arwyn, to Bensor."

"How did you know my name?"

"I know much," he said. "The animals tell me all I need to know of the goings-on in the village. They told me of your arrival."

How was I to respond to that?

"I am Eliendor," he said, walking closer with the help of an intricately carved cane, held firmly in a gnarled old hand. His neck was slightly bent over from an uncomfortable-looking hump that protruded from between his shoulder blades, causing him to turn his head to the side in order to look up at me. He wore a long flowing dark blue robe that shuffled along the ground as he walked. A long, full gray beard adorned his face and a pair of wise old eyes stared from under two bushy white eyebrows. "Does my appearance frighten you?" he asked.

"Your presence did startle me at first, but I don't find you frightening," I answered. "I find myself feeling more curious about you than anything."

The old man chuckled to himself. "Such honesty is rare," he said. "And so, what is it that would make you so curious about an old man?"

"You seem . . . well, different from the others in the village. More learned, I guess, based on the way you talk. And you seem . . . perceptive."

"Such as, knowing you have questions that I may help answer."

"Well, yes."

My new acquaintance sat down on the circle of stone and took a deep breath as he glanced at our surroundings. "Ah, if these walls could talk, what stories they could tell."

"Actually, I'd very much like to know what happened here. This place is so beautiful, and it intrigues me. Can you tell me about it?"

"As I told you, I know much." The old man sat quietly for a moment with a distant look in his eyes. "A great love happened here, a great, doomed love," he said, glancing at the mosaic above. He then looked again at me. "Do you know what this circle is?" he asked, indicating the ring of stone on which we sat. "It is the circle of Omni, the All, the never-ending Giver and Sustainer of Life. The unbroken circle represents His eternal nature. From ancient times until only a few years ago when such was deemed unlawful, people would gather around circles such as this and sing songs to Him and dance joyfully. And," he added, cocking his head at me curiously, "though this one has since dried up, it seems they all encircled water of some form or another. You would not happen to know the purpose for the water, would you?"

How should I know? I was not from around there. The history lesson was all well and good, but there were more pressing matters at hand. I shook my head, unable to recall much about Omni, whatever he had been called where I came from, or anything else for that matter.

"Pity," he replied, looking genuinely disappointed.

I was silent for a moment, a million thoughts suddenly swirling around in my head. But how to phrase them without sounding crazy? "Mr., er, Eliendor," I said at last, "I wonder if you could help me with the rather *unusual* predicament I am in."

"Aye, I have answers, but perhaps not the ones you believe yourself to be searching for."

"But . . ."

"Patience, Arwyn. These walls weren't built in a day, and your answers won't be so forthcoming either." Eliendor stared deeply into my eyes, again giving me the clear sense that he was looking directly into my soul.

This conversation was not going the way I had hoped. "All I want is to find my way home."

"Is home the place where your heart finds peace?"

I thought for a moment, trying to conjure images of the world I had left behind. Nothing. Only a sense of safety and familiarity, and that was peace enough. I nodded slowly.

"Then I can help you . . ." For a moment, I felt a great hope well up inside me. ". . . find peace, though you may not find it where you expect." From nearby there came an alarmed "baa", and into the ruined walls walked a wobbly little lamb, lost from its mother—I knew how it felt. Suddenly, Eliendor rose and walked over to it, scooping it up tenderly in his arms. "Dear little one, have you lost your way?"

"But . . ."

"I will help you on your journey," he said as he turned once more to face me. "And in return you will give company to a lonely old man."

"Okay," I agreed. I had a feeling that he knew more about me than he was letting on and that he had come to the fortress that afternoon knowing

I would be there. But why would he be so interested in me? Did he simply see in me a new friend, someone to keep him company, or was there more to it than that?

Eliendor walked through the archway and toward his waiting donkey, still holding the lamb gingerly in his arms. He moved rather quickly for someone who appeared to be so ancient, making me scramble to keep up.

"But how will I find you?"

"Follow the path of the setting sun," he said. "Ah, there she is." I watched as the old man placed the lamb carefully onto the ground next to its mother, thinking it quite odd how the ewe did not seem afraid in the least of Eliendor. But then again it was hard to be afraid of someone who seemed as gentle as a lamb himself. Oh, how I wished someone would scoop me up and return me to where I belonged!

Despite his frail form, the old man mounted the donkey with little effort. "Talthos, come!" he called with a shrill whistle. A black-as-night raven flew down from somewhere above and alighted on the old man's shoulder.

I watched as the strange company disappeared from view, marveling at the mystery surrounding the brief encounter, and I had a hunch that this man somehow held the secret to my return home.

CHAPTER 12

"It's not fair! It's just not fair!" I wailed from my seat on the couch.

"I can tell you're beginning to feel rather helpless over your, er, situation," the ethereal woman's voice said sympathetically.

I nodded, eyes still shut tight. "This is completely insane, and there's absolutely nothing I can do about it!"

That evening after I returned to the cottage, I casually mentioned my afternoon encounter to Loralon.

"So ye met the old hermit Eliendor did ye?" Loralon replied. "What a strange little man 'e is, livin' in the woods all by 'imself. No one knows exactly 'ow long 'e's lived there, but it's longer than any o' the rest of us 'ave been around."

"What else do you know about him?" I asked curiously.

"'E comes into town once every few weeks, wanderin' about the streets as if lookin' for someone. Rather odd if ye ask me." Loralon stopped talking to guide a thread through a needle. "The children like 'is magic tricks, and some say 'e's a sorcerer with magical powers who kin cast spells 'n talk t' animals. Hunters who 'appen upon 'is cottage come back with stories o' the strangest sightin's of all manner o' creatures, e'en elves."

"He has business with elves?"

"'E apparently 'as some connection with th' elves o' Loth Gerodin. They've been spotted goin' to and from 'is cottage o'er the years, but for what reason's anyone's guess."

"What an amazing person," I said thoughtfully.

"Aye, well, I suppose 'e's 'armless enough, but I still think 'e's verra odd."

And that was the last we spoke of my encounter, but I couldn't shake Eliendor's image from my mind or the idea that he could help me find a way home.

For days there remained a steady stream of onlookers wandering past the cottage, and it was very disconcerting to try navigating the very ill-mannered mule through the garden only to look up and see several amused gawkers standing there. I know they meant no harm, but I rather wished my frustration was not such a source of amusement and that they would have offered a helping hand instead.

Among those I desired least to see was Hamloc, who had an uncanny way of popping up at the most inconvenient moments. Mostly he just stood there and tried to impress me with his tales of prowess and bravery, not ever offering to lift a finger himself. I found him a complete bore and longed to be rid of him so that I could get on with business and go out for a ride. For the beauty of the woodlands, the rolling hills and valleys, and the gentle meandering brooks called to me, and I found myself needing to escape to them every day.

It was on one such afternoon, as I led Avencloe from the stable, that I glanced up the road and saw Hamloc walking toward the cottage. Quickly, I jumped onto Avencloe's back and fled around to the other side of the stable and through the field behind the house, easily jumping the fence and making my escape through the woods to the southwest. There I came upon a road that led past several cottages and followed a stream deeper into the forest. A cooling summer shower had moved across the land a while before, and now wisps of steam rose from the hot, sweating earth, parting in the wake of Avencloe's steps. I urged the steed over an old stone bridge and down the road before spying a path I had not yet explored. I decided to follow it, all the while grumbling about having to act so secretively.

After a while I came upon a small pond covered with lily pads and draped at the edges with graceful willows. A small path led across a neat little bridge at the place where the pond narrowed into a glassy stream and then through a hedge of meticulously kept flowerbeds that lined the far side of the water. Just beyond the flowers, hiding slightly behind one of the willows, I spied a curious round cottage like none I had ever seen before.

I jumped down from Avencloe's back and took him by the reins, leading him across the bridge and down the path toward the cottage, where the shady front lawn came into view. All about the lawn were various animals, including a couple of deer, some squirrels, chipmunks, and a half-dozen rabbits. In their midst, on a bench beside a napping red fox, was a bent-over old man carving a piece of wood with a small knife. The black raven on his shoulder gave a cry as I approached.

"Ah, there you are," Eliendor said, eyes remaining on his work. "I've been expecting you."

"How did you know . . ." I began before I caught myself. There were many things about the old man that were a mystery and would probably remain so.

Eliendor held up the long piece of wood from which a walking cane was beginning to emerge and examined it carefully. "Much work yet to accomplish," he muttered.

I held out my hand to him. "May I?" Eliendor placed the cane into my hand. "Your work is very beautiful," I said, admiring the ornate design already carved into the wood.

"I have always fancied dabbling in woodwork," he commented with a smile.

I looked around the yard and could see numerous birdhouses scattered about on posts and hanging from tree limbs and from the thatched roof's overhang. Each was different from all the others but obviously the work of the same hands. "You have quite a gift," I added.

"We all have gifts to be discovered," the old man said with a twinkle in his eyes. "Have you come to discover yours, or are you here for some other reason?"

"Well, actually, I chanced upon your house while out riding," I began, "but since I'm here, I wonder if you can help me with this problem I mentioned before."

"Perhaps."

I shifted my weight uncomfortably and glanced upward, not knowing exactly where to begin. "Listen," I said at last, "I'll get right to the point. You see, er, I'm not supposed to be here . . . in Bensor, that is. I wonder if you can help me get home."

Eliendor's face showed no sign of emotion. "Why come here at all if you did not wish to be here?"

"Coming here wasn't my choice."

Until now, I had done everything to conceal the mystery behind my sudden appearance at the Guildenmoor Gate several weeks before. Although I desperately needed someone to confide in, I had dared not discuss the event with anyone in the village for fear they would think me even more odd than they already did. As a result, I had locked that memory away in the recesses of my mind, all the while hoping for a way to reveal it with someone who could assure me that I had indeed not gone mad.

The old man seemed the perfect confidant—isolated from the other villagers, a bit odd himself, and so what if he thought I was crazy? He probably was a bit touched himself, I reasoned, even though I had absolutely no real grounds to suspect this, other than Loralon's description of him. And even if word did get back to the other villagers about my story, who would believe an old hermit?

"If you are not responsible for being here in Bensor, then who is?"

"That I don't know. All I remember is that I was happy in my old life, wherever that was. And then one day, while I was minding my own business . . . WHAM! I appear here out of nowhere, with nothing but a few articles of clothing and a horse. No explanation. Nothing."

Eliendor put down his knife for a moment and scratched his chin. "You say you suddenly appeared here with nothing but some clothes and a horse?"

"Yes, and a little bit of money, as crazy as it sounds."

"Do the clothes fit?"

"Yes."

"Then it is obviously *intended* for you to be here," he said as he picked up his knife.

"No, that can't be right!" I protested, feeling my stomach tighten. "If it is, then there's got to be a mistake. I don't belong here! This place is *so* far behind the times, it's not even funny. Where I come from, it doesn't take hours to prepare one meal. All you have to do is pop it into a machine and presto! a full meal in minutes. And laundry! Don't even let me go there!

"And, do you know what's even crazier?" I continued, working myself into a full-blown frenzy. "The things I remember are not the things that really matter, like who my parents are, or the people I knew, or who I was. I remember only the stupid things, like bacteria, traffic lights, and psychobabble."

"Perhaps the things that are most important are buried deeper within, inside your heart," Eliendor said thoughtfully.

I ignored him and began pacing the ground, my voice rising the more incensed I became. I was like a sleeping volcano that had suddenly awakened and was about to erupt. "So, let's assume you're right and someone intends for me to be here. Then why? What purpose could my being here possibly serve?" I demanded, stopping right in front of Eliendor and facing him squarely.

"Each person must discover his or her own destiny," Eliendor said calmly as he went back to his carving. "Yours is not for me to say."

"This isn't fair!" I cried. "I didn't ask to come here! I didn't ask to be given this new body. I don't even know what or who I really am. Do you know what it feels like to be so different and to have people stare at you whenever you walk by?"

"Yes, I do," Eliendor replied quietly.

Okay, he had me there. Feeling slightly ashamed, I had no response.

"Arwyn, you will only find contentment in this life when you accept the fact that sometimes answers are not forthright. But you must trust that eventually they will come. Until then, I can walk with you on your journey."

"How can I possibly accept this? Things like this aren't supposed to happen!" I said angrily. "I can't accept being taken from my old life and away from the people I loved with no explanation. It's not right! And it's not right for you to withhold any information that could help me get home."

"What makes you believe I am the keeper of such knowledge?"

"It's a hunch. You're not like the others in the village. When you look into my eyes, I get the feeling that you already know everything about me."

The look on Eliendor's face still had not changed. He sat there as calmly as if we were discussing the weather. "If be here you must, then I can help you find your purpose. That is all I can promise."

"If you won't help me, then I'll have to find my own way back home." Eliendor remained silent as I turned abruptly and mounted Avencloe. With that, I snapped the reins sharply and took off into the woods.

With hot tears burning down my face, I prodded Avencloe on a mad dash through the forest and back toward the village. The pounding of Avencloe's hooves on the road seemed to echo the weeks of frustration and confusion that had been building in me since that fateful Summer's Eve. With every mile that passed, I became convinced that if I were to escape that place, then I must return to the Guildenmoor Gate. Throwing all caution aside I determined to ride there by myself, through the night if necessary, on the off chance that there I would find the doorway that led back into that other world.

It was not long before I reached the outskirts of the village, where people were going about their daily lives with no warning of the storm that approached. In a fury I charged right through the middle of Baeren Ford, parting people in my wake who were forced to move hastily in order to avoid being run down by what probably appeared a demon-possessed beast. No doubt my escapade would start their tongues wagging again, but at the moment my only concern was to reach the Guildenmoor Gate as soon as I could.

Like a streak of lightning, Avencloe galloped up the hill on the northern end of the village at breakneck speed. Ahead lay the bridge over the Goldenreed, and I knew that I would soon be far beyond the boundaries of the village. Then, only inches from the bridge, for no apparent reason, Avencloe stopped abruptly, causing me to grab hold of the saddle before I tumbled forward. Confounded by my horse's sudden defiance, I rapped my legs firmly against his ribs and sharply snapped the reins. Still he did not budge.

After several moments I realized this strategy was not working. Totally exasperated, I slid down to the ground and stood in front of Avencloe, pulling at his reins in the direction of the bridge. He remained still as a statue.

"Don't tell me you're in the conspiracy too!" I continued to tug unsuccessfully. After several moments, I threw my hands up in surrender. "Fine! It looks like I'll have to see myself to the Gate." I turned away from Avencloe and stomped over the bridge.

Up ahead, I could see the road as it twisted and turned through the high meadow, disappearing far away on the horizon and looking suddenly quite long. I had no food and no protection. What was I thinking?

I looked back across the bridge, where Avencloe had taken to calmy nibbling grass on the side of the road as if he knew I would soon come to my senses and return.

I walked forlornly to the horse's side and took him by the reins. As tears of defeat streamed down my face, I stumbled through the grass along the riverbank until I came to a path that led down to the water. Leaving Avencloe behind, I climbed down the path to the water's edge where I found a large outcropping of rock on which to sit.

Rhododendron and dogwood growing on both sides of the river shaded me from the view of anyone passing on the road above. Kneeling on the rock, I leaned over the water to wash the tears from my face. In the waning sunlight, I caught my reflection shimmering on the surface. Seeing the stranger staring back at me, I angrily smacked the image with my hand, sending water flying through the air. Sitting back on the rock, I drew my knees to my chin and sobbed quietly into the folds of the new frock Loralon had made for me.

It was not until after dark when I finally entered the cottage through the stable door.

"Arwyn! Where've ye been?" Loralon exclaimed as she got up from her spinning wheel. "I've been wairried sick ye were lost alone in the woods, or wairse, knowin' 'ow ye've taken to goin' off on yer own."

"I'm fine," I said quietly.

"Now I kin tell when a pairson's fine and when they're not, an' ye definitely dunna look fine. Did anythin' 'appen?"

"No, nothing happened. It's just that . . . it's too hard to explain."

"Come now. What ye need's a nice 'ot meal to fill yer belly," Loralon offered, gesturing to the pot that sat on the table.

I looked at her with a mixture of gratitude and tears. "I'm really not hungry," I said as I climbed the ladder to the loft.

I didn't care to do anything but disappear. Emotionally drained, I peeled off my clothing and slipped into my nightshirt before climbing into bed. For several moments, I lay there with my face buried in the pillows until I heard Loralon shuffling up the ladder.

"You shouldn't be climbing up here in your condition," I murmured.

"Oh, pish-posh!" Loralon placed a lantern on the bedside table and cautiously sat down on the edge of the bed. "I've always 'aird, 'tis better to speak yer mind than to keep what's eatin' at ye all bottled up inside with nowhere to go," she said.

"You wouldn't understand," I replied without stirring. "No one would."

"Nay, I suppose I wouldna. I've not been but a few leagues from the place o' me bairth. But I do know what the loneliness feels like in the pit o' me stomach e'er time I see Frondamein disappear o'er that hill. I ne'er know if 'twill be me last time to lay eyes on 'im."

I turned over and peered at Loralon through tendrils of hair that had fallen in my face, my eyes welling with tears. "How did you know?"

"'Tis a woman's intuition, dear," Loralon said gently.

"I guess it doesn't take a rocket scientist to figure out that I don't exactly fit in here."

The young woman opened her mouth as if to ask what I meant but thought better of it, and I didn't feel like explaining the dissonance between my world and that one. Instead, Loralon sat quietly for a moment as if trying to get up the courage to ask her next question. "Tell me," she said hesitantly, "what made ye see fit to come 'ere to begin with?"

"I don't know," I said, a new wave of tears overflowing onto my cheeks. "I guess I got lost."

"Then why not retairn to yer 'omeland if ye be so sick for it?"

"If only I could, but I don't know the way," I said, wondering how much of my secret to reveal. "But still, it's so much more than that. Do you know that I can barely even remember what my life was like before? It's like I have amnesia."

Loralon remained silent.

"I hardly remember my own family or my friends or how I learned the things about that life that I do recall," I confided as I squeezed the corner of my pillow with my fist. "And this ring," I said while lifting my hand to show Loralon the deep purple stone that rode on it so elegantly. "This ring was given to me by someone very important in my life, but I can't even remember who!"

Loralon regarded it quietly for a moment. "What a beauty it is." She sighed. "'Tis a pity ye canna remember yer kin. Ever soul needs a place to call 'ome and people what loves 'em."

For a moment, we remained silent. The tears continued to flow as I hid behind my mass of hair. I wondered if I had revealed too much, yet part of me had stopped caring about propriety and only wanted a comforting shoulder on which to cry.

Loralon looked away and cleared her throat. "Er, I suppose Frondamein and I kin be yer family . . . that is, 'til ye see fit to be on yer way . . . not that ye'll be leavin' anytime soon, will ye?"

I looked at the young woman and shook my head slowly.

"Good!" Loralon said as she patted me on the shoulder. "And after a good night's sleep, ye'll be fine. Problems seem all the wairse when the body's weary."

"Yes, I suppose so."

And sleep I did. All night long and then most of the next day, I remained in bed alternating between sleep and periods when all I would do was stare at the thatched roof ceiling above as if in a trance. Having retreated inside myself, I attempted with all my might to conjure memories of my past existence, but all that emerged were sketchy images that floated in and out of conscious thought like ghostly shadows.

For over a day I ate nothing, and no amount of coaxing by Loralon would stir me. It was as though all the life had drained from my body, leaving an empty shell in its wake.

Yet another day passed the same as the one before. The hopelessness I felt had drained every ounce of energy from my body. I lay in my bed, listless, not caring what chores remained undone below or what rumors might be going round about my sudden disappearance after my reckless stampede through town two days before.

All the while, Eliendor's words still rang in my ears, and I was unsure whether to feel angered by them or hopeful. Yet deep inside my heart there still burned a tiny flame that refused to be snuffed out so easily.

CHAPTER 13

"For whatever reason, I guess I'm stuck here, so I might as well make the most of it."

Early the third morning, Loralon awoke to find me dressed and cracking eggs over a frying pan. On the kitchen table was a half-drained jug of milk.

"What else is there to eat around here?" I asked as I noticed her at the door. "I'm famished!"

"What a relief to see ye up and about again," Loralon exclaimed. "I was afraid ye were lost to the wairld."

"Not for long, Loralon. Never for long."

With all the tenacity I could muster, I spent the morning on my chores around the cottage as if to make up for my incapacitation the two days before. As early as I could get away that afternoon, I stole off into the woods, heading straight for Eliendor's house. There I found the old man gingerly pruning a rose bush that grew next to his front door. He glanced up as I approached, seeming not at all surprised to see me there. With great resolve I climbed down from Avencloe's back and walked over to the place where he stood.

"Teach me what you will," I announced. "I'm here to learn."

With sharp, bright eyes that spoke not of an ancient and decrepit old man, but of a mind that remained young and alert, Eliendor gave me a smile. "Come!" he said as he glanced up at the sky. "A cloud approaches and we must seek shelter before it breaks."

With that, he led me through the front door of his rather whimsical-looking cottage and inside, where I caught my breath as I viewed the scene before me. I had entered a spacious round room with a large fireplace in the center that stood open in every direction, still-smoldering embers sending small wisps of smoke up through the stone chimney. A table and two chairs, a large cupboard stocked with a meager supply of plates and cups, a rocking chair, and a small, neatly made bed adorned the interior. Woven rugs like those in Frondamein and Loralon's house covered a creaking wooden floor;

and from the rafters hung countless items, from shiny pots and pans to lanterns and drying herbs.

However, it was the hundreds of books sitting upon curved shelves lining the cottage walls that caught my attention. Everywhere there were books. I went to one of the shelves and ran my fingers along the leather bindings, immediately drawn to the vast library. Eliendor watched my absorption with his collection with an amused twinkle in his eyes.

"You have quite a collection," I commented, picking up one of the books and opening its pages, flipping through the unfamiliar script.

"I have only seen one private library that surpasses it, and it lies in the high elf Valdir Velconium's hall in Loth Gerodin," Eliendor said.

I took the book over to one of the windows on the front of the house to take a closer look. Outside, leaves nodded and danced under tiny wet explosions as a gentle summer shower splattered down.

"I need a purpose," I said at last. "Frondamein has his guard duty and Loralon her spinning and weaving and sewing. I have no way to contribute other than the menial tasks I perform around the cottage. Yes, I know it is helpful and certainly needed, but I need something more, something that gives meaning to my existence here."

Eliendor stood quietly for a moment, staring at me thoughtfully from under his bushy eyebrows. At last he walked over and took my hands in his, studying them carefully in the light from the window. "You've strong yet tender hands, the hands of a healer," he said. "The village is in need of one. The last, old Fradyl, died months ago."

"A healer? You mean a medicine woman?"

"I know of none better for the task."

"But I don't know anything about potions and remedies," I said as I went to sit down at the wooden table.

The old man walked over and suddenly touched my brow with his fingertips. "Healing has less to do with what is in here and more to do with what is in your heart," he said. "You have the heart for the task, do you not?"

"Certainly I like to help others, but . . ."

"I saw how you brought life into that boy who nearly drowned. He would have died had it not been for your healing touch."

"There was nothing magical in what I did. It was something simple that anyone could do."

"Nay, Arwyn, it is much more than that. You have a gift." Eliendor sat down in the chair opposite mine. "As I look into your heart I see much compassion there. You must share this with others."

"But how? I don't know anything about medicine."

"The secrets of medicines have been around for centuries. Open your eyes to the world around you and you will discover them, and I will help you," Eliendor said as a smile passed over his face. "You see, in recent years I've studied the remedies for certain ailments. A rather selfish endeavor, I must admit, as I suddenly found myself an old man needing relief from the aches and pains of this old body."

"A healer," I said thoughtfully. "I do like that idea."

"However," Eliendor continued, "for you to become well-versed in the art of healing, you must learn to read elvish."

I opened the book that lay on the table before me and thumbed through the pages, eyeing the beautiful but unfamiliar script that flashed before my eyes.

"Very few books of late have been written in the language of mortals, and elves are champions of the art," he explained.

I looked up from the book. "Elves, the mythical, magical creatures of the northern forest. I understand you have dealings with them."

"Aye, you have heard correctly," the old man sighed. "The townspeople are obviously more aware of a hermit's comings and goings than I realized. Perhaps I give them something about which to gossip."

"Don't worry about it. Besides, they've turned their attention to me, now. I hear them whispering every time I pass by, and I'm not quite sure what all the commotion is about." I smiled, but in my heart there was sadness. "It's kind of nice to be treated as someone special, but there are many days when I only want to blend in with everyone else." I regarded the old man sitting across from me and hesitated for a moment. "Many of the villagers believe I'm an elf. Do you think I am?" I asked, looking quizzically into his eyes.

"Elves are complex creatures, Arwyn, but to say whether you are one or not, well . . . that may be a bit premature."

"But you could teach me about them . . . their language, their history, how they live, what they eat and drink. I want to know everything," I said passionately. I stopped momentarily, stood, and walked over to the window. "And this country, this beautiful place in which I suddenly find myself—and which I suppose I must now call my home—can you tell me all about it? And maybe, in the process, I can find out why I'm here," I said, surprising myself with how excited my voice sounded. "After all, you've obviously been around a long time; you must know all there is to know about this place." I caught myself, afraid I had offended my host.

Eliendor, who had been listening intently with hands folded on the crook of his cane, looked at me and chuckled. "Aye, I *have* been around for a long time, and I do know much about Bensorian lore. You might even call me an expert on the subject."

"Eliendor, is there any subject on which you are not an expert?"

"Sailing. I've never been out to sea. My expertise lies in the things of the earth and the stars."

I gave the old man an amazed smile. "So, teacher, when do we begin my studies?"

"Right away," Eliendor said, getting to his feet. "It will not be long before you must help to bring a child into the world, and Loralon will need you."

My eyes grew wide at the thought of such a task. Hardly had the thought had time to sink in when Eliendor beckoned to me, moving toward the front door of the cottage. "Come, the rain is over and the forest awaits."

And so began my education. Every afternoon following my chores I made my way through the forest to the old hermit's cottage where he always appeared to be waiting for me. We would spend our time together walking through forest and meadow, Eliendor unable to pass by any growing thing, whether it be leaf, root, or bark, without lecturing on its medicinal properties. Hunters and other passers-by who happened upon us seemed surprised to see such an odd pair—the gnarled old man walking and talking intently with the tall elven maiden. What business we had with each other I'm certain they could not guess. However, as time went by our wanderings sometimes led us closer to the peeping eyes and wagging tongues in the village, where the sight of us together was becoming common.

I was quick to learn all that my mentor had to teach. Every day we waited until the dew had time to evaporate before beginning the task of harvesting the forest's healing treasures. I collected the tender plants in a straw basket and took them home in the evenings where I bound the stems together and hung them upside-down from the rafters in the darkest, driest places in the cottage. And once my collection of herbs grew, I moved them to the loft above the stable. When they had dried, I crumbled their leaves, flowers, and seeds and placed them in glass jars I had purchased at the market.

Next came lessons on transforming the herbs into actual preparations that could be used for treating various maladies. The easiest way to use herbs as medicine was to make them into teas, which were of greater benefit for internal ailments such as colds, fever, digestion problems, and headaches. Pills were a bit more complicated to make, requiring me to mix my powdered herbs with a bit of honey, with the final concoction rolled into balls and dried in the sun.

Even harder to make were tinctures, salves, compresses, and poultices, all used externally for wounds, skin conditions, and swollen glands. Many required a number of ingredients, including oils and vinegar, but the hardest ingredient to acquire by far was beeswax. For that, I would stand away at a safe distance in awe as I watched Eliendor walk casually up to a hollow tree and boldly stick his arm into a swarming hive. His hand would emerge holding onto the plate-like sheets of small white chambers oozing with golden, sticky honey, which he immediately tipped and funneled into a waiting jar. Though startled by the invasion, the bees seemed no more than curious about the giant intruder who casually walked away with the efforts of their labors without so much as a prick. It was altogether intriguing to behold.

Who knew that there was an entire medicine cabinet in the forest? As I learned about a more "natural" way of healing, the more I questioned the efficacy of the more "sophisticated" medical practices I had been accustomed to.

In addition to the lessons on healing, Eliendor taught me the fundamentals of the beautifully lilting elvish language. Soon I graduated to the more subtle nuances, inflections, and meanings of certain elvish words and phrases. To my surprise, I learned that the word *avencloe* in elvish was the term used to describe one who is swift footed. How I could have known this when I had named my beloved horse was more than I could understand.

On those afternoons when the weather prevented us from journeying into the forest, we would sip hot tea together in Eliendor's cottage and talk about all manner of subjects ranging from Omni to the legends of the Eldred, including Elwei. Eliendor spoke of the earliest appearances of the Underlord's servants and the many battles fought, both by Elwei and her followers in Bensor and by those abroad, in the never-ending war against the darkness.

The history of Bensor, I learned, was as Frondamein had told me; however, Frondamein's knowledge of the old legends was limited to the oral tradition that had been handed down through the years. The scholarly lore master talked as though he had been a witness to all these events, even though I knew that no one, except perhaps an elf, could possibly have been alive that long.

I speculated long on these ideas. With memories of my previous existence growing increasingly vague with every passing day, and after the initial shock of my situation had dissipated, I found myself adapting surprisingly well to a more pastoral lifestyle. I was coming to see the Bensorians as a strong but peaceable people, loyal to their country, but with a definite aversion to confrontation. Although the general pacifist mentality was admirable, I worried that this complacency made them perhaps much more vulnerable to infiltration by the enemy.

As for the presence of Dar Magreth to the north, Eliendor's mood became intensely somber when he spoke of it, which only fed the tiny fear that hid deep in my heart. "Mark my words—Dar Magreth's will remains bent on dominating Bensor, yet Bensor would be only the beginning of her ruthless scourge if she at last succeeds," he said once.

I shuddered. "Do you believe the wizard Amiel's prophecy, that a ruler will come to save Bensor?" I wanted to believe the old legends about magical places, immortal beings, talking beasts, and a true ruler who would come to save the Bensorian people. But deep down I remained a skeptic.

"Do you want to know what I think, which really matters not one way or the other, or are you asking this question of yourself?" he replied. It frustrated me when Eliendor did not answer my questions directly, especially when he seemed to know my thoughts better than I did.

"Did Amiel have the authority to make such a prophecy? Yes, he had Elwei's sword, but that was the only proof of his authority. I would imagine that the people would cling to anything that would give them hope."

"Does everything require proof to be true? You see a falcon soaring on the wind, but you do not see the wind. You see a flower grow and believe it is Omni who unfolds its petals, yet you do not see Omni. The fact that you are here at all is a miracle. Look into your heart, Arwyn, for it sees what the eyes do not."

I closed my eyes for a moment, feeling the tears well up inside as a small but familiar masculine voice from my past spoke words I had heard time and time again. Suddenly I was once more sitting in a large room set aglow from the sunlight beaming down through large multicolored windows. "Nothing is impossible for those who have faith," I whispered, and in my mind I could see the vague shadow of a middle-aged man with slightly graying hair speaking from a platform. I knew that although I may not remember the details of my previous life, everything that truly mattered remained tucked somewhere deep in my heart.

I opened my eyes to see a wrinkled face staring back at me. "Hold to that, Arwyn, and you will find your answers."

The hot summer days passed relatively uneventfully, if one can call adapting to a new body and a different lifestyle uneventful. The simple joys of tilling the soil and watching the garden grow and the exhilaration of galloping wildly across fields and meadows as my long hair waved in the wind were enough to pacify my soul in those abandoned moments. The deepening bonds with Loralon and my teacher, Eliendor, also helped to fill the lonely void in my heart after leaving all I had loved before.

It was not long before Frondamein returned home on his monthly leave. There were the inevitable complaints about Festius, yet Frondamein seemed pleased to find his wife's belly growing steadily, to see how orderly he found the homestead, and to know how well Loralon and I were getting along. However, he cautioned me about spending so much time with Eliendor, since most of the villagers viewed the old hermit as strange and slightly mysterious. But I knew better. And I was beginning to care a little less if people thought the company I kept was odd, or even if I was, for that matter.

Life returned to normal following Frondamein's departure for the Guildenmoor Gate, sadly enough for Loralon. She grieved so for their lost moments together, which were becoming even more important as the birth of their child approached.

Despite Frondamein's misgivings, I continued my daily rides to see Eliendor. Between lessons on the healing arts, Bensorian history, the elvish language, and my normal, everyday duties at the cottage, I remained busy. I preferred it that way, for it kept my mind occupied and gave me purpose. However, I was always careful to finish my tasks at the cottage before taking off to follow more scholarly pursuits.

In the late afternoon, I returned loaded down with books, and unless there was canning or other odd jobs to be done, I spent the evening catching up on my reading and talking with Loralon about the day's events. She seemed secretly intrigued at my association with the old hermit and would sit at her spinning wheel and listen intently as I shared my discoveries of old Bensorian legends that had been hidden away in the dusty books for years.

The only growing problem in my new life was Hamloc, who was becoming more of a nuisance as he stepped up his pursuit, showing up on the spur of the moment and following me as I went about my daily business. At first somewhat amused by his failed attempts at charm, I wearied of his overbearing manner, which seemed to intensify with every encounter.

On one such afternoon I was working in a small corner of the garden that had been appointed for my use. I had decided to try growing herbs myself so as not to depend solely on finding them in the forest. As the growing season had almost come to an end, I chose the hardiest varieties to plant, especially those known to aid with the process of childbirth. Carefully I dug small holes in the rich, dark soil and deposited tiny seeds into each one.

"Motherwort here . . . and a little cramp bark there. And . . . perhaps a little blue cohosh as well," I said to myself as I sat on a stool, crouched over my work. "Blue cohosh for a smooth labor," I remembered one of the village midwives suggesting. Suddenly, the sound of footsteps from behind broke my concentration.

"'Ello, me pretty one." I cringed as I heard the deep voice behind me.

"Hamloc," I said as I turned to look up. "To what do I owe this pleasure?" My voice could barely conceal the faint note of sarcasm.

"Just passin' by and couldna help but notice 'ow lovely ye looked sittin' 'ere in yer garden, bent o'er as ye were."

I felt my stomach tighten as I stood to face my visitor, who came dangerously close to stepping on my seedlings. "Business slow at the tavern today?"

"Too slow for me taste, like this town, slow and lifeless," he said with a huff. "A man like me was made for adventure, Arwyn. Someday I'll shake the dust o' this little village and travel the world in search o' me fortune. Just ye wait; I'm goin' to be rich."

"I wish you luck in your travels," I said as I started to turn back toward my work.

"I only need a pretty lady by me side, a feisty one such as yerself," Hamloc said, as he grabbed me by the elbow.

Feeling my temper flare, I forcefully managed to shake his grasp. "No, thank you, but I'm quite content living a 'dull' existence right here."

"Come now, Arwyn, ye know I'm th' only man in town wairthy o' ye. Without me, ye'll likely end up a spinster." I shot him an annoyed glance, but he was too busy touting himself to notice. "Ye need someone strong like me who kin show ye places ye've ne'er been, and protect ye from all o' them nasty, sneaky Gargalocs."

I fought hard to hold my tongue while thinking of a tactful way to respond. "Your offer is kind," I finally said in as polite a tone as I could muster, "but I have a duty here to Frondamein and Loralon."

"Ye dunna know what ye say," Hamloc said, his voice becoming slightly louder. Catching himself, he quickly looked around and then lowered his voice. "Arwyn, I shall confide in ye this day. 'Tis me intention to challenge the Sword of Emraldein. I'm plannin' t' arrange a party to go into Carona where I'll retrieve the Sword from its restin' place."

"You? The true ruler of Bensor?" This time I had to stop myself from bursting into laughter.

"Yes, and kin ye think of one stronger 'n more nobler than I? When I become ruler o' Bensor, I'll 'ave each and every Gargaloc 'unted down 'n killed in every manner imaginable. Ye kin be sure, they'll be shown no maircy. And Emraldein . . . Emraldein Castle'll be restored and 'twill 'ave the biggest and best of everythin'. There'll be servants everywhere to do me biddin', to wait on me hand and foot."

Hamloc suddenly stopped his soliloquy to glance at me; my look of disbelief he surely mistook for awe. "O' course," he said, "ye'll be invited to visit me there." And then he moved closer to me and, as he stared me straight in the eyes with a sly, almost fiendish smile, said in a lowered tone, "I shall even let ye sit on me throne." And I knew exactly what he really meant.

In my anger I glared at the intruder. "If you'll excuse me, I have work to do," I said coldly as I began walking toward the cottage.

In the background I heard him laugh in a most obnoxious manner. "Ye shall come to me yet, Arwyn. Ye wait and see!"

Several townspeople who happened to be passing by on the road shook their heads sympathetically. Although Hamloc's jovial manner was well-liked by those who frequented the tavern, it was rumored that most of the villagers thought he was out of line in his relentless pursuit of me. And I'm sure Hamloc was keenly aware that his reputation as a ladies' man was at stake.

"What a jer . . . boorish rogue Hamloc is!" I said angrily as I rounded the corner of the stable and found Loralon there fetching water from the well.

"And what did 'e say to ye this time?" Loralon asked, as I came to aid her with the bucket.

I quickly related the encounter to Loralon, who shook her head supportively.

"'E is a boorish rogue all right, one what deserves a proper lesson in manners."

"How could he think I would possibly be interested in him? Why, he's almost old enough to be my father!" I exclaimed.

Loralon glanced at me quizzically, and I had to stop and reconsider. I'm sure she assumed I must be ancient, being a supposed elf and all, and maybe I was. But really! Hamloc must be nearing his thirtieth birthday, if he hadn't passed it already—much too old for me. Yet, the idea of courting a teenager seemed just as weird. In fact, the idea of a boyfriend of any age was out of the question. Romance was the last thing on my mind!

A sudden commotion up the road drew our attention. A rider came galloping through the village at breakneck speed. As he passed, we could hear people shrieking as they hurried indoors. The rider soon neared the cottage, and we could hear his cries of warning: "Draigon approaches from the north! Take cover, Draigon is coming!"

Loralon dropped the pail of water as she quickly turned and took me by the hand, leading me toward the front door of the cottage. "Come, Arwyn, we must seek cover!" she said frantically. "If Draigon sees ye and believes ye to be an elf, 'e could cause trouble. 'E mustn't know ye're 'ere!"

Quickly we headed for the shelter of the cottage. Once inside Loralon bolted the front door.

A strange quiet fell upon the town as it awaited Draigon. For several moments Loralon and I sat quietly in the darkness of the cottage until, faintly at first, we heard the rumbling of carriage wheels and beating hooves.

Like a dark cloud descending from the north, Draigon's procession rode through the deserted streets of the village. Riders on black horses escorted a black carriage as it headed in a southerly direction toward Maldimire, fortunately too busy to stop and make trouble that day.

As the procession passed, I peered through the window of the cottage to see the menacing faces of the riders. Each was cloaked in gray with intimidating eyes that dared anyone to hold up their progress.

Inside the carriage I could see the outline of a dark, shadowy figure I was certain must be Draigon himself, the self-proclaimed "ruler" of Bensor. The procession disappeared down the road and into the forest to the south, and a foreboding chill suddenly gripped my heart. Somehow I knew that this first encounter with Draigon would not be my last.

CHAPTER 14

> *"With every day that passes, my anxiety grows. Am I really up to bringing a child into the world?" I said, aware that my brow furrowed with apprehension, even in my semiconscious state. "And to make matters worse, I am forced to deal with this infuriating nuisance. Why can't he get a clue and go bother one of the other village maidens who actually finds him attractive?"*

As if by some mutiny in nature, the warm summer days grudgingly succumbed to the advent of fall. An early first frost seemed to signal the trees that it was time to sprinkle the ground with their multicolored darts, which had already begun to weave an intricate tapestry of reds, yellows, and oranges across the forest ceiling. Looking heavenward, they were a kaleidoscope of vibrant colors against the blue autumn sky. With the dramatic change in the look of the land came also a crispness in the morning air and a subtle change in the position of the sun, which had held out against the fall chill, continuing to beam down upon the earth with its warming, though weakening, afternoon rays.

It was now quite evident that Loralon's time was almost due. The way her belly protruded from her small frame seemed almost unnatural and certainly uncomfortable as the young woman made her way around as best she could with extra weight and swollen ankles. Despite my protests, she insisted on performing the less strenuous tasks around the cottage but found herself tiring much more quickly than normal. When I could get her to sit down and prop up her feet, the warm soaks and borage poultices I made helped to relieve the swelling.

With every visit home, Frondamein seemed more and more anxious about his wife's condition and the health of the unborn child, and I could see the agony in his eyes every time he had to return to his post. Yet he confided to me that my presence there was a comfort, and that felt reassuring. After all, I wanted him to have no regrets about taking me in.

Deep down, however, I was not yet so confident about my ability to bring his child into the world, despite all my talks with the village midwives about the birthing process. How would simple knowledge compare to the real event? I searched my memory for anything that could help me meet this challenge, but to no avail. Yet babies were born every day. How difficult could it be? Simply help nature take its course.

My mind was a tangle of anxiety with every passing day. What if I were out when Loralon went into labor? The thought of being far away when Loralon needed me scared me more than the delivery itself. So I decided to limit my visits with Eliendor during the coming weeks. I did, however, make one last visit to my teacher, who loaded me down with even more books on herbal medicines, ones that I intended to read should I find a spare moment.

As I returned to the village that afternoon I heard a rustling ahead and off the path. I cautiously urged Avencloe on until a horse and rider appeared from behind a stand of alder trees.

The all-too familiar sight of Hamloc was maddening as well as slightly disturbing. For several weeks I had enjoyed a welcome relief from his unwanted attention, during which time he had made one of his wine runs into Elwindor. I had hoped he would lose interest in me during the time away. But to my dismay, he seemed only to have stepped up his pursuit following his return several days before.

"'Tis not safe for a woman to go about in the woods alone," he said. The ever-present gleam in his eyes gave cause to doubt his sincerity.

"Is it concern for my well-being or some other reason that brings you to the forest today?" I said, continuing to press Avencloe onward. Hamloc guided his horse along beside me.

"I kin assure ye, the intentions what brought me 'ere are most honorable." Hamloc suddenly gave a slight bow from his saddle while dramatically removing his hat and waving it in the air in front of him. The roguish smile fixed upon his face made me think that his manner of surveying me was certainly less than honorable.

"I must say, you seem to see danger under every rock and behind every tree, but until now I have seen no reason to be afraid of the woods."

"Ah, love, but the dangers o' the forest are real," he said, glancing over his shoulder in the direction from which I had come. "Ye know, the villagers are beginnin' to say 'ow strange it is ye keep the company o' that crazy old man, Eliendor. Do ye not know 'e talks t' animals as though they kin talk back? And the magic 'e performs: 'tis not natural and is not to be trusted. Mind ye, Arwyn, ye shouldna be associatin' with such pairsons."

The unsolicited advice only irritated me more. "Are you really so threatened by what you don't understand?" I said cooly. "Eliendor is a very wise man and as gentle a person as I've ever met, and mind *you*, Hamloc, I will associate with whomever I so choose."

A brief glint of anger flashed in Hamloc's eyes. "And while we're on the subject o' things unnatural, it's indeed quite strange for a woman to spend so much time with 'er 'ead in a book. What o' cookin' 'n sewin' 'n babies? Ye'd best be wary or ye'll be accused o' bein' a sorceress, what with all that readin' ye do."

"And can you read?"

"Dunna need to," he grunted.

"So you're naturally suspicious of those who do?"

No answer.

"Would you have others as uneducated as yourself?"

"I tell a good story, and people come to me tavern to hear me. They pay me way. What more do I need, I ask ye? And what more do they need if they kin steady a plow and at the end o' the day enjoy a pint for their troubles?"

So much for challenging the Sword, I thought, as if he ever really intended to. I sighed and wished the unproductive conversation would end.

"Ye'll soon find that yer elvish ways will be o' little use to ye here," Hamloc continued. "And as for Eliendor, 'twould be unwise for ye to keep visitin' 'im. I'll not 'ave the woman I'm courtin' goin' off into the woods to see any other man, no matter what 'is age may be."

I was now seething. "Courting? I am not under the impression that we were courting."

Hamloc gritted his teeth in agitation, and I could see the veins on his neck pop out. "Come now, Arwyn, I grow weary o' yer little games. Playin' coy was charmin' at fairst, but I'm an impatient man and expect to get what I want. Ye obviously dunna see 'ow th' other maidens pine for me, or ye'd appreciate yer situation all the more."

"Maybe you would do well to pursue your other opportunities."

Persuasion was not working, but perhaps charm would. "Ah, but, love, th' other maidens 'ave not yer beauty nor yer feisty spirit," he said as he flashed his teeth.

"But as you say, my head is too much in the books. You would grow tired of such a woman in time. I would be much too distracted to attend to your needs."

"Then ye would 'ave to be taught the correct priorities, love."

I halted Avencloe for a moment and looked Hamloc squarely in the eyes, and I could feel a fire burning inside me as I spoke. "Hear me now, Hamloc, you will never tame me, not you . . . nor any man." My words seemed to have little effect, for Hamloc continued to stare at me with a smirk of equal determination, as if winning me over was now more a matter of pride than affection. After all, few of the other village maidens had been able to resist his "charms."

Through the trees I could see the first cottage at the edge of the village and the little lane that led home. With a slight snap of the reins, I pulled away from my unwanted suitor and out of the corner of my eye saw him spit on the ground as I rode away.

Another week passed quietly, aside from the constant work at the cottage. Autumn had come now, in all its brilliance, and with it the sound of crunching leaves underfoot and the smell of hot cider stewing on the fire. Loralon had begun working on new, warmer clothing for me and had already completed a longer, warmer riding gown, a wool skirt and several loose blouses to be worn under a tightly fitting bodice. A warmer sleeping gown and heavier cloak also added to my wardrobe, as well as a pair of leather gloves purchased from the village tanner.

Loralon worked as much as she could, considering the extra weight she carried. But for the most part she busied herself with sewing and other odd jobs that required little physical effort. The more strenuous tasks she had long since relinquished to me, and I wondered what she would have done had I not been there to help. After all, most women in her situation had husbands at home and family nearby.

With every passing day the signs became clearer. Loralon awoke one morning with a cramp in her lower back but forced herself to get up and make breakfast. The intermittent waves of pain continued for the next two days, becoming more and more intense by the end of the second. I remained close at hand but had also made arrangements with Darya, the midwife from across the lake, to assist with the birth when the time came.

At the end of the second day, I crept into bed soon after the evening meal was finished. I had barely drifted off to sleep when a moan from the room below awakened me. I sat upright and listened intently, attempting to shake the sleep from my weary mind. For a few moments the cottage remained silent but for the nightly wanderings of some vermin scratching about in the thatched roof above. I lay my head back on my pillow and for a long while listened in the darkness. I had almost fallen asleep again when another moan, one that sounded distinctly more alarmed, rose through the floorboards from below.

I bolted out of bed and climbed down the ladder, heart pounding with every step as I wondered if Loralon's time had arrived. I entered the bedroom below where she sat on the bed, clutching her belly as the lamplight from the bedside table silhouetted her trembling form. "The babe . . . it's comin'," she said, her voice shaking between heavy breaths. "Me water . . . it broke."

CHAPTER 15

"What am I to do? All my plans are unravelling" I wailed. "Now everything depends on me . . . me, I tell you! And if I fail . . . oh, I dare not think about it!"

My heart was racing. Still groggy, I struggled to remember the steps I had rehearsed a dozen times before. The actual birth could still be several hours away, but I wasn't about to take any chances. I went to the parlor to fetch three of the largest candles I could find and lit them by the smoldering embers on the hearth. I returned to the bedroom and placed them in stands sitting here and there about the room. Another groan came from Loralon, who was sitting propped up on her elbows.

"It won't do for you to ruin that mattress," I said. "I'll need to cover it with a thick layer of blankets. Do you think you can get out of bed for a minute?"

"I kin do better than that. 'Twould do me good to walk a bit."

"You want to walk?" I asked, astonished.

"For a time, at least," Loralon said as she struggled to her feet. Taking my arm, we walked twice slowly around the parlor, until another wave of pain sent Loralon doubled-over on the settee.

"Wait right there while I run fetch the extra bedclothes," I said as I headed toward the ladder to the loft. Up above I quickly retrieved the spare linens that were kept in the bureau and sent an avalanche of sheets and blankets into the room below. Loralon remained on the settee as I returned downstairs and stripped the soiled linens from her bed in hopes that the added insulation from the extra padding would help protect Loralon's mattress from further mess.

"The birthing chamber is prepared," I proudly announced as I appeared back in the parlor. Even in the darkness I could detect the frightened look on Loralon's face and hoped that I would be able to hide the fear in my own voice.

I disappeared again to gather several logs from the woodpile and returned to the hearth where a hastily laid log created an explosion of orange sparks, one of which landed on my wrist. "Ow!" I winced as I quickly retracted my hand. Examining the singed wrist, I could already see an angry burned spot there. I instinctively put my mouth over the spot, for lack of any other relief at the moment.

"Did ye hairt yer 'and?" Loralon said sympathetically as she got up to move around the room again.

"Oh, it's nothing," I shrugged. "With a bit of calendula salve I'll be as good as new."

Attempting to ignore the growing pain on my hand, I roused the glowing embers in the hearth in an effort to rekindle the fire. In a matter of minutes, a single yellow tongue of flame appeared, and it was not long before others like it started gnawing away at the log.

A chill ran down my spine as Loralon clutched her belly and let out a cry. Alarmed and quite shaken by my friend's outcry and my own sense of helplessness, I hurried to Loralon's side and placed a supportive arm around the soon-to-be mother.

"Arwyn, the pain," Loralon cried. "'Tis more than I kin bear."

I gritted my teeth, knowing the worst was yet to come. "Give it a moment and the pain will pass. I'll have you something to ease it as soon as possible, but for now try to breathe in and out slowly," I said in as comforting a tone as I could muster while gently brushing the hair from Loralon's damp brow. "Let me help you back to bed."

"I dunna think I could stand to lie still e'en if I were to try," Loralon said.

"Hmmm, perhaps staying on your feet *would* allow gravity to take its course," I reconsidered.

"I dunna know what the 'gravity' is, but if 'twill 'elp, then walk I shall."

"Why don't you keep walking around for as long as you feel like it? I'll go fetch the midwife after I put some water on to boil."

Loralon nodded her head as I left the room and went out into the chilly night air to the well, too intent on the task at hand to be concerned at how inadequately clad I was. Down the road several rather inebriated tavern patrons were heading home as best they could, albeit in the opposite direction, singing a rowdy folk song.

I uncoiled the water bucket, sending it down into the depths of the well until I heard a muffled splash from below. After a moment, I hoisted the full bucket to the surface and took it inside where I emptied the contents into the kettle above the now-blazing fire.

Quickly I returned up the ladder to the loft where I pulled off my long sleeping gown and climbed into a tunic and long skirt. Once my boots were on, I descended the ladder into the parlor below. "I'm going to get Darya," I announced. "I won't be long." Loralon merely looked at me and nodded.

I turned and headed for the stable door. It would take several minutes to harness and saddle Avencloe, but the able horse would provide the fastest way to get to the other side of the lake. Grabbing my riding cloak from a peg next to the door, I entered the stable and it was not long before Avencloe and I disappeared into the darkened streets of the village.

With help from oil lamps that dotted the streets and a host of friendly lights that shone through cottage windows, I navigated the quiet streets of the village. The night air was chilled, and I could see my breath in the lamplight, prompting me to pull my cloak more tightly around my shoulders.

At last I arrived at the midwife's home, a neat little cottage with a path of stone that led up to the front door. I dismounted and followed the path I had become all too familiar with over the past weeks when I had made visits to seek the experienced older woman's birthing advice. It was a relief to see a light glowing from inside the parlor and hastily I rapped on the front door and waited for an answer.

"Now who could that be this time 'o night?" came a voice from within. "State yer name and what be yer business?"

"It's me, Arwyn."

"Well, why did ye not say so to begin with, child? I'm afraid I'm in no condition to come to the door, but ye kin let yerself in if it please ye."

I did not need to be invited twice. Quickly I opened the latch and entered the room, breathless. "Loralon's time has come," I said, my words dying even as I spoke them. Before me, the woman I had been depending on to help with the birth sat with a rather swollen ankle propped up on a chair in front of her.

"Tch! I was afraid 'twould be so," Darya replied. "Twisted me ankle this mornin' I did, while chasin' me goat after 'e tried t' eat at the laundry. Miserable creature! 'Twas a nasty fall I took and 'twill be the death o' me if I have to take e'en one step, much less go to th' other side o' the lake."

"But what am I to do!" I cried frantically. "Loralon's over there right now, and she's in a lot of pain."

The normally robust midwife winced as she shifted her position on the settee. "There's nothin' to bringin' a babe into the wairld. Done it dozens o' times and not a one of 'em lost."

"But this is my first time. Surely you can understand my concern."

"Aye," Darya sighed. "I suppose ye could go to that *other* midwife—although she doesna have the delicate touch that I possess."

"You mean Ismei, the tanner's wife?" I had already heard rumors of the ongoing rivalry between the two primary village midwives and thought it quite silly for two grown women to carry on as they did.

"Aye."

"Then I must go to her right away."

"Mind ye, ye'd be better off seein' to the bairthin' yerself."

I dismissed Darya's grim portrayal of her rival and headed for the front door. Remembering my manners, I suddenly stopped and turned, "I'm truly sorry you hurt your ankle. Maybe when this is all over, I can come and help out while you're still on the mend."

"Tch! I'll be up and about in no time. It takes more than a twisted ankle to keep this old mule down for long."

"I'd better be on my way."

"Remember what I told ye and ye'll do fine," Darya called as I shut the front door behind me.

Outside, Avencloe waited patiently as I climbed onto his back. With a click of my tongue he set out again under a sky filled with a million twinkling stars that easily veiled the new moon with their light. My heart beat faster with every step of Avencloe's hooves along the cobblestone lane. Ahead was the village square, its shops long-since darkened as their owners settled in for the night. I rode swiftly up to the front door of the tanner's shop and slid down off Avencloe's back, ran up to the door of the shop, and knocked loudly. It seemed like forever until I saw through the window a tiny light that seemed to float through the gloom within. The opened door revealed the tanner standing before me in his nightshirt and cap. Cautiously he lifted a candle up to my face.

"Miss Arwyn!" he exclaimed. "What brings ye out at this hour o' the night?"

"I need to find your wife," I explained breathlessly. "Loralon's about to give birth and I'm going to need help."

"Help ye she would, but she canna."

"Why not?" I asked, unbelieving.

"She's o'er in Farnmoor, thirteen miles away, visitin' 'er sister. Took 'er there only two days ago, I did."

"When is she due back?"

"Not for another week at least," the tanner replied. "Not soon enough, it seems."

"You're right about that," I said anxiously.

"Now, ye'll not let on to me wife I told ye this," the tanner confided, "but ye kin always seek the help o' Darya o'er on the east side o' the lake."

"Yes, I suppose I can," I said weakly, my stomach beginning to churn unmercifully.

"I wish ye luck, Miss Arwyn," the tanner said, as I turned away.

Disheartened, I took a deep breath and mounted my horse again. As I made my way over to the far side of the lake, my mind was a whirlwind of the instructions I had gathered over the past weeks as I had prepared for the task that lay ahead. Feeling quite overwhelmed, I approached the cottage with a great sense of dread. In this primitive place lacking of modern medicine,

The Healer of Guildenwood

anything could happen. Was I prepared for all the possibilities? How could I stand it if anything happened to Loralon or the baby? What would I tell poor Frondamein?

Wait! There was no sense getting that worked up, or I surely *would* make a mistake. Determined to bring this child safely into the world, I gritted my teeth and walked in the door—just as Loralon was seized by another spasm of pain. I ran to her side and helped her to the settee.

"What took ye so long?" Loralon asked once she caught her breath. "And where's Darya?"

"Well . . . actually . . . Darya had an accident today and won't be able to come."

"She what!" Loralon exclaimed, eyes wide with shock.

"It's true. She can't leave her house."

"Not to wairry. Ye'll 'ave to go fetch Ismei instead; although the woman's a bit too 'ardheaded if ye ask me. Likes to take charge of everythin' from what I 'ear."

"Er, well, it seems Ismei's on holiday in Farnmoor."

The look on Loralon's face was one of panic. "What shall we do! I canna tell the babe to wait until a more convenient time to make its entrance into the wairld."

"Don't worry, Loralon," I said in as calm a voice as I could muster. "You'll be fine—I'll see to that myself."

"But . . . 'ave ye e'er bairthed a babe afore?"

"Well, yes, I'm sure I've seen it done," I fibbed.

Loralon took several deep breaths. "I'd best get to bed. The pains, they're a-comin' closer together now," she said, as she took my arm and made several cautious steps toward the bedchamber. Once inside, I helped her onto the bed and arranged several pillows to support her back.

Hesitating for a moment to try and remember all that the midwife had explained, I took a deep breath and returned to the well for another bucket of water. Using a bar of homemade lye soap, I scrubbed my hands from fingertips to elbows, which only irritated the singed welt on my wrist all the more. I made a mental note to treat the place with salve as soon as I had the chance.

Carrying a damp rag, I reentered the bedroom. "This will help you cool off." I placed the rag on Loralon's forehead, who smiled gratefully at her physician in training. I returned the smile, trying to look as courageous as possible. "Try to rest for now. You'll need your strength for the next wave."

Loralon reclined on the pillows as I went to check on the water I had put on to boil. At the bottom of the black kettle tiny bubbles had begun to form and float dreamily to the surface. How long it took for water to boil in this primitive manner!

While waiting, I took a lighted candle and went down the steps at the other end of the room and into the pantry. The dark, cool underground room had been the perfect place to keep my herbs, especially during the hot summer months. One whole shelf was brimming with apothecary jars full of dried herbs, each one carefully labeled with elvish letters. The ones I had anticipated needing the most I kept close to the front so as to be located quickly and easily when the time came. For several weeks, I had been giving blue cohosh tea to Loralon every day so that her labor would go more smoothly, and I now prayed that the herb would live up to its reputation. I quickly grabbed two jars, one labeled "Cramp Bark" and the other "Anise" and returned to the hearth where the water had at last begun to boil.

From the bedroom another painful outcry arose, this one arriving several minutes quicker than the ones before as her contractions became more intense. I appeared at the doorway, dreading what had to be done next. Even in the glow of the candlelight, I could see the fear in the young woman's eyes. So innocent and childlike they were, it seemed strange that one barely a woman would be having a child herself.

As for me, most days I still felt like a girl myself—certainly not someone strong enough yet to accomplish such a feat as birthing a baby. What in the world was either of us thinking?

Better to just suck it up and do what needed to be done than to dwell on my inadequacies. I took a deep breath and kneeled at the foot of the bed, urging my patient's legs apart. Becoming this intimate was not exactly comfortable, but I had no choice, especially if I was going to be a healer. Feeling a bit light-headed, I took yet another deep breath and, with a grimace plastered on my face . . . well, I had to go searching with my fingertips, not exactly sure what I was feeling for, and all without rubber gloves. Ugh!

I forced myself to concentrate on the task at hand until I thought I could detect some sort of opening at my fingertips, which seemed to be about an inch in diameter. Then as fast as possible I withdrew my fingers and immediately ran to the bucket of water to wash, willing myself all the while not to faint.

During the brief interlude, I took the cramp bark and anise from their jars and placed them upon a piece of muslin cloth, which I then tied up with a coarse piece of string and set inside a mug along with the boiling water. While waiting for the pain-killing tea to diffuse into the water and cool enough to drink, I prepared more of the same to be used later. It was promising to be a long night.

For the next several hours, I sat by Loralon's side attending to her every need, medicating her as much as possible with the homemade analgesics and reminding her to keep breathing steadily when the waves of pain hit. Once more I had to check the size of Loralon's opening, which was now almost three times as large as before, but this time I could feel a firm mass on the other side.

Soon the contractions came at a more constant rhythm. The herbs had helped to ease them somewhat, but still the pain remained intense. Once again, I checked my friend's progress, trying to get what must be done over with as quickly as possible.

"Finally," I announced with much relief, "you may push."

Loralon clenched her teeth and with my help, sat up and clutched her knees for several seconds. "I canna . . . I just canna," she wailed, falling back onto her pillows.

"Yes, you can, you must," I encouraged. "Rest yourself for a minute and we'll try again."

For nearly an hour I remained by Loralon's side as the young woman struggled to bring her child into the world, but the anxiety was almost more than I could bear. It was terrifying to think of anything happening to someone I had grown to care for so.

Loralon, soaked in perspiration, cringed with every grueling push, begging for the ordeal to end. She turned her head upward with a panicked look in her eyes. "Arwyn . . . ye must promise me this," she said between staggered breaths. "Promise me ye'll look after the babe . . . should me soul leave this wairld tonight. Mind ye . . . see that it grows up healthy and strong."

My brow furrowed. "Nonsense! You'll no doubt see to that yourself."

Loralon's expression was determined. "Promise me now . . . or next time I scream 'twill be to wake the dead!"

"I give you my word," I said solemnly.

"And ye must watch o'er me darlin' 'usband. See that 'e 'as warm clothes to wear when the snows come."

"I promise." The conversation was more than a little disconcerting.

The candles that had illuminated the room throughout the night had almost been consumed when at last a tuft of red hair on a tiny head appeared in view.

"No more," Loralon cried as she collapsed onto the disheveled pillows on the bed. "I kin bear no more." Her voice was a whimper.

"You musn't give up," I encouraged. "I'm seeing the baby. A bit more and it will all be over; then you may rest."

Loralon lay still for a moment and then, with face contorted, she mustered the strength to push yet once again.

Red streaks of dawn had begun to appear across the eastern sky when at last the child made its entrance into the world. Covered with blood and mucous, he protested the rude awakening from his warm, blissful home as

I cut with a sharp knife the cord that had attached him to his mother these many months.

"You've got yourself a handsome little boy," I announced.

"Thanks be to Omni," Loralon said, as she collapsed onto her pillows.

Cradling the slimy, squirming, and screeching baby carefully in my arms, I excused myself from the room, completely humbled by the miracle I had witnessed. I dipped a clean cloth into the now-lukewarm kettle of water and used it to wash the newborn, revealing a child of fair skin and wisps of soft reddish hair above his forehead.

Wrapping the baby in a blanket crocheted by his mother, I returned to the bedroom where Loralon lay calmly upon the bed, hair still pressed to her wet forehead. Her eyes were fixated upon the bundle in my arms, which I placed gently into her own. A broad smile spread across Loralon's face as she nuzzled the newborn and held him to her body. With a great sense of awe I watched as mother and child came face-to-face for the first time. Much to my extreme relief, my first two patients were alive and appeared to be doing well.

Though the ordeal was over, the full impact of the night's events hit. I was exhausted, both physically and emotionally. All the anxiety over planning for the birth and then, at the last minute, having to do it without the help of an experienced midwife was more of a challenge than I had bargained for.

After tending to Loralon and cleaning up the inevitable mess, I collapsed on the rocking chair beside the fireplace, allowing myself to relax the knot in my stomach that had been twisting and turning since Loralon's first cry the evening before.

As I stared pensively into the dying embers in the hearth, I suddenly remembered the burn on my wrist that I had yet to attend to. With all the drama of the night, I had simply ignored the pain and had not been able to treat it. I carefully examined my hand and was surprised to discover no sign of a burn anywhere on my flesh. Where the spark had left its mark, there was now only smooth, milky-white skin. I quickly examined the other hand, thinking that perhaps I had been mistaken as to the location of the burn, but no blemish could be found.

"How odd," I said to myself, totally bewildered.

As I pondered the mystery of the disappearing burn-mark, the sound of creaking wagon wheels passing jolted my mind back to the beckoning duties of the day. I immediately arose to prepare a sizzling breakfast over the resurrected fire, which I later brought into Loralon's room on a tray. I was surprised to see how voraciously the young woman devoured the meal, but reasoned that anyone would be famished following such an ordeal. It also served to remind me of my own hunger, now quite ravenous. I returned to the kitchen and to my own breakfast, where I cleaned every bit of egg from my plate and then consumed nearly half a loaf of bread and two large mugs of milk.

"Ne'er 'ave I seen anyone eat as ye do," Loralon commented.

I looked up from my plate to see Loralon standing in the doorway to her bedchamber. "Birthing babies, as long as one doesn't dwell on the more unpleasant aspects of the process, can make a person quite famished. Now what are you doing out of bed?"

"I've nursed the babe, and now there's work to be done while 'e sleeps."

"Don't be silly!" I protested. "You're in no condition to be moving around. Save your energy for your child, and I'll see to the animals and the cleaning."

"'Tis true I'm quite sore," Loralon relented, wincing as she shifted her weight.

"Then go take a hot bath while I change your bed linens," I suggested. "I set the peat burning a while ago. The water should be warm by now."

"Such a dear! Always knowin' what I need afore I know meself."

Tired as I was, I forced myself to strip Loralon's bed of all the blankets and bedclothes used during the birthing, and then I scrubbed them and boiled them. The day had turned out to be rather warm for autumn, as if summer were making one final appeal before the deep chill set in. Taking advantage of the warm spell, I put the blankets out to dry on a clothesline strung from the corner of the barn to the covered well. To anyone who happened to stop by, I eagerly shared the happy news of Frondamein and Loralon's firstborn. But secretly I was glad for having further proved my worth, for I was sure there were those who questioned Frondamein's wisdom in taking in a perfect stranger.

I worked throughout the day to catch up on all the work that had to be done, yet the women of the village were good to come by bearing food, curious to see Loralon and Frondamein's firstborn. The last of the visitors left by dusk, when dark clouds billowed in from the west, their deep rumblings signaling an approaching storm. There was a sudden chill to the air, and I rushed to remove the partially dried items from the line so that my efforts would not be in vain. I took them into the barn and draped them as best I could from rafter to rafter.

It was not long before the clouds broke, and a deluge of heavy raindrops pelted the cottage. Loralon and I ate a quiet dinner beside the fireplace, listening to the rain thud against the thatched roof above and feeling very grateful to Frondamein who had reinforced the roof with extra reeds for insulation. Not a drop leaked into the room below.

After dinner, we sat silently before the crackling fire, thankful for its

Mary E. Calvert

warmth. As the tiny baby suckled at her breast, Loralon sipped on a painkilling concoction of motherwort and meadowsweet that I had prepared for her. I sat on the padded settee with my head back, too weary from the eventful day to read as I usually did in the evenings.

I had begun to think of heading up to the loft for bed when suddenly there came the chilling sound of someone opening the stable door. Loralon and I sat upright as Avencloe neighed loudly from within the barn. Who would be coming to call so long after dark, especially on such a stormy night?

And then came a dreadful thought—what if the person who had opened the barn door . . . was not a person at all?

CHAPTER 16

"How much can a person take? I finally snapped, and my body somehow knew what to do!" I groaned.
"It sounds like you had been pushed to the limit."
"Yes, but I bet they'll all hate me now for sure."

Swallowing my fear, I jumped to my feet and quickly grabbed a lantern as Loralon clutched her child. I hurried to the door leading from the house into the stable and opened it cautiously, not knowing exactly what I would do if the worst came to pass.

Outside the rain thudded mercilessly on the roof. A flash of lightning lit up the gaping stable door and silhouetted the form of a man leading a horse by the reins into the dryness inside. I lifted the lantern and recognized Frondamein as he shed the soaked hood of his cloak.

"Frondamein, you gave us quite a scare. We weren't expecting you," I said, releasing the air in my lungs with a whoosh. With everything else that had happened, the fact that there had been a new moon the night before barely registered.

Immediately the relief of seeing him there dissipated as I could tell that something was dreadfully wrong. His face appeared quite pale in the lamplight, which only made the dark circles around his eyes appear even more ghastly in contrast. "What's wrong?" I rushed to his side and took Haseloth's reins. He gladly relinquished them without protest.

"Feelin' a bit under the weather is all," Frondamein said, attempting to smile.

I lifted my hand to feel of his forehead. "You're burning up. Get inside. I'll take care of the horse, but you'll have to be quarantined. You shouldn't get close to your son until you're well."

"Me son?" Frondamein turned to look at me, eyes brightening despite his discomfort.

"Yes," I replied with a smile. "Born this morning. Both he and Loralon are doing well," I said over my shoulder as I went to shut the stable door.

Frondamein let out a relieved sigh. "Thanks be t' Omni," he whispered.

I led Frondamein's horse into the stall next to Avencloe as Frondamein propped himself up against a post. Then, taking the visibly frail man by the arm, I led him into the house. Loralon was standing next to the fire with the baby in her arms, her face alight with joy.

Frondamein looked at them both and smiled weakly. "I'm sorry I've gone and got meself sick, love, but I willna be 'oldin' me son this night."

The smile on Loralon's face melted into a frown of concern.

"Can you make it to the loft?" I asked. "It won't do for you to spread germs to the baby."

"What is 'germ'?" Loralon asked, the look on her face growing even more alarmed.

"A germ is a microscopic organism . . .," I rattled off from somewhere in my memory. "Er . . . A germ is the thing that carries diseases from one person to another. As long as Frondamein has a fever, he'll be contagious."

"I'll try, though I'm at the end o' me strength," Frondamein said wearily. "'Twas all I could do to make it to Baeren Ford without fallin' off the back o' me hairse."

It was difficult to watch Frondamein slowly hoist himself up the ladder, one agonizing step after the other. Once at the top, I heard him groaning as he peeled off his wet clothing and collapsed onto my bed.

Loralon's brow was furrowed, and she started toward the ladder herself. "No, you musn't," I warned, putting a hand on her shoulder. "You can't get sick or you could make your son sick too."

The young woman's eyes widened with concern. "But . . ."

"Don't worry. I'll take care of him."

"But ye've barely 'ad a rest yerself."

"I'll be fine on the settee. Remember, I'm not the one who just had a baby, and from what I can tell, I definitely had the easier job," I said with a smile, trying to be reassuring. Just then, the newborn in her arms stirred. His face contorted into a look of displeasure and then turned beet-red before he let out a high-pitched wail. "Now go on to bed and see to the baby while I see to Frondamein."

"Very well," Loralon relented, hurrying into her bedchamber.

It was not long before I had mixed a concoction of yarrow and elderberry root to bring down Frondamein's fever, along with a bit of valerian root to make him more inclined to sleep. I climbed the ladder and found his soaked clothes strewn about the floor. Poor Frondamein lay under the covers shivering even as beads of sweat glistened on his brow.

"Here, drink this," I said, offering him a mug of the medicinal cocktail. My new patient unquestioningly accepted the brew, and as there was nothing else I could do for him, I left, hoping he would soon settle into a slumber.

After feeding Frondamein's hungry horse, I returned to the parlor and collapsed on the settee underneath a quilt. Folding my tall frame as best I could onto the inadequate piece of furniture, I eventually fell into a shallow slumber myself. However, I found it frequently interrupted during the night by the sounds of Frondamein tossing and turning in the loft above and the occasional sounds of the crying baby. My herbs I kept close at hand and a large pot of water simmering on the hearth throughout the night.

The next morning, I roused myself from the settee to place another log on the fire when I woke to find a chill in the air. Outside, the rain continued to fall steadily and tiny rivulets streamed down from the overhanging eaves and onto the soaked ground below. In the bedchamber, Loralon tenderly held her child to her breast, but I could see her cringe whenever a groan came from the loft above.

I placed two more logs on the fire then went to check on Frondamein, whose misery raged on. Sweat continued to break out on his forehead, yet he would kick off his covers only to shiver with chills a moment later. But without the instruments to measure his temperature, how was I to know if my medicines were working?

Loralon did what she could to help when the baby slept, but she was even more exhausted than I. So I put on a stiff upper lip and told her to go back to bed. After all, I wasn't the one who had just given birth, and I couldn't even begin to imagine how sore she must have been—I had seen quite enough to convince me of that.

To everyone's relief, Frondamein's fever broke by midafternoon, and as he rested more easily I slowed down a bit. I had been attending to everyone in the house, both human and animal, for two days, and my body was starting to tire out from the relentless pace. Following a rather haphazardly thrown together meal of sliced roast beef between two slices of bread with a dollop of horseradish, I quickly washed the plates and collapsed on the settee for a fairly uneventful night of sleep. My body, however, had still not become accustomed to such cramped sleeping arrangements nor to the intermittent cries from the hungry child in the room next door.

The crowing of a rooster came much too early the next morning, and I groaned as I forced my body to rise from its resting place. At least the day promised to be brighter than the one preceding. From the windows situated on the eastern side of the house, I could see that golden streaks had already begun to creep across the sky from the east, transforming the darkness into a brilliant pale blue, like a wave rippling across the water.

I climbed to the loft to check on Frondamein, who was still resting peacefully, and I could hear Loralon and the baby beginning to stir below. I returned shortly downstairs and grabbed the egg basket before disappearing into the stable. Still feeling rather groggy and wishing for another few hours of sleep, I gathered as many eggs as the hens had offered and placed them in the basket. Grabbing a stool and a pail, I pulled up beside the cow and began the process of procuring milk from the rather temperamental bovine, which took a step backward and kicked over the contents of the bucket, spoiling my efforts. Cursing under my breath, I retrieved the now-empty pail and began the task again, this time careful to pay closer attention to the cow's movements.

Gathering the pail of milk and basket of eggs, I returned indoors where I found Frondamein sitting in the rocking chair next to the fire as Loralon stood nearby with the baby in her arms.

Frondamein looked up and smiled as I entered. "Good mornin' to ye," he said cheerily.

"It appears as though you're feeling much better," I commented.

"That I am, though still a bit weak," he admitted. He looked up at his wife and to the peacefully sleeping newborn. "Miss Arwyn, ye've done so much for this family since ye came to live with us a while back, but nothin' as much as what ye've done the past few days. Dunna know what we'd 'ave done without ye, and Loralon, Amerigo, and I would like to tell ye 'ow grateful we are."

"Amerigo?"

Loralon smiled expectantly. "Do ye like it, Arwyn? 'Tis a groovy name, do ye not think? 'As a different ring to it."

"Well, yes, I like it very much," I answered, although taken back a bit by the unexpected announcement. "It befits a person of greatness, as I'm sure he'll be."

Loralon and Frondamein almost seemed to sigh simultaneously with relief . . . as if their son's name were dependent on *my* opinion . . . as if *I* were now a part of the family.

I returned to my morning duties with a renewed vigor, feeling both relieved and happy over Amerigo's safe entrance into the world and the fact that Frondamein was well on his way to recovery. Not to mention the fact that I was finally feeling like I *belonged*.

However, the warm feelings soon dissolved when I discovered I had left the eggs in the skillet too long and that they had become an unrecognizable blackened mass. Grumbling, I had to scrape out the caked-on pan as best I could before any of us were able to eat breakfast. Yet even after a full stomach, nothing could be done for the overall weariness that had plagued me those past few days. Even though I had managed to find a few winks on the settee, it was still not the deep sleep I had become accustomed to in my own bed.

But there was work to be done. So, following breakfast I went out to sweep the stable and give the horses fresh hay.

"I know I've been neglecting you lately," I said as I stroked Avencloe's muzzle, "but I promise to start going on our afternoon rides again as soon as possible."

"So ye've started talkin' t' animals same as yer friend Eliendor." I knew the voice without having to turn my head. There standing in the opening to the stable was Hamloc, his leering form darkening the entrance as the sunlight at his back cast a long shadow within. "'Aven't seen ye lately in the village," he said as he invited himself in.

Perturbed, I grabbed a broom and swept stray pieces of straw back into place. "I've been rather preoccupied lately. You know . . . birthing babies, tending the sick. I haven't had the time for carousing at the tavern."

"What a pity," Hamloc said, inching closer. "I've missed yer pretty face."

Suddenly he reached out and touched me on the cheek. Such an intimate gesture I had not expected, even from him. I turned quickly toward the side door of the stable and attempted escape, but Hamloc stretched out his arm to the edge of the doorway, blocking any exit.

"So much for pleasantries," I quipped. "I suppose you've given up that little charade." Somewhere deep inside me a fire ignited. *Come on*, I thought, *make my day*.

"Ye've been resistin' me long enough," he said, backing me into a stall. "It's about time ye find out what ye've been missin', then perhaps ye'll respond more proper to me affections."

Like a snake moving in to strike its trapped prey, Hamloc slithered in closer. And I, cornered like an animal caught in a snare, could feel my fingers curling into a fist. "I'm warning you, come no closer!"

"Come now, Arwyn. No need to be so skittish."

"Back off!" I yelled, heart pounding.

As Hamloc reached out to grab me around the waist, my left arm went instinctively up to block any blows that might be forthcoming. "Kaia!" I yelled. Quick as a flash, I struck at the middle of his face with my other hand, sending his head springing backward then rebounding as he held his nose. I brushed past him and headed toward the front door of the stable as Hamloc shook his head, no doubt all thoughts of an amorous encounter forgotten.

Outside on the road several passers-by turned their heads and stared as I stormed through the entrance of the barn. In close pursuit was Hamloc, who angrily grabbed me above my left elbow. Instinct took over, and with my left heel, I struck Hamloc's shin below his knee. And then, as Hamloc fell to one knee, holding onto his leg in pain, I pivoted around and kicked him on the side of his head, sending him sprawling backward onto the ground. There he lay in agony, holding onto his lower leg as blood trickled down his face.

To the sound of stunned gasps coming from the spectators on the road, I tossed my head back and walked indignantly past the writhing body in the dirt. I headed for the front door of the cottage, wondering how on earth I had known how to bring down a man of Hamloc's size. My reaction had felt all too natural.

Suddenly I heard the sound of laughter coming from the spectators on the road. By then a small crowd of both men and women had gathered to gawk at the spectacle of the town "hero" brought to his knees.

And there Loralon stood at the front door of the cottage, bucket in her hands as she stared at me, open-mouthed. She had witnessed the whole unfortunate event. I stormed toward her brazenly, until I heard a man on the road yell. "Seems Hamloc's finally met 'is match!"

"Aye, to think all this time 'e's been a regular lady-killer. Seems it takes a lady to bring 'im to 'is knees."

"Why dunna she castrate 'im now and be done with it?" an old woman cackled. "No doubt the thought 'as crossed 'er mind a time or two."

Amidst the jeers of the crowd, Hamloc struggled to his feet and limped away like a beaten dog, tail tucked under its rump. Head down, he took off in the direction of the tavern.

As I burst through the front door, Frondamein looked at me with wide eyes from his viewing spot at the front window. I stopped and looked at him unapologetically. "He had it coming!" I said. "I could only take so much harassment."

Frondamein shrank back slightly as I brushed past. "Believe me, miss, I'm not one t' argue with ye."

"If only more men could be like you, Frondamein," I said, throwing my hands into the air.

"I daresay there's plenty a man better than I."

I went over to the settee and sat down, still quite shaken, as Loralon came through the door. "Arwyn, 'ow did ye . . . ? Why, he's a man and ye're but a woman, same as me."

"I'm sure I couldn't explain it to you, even if I tried. Something inside snapped when he grabbed me." I groaned and leaned against a knee, propping my forehead on my hand as though I had a headache. My hair obstructed my face as the full weight of my actions began to sink in. "Right when I was starting to fit in . . . well, a little at least . . . I go and beat up the town 'hero,'" I lamented. "Now they'll really think I'm weird, or worse."

To my great surprise, rather than a word of sympathy, Frondamein burst into laughter. I looked up at him through a loose lock of hair. "On the contrary, Miss Arwyn, on the contrary," he said at last.

Loralon could hold her mirth no longer. "Aye, 'twill be a story what'll provide many a day's gossip to be sure," she chuckled.

"What shall I do? How will I ever face them again, or him for that matter?"

"Ye needn't wairry yerself about 'Amlock, Miss Arwyn," Frondamein said. "I'll wager 'e'll not be givin' ye any more trouble. And as for th' others, ye may find ye've improved yer lot by standin' up to the rogue."

"Do you really think so, Frondamein?"

"Aye, and I'd e'en go so far as to say ye'll be the *new* village hero."

The village hero? I shook my head dubiously.

Yet there *was* one thing I knew for certain after my explosive encounter with Hamloc—no matter what I did, I would always stick out in the village like a sore thumb.

CHAPTER 17

"Thank goodness I have achieved some degree of normalcy and peace. Yet as the air thickens with the smell of snow, I somehow feel compelled to give gifts to the people who have come to mean the most to me, like it's a natural thing to do at this time of year."

I stopped speaking for a moment and was vaguely aware that a smile crossed my face.

"What makes you smile?" the woman's voice asked.

"Eliendor," I replied. "He has an uncanny way of anticipating what I need right when I need it."

Little more than a fortnight passed since the incident with Hamloc when he made a quiet departure from Baeren Ford, "leaving to seek his fortune" down south in the city of Maldimire. But I knew the real reason he left, and based on the tittering and whispers of the villagers every time he passed by, I imagined they did, too. Such a man could hardly bear such a blow—both literally and figuratively—to his ego as my stinging lesson in manners had accomplished.

As for me, I felt like celebrating his departure, yet my gloating was tempered by the knowledge that several of the village maidens were not at all pleased with me. After all, I had single-handedly run off the most eligible man in town. But as far as I was concerned, they should have thanked me.

Yet the incident with Hamloc had done more than solve my problem and create gossip—it had awakened in me a fire and, along with it, memories of movements and postures I had known well, long, long before. And so, with Frondamein gone once more, in the early mornings before the sun rose I took to stealing quietly into the stable dressed simply in my pantalets and bodice where I was sure to be seen by no one save the farm animals. There I engaged in a series of rhythmic pivots on my long legs, at the same time making sweeping motions with my arms and jabs in the air as if battling some unseen foe.

Though it occupied a new body, my mind recalled routines learned long ago and began to train my new arms and legs and hands to move with as much stealth as those I used before. All semblance of my earlier clumsiness gone, my body took to this new regimen very well as it fluidly stepped across the stable floor in steady patterns. Clearing my mind of all other matters to focus solely on forcing air in and out of my lungs, I allowed the hidden parts of my mind to guide every movement.

It was only a matter of time before there came a quiet crack in the stable door as a pair of curious eyes watched from the warmth on the other side. Feeling at one with the thick scent of hay that permeated the air and with the sound of my own breath, I hardly noticed the spy until the tiny bundle in her arms betrayed her presence.

I stopped cold when I heard Amerigo's cries coming from inside the cottage and turned in time to see Loralon darting into the shadows behind the door. My secret had been discovered.

"Er, I suppose you wonder what I'm doing," I called, blushing.

Loralon reappeared in the doorway with a sheepish expression on her face. "I'm not usually one to spy, but I couldna help but wonder why it is ye've taken to risin' so airly and goin' to the stable. I know 'tis not been to milk the cow."

"Well, no," I admitted. Such behavior must certainly look bizarre, and I had known I would eventually have to explain myself once Loralon took a mind to investigate my early morning activities. "Do you remember what I did to Hamloc a while back?"

"Remember? The sight of 'im lyin' there on the ground is one I'll not forget 'til the end o' me days," Loralon laughed. "I'll ne'er know 'ow ye did it."

"It was a simple self-defense technique. It's really very easy once you get the hang of it, but it does take a lot of practice. That's what I've been doing out here in the mornings—practicing."

As Loralon stood inside the doorway, a faint, mischievous smile crept across her face. "Arwyn, I wonder if ye'd 'ave a mind to teach me these . . . tech, um, niques?"

I couldn't help but smile myself at Loralon's spunk. "I'd love to."

"Then get yerself into th' 'ouse. Ye'll catch yer death out in this cold stable with just yer skivvies on."

"Funny, I hadn't even noticed the chill," I said as I stepped into the warmth of the cottage, grateful that this most recent nonconformity had been met with approval.

Soon martial arts lessons became part of the morning routine. I would often have to coax Loralon out from under her warm woolen blankets and into the flickering darkness of the parlor where I had already built a roaring fire. The shades we kept drawn, lest any early travelers out on the road should look inside and see us gallivanting around the room making all manner of absurd-looking motions in nothing but our unmentionables.

I had to stifle a smile at Loralon's awkward and often unsuccessful attempts to balance on one leg while kicking into the air with the other. Yet with a little patience and prompting, she focused on her breathing and on mastering the simpler techniques first. But most importantly, she did not give up—that is, until Amerigo awakened in the next room and demanded his breakfast.

The first dusting of snow conjured images in my mind of trees covered with brightly colored lights, the smell of evergreen, and packages wrapped neatly in red and green paper. These past weeks I had attempted to push my longings for that previous life aside, but now I found myself yearning again for the familiar sights and sounds of home. With no known way to satisfy the need, I sublimated my ache for the past by doing what only seemed natural for such a time—giving gifts to my friends.

Loralon's eyes filled with tears when I presented her with a lavender sachet tied decoratively in a lace cloth and a jar of sea salt mixed with rosemary oil. But I believe she was even more surprised to discover that I had been secretly borrowing her sewing tools and working up in the loft late in the evenings on a gift for Amerigo, a soft doll that looked something like a bear, albeit slightly disfigured. Still, it was soft and warm and its charming button eyes already seemed to captivate the infant.

During Frondamein's last visit home before the deep snows of winter set in, I presented him with a jar of calendula salve to help combat the effects of the dry, cold air on his exposed skin and a pair of leather gloves I had purchased at the market. The blushing Frondamein accepted the gifts gratefully and though he said little, I could tell by the smile upon his face that he was touched.

"There's no mistakin' the smell o' snow in th' air," he commented on the morning of his departure for the Guildenmoor Gate. "I'd best be leavin' for the Gate afore it sets in."

"Ye'll keep the scarf I knitted tight 'round yer neck," Loralon said. "I wairry about ye enough than to fret ye'll catch yer death in the cold."

"Aye, woman, ye needn't wairry yer pretty little 'ead what with me woolen scarf and cloak and the fine new gloves Miss Arwyn was kind enough to give me."

"Ye know I canna help it."

Outside the window a scant few flakes of white floated dreamily down from the sky, like fairies dancing down from the heavens. Frondamein sighed and pulled himself away from the kitchen table and walked over to the window. "With the snows a-comin', 'tis likely I willna make it 'ome again 'til th' end o' winter," he said quietly.

The Healer of Guildenwood

"Then we'll pray for an airly spring," Loralon said, as she went to her husband's side. Quietly they held each other and wept, their bodies silhouetted in the dull light emanating from outside the window.

I remained at the table holding little Amerigo in my arms, and I felt the sting of tears in my own eyes as my heart broke for the two whom I had come to love so dearly. So angry and helpless I felt at the cruel injustice they were made to suffer. Yet what could be done to change it?

Horse saddled and supplies packed, Frondamein bid me farewell with a quick embrace, the first such gesture he had bestowed upon me, and one that was certainly heartfelt. He smothered the faces of Loralon and Amerigo with kisses before climbing atop Haseloth and setting off once again for the north, perhaps not to return again until the coming of spring.

That afternoon the snow fell in earnest. I bundled up in my blue riding cloak and set off through the woods in the direction of Eliendor's cottage. I knew from what I had heard in the village that the winter snows were often quite deep and that travel, even from one side of the village to the other, was quite limited on days when the storms were the fiercest. During such times the villagers tended to stay to themselves, hibernating in the comfort of their warm, fire-lit parlors.

Knowing that Eliendor must spend the cold winter alone in his cottage in the woods made me worry all the more about him and the possibility that it may be weeks before I would be able to check in on him again. Bearing a variety of herbal teas already bound and tied in muslin cloth as well as the heaviest quilt I could find for sale at the market, I entered the old man's cottage. With a twinkle in his eyes, Eliendor graciously accepted the unexpected gifts.

"As it so happens, I also have something for you," he announced, after pouring me a cup of hot, steaming tea. He then went across the room to the corner of his cupboard and retrieved two items before returning to his seat before the fire. There he handed me a beautifully carved bow and a quiver full of arrows. I ran my fingers along the smooth finish, admiring the workmanship that had gone into its making. How Eliendor could have known that the giving of gifts was so important to me at that time of the year was more than I could understand.

"This is the coolest, I mean, nicest gift anyone has ever given me," I said, as tears welled in my eyes. "I will treasure it always."

"I hoped you would like it," Eliendor said. "Of course, you must first learn how to use it. Although I don't care for meat myself, it is your duty to help provide for Frondamein's family as best you can. If that means hunting game from time to time, then so be it. However, you may even find that learning to shoot could help in other ways."

I shuddered to think what he meant but pushed all disturbing thoughts aside for the moment. "I've seen the hunters when they return from a day in the forest, and I've watched them practice at the range. Yes, I would very much like to learn their skill as well," I said enthusiastically.

"Then come," Eliendor said. "The daylight wanes and the snow deepens. If nothing else I shall send you home with at least the rudiments of good shooting. The rest you may practice as the weather allows, more so as spring approaches."

Warmed by the tea, we walked out behind the cottage to the small stable where the old donkey made its home. There, Eliendor had painted a bull's-eye on the side of a stuffed burlap bag set atop a pile of logs. He counted ten paces from the target, turned around, and handed the bow to me. Slowly I pulled on the taut string, marveling at how much effort it took to draw it back.

"First, you must learn how to hold a bow correctly," Eliendor said as he positioned my left arm out in front of me, slightly bent at the elbow. "Good. Now you're ready to nock your arrow." Eliendor retrieved one of the deadly shafts from my quiver and placed it in my right hand. Awkwardly I fingered the feathered fletching and placed it upon the string, trying at the same time to keep the shaft balanced against the bow.

"Using your three middle fingers, draw the string straight back," Eliendor instructed. "Now, line up the target with the sight on the bow and release the string."

Closing one eye, I lined up the target as best I could through the falling snow. Holding my breath, I let the string loose. *THWAP*! "Ouch!" The wayward arrow whirred through the air, hitting the stable sideways and bouncing down into the frosted grass.

"You straightened your left arm," Eliendor observed. "No doubt you shall have a nasty bruise there this eve."

I winced as I rubbed the sore spot. "This is much harder than it looks."

"Yes, but with practice it will come."

For a while longer I eagerly practiced my new sport until Eliendor's yard was littered with arrows that had bounced off the side of his stable, some actually lodging there in the wood. By the end of the afternoon, however, I was beginning to actually hit the target with more consistency.

"Well done! You learn quickly," Eliendor commented with an amused twinkle in his eyes.

Were it not for the failing light, I would have liked to have stayed a while longer. Even the deepening snow did little to squelch my excitement. Yet home beckoned, and I dared not get caught out in the woods after dark with the snow falling as it was.

Kissing Eliendor on the cheek, I bade my friend farewell, as it was likely that I would not be able to journey into the forest for several weeks. With quiver strapped firmly to my back and bow slung across my shoulder, I accepted from Eliendor a half dozen more books that I wished to peruse over the coming weeks. Feeling a great deal of misgiving, I forced myself to leave the old hermit to his solitary lifestyle for the remainder of the winter.

CHAPTER 18

"The seemingly endless snows are enough to make anyone go mad, and yet the quiet it affords gives me the chance to delve a little deeper into the questions that continue to haunt me. Am I elf or am I mortal? Why does my apparently elvish nature seem to be such a big deal to everyone around me? And for that matter, I still would like to know why I am here, why I am really *here."*

Back at the cottage, the short winter days crept by. Outside, the snow continued to fall until the drifts covered the entire bottom half of the first floor windows. Days were spent in the parlor, and on the coldest nights Loralon and I gathered every blanket in the house and slept with Amerigo between us on the floor before the fire.

I tended to the animals in the stable as best I could, all the while worrying that this sudden sedentary lifestyle could not be good for Avencloe, a beast that thrived on movement. On days when the snow slackened, I saddled him up and rode through the streets of Baeren Ford so that the horse could at least get some exercise during the long winter months. Sometimes we met other brave souls who had ventured forth from their homes, and I was secretly grateful for the opportunity to hold a conversation with someone besides Loralon. I attempted to visit Eliendor on occasion, but the untended drifts on the paths that lay out from town were too deep even for Avencloe.

Loralon spent her days at her sewing wheel and weaving loom; however, much of her attention had been taken over by Amerigo, whom she coddled next to her for hours on end. She also spoke frequently of Frondamein, wondering often if he had enough hot food to eat and warm clothing to wear. As best I could, I tried to reassure my friend, but in the end nothing could have comforted her but to see her husband standing at the front door.

I spent my days pouring over the stash of books on loan from Eliendor, not only learning the complexities of medicinal herbs but also Bensorian lore. By then I had become a proficient reader and had taken to the elvish language like second nature. In the evenings by firelight I entertained Loralon with readings in the beautiful dialect, but there was one book in particular that held my rapt attention. A rather illustrious mortal who had set out to study the elvish race and all the many facets of elvish life had written it almost two centuries before. I poured over its pages, hoping that it would illuminate the mystery of my own nature. Instead, it only deepened it.

Physically, I seemed to be quite elvish. It was true that, like the elves, my senses were certainly heightened, allowing me to see the color of a man's eyes as far away as the tavern and to hear even the smallest bird alighting on the roof, when I had a mind to notice such things. My body also seemed to heal itself more quickly than usual, and I never seemed to come down with the various illnesses that plagued the other villagers. Even extremes of heat and cold had little effect on me. I hardly ever broke a sweat, and though it felt good to sit beside a warm fire when the snows hit, I could walk outside with little more on than my wool cloak and only feel a little tinge of a chill.

Then there was the issue of my ears. In every other respect I *looked* elvish—tall, with long flowing hair, and eyes that Frondamein described once as "piercing." Yet my ears were distinctly human, with none of the pointed features of the nobler race. And so, they remained hidden beneath my mounds of hair lest anyone begin to ask questions I was not prepared to answer.

Despite my physical "giftedness," there were many ways in which I felt much more an earthy human, particularly in regard to my temperament, than a cerebral elf. Yet, like my ears, my passions I kept hidden behind a mostly calm, refined exterior, quickly roused when need arose. Hamloc had been a case in point. I wasn't certain if a true elven maiden would have handled his advances any differently, but I was sure that there would have been more brain cells and fewer fists involved.

Finally, there was yet one other aspect of elves I was not fully certain I understood, much less possessed, and that was their seemingly mystical connection with nature, a quality that was almost magical. And although I felt a deep respect and love for the things of the earth, my relationship with it seemed certainly less than mystical.

I quietly pondered these matters as I gazed out at the falling snow, yet I spoke of them to no one, not even Loralon. If the villagers wished to think of me as an elf, then so be it. I only hoped that there would not come a day when being an elf would prove a liability.

Just as I believed I would go mad if I had to endure another month confined to the small cottage, the heavy snows lessened. It was at such a time, when every villager could no longer bear the icy prison of white that encapsulated the valley, that we all ventured from our warm homes to celebrate the annual Blizzard Feast and the end to our relatively isolated lives.

And what a celebration! There was pork skewered and roasting over a blazing fire, roasted chestnuts, with hot cider and strong ale. Nearby, children slid down the hill north of town on homemade sleds while young and old alike skated across the frozen lake.

There in the snow-covered streets the villagers danced around huge bonfires to raucous jigs and old Bensorian folk songs until the wee hours of the morning. And I was very happy not to spend the evening as a wall flower, thanks to Loralon, who had for weeks been preparing me for the festivities by teaching me the most popular dances, whistling tunes as best she could as we spun around the parlor floor. I felt rather foolish, yet no more foolish than I did during our early morning self-defense lessons. Still, the practice paid off, and there were even several young men at the feast who asked me to dance. And although Loralon had prepared me well, the music was so hypnotic that I caught myself swaying my hips and bobbing my head as it seemed I had in the past, only to realize that my odd dance moves had drawn more than a few strange glances. But I at least managed to keep from stepping on anyone's feet.

Breathlessly, I twirled around in the snow to the sounds of rather lively folk songs as my partners blushed each time I smiled at them. At the end of the day I walked home with Loralon, who held tightly to the well-bundled Amerigo, still feeling the warmth of the bonfire and the hot mulled wine I had indulged in at the insistence of Padimus the taverner. In all my months in Bensor, I could not remember ever having such a good time.

In a matter of weeks, winter's icy grip surrendered to an early spring, and life returned to normal. The world shed its white cloak for one of green, ornamented with splashes of brilliant pinks, yellows, lavenders, and whites. Outside the cottage, daffodils, tulips, and forsythia seemed to emerge overnight on the front lawn. Never before did I remember seeing such a glorious springtime as that which had come to Bensor, and it was invigorating.

Frondamein returned home as soon as was possible, and Loralon could not have been more relieved that he had made it through yet another bone-chilling season at the Guildenmoor Gate. At my first opportunity I went to visit Eliendor and found that he had survived the harsh winter on his store of firewood, his books, a harvest of dried fruits and nuts, and many jars of vegetable stew. I quickly resumed my visits to his home as well as my afternoon rides through woodlands teeming with new life.

Word had long since spread throughout the village of the smooth birth of Amerigo, yet it was not until we were well into the month of First Winter when one brave soul ventured to knock on my door when the sniffles hit town. It was Kiril, the rather oversized boy of perhaps nineteen with wavy brown hair, who had taken Hamloc's place at the tavern. Coughing and feverish, he showed up unexpectedly one morning before the snows hit and asked to be seen by the "healer." I promptly prepared several tea bags filled with elderberry flowers and sent him on his way, cautioning him to go straight to bed and to drink nothing stronger than apple cider. Three days later he appeared again to thank me for curing him and to offer whatever of his services the newest village healer required.

I never forgot his offer, and so when spring arrived I invited him to join me on my plant-finding outings when he was not busy at the tavern. Together we ventured into the forest where he followed dutifully behind as I led him through ravines and across brooks, often getting caught in brambles and on occasion finding himself with a case of poison ivy. Still, he followed, collection basket in hand, desiring no more reward than a smile of gratitude.

Our wanderings led us southeast of the lower lake to a cottage in the forest where his uncle Leoric, a huntsman, lived. A narrow deer trail led past the cottage and into the woods on dry, flat ground along a bog where there grew an abundance of bilberry, which I found useful for treating digestive problems. Once, Kiril and I followed the trail as far south as the road to Wittering, where I found myself looking longingly eastward, wondering if I would ever travel beyond the borders of Baeren Ford.

"Ye've a restless 'eart, one what longs to see the wairld beyond this wee village," Kiril observed as he watched me staring down the road.

I turned to him curiously. "And what of you? Do you ever wish to see what lies beyond?"

"Aye. Been to Maldimire, I 'ave, which I suppose is more than most. But truth be told, I wish to see th' Andains. Loth Gerodin, too, but I know 'tis but a dream, the way thin's are." He sighed. He then gave me an encouraging smile. "Dunna ye wairry, Miss Arwyn, I'd wager someday we'll both see what lies beyond that bend."

"I do hope you're right, Kiril," I laughed. "I do hope you're right."

It was not that I needed an assistant, but Kiril was good company as he knew all the village gossip and a good many tall tales, having worked for Padimus doing odd jobs around the tavern since he was a child. Though our conversations were certainly not as deep as those I had with Eliendor, when I was with Kiril I laughed often. He was also bright and, as his grandmother had taken over his education when schooling had been all but banned by Draigon, he was one of a few in the village around his age who knew how to read and write.

I also suspected that Kiril had had something to do with the fact that I found several more of the villagers on my front doorstep seeking relief from all manner of irritations: headaches, upset stomachs, flatulence, menstrual pains, and the like. Nothing major, but it was a start. And maybe, just maybe they were starting to see me as something other than the town anomaly.

It hardly seemed like the village had recovered from the raucous merrymaking at the Blizzard Feast when the annual spring festival rolled around, right in time for the month of Second Spring, and with it came all manner of traveling minstrels, jugglers, acrobats, and magicians. It was one of the largest celebrations in the Bensorian year and one that was anticipated greatly following the relatively quiet winter months. This year was to be no different. The whole village was practically giddy with anticipation as we watched from the village, as the various booths and tents were set up on the high meadow above. A traveling troupe arrived and brought with them wagons full of exotic foods and candies, games of skill, and unusual trinkets from faraway places.

Draigon may have squelched many things for the Bensorian people, but their celebrations were not one of them. If there was one thing I was learning, it was that the Bensorians loved them, and for two days the inhabitants of Baeren Ford put aside their work and enjoyed friendly competitions and sporting events amidst a carnival-type atmosphere, culminating the afternoon of the second day with the famous Baeren Ford-Isengrass horse race.

As luck would have it, the festival fell on the very days that Frondamein was at home. He, Loralon and I, with Amerigo in tow, walked leisurely through the gaily painted booths, enjoying all the many delicious aromas and tastes within. Huge roasted turkey legs, fried pickles, and sweet taffy were but a few of the fair's offerings, and of course, Padimus and his huge kegs of ale were highly visible and very popular with the festivalgoers. We laughed at the antics of a group of comedic actors and were awed and delighted when a skilled magician took the stage. There were log-cutting contests and jousting competitions, yet it was the archery contest that most held my attention.

I was nowhere near proficient enough to join the competition—yet. But as soon as the weather had begun to improve, I was out practicing my new sport at every chance. Late in the afternoons, after most of the village hunters had long since left their target practice for the forest, I would steal off to the archery range north of Arnuin's Hold where a handful of women archers went to practice their skills. There I sought guidance from the more experienced women, who gave me all sorts of advice regarding my stance, how I held the bow, and how I lined up the target with the sight. And although I was still far from being considered good by village standards, I had at least learned to hit the target consistently. "Perhaps next year," I thought, as I watched both male and female archers stringing their bows and checking their fletching in preparation for the contest.

But there was one contest I simply *had* to enter, the much-anticipated horse race. From villages and tiny hamlets all over people had come to the high meadow of Baeren Ford in order to see which horse could span the two miles from Baeren Ford to Isengrass and back again the fastest. In my heart I knew Avencloe could fly like the wind, yet I needed to prove to myself that he was indeed the quickest around.

Master Ingmar, a grain merchant and the richest man in Baeren Ford, stepped up to the podium dressed in his best finery. "Last call," he announced as the racers made their way to the starting line.

Confidently Avencloe and I approached the starting line with at least a dozen other contenders. Even the majestic horse seemed excited, anxiously neighing and pawing the ground as if he were ready to leave the others in the dust. Our presence there was met with a mixed reaction from the competition. Some gave me looks of dismay as all hope of winning the competition drained from their faces. Then there were others who looked at me smugly, eager to disprove all the village gossip concerning my unnaturally fast "phantom horse," as they called Avencloe.

"Ye know the rules," Ingmar announced. "All the way 'round the fountain in Isengrass and back. And lest there be any funny business, ye must retairn with a streamer from the proctor." With that, he walked out into the middle of the field, and with a blare of trumpets, Ingmar lowered the starting flag.

In an instant, all the horses took off in a gallop across the wide field and rolling hills toward the village of Isengrass. It was only a matter of seconds before Avencloe had sprung several lengths ahead of the competition, and it was not long before the other horses had little chance of catching up to him at the speed he was running. Their only hope was the possibility that the great horse's burst of energy would be short-lived. I, however, knew better. In fact, I knew that Avencloe could have even gone faster had I desired it.

Along the route, onlookers stood by with gaping mouths as the white phantom dashed before them far ahead of the other horses. Up ahead in the village of Isengrass a crowd had gathered in the town square to witness the grand event. Avencloe and I alone approached from over the hill and sped toward them as though demon-possessed. One race official stood on the fountain that lay in the middle of the square and waved a flag as we drew near. Pulling slightly on Avencloe's reins, I slowed enough to grab a red streamer from his hand and stuff it into my belt before beginning the ride back toward Baeren Ford.

Up ahead and over the hill I could hear the thunder of hooves as the others approached. With a bit of maneuvering I swerved to avoid a collision, and Avencloe and I raced onwards.

After only a few minutes, we crested the last hill and looked down upon the familiar sight of the village nestled in the valley below Arnuin's Hold.

Mary E. Calvert

Amidst the sounds of cheering and great celebration, Avencloe galloped past the finish line and into the middle of the waiting spectators, hardly affected by what was to him a mere afternoon jaunt.

The villagers soon turned their attention back to the hill in anticipation of the next horse, yet there came no sound of approaching hooves for several minutes. Eventually a second racer came into sight, determined to finish the competition. It was not long before others appeared as well; although several, seeing that they had no chance of winning, became disheartened and abandoned the race altogether.

Ingmar eyed me suspiciously and started whispering something to one of the other race officials. I'm certain they were trying to decipher how anyone could have ridden so far in such a short time. Something was definitely amiss.

Yet in the midst of all the hubbub of celebration, disappointment, and suspicion, a lone rider appeared over the hill and galloped to the place where the crowd was waiting. Even from afar I recognized him as the man holding the streamers at the fountain in Isengrass. Deftly he dismounted and walked over to the place where Ingmar stood. As the two talked, Ingmar's eyes grew wide and he turned to me.

"'Tis official! Miss Arwyn o' Baeren Ford is the winner o' this year's competition," he announced as a great cheer arose from the crowd.

I walked up to the podium where he stood, thanking him sincerely for the honor and for my award, which amounted to six pieces of silver and a prize ham donated by Manyus the butcher. The crowd clapped gleefully as I accepted my prize. That is, except for a small group of village maidens who clapped halfheartedly. They still had not forgiven me for Hamloc's disappearance.

As I descended the makeshift platform, I looked out into the audience and caught a glimpse of Eliendor standing at its edge with a faint smile on his face, Talthos sitting dutifully upon his shoulder. Attempting to make my way through the crowd to greet my friend, I was stopped by many who paused to offer their congratulations. But when I finally found the place where Eliendor had been standing, he was nowhere to be seen.

CHAPTER 19

"It has been exactly one year, three hundred and ninety-two days, to be exact, since I came to Bensor. I guess it's a birthday of sorts."

———◆———

Summer's Eve came at last, its approach heralded by the return of summertime warmth to the valley. It had been exactly one year since I had so mysteriously appeared at the Guildenmoor Gate and been befriended by Frondamein.

Quietly I went about my daily business, choosing to remember the event privately. I was therefore glad when Loralon asked me to go into the woods to pick a basketful of freshly ripened blackberries. Relieved at the idea of solitude and a time to ponder things anew, I willingly harnessed Avencloe and slipped into the forest. There I found a large hedge covered with thousands of blackberries sitting on a bluff above a large stream. I could hear the water gurgling below, and it soothed my soul as I took my time filling the basket.

At this, my first anniversary in Bensor, I had settled into my new lifestyle and now rarely thought of—or allowed myself to long for—that distant life I had left behind. There were even days when I wondered if all that had happened to me before my arrival at the Guildenmoor Gate had really been nothing more than a dream, and that, in this world where magic and mysteries seemed to hide a little beyond reality, perhaps I was merely a servant sent by Omni to help this poor family until the day came when Frondamein and Loralon would no longer have to be apart.

That explanation was enough at times to satisfy attempts to rationalize my situation, yet deep down I knew that I *had* lived another life in an entirely different place, and that my reason for being in Bensor went much deeper than simply watching over Loralon and Amerigo. Someday I *would* discover that reason.

I had long since filled my basket with blackberries and was sitting in the tall grass enjoying the breezes that swept down from the fields beyond when there came a loud splash and some ugly grunting noises from below. Intrigued

Mary E. Calvert

by what could possibly be making all the commotion, I girded up the hem of my gown, tucking it under my belt, and quietly crept through the brambles to the edge of the bluff where I peered down onto an amazing sight below.

To my surprise, next to a sandbar that jutted out into the stream, two Gargalocs who had stopped to make camp were thrashing about wildly in the water. In the past year there had only been infrequent rumors of the foul creatures passing through the village after nightfall, yet they generally had no business in the town that made them linger, and it had been an entire year since I had encountered the creatures. My first instinct was to creep quietly away lest they discover me, yet there was something in their manner that kept me spellbound and crouched upon the ground. What on earth could possibly be causing them to behave so?

It was not long before I discovered the cause of the commotion. There in the water the silvery shadows of darting fish parted in the wake of the huge Gargalocs in an effort to avoid being snatched up in a hideous, claw-like hand. There seemed to be no strategy involved in their efforts, and I wondered why these creatures, which had swords and other tools nearby on the ground, had not discovered a more efficient way to retrieve fish from the stream.

Suddenly a hulking third Gargaloc emerged from the trees carrying a load of twigs and limbs that he threw haphazardly on a pile that had already been laid nearby. He plopped down next to the pile and picked up two stones from the ground nearby and struck them together. Then it dawned on me—these were not fierce, cunning creatures at all, but more like mentally limited children, easy pawns in the hands of some more sinister being. Still, I did not care to meet one alone in the forest.

Shrouded under a veil of rhododendron, I spied on the scene below for several more moments, feeling almost sorry for the poor creatures. As I was about to slip away, a single fish went flying through the air and landed on the rocks beside the stream. The slimy, helpless thing writhed about for a few moments until one of the Gargalocs hit it over the head with a large stone and lumbered over to the place where the third was still trying to light the fire. The small success had caused a good deal of excitement below, as evidenced by all the grunting, and I decided that it was a good time for me to make my escape.

Quietly I crept out from beneath the underbrush until I was well out of sight of the stream. Gathering my basket of blackberries, I mounted Avencloe and headed for home in a rather roundabout way so as to avoid any other Gargalocs who could be in the area.

I pondered the strange encounter until I arrived back at the cottage and opened the stable door. Inside I saw Frondamein's horse and remembered that it was time for his monthly visit home. After seeing to my own horse, I opened the door into the cottage and was even more surprised to see not only Loralon and Frondamein but also Eliendor and Kiril, all with large grins on their faces, sitting around the kitchen table where a cake, my favorite of Loralon's many tasty specialties, had been placed. Even Talthos the raven was sitting upon one of the rafters, making quite a raucous cawing noise as I walked in.

Loralon smiled and walked toward me. "Oh, Arwyn, we were 'opin' to surprise ye, this bein' the fairst annivairsary o' yer arrival in Bensor 'n all. Ye're surprised, are ye not?"

The words would barely come through the tears that welled in my eyes. "That I am."

"Left extra airly from the Guildenmoor Gate, I did, all so as I could be here in time for the celebratin'," Frondamein added, with a twinkle in his eye.

"Eliendor, how did you . . . ?"

"That fine loaf of sweet bread Loralon was kind enough to have you bring me a week or so ago? She cleverly discovered it was a good hiding place for an invitation," the old man explained.

"Miss Loralon's 'ad me runnin' around all week, 'elpin' with th' arrangements. Run me ragged she 'as," Kiril added with a smile.

I could not help but smile myself. "I'm so glad you all are here together," I said as a tear trickled down my cheek. "All of you have helped me adjust to this, er . . . new life, and I have come to love each of you dearly."

"Hear! Hear!" Frondamein said. "But enough o' the speeches. This hungry traveler, for one, is ready to eat."

With that we all took our seats around the kitchen table and prepared to feast on the delectable roast beef with carrots and potatoes, creamed corn, cooked spinach, and freshly baked bread that Loralon had been working on all day. We also enjoyed a bottle of Elwindor's finest wines, donated to the cause by Padimus, with his best wishes. It was like any other Bensorian birthday celebration, but as I could not seem to recall the date of my birth, the anniversary of my arrival in Bensor seemed the next best day to celebrate.

As we ate, Frondamein and Loralon glanced every now and then at Eliendor, who had a habit of staring at people in a way that made them feel their entire lives had been laid out on a platter and served up for his scrutiny. It was certainly difficult to keep any secrets from him, intuitive as he was. The old hermit offered little at first to the conversation, preferring to sit back and listen to what began as strained talk but later turned to relaxed chatter after we had all had a glass of Elwindor's finest.

After a while even Eliendor was convinced to join the conversation when Loralon shyly asked him to recount the love story of Elwei and Arnuin. All sat mesmerized as Eliendor sat back in his chair and told about the lovers with more detail than any of us had ever heard. Even Eliendor appeared to enjoy himself, much preferring a discussion on lore to the gossip of Baeren Ford.

Mary E. Calvert

Following the storytelling, as if anyone still had any room left under their belts, Loralon cut the cake, a chocolate one—quite a delicacy in those parts.

Everyone contentedly full, we all pushed our chairs back from the table, and the two older men filled their pipes with tobacco.

"Beggin' yer pardon, Miss Loralon, but me duties at the Blue Willow call, and I'd best not let Padimus wait," Kiril said. "There'll be a crowd tonight, seein' as it's Summer's Eve and all, and with all the celebratin' 'e'd be cross if 'e were left to fend for it all by himself. I'm late enough as it is, but I thank ye for the fine food as well as the fine company. And, Miss Arwyn, may yer second year in Bensor suit ye as well as the fairst."

"Thank you, Kiril. I'm sure it will," I replied.

His good-byes said, Kiril slipped out into the warm evening air and was gone. Amerigo, who had been sitting on his father's lap, began to cry and squirm to return to his mother's arms.

"The lad's 'ungry," Frondamein observed. "Ye'd best go and nurse 'im afore 'e causes a scene."

"Aye," Loralon said as she took the babe into her arms. "And I'll thank ye to clean up this mess in the meantime."

"A man gets no rest, not e'en in 'is own 'ome." Frondamein shrugged and grinned.

"I'll help you," I offered as I rose from my chair.

"Nonsense," Frondamein protested. "Ye're not expected to lift a finger on such an occasion."

Eliendor stirred anxiously in his chair. "Arwyn, it *is* a fine evening outside and I have a mind to take a walk. Perhaps I could even interest you in a lesson on the stars," he said with a mysterious gleam in his eyes.

"You're right, it *would* be a nice night for a walk," I agreed.

"Aye, 'tis a fine night indeed, not to be wasted indoors," Frondamein said. "P'rhaps Loralon 'n I'll take the babe and go up the road to tavern for a pint after he's finished eatin'. May e'en save me from havin' to finish the cleanin'."

"Ye'll not get out of it so easy," Loralon said as she appeared at the door to their bedchamber. "And besides, the tavern's no place for a child this time o' the day."

"Aye, I suppose ye're right, love."

"Miss Loralon," Eliendor interrupted, "I want to thank you for a very pleasant evening. I had heard you were one of the best cooks in Baeren Ford, and now I know those rumors to be true."

Loralon smiled shyly and blushed. "I'm glad ye were able to join us."

"Frondamein, you have a lovely wife and handsome young son. You must be very proud," Eliendor added.

"Aye, that I am." Frondamein beamed.

"I will then bid you a good night and take my leave with Arwyn," the old man said as he grabbed his cane at the front door. And then, turning around, he added, "Lessons concerning matters of the stars can be rather lengthy. I wouldn't wait up for Arwyn's return home unless you mean to arise late tomorrow. Talthos, come!"

Like a shadow the pitch-black bird swooped down from the rafters above and alighted on his master's shoulder.

I turned to Frondamein and Loralon and shrugged, not knowing exactly what Eliendor had in store for the evening. He was acting very mysteriously, yet I willingly followed along as the old man disappeared out the front door with pipe in hand.

The first stars had already begun to appear in the night sky overhead, and over in the lake the bullfrogs had begun their nightly chorus. We walked silently along the darkening road toward the village as spirals of pipe smoke wafted above Eliendor's head for a moment before disappearing in the breeze.

I could not help but smile as I thought of how kind my friends had been to give me such an evening. They were my family now, as memories of my long-ago family were lost somewhere in the deep corridors of my mind.

As we reached the foot of Arnuin's Hold, Eliendor took off from the road and went up the path toward the ancient fortress. Up ahead its eerie gray walls loomed like ghosts in the emerging starlight, more silent and foreboding even than during the daytime. Deftly he traversed through the maze of broken walls as if he knew them well, and walked up to the building on top of the hill where he and I had met almost a year before. Up in the rafters the pigeons had long since turned in for the night under the twinkling stars in the sky above. How peaceful and quiet it all was, I thought, enchanted by the serenity.

Without saying a word, Eliendor led me up to the edge of the Circle of Omni and turned to face me. "There is a reason I brought you here this evening."

I smiled. "I sensed there was."

"You did, did you? I would imagine you sense a lot of things others around you do not."

"You may be right," I replied hesitantly, not exactly certain where this was leading.

"It has been exactly one year since your arrival in Bensor, and in that year you have learned much, have you not?"

"Yes, of course. You have taught me much about healing and about Bensor, among many other things."

"Yet there is so much more you need to know in order to grow and to become what you are meant to be," Eliendor said solemnly. "It is time for you to enter the next level of your education."

"I don't understand."

Eliendor stared squarely up into my eyes, and even in the darkness I could see their intensity, as if what he had to tell me was of dire importance. "What I have left to teach you comes not from a book. What you must learn you already possess deep within your soul."

I shifted uneasily at the old man's words.

"Arwyn, you have indeed observed how keen your physical senses have become, have you not?"

I nodded.

"Yet there is a deeper sense inside you, a 'gift,' so to speak, of special abilities that very few possess."

"I'm not sure I know what you're talking about," I said honestly, shaking my head.

"You're not sure, are you?" Eliendor challenged. "What about the way you sense a person's character even before you really know them? And your ability to heal the sick? And the uncanny way you and your Avencloe seem to know each other's thoughts?"

"Well, I don't know about that, but I do remember Frondamein saying that you can tell a person's character by looking deeply into his eyes."

"Frondamein is a wise soul, much wiser than he believes himself to be. Perhaps he has a touch of the 'gifts' as well—most people do, but few realize their potential."

"What are these 'gifts' you speak of?"

"I am speaking of the Gifts of Old—inherent powers given by Omni to all people, yet in some they are stronger than in others. They were especially strong in the Eldred. Elwei, for one, used those gifts to help cultivate her land. The elves know of them, and many have studied and honed their gifts to a great degree."

"Yes, from what I understand of elves, they have a sort of magical, er, quality. Is that what you mean?"

"Yes, exactly."

"But special 'powers'—isn't that like sorcery, and therefore evil?" I asked.

"Arwyn, any gift from Omni is good, and here in this world, where everything is not always as it appears, you will find that it takes the power Omni gives, what you might call magic, to fight the Darkness. Yet, as it is with anything, the Gifts can be twisted and turned to evil," Eliendor explained, his bushy eyebrows furrowed grimly.

I remained silent for a moment and shook my head slowly. "But why me? Who am I that I should be so honored?"

"Arwyn, you have the potential to do great things to fight the Darkness that is gathering," he said, his voice forceful with a note of urgency. "I know you believe yourself to have a purpose here in Bensor that goes beyond being a healer. Perhaps my helping you become aware of what is truly inside you will help you find your destiny."

"This all sounds so mysterious." I sighed and remained silent for several moments, contemplating the seriousness of Eliendor's words and whether I was really up to such lofty expectations. "Tell me, Eliendor, what exactly will this mean to me? What exactly are these powers you speak of?"

Eliendor shrugged. "As I told you, you already have the power to sense things others do not, but that sense will continue to increase in manifold ways. And when you look into a person's eyes, you will have a greater awareness of their character, whether good or evil."

The old man stopped speaking for a moment. He turned and looked out over the twinkling lights of the village below and sighed. "Here in Baeren Ford you have remained sheltered. Would that there were more such bastions of innocence! Beyond the borders of this town there may be others who, attuned to the Gifts themselves, will have the ability to hide their true nature from you. They may appear fair, yet inside, their hearts have turned to stone. Therefore you must always be on guard."

"Why I would have dealings with any such person, I don't know. What would they want with me?"

"Someday you may yet spread your wings and fly beyond this valley."

I wanted to believe him, but at the moment I rather liked the thought of staying safe and secure within the borders of Baeren Ford.

"Now, concerning the Gifts . . ."

"Yes, please go on."

"You may find yourself with the ability to change the appearance of objects," Eliendor continued, "and those who have studied the gifts for some time can change their own appearance."

"You mean, a human could take the form of, say, an animal?" I asked, stunned.

"Aye, it has been known to happen," he explained. "But, mind you, Arwyn, such will *never* change a person's or an entity's true nature, for that which is in the heart does not transform so easily."

"Er, anything else?"

"You may even be able to communicate, albeit without the use of words, with certain animals who are willing to talk to you. Furthermore . . ."

"It sounds like you possess the 'gifts' yourself."

"Shhh!" Eliendor insisted, pressing his forefinger to my lips. "Time is waning, and there is still much to accomplish. Now, as I was saying, your gift of healing will be expanded a hundredfold. Some who possess the Gifts have even been known to heal the ills of others simply by laying their hands on them, but only in rare cases.

"You may also have the ability to command objects to move and they will obey. Such is a gift of Omni, though He saves the more spectacular phenomena for Himself," Eliendor added with a smile, "like creating something out of nothing. No mere person, no matter the degree of skill he or she may have with the Gifts, could ever accomplish such a feat."

"Yet these are *indeed* useful skills to have," I commented, astonished. Why, telekinesis alone could make life much easier . . . but wait! Was I really starting to believe all this? It sounded so bizarre, yet over the previous year I had begun to learn there were many things in the world that could not be easily explained. Like my being in Bensor. So, I was not as quick to dismiss his words as perhaps I would have in the past.

"And I shall give you a stern warning: though you may possess the *Gifts* of Omni, you should *never* act as though you were Omni, nor think of yourself as Omni, for these gifts are but a shadow of His might. You will remain Arwyn of Baeren Ford, and you must use your gifts sparingly, for the good of others, and for no selfish purpose, lest you wish to answer to the All Himself."

I gulped, hard.

"As it will be with Dar Magreth, who dabbled in the Gifts of Old and bent them to her own will, rejecting those belonging to Omni. How innocuous the Dark Gifts seem at first until they trap the user in a downward spiral into darkness, as it was with her. And when an elf such as Dar Magreth, normally with an enormous inclination for goodness and beauty, turns to the Dark Gifts, then he or she becomes altogether evil in the worse sense."

My brow furrowed. "I do not understand. I believed elves to be marvelous creatures, full of magic."

"And indeed they are. Most can handle the temptations that come with such power. Although"—he chuckled softly—"having known a few in my time, I must say that most do have one or two minor shortcomings that are hardly apparent to most."

My eyes turned to the image of the woman staring down at us from above, forever trapped in stone. "And what was Elwei's, I wonder?"

Eliendor opened his mouth as if he were about to answer, and then his eyes strayed to the same spot on the wall and the silent, ever-present guardians of the Circle. "It was said that she was, er, *spirited*," he said slowly.

"What of mortals? Do any possess the Gifts?"

"Why yes, they all possess the potential. On the other hand, mortals tend to be ruled by their flighty emotions and are therefore much more subject to corruption. I suppose that is why most are ignorant of the Gifts. Yet, even when a mortal does happen to stumble upon them, it is rare for him to handle them without making a mess of things."

I shuddered to think of the immense responsibility that he offered me.

"But which path is it my nature to choose?" I asked, half to myself and half to Eliendor. "The way of the elves or the way of mortals?"

Eliendor smiled gently. "The fact that you would ask such a question tells me that you will be wise in their use."

"This is both wondrous and terrifying all at once," I said, my mind spinning. "Life seemed much simpler before I knew such Gifts existed."

"Ignorance would indeed make life more simple, more secure. In fear, you may choose to ignore all I have revealed, but if you do, then you will never know all you are capable of."

I looked at Eliendor almost breathlessly. "Eliendor, I have always trusted in your guidance, and yet I fear I am at the threshold of some force I do not yet understand."

Eliendor smiled. "You will come to understand many more things in time, but for now you must cling to the trust you have in me and in the One who is far greater than I."

"But how must I realize these gifts—what must I do?"

"Come." Eliendor motioned to the stone circle next to us. "All you need do is step inside this circle. The gifts flow from Omni, and it is therefore fitting that you are inside one of His circles when you come to realize them."

Something stirred inside me. Knowledge, perhaps, that I stood at a crossroads. One path led down a very straight, safe, predictable road. The other, up a mountain full of sharp, shadowy crags and dangerous precipices, but at the top was sunshine, and the most amazing vistas imagineable.

I gazed inside the dark circle. Many times I had visited that place alone, finding temporary solace between its weathered and mossy walls. It had always held such fascination, and when I was there I had always felt a comforting presence that could not be explained. Yet as I looked into the cracked stone circle overgrown with weeds, I found it hard to believe that it held such mystical powers. Then, taking Eliendor's outstretched hand, I slowly stepped into its midst.

CHAPTER 20

"Such wondrous and frightening things, I could scare imagine before this night."

―――◆―――

Eliendor took both of my hands into his and spoke again. "This Circle of Omni will show you many visions, yet they are only shadows of the past and present, which may hint of things yet to be. But of what is to come you will not see, for Omni alone can know the future, and to try to see it would be folly."

I nodded slowly, my eyes wide with wonder.

Without warning, Eliendor closed his eyes and broke into a language unknown to me. The intonation in his voice rose and fell and a thick mist rose from the middle of the circle and enveloped us both. For a moment I wanted to turn and leave that place for the security of the cottage. Yet something held me steadfast—perhaps nothing more than the trust I had put in Eliendor. That, and two weathered old hands which held onto mine with an iron grip.

The walls of Arnuin's Hold and the bent-over shape of Eliendor suddenly melted into the darkness, leaving me a lone soul on an island in the midst of the cosmos. Up above my head I could see a blur of stars trailing stardust behind as they spun overhead. So dizzying and exhilarating it was, all at once, until the stars were all orbiting, nay, dancing it seemed, around *me*, like fireflies on a summer night. I was shrouded in a sea of golden, sparkling light, fighting to maintain control as a tingling, ethereal sound filled the chasm, like the sound of singing.

With no warning whatsoever, I abruptly found myself in the middle of an emerald forest, silent and fragrant with the scent of evergreen and lavender. I was standing on the edge of a perfectly round pond of water so clear and still that the bottom seemed just below the surface and yet an abyss all at once. Next to it towered a huge willow tree, the largest I had ever seen, with a strong, thick trunk and graceful branches that hung down and caressed the surface of the little pond as if sheltering it lovingly.

My eyes were drawn back to the water, where something billowed up from deep below the surface. As I looked closely, it was a very small mountain that had suddenly thrust up from the bottom of the pond, like a nail pounded through a board. Soon, other mountains sprang up, tiny volcanoes erupted, seas frothed and foamed as they bashed into formless shorelines, and great waters bubbled forth from the earth like fountains, carving deep valleys as they made their way to the raging sea. And in the water I could see the reflection of a million stars, each bursting into brilliant life like the lights of a great city at twilight. Yet for all the power I had witnessed in the little world below the surface of the water, it was completely void of color, only dull greys and browns.

As I came to this realization, all grew still and quiet in that little world, as if it waited, trembling, in anticipation of what was to come. Looking down through the window of water, I caught a glimpse of green, and then a spray of violet, followed by a yellow and then a red. On and on faint colors splashed onto the palette before me, seeping together, growing ever more brilliant as they blended, creating even more colors until I realized that I was staring at an incredible, intricate tapestry not even the most skilled artist could possibly duplicate.

As I stood there witnessing the drama unfold, the tapestry seemed to move as if the colors themselves were alive. My eyes were mesmerized by all that I saw, until I realized that what I saw moving were millions upon millions of living creatures, from animals of all shapes and sizes to the peoples of the earth: elves, dwarves and humans, and strange and mythic beings I had only heard of in legend. And to my surprise—they were all dancing. Joyously they moved and lifted their hands and swayed to a deep pulsating murmur coming from within the earth and to a light, melodic tune that reverberated through the air. Like children they were, innocent, happy, with not a blemish or care in the world. And how I wished to join their merry celebration! It was all I could do to keep from plunging into the pool myself.

Then, without warning, the dancing came to a halt as a shadow clouded the faces of the dancers, erasing the joy within their eyes one by one. I looked above the surface of the water in time to see the source of the disturbance— an apple, half-eaten, tossed into the middle of the pond with a great splash. The ripple effect was instant as I watched a wave radiate from the center, polluting the beautiful, clear water with a dark cloud of red as it headed toward the shoreline where I stood, devouring everything in its path. And all the beautiful creatures, and the light in their eyes—obliterated. I felt like weeping, weeping for the loss of joy. What horrible thing had stolen the innocence from the little world in the pond? And I could but stand there, helpless to do anything to stop it. How my heart went out to the little creatures below the surface of the water.

All at once I found myself briefly standing in the glade of some other ancient forest, witnessing the embrace of two lovers in the moonlight. The statuesque woman's dark hair was long and smooth as silk, and although I could not see her face, I guessed that she must be very beautiful, for the handsome, noble man who held her in his arms looked upon her with an expression that was a mixture of great passion and tenderness. Then from somewhere in the darkness came a snarling sound, like from that of a great cat, culminating in a spine-chilling roar that shattered the image of the lovers like glass breaking into a thousand pieces, leaving me alone on a barren landscape.

A great shadow moved across the face of a pale moon, and all I could see around me was a barren wasteland filled with marching armies, violent battles, and cities that lay in ruin. Fear gripped my heart, and I felt vulnerable and exposed. Yet there was nowhere to hide.

Just when I thought I could bear it no more, the image changed again, and I found myself in a beautiful white city on a hilltop at sunset. Effortlessly my mind followed a cobblestoned pathway between two impressive buildings with balconies overlooking a street, and I caught blurred glimpses into inner courtyards where fountains flowed and flowers grew in hanging baskets. Up ahead the passageway opened onto a parapet overlooking the city terraces that cascaded down to a large body of water where majestic ships lay in the harbor.

On the parapet there stood a man dressed in finery with dark hair clasped at the back of his neck. With the setting sun to his back, he looked to the eastern sky where Elwei hung in the far distance, but he hung his head as if he carried a great burden. As I drew near, he seemed to sense my presence and was about to turn toward me, but before I could see his face the scene changed once more.

This time I was staring at a tower so high that it seemed to pierce the darkened sky above. I was shrouded in gloom and there arose a stench so foul that I thought I would be ill. From a place nearby came the terrifying howl of some unspeakable creature that made me shiver with dread. So eerie and desolate was this place and so disturbing it was, I longed to be rid of the vision. Yet suddenly I was thrust onto the upper reaches of the tower, and as I looked far down into the shadows below, I saw a sea of humanity, clothed in rags, staring up to the place where I stood with hungry, hollow eyes.

A gasp of horror escaped my lips. My heart felt such pity as I looked upon them, and they were all staring at me, as though they expected me to do something. Yet I felt absolutely helpless to do anything to improve their condition. Who was I that they would be looking to me for aid?

Just when I thought I could bear the image no longer, I opened my eyes and found myself once more in Arnuin's Hold with Eliendor standing before me, holding my hands in his.

A beacon of light had reached down from the heavens and bathed the circle in which we stood with a crown of golden light, more beautiful than anything I had ever seen before. Eliendor was still speaking in the strange tongue, the intensity in his voice growing more and more until he suddenly fell quiet.

Then there was silence. It was the silence of the country, the silence of humans asleep at home in their warm beds as the crickets and the owls graced the night air with their chirps and calls. It was the silence of peace and safety that I had come to love as I snuggled into my own bed each night.

"It is done, Arwyn," Eliendor said in a hushed tone.

"What wondrous and frightening things I saw." I turned away, my mind reeling from the events I had witnessed. "What sense am I to make of it all?"

"It is for Omni to reveal to you when the time is right."

"Who are you that you know so much about the ways of Omni?" I asked, knowing that there was much more to him than an old hermit who happened to know a little about medicinal plants and the local lore.

Eliendor simply smiled his serene but evasive smile and replied, "As I said, all questions will be answered in due time."

Several hours had passed since we made our way up to Arnuin's Hold. The taverngoers had long since gone home and were now comfortably in bed. I bid Eliendor farewell before stealing quietly into my own home and my own bed, trying hard not to wake the three who were sleeping in the room below.

As I lay there in the silence of the loft, I thought back over the strange events of the evening and the bizarre images I had witnessed. How I had been made privy to such astonishing things was more than I could comprehend. And the thought of having special gifts, indeed, special *powers* . . . was frightening. Was I strong enough to use my powers well, or would I fall into the same trap that had ensnared so many others? Would I rise to a more lofty, elvish nature, or would I discover that I was a weak human after all? And by then, would it be too late for me to be saved?

CHAPTER 21

"I am no longer the person I was. Something inside me has changed, allowing me to see the world and all its beauty with greater clarity. Yet with my newfound awareness, I am also able to gaze into the heart and see evil at its rawest."

In the months that followed, I was keenly aware that a change had come over me. My girlish ways were gone—it was like I had become an adult overnight. I felt more serene, more thoughtful, less ruled by my emotions.

My senses had become even more sharpened, particularly my ability to read a person, or even an animal, simply by looking into their eyes. With great concentration, I found some animals with whom I could communicate without one spoken word. Even the stubborn old mule, who had given me such grief out in the garden the planting season before, now plowed a line as straight as an arrow at my bidding. With the people of Baeren Ford, on the other hand, I discovered that some were easier to read than others, requiring only a quick glance in passing for me to know where they were going or what cares they bore. But one fact remained true of all of them-- though they went about their days with a great deal of neighborliness and pleasantries, there was a void in each of their souls, a void that cried out to be satisfied by something that could not be seen with the eyes.

My other "abilities," though, I was more hesitant to test. However, one rainy summer afternoon, curiosity got the best of me. I broke from reading, sat up in the loft, and with much apprehension quietly willed the pages of my book to turn on their own. As the pages flipped one by one, my heart leapt with a sense of awe. In my wildest dreams I never imagined being able to perform such feats—ever!

Anxiously, I slammed the book shut. No one, not even Loralon, would discover my secret. I would only use it sparingly and when absolutely necessary.

The warm days of the Bensorian summer passed uneventfully. I continued to practice with my bow and arrow as often as I could, hitting targets, even

The Healer of Guildenwood

moving ones, with as much accuracy as the best archers in Baeren Ford. Secretly, I wondered how much of this newly found precision was due to skill and how much to my ability to will the arrows to land precisely.

My afternoon visits to Eliendor's home occurred almost daily, and when we were together we spoke almost exclusively in the elvish language. However, as my reputation as a healer spread throughout the village and to the countryside beyond there came at least one knock on the door each day from someone seeking my services, and I found it increasingly difficult to break away in the afternoons for long periods at a time. I had already delivered one more baby to a young woman who lived in the woods beyond Arnuin's Hold and had been approached by two more expectant mothers about delivering their own children. Yet out of respect for Ismei and Darya, I opted to simply assist the more experienced midwives. After all, there was still so much more for me to learn about being a healer.

From time to time, I retreated to Arnuin's Hold, drawn back to the place that had held so much meaning for me in days past. There I lay down on the grass in a ray of sunshine and stared past the ruined walls into the clear blue sky above. At such times when I was so attuned to the simplicity of the sun's warmth and the scent of the grass beneath me, it seemed an unlikely place to harbor such a mysterious force. Yet I remembered well all that I had seen and heard on that starry Summer's Eve.

Summer soon merged into fall, and with it came Amerigo's first birthday on the twenty-fifth day of First Autumn. The baby boy had begun to take his first steps a month earlier and never ceased to charm Loralon and me with his babblings. It was difficult to imagine how close we came to losing him.

It was a fine, warm autumn day. Eliendor and I had finished a walk through the woods and had returned to the old man's cottage, all the while discussing ancient lore, when I happened to notice a curious, beautifully carved wooden box sitting partially hidden on one of the rafters above. I stood up to take a closer look.

"What a beautiful chest," I commented. "It looks like it holds a treasure."

Eliendor avoided my questioning gaze. "Only a dusty old memento of sorts," he said, brushing his hand as if to dismiss the subject. Which, of course, only made me more curious.

"May I see?"

"No key," he said with a huff.

I was about to suggest that he use the Gifts, but then I noticed his brow furrow as his hand went to his chest.

"What is it?" I asked, yet I had felt it too—the distinct sense that something was going terribly wrong.

Eliendor spoke hurriedly. "Arwyn, you must return home immediately. Something is happening there—I cannot see what, but Loralon needs you."

All thought of the mysterious chest forgotten, I took off across Eliendor's front lawn and climbed atop Avencloe. Ever at the ready, the steed bolted into the woods. Overcome with worry, I urged him onwards through the trees, leaves crunching furiously underfoot as he ran.

As we approached the village of Baeren Ford, I could tell that something was very much amiss. Even through the line of trees on the edge of town I could see that the streets were empty save for black horses and their gray-clad riders who were scattered in groups all about the village. As Avencloe reached the main road and turned toward town, it became evident that one such group had stopped in front of Frondamein's cottage and was standing next to a large covered carriage of black etched in gold.

Amidst the sound of shouting voices, I could hear Loralon screaming, and in horror I saw that two of the men dressed in gray were trying to restrain her as best they could against her wild struggling. It was not long before I could see the cause of her distress— walking toward the front gate a third man held a crying Amerigo in his arms.

A look of utter contempt covered his face, until he turned to see he was only inches from the tip of a very sharp arrow pointed right between his eyes.

"Return the child to his mother at once!" I commanded.

The man shrank back, but he made no effort to hand over the baby.

"What is the cause of this outrage?" I demanded, my hands still holding the bow and arrow steady.

"This woman 'as not paid 'er taxes," said one of the men as he tightened his hold on Loralon. A trickle of blood ran from his nose where he had been struck. However, Loralon had been no match for the two burly men together. "P'rhaps holdin' 'er child will persuade 'er to hand it o'er," he said viciously.

"Do you not think that any woman would relinquish her last coin rather than see her child kidnapped by a group of heartless minions?" I said through clenched teeth.

Suddenly the door to the carriage creaked open and out came a wooden stump, followed directly by the sinister-looking man to whom it was attached. Every feature of his face was pointed, from his dark crimson hairline to his eyebrows and nose and the tip of his red goatee. He reminded me altogether of a viper.

With an air of command, he walked boldly through the front gate and onto the lawn as if he were doing no more than paying a social call. I had come face-to-face with Draigon himself.

"Is there a problem?" he said in a very controlled tone of voice, his steely, snakelike eyes staring all the while at me.

"Is it a policy to allow your henchmen to harass innocent people, your own subjects, into giving up all they have in order to fill your own coffers?"

"My dear . . . I am so sorry, but I did not catch your name."

"My name is Arwyn."

"My dear . . . *Arwyn*, there is no need for you to keep pointing that arrow in the face of my lieutenant. I am sure that whatever misunderstanding has arisen can be corrected."

"Tell him to hand the babe over to his mother."

"It is done," Draigon said as he snapped his fingers.

Loralon, released from the clutch of her captors, ran across the front lawn and gathered the crying Amerigo to her breast.

"Although my lieutenants do sometimes act hastily, the matter still remains concerning the payment of taxes," Draigon said. "We have been more than fair over these past years and have made few demands of the people, but the time has now come to pay."

"Do you not realize that this woman and child are the family of one of your own guards, the same guard who saved your life several years ago? Without him, you would have lost more than your leg," I said, glaring down at the stump that protruded from under his cape. "It seems you are the one who owes *him*."

Draigon's eyes widened for a moment, as though I had brought up a sore subject he hoped had been long forgotten. Then his eyes narrowed.

I did not budge.

"After considering the circumstances, I shall indeed extend mercy to this woman," he said coldly. "But hear me now, Arwyn. After this day, I am indebted to no one."

"Then begone, and trouble these poor people no more."

I could see the veins virtually pop on his forehead as he motioned toward the road with a jerk of his head, eyes still fixed on me. "You are very self-assured, an elf living so far from your kin."

"You presume me to be an elf?" I asked, as I brushed the hair back from my right ear.

"Elf or no, I do not take kindly to insolence," he hissed. "Cross me again and you may find yourself in a rather undesirable situation."

I would not allow my gaze to break away as I stared down into Draigon's eyes from Avencloe's back, and from my perch I could see into the blackness of his empty heart. So twisted and evil it was. But there was something else there, hidden even deeper—cowardice! So miserable a wretch he was, I almost pitied him. Almost.

With one last spiteful glance, Draigon turned and motioned for his henchmen to follow. Together they walked back through the front gate, carelessly trampling the pansies Loralon had so carefully planted several weeks before. Draigon disappeared into the darkness of his carriage while the others mounted their black steeds. Ever vigilant for a sign that Draigon would change his mind and return, I watched as the company headed down the road and into the forest beyond the village.

I ran to Loralon, who still clutched the crying Amerigo to her side, and ushered her indoors. As I locked the front door, Loralon collapsed, sobbing, onto the parlor floor.

Amidst tears of terror mingled with relief, I tried to comfort her as best I could.

"'Ow kin I e'er thank you?" Loralon whimpered through convulsive gasps. "If ye'd not come around when ye did . . . why, I dare not think of it."

My own tears flowed freely, but the words simply wouldn't come. All I could do was crouch beside her with my arms enveloping both mother and child. Yet in that moment, I was certain the tiny flame deep within me had been fanned, and it would continue to grow, consuming me until the day when Draigon no longer sat on the throne of Bensor.

CHAPTER 22

I must have sat there silently for several moments, burning at the memory of my encounter with Draigon, for after a while Dr. Susan's voice broke through with some insistence. "Please, continue," she urged.

"Surely I have placed myself in greater danger now that Draigon knows of my presence, and to aid my new friends will only place me at even greater risk." I could feel a mischievous smile spread upon my face. "However, I rather fancy the idea of defying him in secret."

"New friends?" Dr. Susan questioned. "I think your memories have skipped ahead. Perhaps you can back up a bit and fill me in."

Another year passed in Bensor, and soon I celebrated the second anniversary of my arrival there. Ever since my run-in with Draigon, life had been fairly normal, though talk of the altercation continued throughout the village for a long while afterward. I suppose I became somewhat of a hero in the eyes of the villagers for standing up to Draigon and his henchmen, but I only did what I did because someone I loved was in danger.

However, in the weeks that followed, men in gray were seen riding through town on a more regular basis. They must have gleaned from the locals where I lived, for always they seemed to linger at the edge of the woods with their eyes upon our small cottage before moving onward.

Upon hearing of my clash with Draigon and his lieutenants, Eliendor warned me to be wary because, even though Draigon was a counterfeit ruler, he held great power and sought to crush anyone who threatened his position. And, as he warned, Draigon could have a bearing on my own fate.

But I attempted to shrug off the whole incident. "What importance could I possibly be to Draigon?" I asked, to which Eliendor responded by becoming contrary and brooding.

The winter snows eventually arrived, though with less intensity than my first winter in Bensor. Spring soon followed, turning the landscape into a dazzling cornucopia of sights, smells, and sounds. With it came the annual Spring Festival and all its amusements and competitions. Believing myself to have an unfair advantage with Avencloe, I quietly bowed out of the horse race.

But I needed to prove to myself that I had become a competent archer, so I entered the archery competition. Trying not to employ my giftedness, I still hit each target with more precision and consistency than I ever thought possible, easily winning the competition, even over those who had been shooting for years.

Summertime soon returned to Bensor, with its longer days and warmer temperatures. The second anniversary of my arrival at the Guildenmoor Gate came and went with the same intimate celebration as the year before. After recovering from the trauma of the previous autumn, Loralon remained as she had always been—content as long as her husband was home and her child happy.

Carefree Amerigo grew more every day, amusing the adults in his life as he explored his world around the cottage on two wobbly little legs. To him I was "Ah-wyn," an auntie of sorts to whom he ran when his mother was not readily available. But it was clear that he and his mother doted on each other by the way he shadowed her wherever she went.

Frondamein, however, had taken to brooding about the house as though he carried the weight of the world upon his shoulders. There had been no way to shield him from the village gossip. Upon hearing that his son had almost been kidnapped and held for ransom, possibly never to be seen again, his whole manner changed. A bitter shadow rested on him, replacing the merriment in his eyes with lines of fear and doubt. He was like a long-dormant mountain of fire, sullen and quiet on the outside while inside a cavernous pit burned. He smiled weakly at our attempts to cheer him up, but they were never enough.

My life had changed little, except for having become the most sought-after healer around. With all the inquiries I received regarding matters of health, it was getting so that fewer of my afternoons were free to visit Eliendor or simply to take long rides through the countryside. Whenever possible I saddled Avencloe and stole into the woods for a few hours of peace and solitude.

On one such afternoon, a stifling heat bore down on the land as I rode to one of my favorite secret places beside a small stream. I climbed down onto a large rock and splashed the cold, clear water onto my face. I looked up in time to spot a curious sight on an ancient oak that stood on the opposite bank. Peering through my fingers it seemed to me that a pair of eyes stared back from the trunk of the gnarled old tree.

Believing myself to be slightly touched by the heat, I sat back on the rock

The Healer of Guildenwood

under the shade of a river birch, humming a tune. Every few moments I glanced over toward the oak. I could have sworn the position of the eyes changed slightly, and there was not one pair of eyes but two. Making myself comfortable in the cool shade, I sat with my back against the tree and closed my eyes.

"Achoo!"

I quickly opened my eyes to see a scowling face carved into the tree trunk that had not been there before.

I settled back against the river birch, feigning deeper sleep as I peered through my eyelashes. For a few moments nothing unusual happened. Then there was another distinct sneeze and I jumped to my feet in time to see the oak tree appear to sprout legs.

Two little men with long beards, one of brown and one of red, fell from the tree and onto the grassy bank beside the stream. They were gaunt, and their clothes were ragged, as if they had been worn for weeks.

"Did I not tell ye to be quiet!" the one with the red beard yelled, as he pounced on the other.

"That ye did, but me nose takes orders from no one," the second said, trying to ward off his attacker.

Together the two struggled on the ground, not noticing as I traversed the stream on stepping-stones and stood over them. I cleared my throat and the two little men jumped to their feet, clutching each other in fear.

"'Tis an elf!" the one with the red beard said, panic-stricken. "Please dunna put us under a spell."

I could not help but laugh at the notion. "Be assured, I mean you no harm."

Gathering a great deal more courage, the little man with the red beard eyed me with much suspicion. He barely came up to my waist. "Say, what's an elf doin' so far from Loth Gerodin?"

"I might ask the same question of you," I replied. "You are dwarves, are you not? What brings you so far from the Andains?"

The brown-bearded dwarf was about to answer when the other turned and gestured for him to remain quiet. "Our business shall remain our business," he said rather rudely.

"Very well, I see that this brief encounter will remain as such," I quipped as I turned to leave, "but I am not the one going to sleep tonight on an empty belly."

From the corner of my eye, I could see that the red-bearded dwarf stood planted by the tree, his arms crossed defiantly. The other stepped forward as I was about to cross the stream. "Will ye not help us?" he pleaded pitifully.

"Hutto! Be quiet afore she sends us to Dungard!" the red-bearded dwarf yelled.

"If it's Dungard you fear, then you worry for naught," I said. "But if your greatest concern is where you will find your next meal, then I may help you."

"An elven maiden would give aid to two poor dwarves lost in the woods?"

"Why wouldn't I? I have no quarrel with you."

"Goodren, we've no choice but to trust her," the brown-bearded dwarf said.

"One canna tell who's evil and who's good, nowadays. Why, she could be an elven witch."

"There's no such a thin', unless o' course ye consider the nameless one to the north, and I dunna think ye'd find *her* strollin' about in the forest o' Guilden," Hutto argued. "And did ye consider the possibility that this fair maiden could be an angel sent to help us?"

This banter went on for quite some time as I stood there quietly, studying the two with amused delight. Never before had I seen such persons—each standing less than four feet tall and sporting thick, scraggly beards that had grown well below their waists.

Despite his overall haggard appearance, Hutto's cheeks were ruddy and dimpled, and deep in his eyes there was merriment. Goodren, however, had a weathered look about him as though he had lived for many, many years, and his shifty eyes had not let down their guard for one moment. Eliendor had told me it was difficult to guess a dwarf's age, for they often lived for hundreds of years, and even the younger ones tended to look ancient.

Patiently I waited until the dwarf called Goodren snorted loudly in one last act of protest.

"I say we trust her!" the other exclaimed.

"Suit yerself, but if we find any o' Draigon's lieutenants pokin' about, we'll know who's to blame."

The brown-bearded dwarf ignored the last comment and turned to me. "Please forgive me friend's disagreeable mood. He's been through a lot o' late—we both have," he said. Suddenly, the dwarf bowed low to the ground. "Hutto, at your service, and this is Goodren."

"And I am Arwyn."

"Pleased to make yer acquaintance," he replied. "Come, sit down, and we . . . that is, I will tell ye of our plight."

I sat down upon the grass beside the funny little man, as Goodren remained standing, with arms crossed and face contorted into a cantankerous scowl.

"Our home is in the Andain Mountains where we mine gold and precious jewels," Hutto began. "Yet as o' late they've become a bastion o' Draigon, perish his abominable name!"

"Aye, may his beard be infested with the fleas of a thousand mongrels!" Goodren piped in.

"There he has stationed men, e'en Gargalocs, to do his biddin', to oversee the minin' that has been controlled for generations by us dwarves. Ye see, afore Draigon come along, those in charge left matters o' minin' to us as long as we gave half of our spoils back to Bensor. Back then, 'twas used for the buildin' o' the great Bensorian cities—Maldimire, Gildaris, Grandinwolde and its castle . . . e'en Emraldein . . ."

"May Maldimire crumble up to his ears! He's not desairvin' o' such a fair city."

Hutto turned and huffed at his friend. "I'll thank ye not to interrupt unless ye'd like to join us proper." Goodren merely stood firm and, with bottom lip protruding stubbornly, turned his gaze to the branches above.

"Yet now, most all we mine goes straight to Maldimire, leavin' us with little. Our cities are decayin' and in gross need o' repair, and there always seems to be a shortage o' food. We're forced to work long hours and are not allowed to leave our villages. 'Tis like we're prisoners in our own homes."

With each word, Goodren stoked my inner fire, and I could feel its tongues fueling my sense of the injustice being done. . . and my utter contempt for Draigon.

"To make matters worse, our 'watchers,' if ye will, have taken to all manner of abuses when they see fit to keep one of us in line," Hutto continued. "Me own brother Anglin was killed by one gone mad, just waitin' for one of us to step out o' line. Poor Anglin was 'is victim—had worked all day and all night, too, and refused to lift another stone 'til 'e could lie down and rest for a time."

Hutto stopped speaking for a moment and gave a sniffle. "The guard beat him to death, moreso to keep the rest of us in line than anythin'. 'Tis a sight 'twill haunt me the rest o' me days." The dwarf's voice trailed off and he had a sad, faraway look in his eyes.

"I am sorry for your loss," I said quietly.

Hutto looked at me and sighed. "'Twas then that the lot of us decided to rebel. We gathered what weapons we could and attacked the tyrants, but to no avail, for they had caught wind of our plan. Several of us they killed, and the rest they rounded up to take to Dungard. I hate to say it, but I'd almost rather be in the bowels o' that dungeon than to stay and witness what Draigon's minions are doin' to me people in the Andains."

"And how is it that you came to be here?"

"Those of us they captured, they bound by rope and placed in two caged wagons to begin the trek to Maldimire. The journey from the Andains through Gildaris and on south was long. We were but two days from reachin' Maldimire when we stopped near the place where the East Road meets the road headin' south. As we crossed o'er a stream, our guards allowed us to climb out of our confines to relieve ourselves and get a drink o' water.

"As one of our guards bent down to get a drink at the stream's edge, he failed to notice that the knife he wore in his belt loop had become unleashed and slid down into the mud. Havin' witnessed this fortuitous opportunity we made our way o'er to the place where the guard had been squattin', and Goodren here was able to hide the knife under his tunic.

"Fortuitous, indeed! We'd be better off with our captors. At least they gave us bread and water," said Goodren with a huff.

Hutto rolled his eyes. "The guards paid us little mind once we were back on the wagon, and the other group we'd been travelin' with had lagged behind and had not been seen for a while. If we didn't act quickly, we'd lose our chance for escape.

"As we got underway, Goodren retrieved the knife and quietly sliced away at our bindin's. Once freed, Froilin, the strongest of us, reached through the bars of our cage and held the knife to the throat o' the driver, demandin' our captors shed their swords and give us the keys to our cell. Knowin' the strength o' dwarves is indeed mighty, the coachman begged the other to give in, and seein' as we were about to go plungin' off a steep embankment, 'tis indeed what they did."

"Froilin kept the knife to the driver's throat until the rest of us made our escape. Just then the other wagon came barrelin' down the road behind us, and then 'twas mayhem all about. The last I remember, poor Froilin remained trapped inside the carriage while Zedlem and Balgrum fought against the reinforcements, all the while yellin' at Goodren and me to escape.

"There was naught we could do to help our friends, so we took off into the forest, runnin' as fast as our legs would carry us. One of our guards pursued us, though I'd wager the others had their hands full with Zedlem and Balgrum, for a weak lot they're not.

"Now, Miss Arwyn, as ye've already discovered, we dwarves do have a way of blendin' into the landscape when we take a mind to it, so it wasna long 'til we lost our pursuers. And for a long while we waited for any sign of our friends, but alas, we may ne'er know their fate . . ."

I glanced at Goodren, who remained stiff as a board and wore a scowl. Yet I thought I detected a small tremor in his lower lip and an odd glistening in his eyes.

"In the darkness of a passing thunderstorm in the dead o' night, we crossed the road that leads north to Baeren Ford, and for several hours more we trod, tryin' to get as far west o' the road as possible. When we were sure our trail had been lost, we slowed our pace. These past two days we've been a-wanderin' the forest o' Guilden, survivin' on little more than roots and berries. We'd discovered the hollow o' this old oak tree and thought it safe for a time at least, that is, until ye discovered us."

I sat pensively for a moment, surveying the oak tree. "Such shelter will not do for long. You will need something more adequate while you are here."

"Which will hopefully not be verra long," Hutto added. "'Tis our wish to return as soon as possible to the Andains."

"Do you not fear capture again should you return?"

"The Andain mountain chain is verra large. 'Twas in the southern Andains where our troubles started. After time has passed, we could return to the northern branch o' the mountains where there are small pockets o' dwarf colonies. We would be given refuge there."

"Shhh, Hutto!" Goodren warned, breaking his silence. "Ye give away too many of our secrets, and to an elf at that."

"And what quarrel do ye have with the elves?" Hutto asked.

"Hmph! Elves and their high and mighty language what no common person can understand! They live on the verra edge of our mountains and could verra well come pokin' about in search of our mines should they take a notion," Goodren said gruffly.

"Ah, but ye forget," Hutto said. "We dwarves have our own ancient language as well. And as for the elves, there are some what's been around long afore our ancient mines were discovered, who probably know o' their whereabouts e'en better than we."

I smiled. "I can assure you I have no need for your treasures, though great they must be. However, it may be some time before you are able to return home, and until then we must find you a safe place to stay. For there are no doubt those who still pursue you, and the sight of two dwarves traveling alone together in this region would raise suspicion."

"So ye'll help us?" Hutto said expectantly.

"Yes," I replied. "I harbor my own grudges against the powers that be and would gladly help you to escape Draigon's wrath and those who work for him."

"Bless ye, Arwyn!" Hutto exclaimed as he jumped to his feet. Goodren still had not moved and continued to regard me suspiciously, his eyes darting away and a faint tinge of red rising in his cheeks every time I looked at him.

"Come," I said, as I stood up. "I have a friend who can help you. His cottage is not far from here."

"What? Another?" Goodren protested. "Soon the whole o' Guildenwood will know of us!"

"Goodren, mind what ye say! We're in no position to question the lady's help, for surely she places herself in peril's way by givin' us aid."

Leading Avencloe by the reins and keeping well away from the roads, I walked through the woods with the two dwarves by my side. It was not long before we arrived at the house of Eliendor. As usual, I found the lore master sitting quietly on his front lawn smoking a pipe with Talthos perched on his shoulder. The black-as-night raven gave a raucous call as we approached.

"Welcome, Arwyn. I see you have brought visitors," Eliendor said.

"May I present Masters Hutto and Goodren. I have only recently made their acquaintance," I said.

The two dwarves bowed low to the ground out of respect for the ancient-looking man, although it was clear that Goodren remained cautious by the way his eyes stayed fixated upon Eliendor as if sizing him up.

"How peculiar it is to see dwarves in these parts. You must indeed have quite a story to tell, being so far away from home."

"Indeed we do sir . . ." Hutto replied.

"But perhaps the story can wait until their bellies are full," I suggested. "I am afraid they have had little to eat these past days."

"Then by all means, please step inside my home. It so happens I have a pot of stew simmering over the fire even as we speak." Eliendor motioned toward the cottage.

In the end, it took little convincing for the dwarves to enter as the aroma of hot food wafted out the front door. Hungrily they devoured the stew and a whole loaf of bread. Eliendor sat back and smoked his pipe as he watched the two consume what was to have been his dinner. However, the dwarves were considerate enough to leave at least some at the bottom of the pot for their host and for me. Afterward they sat back in their chairs with hands resting on their bloated bellies and told Eliendor their tale.

"And now we fear for our fellow dwarves, not knowin' what befell 'em back on the East Road," Hutto said grimly. "If alive they be, then they'll surely receive greater punishment for their revolt."

Eliendor puffed thoughtfully on his pipe. "Only Omni can help your friends now," he said at last. "We must first attend to your situation, which is certainly precarious. You must find a warm and dry place to stay until you are able to return to your home. Until then, you are welcome to remain here. The floor is hard, but I would imagine that with a few quilts it will be more comfortable than the floor of the forest."

"We'd be most indebted," Hutto said. Goodren confirmed with a nod.

"There is a small cave not far from here that may suit you well," Eliendor added. "It was once a den of pocaburs, but it now seems to be uninhabited. With a little work, you may feel right at home. Yet you must always be cautious lest some hunter or wanderer comes seeking a bounty for your capture."

"And are they to hope for a return to the Andains?" I asked.

"That is not a problem we can solve at this time," answered Eliendor. "Perhaps when the furor over their escape has died down the answer will come to us."

As the light faded to the west, I bid my new friends good-bye and headed home. There I confided in Loralon, whose eyes grew wide with wonder at the telling of the dwarves' plight.

"The poor thin's," she said, shaking her head. "No doubt they'll need new clothes. The ones they 'ave must be a sight."

"That they are, Loralon. I'll go to the village first thing tomorrow after my duties here are finished and buy some fabric. Would you then be a dear and make them some new garments?"

"Aye, but I'd best get their measurements fairst. I've not sewn for the little people afore."

"Then I shall take you to the woods after lunch."

"They'll be needin' much more than clothes, it seems."

"Yes," I said pensively, "I have already begun to consider how we shall go about getting the items they will need, but I will wait until tomorrow before I think of it further. My head is weary and I need to rest."

The next day I finished my chores at the cottage and made my way into the village to pay a visit to Feyla, the dyer's wife.

"'Tis rather crude material for someone such as yerself," the nosey shopkeeper commented. "Would ye not prefer somethin' with a little more color to it?"

"This will be fine for my purposes," I said, slightly perturbed.

Just then the door into the dyer's shop opened and a rough-looking man dressed in gray walked in. Feyla and I grew quiet.

"We've come bearin' notice to all the business owners in the village that they're obliged to post this sign on the outside o' their establishments," he said gruffly, holding up a hand-written piece of paper. It was a notice about two dwarves who had escaped somewhere in the area and were fugitives from the law. The notice also mentioned a reward for their capture but failed to mention how much. Regardless, it did not bode well for Goodren and Hutto's friends, for only two dwarves were mentioned.

Feyla walked over to the man and regarded the notice indignantly. "Verra well, ye kin nail it there if ye wish, but little good it'll do if none kin read it, thanks to yer boss who's banned us from educatin' ourselves."

The man grunted and exchanged unfriendly glances with the gutsy shopkeeper. He peered over at me, and his expression turned from one of surprise to intense loathing. It felt more than a little disconcerting to be hated simply for *being*, but I did not back down from his gaze.

The man turned and left the shop, and within moments we could hear him hammering the sign onto the door outside.

After I finished my business with Feyla, I hurried back to the cottage and discovered that numerous notices concerning the two dwarves had been posted throughout the village. That afternoon Loralon and I left Amerigo with a neighbor and with a borrowed horse stole quietly into the forest to Eliendor's home. As we approached, Loralon smiled with delight when she saw the oddly shaped cottage and lily pad-covered pond.

"Ah, Arwyn, Loralon, good afternoon," Eliendor greeted cheerfully as if nothing were out of the ordinary. In his hand was a sack full of seed he was using to fill his bird feeders. Talthos perched nearby on one of the tiny houses hanging from the tree limbs that branched out over the yard. "The presence of your friends has already brought their would-be captors into my woods. Two riders came through this morning, poking about and asking all manner of questions."

"And the dwarves?" I asked anxiously.

"They are safe in the cellar." The old man paused for a moment. "Er, you did know I had a cellar, did you not?"

I shook my head.

"The doorway lies under the rug that sits beneath the kitchen table. Quite a bother to get to, and that is why 'tis rarely used."

"Loralon has come to offer her seamstress services."

"Ah! Then our friends will be well robed indeed!" Eliendor exclaimed, and Loralon blushed. "Come, we shall coax them from their hiding place." With that, he led the two of us inside his cottage.

Upon entering, Loralon stared in amazement at the hundreds of books that lined the rounded walls. "Ne'er 'ave I seen so many books in one place!"

"I'm quite the avid reader," Eliendor confided as he leaned in closer. Altogether he was in quite a jovial mood, much more so than usual.

"I should 'ope so! 'Twould be a pity for so many books to go to waste," Loralon said.

Again surprising me with how strong and agile he was for such an old man, Eliendor quickly moved his kitchen table and chairs out of the way and threw back the rug beneath, revealing a square door with an inlaid handle. First knocking three times, we heard the door being unlatched from the other side, and then we opened it revealing the cellar below, where Hutto and Goodren had been sitting in the darkness. They squinted as the light from above hit their eyes.

"See, Hutto, I told ye they'd be comin' for us," Goodren said. "This cellar's been nothin' more than a holdin' place until our arrest. The whole town probably knows of our presence by now."

"Loralon is hardly the whole town," Eliendor retorted. "And if you'd like to run around in something more than rags, then I suggest you get yourselves up here and be measured."

Hutto came scurrying up the ladder. When he emerged at the top, he gave a bow toward the two of us. Goodren soon followed, peering cautiously at his surroundings before finally climbing out into the parlor. Loralon stared in wide-eyed wonder at the two little men standing before her.

"Forgive me, kind sirs, but 'tis been years since I've laid eyes on yer kind," she apologized. Then she sat down on one of Eliendor's kitchen chairs and took out her tape measure. "Come, it willna do for two fine gentlemen such as yerselves to be goin' about in tatters."

While Loralon worked doggedly at her task, I informed the dwarves of the situation in the village and the unknown bounty that had been placed on their heads.

"You had best remain here a while longer until the hunt for you dies down," Eliendor added. "There will no doubt be scouting parties in the woods until they determine that you are either dead or well on your way back to the Andains." He placed another log on his dying fire. It was almost time to make tea. "I took the liberty of visiting your future home this morning, well before you stirred, and I found it to be very suitable for two dwarves. With a little work, it should be an adequate though modest abode, at least until you are able to return to your kin. Still, we should wait until the search for you dies down before I take you there."

In the days that followed, Goodren and Hutto settled into the abandoned cave that lay less than a mile to the west of Eliendor's home. Kiril was the only other person I told about the dwarves, and in normal Kiril fashion, he made himself useful, gathering pots and pans, tattered old blankets, and an assortment of gadgets that had been lying unused in his parents' house. He even managed to finagle a pair of mattresses, now too small for the tanner's growing twins, explaining that he needed them for added insulation in the walls of his attic bedroom.

Under cover of night, Kiril and I hitched and loaded his father's wagon and then made our way as best we could into the forest to deliver the goods. With some effort, in two trips we were able to carry most everything by foot the remaining distance off the trail. Whatever else the dwarves needed, we delivered in bits and pieces by daylight.

Loralon worked tirelessly until Hutto and Goodren each had two new outfits. The clothes were nothing elaborate. It was well-known that dwarves were particularly unpretentious and favored comfort and durability over style. However, each article of clothing was adorned with Loralon's signature lavender sprig, embroidered on an inconspicuous spot in every garment she made—her small feminine touch to an otherwise drab ensemble.

Eliendor found himself carving small bows and arrows so the dwarves could begin to hunt for their own food. He even let them borrow a stack of his books written in ancient dwarvish for them to peruse by candlelight during the long, monotonous hours in the cave.

As often as I could, I stole into the forest and visited the dwarves, whom I found to be quite amusing and knowledgeable folk, having lived generations longer than most mortals and witnessed so many extraordinary events in their long lives. Why, just hearing of their cities carved from stone made me wish all the more to someday take a holiday from Baeren Ford.

"And me great-grand-da, he told o' the days when Elwei walked the earth. 'Twas back afore the star stones grew cold and silent."

"Star stones?" I questioned, to which the dwarves glanced sidelong at each other as if they'd revealed too much.

"Please, Miss Arwyn, have yerself some more tea," Hutto said hurriedly in a not-so-subtle attempt to change the subject. Eliendor merely sat there with a gleam in his eye, as if he knew exactly what they had referred to, but it was days later when I remembered to ask him what star stones were.

"Arwyn, one thing you must know about dwarves is that they often exaggerate the beauty and worth of this stone or that," he explained. "I'm certain that star stones are simply one of many they determine to be enamored of on any particular day."

"But it wasn't like that," I wanted to say. However, I knew that Eliendor was not one to budge when a topic arose that he did not wish to discuss.

Once convinced that I did not mean to turn them in to the authorities, even Goodren warmed up to me and together he and Hutto began to teach me the fundamentals of the dwarvish language.

Yet even as they seemed to be adjusting to their lives as fugitives, I knew that the hideout in the cave was only a temporary solution. Somehow, I would have to find a way to get the dwarves back to their home—but how? I had to remind myself that the dwarves weren't the only ones with a target on their backs. I had one, too, ever since the day I so brazenly stood up to Draigon. One false move on my part, and I could very well end up in Dungard myself.

CHAPTER 23

"The chance to see the world beyond Baeren Ford breathes new life in me, and although I admit that Eliendor's stern warnings are cause for some misgiving, I shall not let that ruin this grand adventure."

The heat of midsummer billowed in from the south on gusts of hot air and with it came a decree sent from Maldimire. A herald galloped in after daybreak one morning, proclaiming throughout the village that all were to convene in front of the old mill at noon for a meeting of great importance to the land of Bensor. Frondamein was home on leave, and we had just begun the morning chores in the garden when the messenger passed by. We exchanged puzzled glances, wondering what news could possibly be so dire. Before the noon hour arrived, we gathered Amerigo and made our way over to the mill where a throng of villagers had already congregated.

As I made my way through the crowd, I could see the faces of the people were full of anxiety. Whatever came from Maldimire could not be good, and the townspeople braced themselves for some new rule or regulation that would cause even more unrest. Amidst the drone of anxious murmurings, the herald took to the steps in front of Ingmar's mill and motioned for the crowd to hush. As if sensing the villagers' response to his message, the young gray-clad herald, perhaps only in his early twenties, shook nervously as he unrolled a bundled-up piece of paper. How could one so young work for Draigon? Perhaps he was no more willing than Frondamein.

Uneasily the herald cleared his throat and read from the paper. "It is hereby decreed by the law of the land that all the peoples of Bensor shall be counted for a census. Representatives from each village, one for every fifty persons, shall report, before First Winter, to the designated city in their region: Stone Harbour for the region of Loth Gerodin, Floren for the region of Elwindor, and Maldimire for the region of Guilden. Each representative shall be prepared to give the names, ages, and residences of each and every person that has been assigned to them. Failure to comply will result in severe consequences, even imprisonment in Dungard."

A sharp, angry cry arose from the crowd. "Why's ol' Peg Leg so curious as to our whereabouts?" someone yelled. "Soon 'e'll be a-wantin' to know the number o' hairs on our 'ead."

The area surrounding the old mill suddenly erupted in a chorus of angry voices. The herald lifted his arms in an effort to restore order. "The purpose . . ." he began. The hubbub at last died down and he continued to read. "I say, the purpose of the census shall be to aid in the collection of taxes, to make it a more orderly process for all parties involved."

"And what o' the elves?" a man shouted, glancing quickly over in my direction. "Draigon'll 'ave quite a time findin' 'em, much less countin' 'em all. It'll be us mortals who'll end up payin' while the elves'll still go about their own merry lives deep in their forest."

"Draigon's always 'ad 'is ways o' squeezin' our 'ard-earned money from us. Why's 'e need a census now? And why must the lot of us go to the trouble o' travellin' all the way to Maldimire? Why kin the census not come to us?" Padimus yelled. An angry din rose again from the crowd.

Feyla, who was standing close to me, leaned over and confided, "I meself wouldna mind a trip to Maldimire. They've the finest fabrics from all around an' 'twould give me the chance to do a little shoppin'."

"What about your husband and children?" I asked.

"Not to wairry! Me husband kin keep the shop 'n me children are old enough to fend for themselves."

"As I said," the herald retorted, "representatives will return in the spring to make sure everyone has been accounted for. Those who have not will be sorely punished, so I suggest you elect your delegation to Maldimire soon." The look on the young man's face had turned to a scowl, making him lose whatever air of innocence he had before. Suddenly he made his way through the crowd to his waiting black mare, ignoring the shouts hurled at him. Without saying another word, he climbed upon the back of his horse and rode away north to the next village.

A clamor of anger and confusion spread throughout the gathering, becoming louder and louder until Ingmar took to the steps in front of his mill.

"Settle down, settle down," he said. Finally, the noise diminished. "Does it not seem odd to ye, people o' Baeren Ford, that Draigon's tryin' to keep such a close eye on us?"

About a dozen or so ayes arose from the crowd in response.

"I say we rebel!" someone yelled from the midst of the throng. "Let's show 'im 'e canna control us no longer!"

Frondamein stepped up to the place where Ingmar stood. "Ye dunna know what ye say!" he said, nervously glancing around the crowd. "Draigon's more powerful than ye kin possibly know, and 'is spies are everywhere."

The Healer of Guildenwood

"Frondamein, ye're a guard at the Gate," Ingmar said. "Tell us what ye know."

"More than most o' ye are aware," Frondamein said. "Them evil Gargalocs come in 'n out every day. Where they go is anyone's guess, but I daresay the powers that be know they're 'ere. But beyond that, there are those of our own kind who've sold o'er to him as well."

"'Ave ye any news from the northern forest?" asked a thatcher who lived along the upper lake. "We've been so long separated—do they know of our woes?"

"Aye," Frondamein said slowly. "There are even rumors of . . ." Suddenly he stopped speaking and looked nervously at Ingmar, who shot him a glance of warning.

What sort of secret did the two share? I wondered.

"Er, now's not the time nor the place to discuss such thin's."

"What does it matter about the elves?" asked Emiloth, the village blacksmith and one of the few who made it clear he remained suspicious of me and elves in general. "We'd like to know 'as there been any news from the south?"

"Aye, when will our true ruler come to save us? That's where our 'ope lies—not in that o' the elves," yelled Manyus the butcher as he glanced over at me apologetically. "Beggin' yer pardon, Miss Arwyn," he added.

A general buzz arose from the crowd, people asking questions and making comments about the prophecy.

"Dunna be daft!" An old man stepped up before the throng. "There's no true ruler. The wizard came years afore I was born, and I'm now one hundred and thirty. I say if there be any 'ope, then it is in ourselves!"

A mixture of cheers and misgivings went up from the crowd.

"I agree with th' old man!" Frondamein shouted.

For as long as I had known Frondamein, he was a man who earnestly hoped in the old prophecy, and I was taken aback at his words.

"Though I've not lost all faith in the prophecy, the wiser part o' me says we mustn't wait around for '*im* t' arrive while our country falls apart around us. Still, now's not the time to do anythin' foolhardy."

"I would 'ave t' agree," Ingmar announced. "Though we dunna like th' idea o' the census, we must obey the law as it stands and 'opefully we'll be no wairse off for it than we are now." Murmurings of concurrence spread throughout the multitude. "Is it then decided that we'll be takin' a delegation to Maldimire?" A wave of cautious "ayes" arose from the crowd. "Then I shall be the fairst to sign up," Ingmar announced. "And who'll be next?"

After several moments three men from the audience raised their hands. Feyla suddenly stepped forward. "I'll go!" she announced.

"Ah, a female!" Ingmar said. "Will there be others?"

"I, also, will go." A hush spread throughout the crowd as I stepped forward.

"Miss Arwyn," Ingmar said awkwardly, "the trip'll be a difficult one for a lady."

"An' what would that make me?" Feyla protested.

Ingmar ignored the crowd's laughter. "There'll be no soft beds along the way, and we'll spend our nights a-sleepin' on the ground."

"All the better," I said. "I'm up for an adventure."

Ingmar shrugged. "Suit yerself, but dunna say ye've not been warned."

I returned to Loralon's side as several others raised their hands to volunteer. "I hope my absence won't be a problem," I said. "For so long I have wanted to see the great city of Maldimire."

"Then go ye must," Loralon said. "Ye'll only be gone a few days, and we kin manage fine."

"I'm afraid ye'll not see the grand and glorious city of old," Frondamein said bitterly as he rejoined us. "A lot 'as changed these past years."

"Just do yerself a favor and not cross Draigon," Loralon added in jest.

"He'll not even know I'm there."

By the end of the afternoon, the delegation had been chosen, one representative per fifty villagers—four women and eight men in all, including my friend Kiril. We decided to leave in the early fall when the weather would turn cool, for the summers in Maldimire could be scorching, but autumn on the coast was generally warm and pleasant.

"It is foolish for you to go to Maldimire!"

I had never seen Eliendor so impassioned. The bent-over old man paced the floor of his parlor with fervor. "You will be walking right into a pit of snakes, right into the very bastion of Draigon."

"I very seriously doubt that Draigon will be personally conducting the census. With all the people who will be there, I will blend right in."

"Arwyn, have you noticed that you simply do not *blend in* anywhere you go?"

It was hard for my eyes to conceal the hurt I felt, knowing my efforts to assimilate into village life were so obviously futile.

"Have you any idea what is at stake?" Eliendor said more gently.

"What *is* at stake, Eliendor?" I challenged. "My life? My freedom? What about my peace of mind? What about the fact that I have barely been four miles outside this small village in the past two years—that I long to see what lies beyond? I refuse to allow Draigon, or anyone else for that matter, to control me," I said defiantly. "If they will be waiting at the front gates of

The Healer of Guildenwood

the city with nets in hand, ready to capture any elf who dares enter, then you must tell me. Otherwise, I will take my chances."

Eliendor turned quickly, muttering something, but all I caught was "stubborn" and "mother."

"*What* did you say?"

"You're as stubborn as a mule," he said, turning to face me. "You won't listen to reason and are bound and determined to do as you wish," Eliendor sighed as he sat down on the edge of his raised hearth. "Go if you must. We'll pray to Omni that Draigon will not be in residence at that time, or that rumors of an elf in Maldimire—and there are sure to be rumors—will somehow not reach his ears."

The remaining weeks of summer came and went, ending abruptly with an early first frost. I had gone about my days much as I always had, with household chores in the mornings, afternoon rides and visits to see Eliendor and the dwarves, and tending to the almost daily stream of patients who came seeking treatment of one kind or another for their infirmities. Longing to experience something new, I anxiously awaited the day when the delegation from Baeren Ford would leave for the south. Already there had been an influx of fellow sojourners traveling from the north on their way to the census in Maldimire. Widow Pelipin's inn and the Blue Willow had fared especially well from the surge in business, and there were others in town who had opened their homes to help take care of the overflow at the inn.

The morning the delegation set out for Maldimire was a chilly one. All eight men and four women congregated in front of the mill with their horses, an extra supply horse named Ansel, and family members who gathered around to send them off. Bundled up in my woolen cloak, I gave Loralon and Amerigo quick embraces before mounting Avencloe. Behind me there rode a knapsack bearing two changes of clothing, several apples, two sandwiches, and three loaves of pumpkin bread to be shared with the other travelers. I also carried a small purse that held medicinal herbs bound in individual pouches, should anyone in the group suffer from any traveling maladies, as well as several coins I intended to use at the shops in Maldimire. Finally, I carried the list of those villagers I was meant to represent at the census.

It was not long after sunrise that the delegation got under way. Though the air was crisp, the sky was clear and rays of sunlight illuminated the exhilarated mood I felt as I anticipated the adventure before me. For most of the morning I rode beside Kiril, enjoying his merry yet relaxed nature. Along about the noon hour, I heard a familiar cawing noise and looked back to see Talthos perched behind me on Avencloe's rump.

"Ah, I see Eliendor has sent you to keep an eye on me," I said, as a smile crept across my face. The big black bird gave another cry as if in answer. "Very well, you may travel with me, but only if you remain quiet. I will not have you screeching in my ears all the way to Maldimire." The raven simply cocked his head as if nothing could deter him from his mission.

The road to Maldimire followed the twisting and turning River Goldenreed throughout the day, and I was no less enchanted by the beauty of the landscape and the quaint villages through which we passed than I had been on that day long ago when I had first come to Baeren Ford.

The company made several stops along the way to give ourselves and our horses a rest. By midafternoon we had all shed our cloaks.

Before sunset, the delegation stopped to camp for the night in a field beside the road. Ingmar, being the wealthiest among us, had purchased a slab of ham and several loaves of bread in one of the villages we had passed. By firelight, all twelve travelers waited patiently for the ham to roast, passing the time talking about the day's journey. After all were sufficiently full, we told stories and sang old Bensorian folk songs until late in the evening. As the fire died, I wrapped myself in my thick, warm blanket and fell asleep among the other women, several yards away from the men.

The next morning came early, and at Ingmar's insistence the delegation was fed, packed, and ready to leave right after sunrise. Talthos, who had flown off to some unknown spot for the night, suddenly showed up again on Avencloe's back soon after we departed.

The second day of travel was much like the first, with little change in the landscape. However, the air temperature was noticeably warmer the farther south we went, and I seemed to detect the smell of salt air as the day wore on.

As the sun sank low in the western sky, the delegation from Baeren Ford crested a hill that looked down on a plain—about a mile in length—that separated us from the city of Maldimire. For a moment the delegation halted its progress to soak in the sight. My heart beat a little faster to see this wondrous city and catch a glimpse of the vast sea beyond.

To our right the Goldenreed cut into the valley to the west, and I could see where it made its final journey across the plain and ultimately emptied into the bay below the city. To our left another road veered off to the east, and Ingmar commented how following that road would eventually lead to the doorstep of Emraldein Castle. My heart trembled at the thought.

But it was the shining city of Maldimire set high atop a cliff overlooking the cobalt blue Eleuvial Sea beyond that really caught my eye. Even from afar I could make out Maldimire's grand Palace of Lords. There it sat atop the hill like a crown of ivory, its center dome rising from the midst of five smaller domes, and eight buttresses flaring out on all sides to six tall towers. And if the palace was the crown, then the mass of white buildings that spread from the top of the hill and down to the bay were golden hair, shimmering in the light of the setting sun.

The company pressed onward once more, riding down the hill and onto the plain where already many groups who had come for the census were setting up camp along the road. Most had vied for positions along the Goldenreed and remained to the north of the city. Ingmar, however, who had traveled to Maldimire on numerous occasions, knew of a spot toward the east and closer to the Silvendell and the city walls where we could get both food and water for our tired horses. Not to mention, the position was much closer to the city's entrance, and the earlier the delegation would be able to enter the city and beat the crowds the next morning, the better.

The imposing white walls of Maldimire loomed above, shading us from the remaining sunlight as we at last reached our destination for the evening. There were several groups from other villages who had also come to camp along the Silvendell, but their numbers were fewer, as the villages that lay to the east between Maldimire and the forbidding jungle at Carona were scant. The vast majority of Guilden censusgoers would arrive from the north and west.

Ingmar decided to set up camp beyond the eastern wall of Maldimire at a spot between the Emraldein Road and the River Silvendell. Many miles east of the city, north of where it would have emptied into the sea, the Silvendell made a sharp turn to the west, cutting a dramatic canyon that eventually ran right through the center of Maldimire where it joined with its sister, the Goldenreed, and emptied quietly into the bay.

Even from outside the city walls, I could see that many dwellings had been carved into the far side of the gorge, connected by steep stairways that twisted and turned as they made their way from one residence to another. Wild bougainvillea in bright purples and fuschias sprang up in cracks and crevices along the wall of the ravine. All in all, despite their precarious position, these dwellings looked to be rather pleasant places to live, with their striking views of the river and the forest of Guilden that lay to the north.

As the company made ready to settle in for the night, Ingmar took Kiril and me along with him to find dinner while the others stayed behind to water the horses at a nearby well used primarily by travelers. Outside the eastern wall of the city were several houses that sat next to the river. There we found a set of stairs that led down to the water's edge. The northern embankment of the ravine was less steep than the southern side, and it did not take long before we reached the bottom. Several fishing boats were tied to a dock, their owners having long since returned home for the evening. One lone fisherman remained sitting in his small boat, cleaning his nets with a pile of a dozen or so fish at his feet.

"Good day for fishin'?" Ingmar said in his booming voice, as the three of us approached.

"Does it appear 'twas a good day?" the fisherman asked rudely, not looking up from his net.

"Er, 'ow much for the lot o' yer catch?"

The fisherman at last looked up at the rather unlikely group standing before him on the dock. His face was weathered and his eyes shifted suspiciously as he surveyed us, glancing longest upon me. "A quiddel, and not a penny less," he said at last.

"A quiddel! Why, 'tis nothin' but robbery!" Ingmar complained.

"Ye kin take it or ye kin leave, but as ye kin see, I'm th' only one left. So if it's fish ye're wantin', there's more to be found in the city."

Ingmar glanced far downstream at the bridge that spanned the gorge. To go into the city at this late hour would be an errand that could take most of the evening. "Blast! Here's your stinkin' quiddel," he said as he dug into his pockets.

Quickly I rummaged through my own purse until I found a coin to hand to Ingmar. "Please, take this," I said.

"Not to wairry, Miss Arwyn. Me pockets are deep, but I dunna take kindly to those who would pick 'em," Ingmar said as he glanced toward the fisherman with an annoyed look.

The fisherman took his payment and quickly slipped it into his back pocket before placing the slippery fish into the sack Ingmar handed him.

"Been a lot o' visitors to town?" Kiril asked uncomfortably.

The fisherman grunted. "I ain't 'ere to conversate with. That be what the taverns is for. I dunna take kindly to conversin' with all the foreign folk about."

"Then we'll take our fish and be out o' yer hair," Ingmar said indignantly. With that, he snatched the sack from the fisherman's hand and turned toward the stairs. "Come, we've no more business 'ere."

"What a disagreeable person," I commented as we ascended the staircase.

"Aye, Miss Arwyn," Ingmar said. "I'm afraid there be a lot o' disagreeable sorts in this city. 'Tis not what it once was afore Draigon came years ago. 'Til then, the folks o' Maldimire were as fine as any Bensorian." He sighed. "I suppose years o' livin' with a tyrant at the back door is enough to make most develop an unpleasant disposition."

Once back at camp, the delegation went about the task of preparing our evening meal of fish, bread, and potatoes purchased from a woman peddling fruits and vegetables from a pushcart to the many censusgoers camping out before the city gates. The weather was happily mild and dry, and a million twinkling stars spread out over the vast night sky, easily seen from our vantage point on the plain.

Drowsy, following the evening meal and long day on the road, I settled between the folds of my sleeping roll and stared for a long while at the celestial spectacle before trying to fall asleep. But throughout the night rowdy noises from the taverns and streets of Maldimire floated down from above, making sleep elusive for the party from Baeren Ford, who were more accustomed to falling asleep to the sounds of the crickets and bullfrogs. As I drifted in and out of a restless sleep, I was conscious that men dressed in gray were riding slowly past, eerily patrolling the sleeping crowds. It was enough to make me shiver and pull my blanket closer.

CHAPTER 24

"The outward shell of Maldimire's beauty is but a mask for the filth and corruption within. Still, there is some good here, though I do not wish to linger for long."

The sun rose much too soon the next morning. Sleepily, our company consumed the special peppermint tea I had prepared, which helped give our clouded minds a jolt. The anticipation of entering the beautiful city of Maldimire was enough to get my blood pumping, even after a less than restful night of sleep.

Following a hasty breakfast, the delegation walked the distance along the Emraldein Road from camp to the front gate of the city, leaving behind a young man from the outskirts of Maldimire to tend to the horses in our absence until someone could return to relieve him later in the day. It appeared as though other groups also had the idea of beating the crowds into the city that morning, for a throng of censusgoers were already making their way through the gates. The going was slow, but eventually we found ourselves inside the city and on our way up the gradual slope to the bridge that spanned the tall gorge. As we crossed over, I looked down from the dizzying height to the surface of the Silvendell some two hundred or more feet below, marveling that such an amazing feat of engineering could have been accomplished in such a place.

Once inside the city proper, Ingmar gathered us all to him. "No doubt there's a long line what's already formed. We'd best take turns waitin'. If the women would see to their shoppin', then the men kin stand in line, though I'd suggest an escort go with 'em, for the city's no place for a woman to wander alone."

It was then decided that the four women would break up into two groups, one accompanied by a farmer by the name of Zedrick and the other by Kiril. I was happy to set out on my shopping excursion with Feyla and Kiril, for I very much enjoyed the company of both.

"Where would ye ladies care to go fairst?" Kiril asked.

The Healer of Guildenwood

"I come all this way for the fine fabrics o' Maldimire, 'n ye ask where it is I care to go?" quipped Feyla.

"Miss Arwyn, what be yer desire?" Kiril ignored the feisty dyer's wife.

"I wish to gaze upon the sea," I said without hesitation.

"Fine, to the sea it is," Kiril said. Feyla was about the protest when he put his hand up. "Tch! Ye'll 'ave time to look for yer precious fabrics, but for now it's to the sea we go."

With that, Kiril, the grumbling Feyla, and I made our way through the crowd and up the main street through the city. Along the way we passed buildings in various states of disrepair, eyesores compared to the illusion of quaint whitewashed structures as seen from afar. In the streets garbage lay strewn about, and the foul smell of decaying food and worse permeated the air. Everywhere, mangy-looking dogs lurked in the shadows, waiting for someone to drop a morsel of food for them to devour. Recovering from a night of debauchery, disheveled men reeking of ale lay about under trees and in doorways. It made Feyla and me cringe with disgust as Kiril glanced about warily, ushering us quickly past.

The road that led up to the highest point in the city was steep and ran parallel to the palace walls, outside of which the census was being held. Once we had passed the main boulevard into the area surrounding the palace, my companions and I crested the top of the hill and found that the road we had been walking along ended abruptly where another, narrower one, took off to the east. Kiril led the way through the small shops and houses that began where the hill started to slope downwards until we came out abruptly onto a landing with a dramatic view of the sea far below.

Drawn to the very edge of the landing, I stood captivated by the unfolding scene beneath the city. Before me the blue Eleuvial shimmered in the morning sun and a gentle breeze caressed my face with warmth. The city itself seemed to have overflowed onto the towering cliffs above the sea, littered with whitewashed dwellings built precariously hundreds of feet above the crashing waves below. Narrow, twisting walkways and staircases connected them one to another, and each dwelling had its own veranda, covered with pots filled with a rainbow of flowers. *This* was the real Bensor, I thought, not that stinking part of town that lay at the top of the cliff.

For several moments I stood still, soaking in the warmth of the sun and breathing in the scent of salt air and orange blossoms. As I closed my eyes, a vision dashed through my mind of a young girl building sandcastles beside the water, the shadows of a man, woman, and boy not far away. In an instant the image was gone, and I was again looking down upon the pounding surf at the bottom of the cliff.

A large ship left the port below, heading toward the west, its sails unfurled in the strong breeze. When I saw it, a wave of sadness passed over me, as if the sight of it sailing westward held some dark sense of foreboding. But did such a baffling feeling brought on by no apparent reason hint at my future? Or my past? Eliendor warned me that, like the images I had seen at Arnuin's Hold, fleeting premonitions were all part of having the Gifts. But what could it mean?

I could have remained there all day, content to soak in the beauty around me, yet time was precious, and we had to go on. For a while Kiril, Feyla, and I followed a narrow walkway along the edge of the cliff until we found ourselves once again engulfed by buildings, heading downhill toward the bay. This particular area of Maldimire would have been charming but for the overall unkempt appearance and the garbage lying about the streets. Somehow, however, wild bougainvillea, oleander, and hibiscus managed to flourish, untended, in cracks and crevices between the buildings or adorning archways and creating shady canopies for the sun-drenched sidewalks.

For the remainder of the morning we made our way slowly through the labyrinth of narrow streets and alleyways that seemed to have no particular pattern and were very disorienting, stopping in some of the many shops along the way. I bought a handful of fish scales, very useful as nail files, a few containers of dried herbs that could be found nowhere around Baeren Ford, and several small boxes of chocolates that had been imported from faraway. I also paid dearly for a more comfortable new corset than the ones found in the villages. Such comfort was a luxury, but one worth the price.

Though the streets of Maldimire were crawling with scores of exotic-looking people of every skin tone under the sun, it seemed to be my presence that created the most stir among the people I met along the way. For an elf to venture into Guilden was one thing, but to come right onto the very doorstep of a tyrannical ruler who hated elves was another. And it was evident, based on several of the looks I received, that not everyone in Guilden held such high respect for elves as those who lived farther north. Poisoned for so long by Draigon's suspicions, mistrust of the elvish people had no doubt crept into the hearts of those around him like a plague. I, for one, was very glad to have a young man of Kiril's size in our company.

Quite pleased with the results of the morning's shopping spree, Kiril, Feyla, and I made our way down to the edge of the bay, where we stopped at a stand on the wharf for fish sandwiches. Sitting on a nearby bench to eat our lunch, we watched the fishing boats coming in and out of the bay. On the far side of the water two tall ships were docked, and again as I looked at them a sudden and inexplicable wave of sadness overcame me, broken only by the drone of Kiril's voice as he explained how the low-lying area of Maldimire that lay on the other side of the bay was filled with canals, and that those who lived there got about on footbridges or by boat. A bridge over the River Goldenreed was the only thing that physically connected the western end of the city with the eastern.

The wave of sadness retreated as quickly as it arrived, fended off by the glorious sunshine. I smiled contentedly as I finished my sandwich and stared at the water shimmering in the bay. Out of the corner of my eye I could see a familiar black shadow sitting on a nearby piling. Throughout the morning, I had caught glimpses of Talthos every now and then sitting in a tree or on top of a building, his sharp black eyes always fixated upon me as if he had been sent to keep me in line. It was more than a little unnerving how he seemed to pop up in the most unusual places.

"It's time we join the others," Kiril announced, looking up at the sun that was now directly overhead.

"If we must," I commented, "though what a lovely morning it has been."

"Aye," Feyla agreed, "but we'd best do what it was we came 'ere to do."

As we looked back up the hill from which we had come, the palace towers on top seemed very far away. Not knowing exactly which of the tangled streets to take, we determined that any path heading uphill was bound to get us to our destination. At last we emerged onto the broad thoroughfare we had traversed earlier, where a large crowd of people blocked our way.

Peering over the heads of the crowd, I saw a sight that made me sick with disgust. There, on a raised platform, were a dozen dwarves, bound in chains and looking downcast and dejected. Their eyes showed none of the fire I had seen in my two friends, Goodren and Hutto, as if their wills had been utterly broken. To make matters worse, this seemed to be some sort of slave auction. A man in gray called for bids as he brought one of the dwarves up before the audience.

"This one's strong indeed," he bellowed. "He'd make a fine dock 'and or p'rhaps 'e'd be good at shovellin' manure."

Amidst the sound of snickering at the auctioneer's jeering comment, several hands shot up in the air and murmurings about the dwarf spread through the crowd, most quite disparaging.

Incensed by the spectacle going on before me, I wished there was something I could do—anything!

As if reading my mind, Kiril grabbed me by the elbow. "It's no use, Miss Arwyn. Them what live in this city have become as cruel-'earted as 'im what lives in that palace."

I shook my head sadly and turned away. "Then come, I can no longer bear to watch, especially when there is nothing that can be done to right it."

We made our way toward the palace walls on an avenue lined with palm trees. A long line of censusgoers remained, yet we were relieved to discover that the group from Baeren Ford had made much progress toward the front and would only need to wait a little while longer.

Still, the line that led to the census area moved painfully slow in the heat of midafternoon. Nearby, the rowdy sounds of drunken revelry spilled out of a local tavern.

As we waited, the officials at the census barked orders at a girl of perhaps sixteen or seventeen every now and then. She would disappear for a few minutes and return to the officials with water or some other item such as food or ale in hand. I immediately felt pity for the girl dressed in little more than rags and dark hair with blondish streaks, lightened by the coastal sun. It was cropped short below her chin, making her look almost boyish. In the girl's eyes I could see despair and loneliness, as if the hapless streets of Maldimire had long been her home. Such a place was not for a child, and so young she was to be the maidservant of men who gave her little more than a grunt for her efforts.

"Step to the front o' the line!" a garbled voice called, breaking into my thoughts.

With my list in hand, I stepped forward toward a table where one of the census officials sat. He looked up and sneered as I walked toward him. "'Ave ye not heard?" he said in a rather unfriendly manner. "Ye're in the wrong place. The correct census location for *your* kind is Stone Harbour."

"I was under the impression that the location is based on one's residence and not one's kind," I answered.

"And where is it exactly ye hail from?"

"I am from Baeren Ford."

"Baeren Ford, is it? Now that's an odd place for an elf," he said in a tone that was none too friendly.

I bit my tongue to keep from responding in like manner.

The official gave me a most distasteful look. "Verra well," he said as he reached beneath the table and fumbled through a stack of rolled up papers. He unrolled on the table before him a large scroll that contained a crude map of the village of Baeren Ford. "Now, what be yer name?"

"Arwyn."

"Well, *Arwyn*, would ye be so kind as to show me exactly where on this map ye live."

I pointed to the plot of land that lay on the main road at the edge of the village. The official scribbled my name on the same spot, writing the word *elf* beside it in bold letters.

"And what be yer age?"

I was still not entirely sure of the answer.

"Eh, what does it matter?" the official said, waving his hand at me.

"What's age to an elf? Most o' yer type have lived so long ye've no idea how old ye are, anyhow."

My face remained expressionless.

"Now, do ye live at this location alone?"

"No."

"And who is it what lives with ye?"

"I live there with a woman named Loralon and her son, Amerigo."

The official lifted an eyebrow. "There's no man about the house, eh?"

"Her husband resides at the Guildenmoor Gate where he has been assigned guard duty."

"Why's an elf livin' in such an arrangement?"

"Is that question part of the census?" I asked.

The official merely grunted and continued his questioning. I found his manner most irritating and longed to be done with the whole ordeal and on my way. I had experienced enough of Maldimire and wished to return to the camp. Yet it took a while longer with the official before he was finally through reviewing my list of Baeren Ford residents, and I thought it odd that a census meant to make the taxation process less complicated asked no questions concerning the trades of my assignees.

At last the questioning was complete and I turned to go. I looked through the crowd for the other representatives from Baeren Ford and was glad to see the friendly face of Kiril, who had completed his own questioning and was now waiting to accompany me back to camp.

Suddenly a commotion broke out behind the line of census officials. I turned in time to see a rather large and scruffy dog shoot out from under a table in hot pursuit of a terrified cat. The dog crossed the path of the young girl I had been watching before, who lost her balance and sent a jug of water spilling all over the official I had been dealing with.

"Ye fool of a ghel!" he yelled as he sprang to his feet, striking her with the palm of his hand. The girl fell to the ground, cowering pitifully. "I'll teach ye to be clumsy!" With that he unstrapped the belt from around his waist and readied it to strike.

Don't get involved, I told myself. Yet when I looked into the eyes of the frightened girl, I knew this wasn't an option. So I stepped up and grabbed his arm. "Leave the girl alone!" I pleaded.

The official turned to see who had grabbed him, and he glared at me. Roughly he jerked his arm out of my grasp. "Begone with ye. The ghel needs to be taught a lesson."

"What has she done that you would treat her as you would an animal?" I said, stepping in between him and the young girl who remained on the ground.

By now a crowd had gathered to witness the scene. Red-faced, the official persisted. "This matter is o' no concern to you!"

"I will buy her, whatever you wish. Just please do not hurt her!" Out of the corner of my eye I could see several members of the Baeren Ford delegation trying frantically to get my attention and persuade me to let the matter rest.

"I'm warnin' ye—cross me no longer and allow me to do me job," the guard said as he raised his belt in the air.

Instinct took over and I fell to the ground, shielding the girl with my own body. "Then you will have to go through me," I said, even as tears welled in my eyes. I did not relish the idea of being beaten, especially by one so loathsome, but there was something about the girl that made me feel protective of her.

I closed my eyes and waited for the first blow as I held my breath, yet when no pain was forthcoming, I began to hear the sound of jeering coming from the crowd. I opened my eyes to see the official surrounded by a mob of censusgoers who had become incensed by his actions, and by his reluctance to strike, it appeared they were having an effect. With any luck, he would back down and let us both be gone.

"Ye've angered me enough. Now you and the ghel must both answer to me master."

"You would trouble your master with a matter such as this!" I protested. "What laws have been broken here, I ask you?"

"Interferin' with an officer o' the law," he barked. Suddenly he reached down and pulled the terrified girl to her feet.

"Leave the girl out of this," I pleaded. "She has harmed nothing other than your pride."

"Her actions were no accident. This waif of a ghel 'as been waitin' to seek vengeance since this mornin' when I refused to pay her for a loaf o' stale bread she delivered."

"'Ow was I to know 'twas stale?" the girl protested. "I didna taste it afore I give it to ye. And what 'appened now 'twas an accident, on me honor."

"Ye're nothin' but a wench. What do ye know of honor?"

"More than you," the girl mumbled.

"I've 'ad enough o' yer insolence . . . and yer's as well," he said, turning to me. "P'rhaps a meetin' with the law o' the land will teach ye to be more respectful."

A shocked murmur arose from the crowd. The law of the land rested with one person—Draigon, and a meeting with him almost certainly meant a trip to Dungard.

Suddenly chaos ensued. A second official stepped up and grabbed me by the arm. I turned to see a frantic Kiril edging his way toward me as I was led away. "Miss Arwyn, what shall we do?" he shouted.

The Healer of Guildenwood

"Here! Take my bag," I yelled, quickly tossing my knapsack to him. My purse I continued to cling to.

"Now ye've gone 'n done it!" he exclaimed.

By now Ingmar and several others from the Baeren Ford delegation had made their way to the edge of the crowd, watching helplessly as the two guards led the girl and me toward the palace. And with every step I took, I wondered if my impetuous nature had finally caught up with me.

CHAPTER 25

"I should have listened to Eliendor!" I wailed from my seat on the couch. "Oh, what have I done?"

The crowd parted in the wake of Draigon's lieutenants, who roughly thrust the girl forward toward the palace's outer walls. With me they were more restrained, yet the guard maintained a firm grip on my arm, and I wondered if there was an underlying fear of the elves that stayed him, a fear that fueled their hatred. The heavily guarded iron gates leading to the courtyard of the palace opened as we approached. Soon we were inside the palace walls and away from the noisy throng of curious onlookers who had gathered to see what they could of our fate.

Unwilling to show any hint of fear, I walked with my head held high. Yet inside I felt a pang of remorse for not having heeded Eliendor's warning. When had I become so brave . . . or so foolish?

As we approached the white outer towers of the Palace of Lords, I could see the courtyard was in a sad state of disarray. What were once bubbling fountains standing before the entrance were cracked and empty piles of stone. The long-neglected pavement on which we walked was littered with weeds that had managed to spring through cracks in the surface. Even the palace itself, white and full of splendor from a distance, was covered with pock marks of chipped paint and an occasional broken window, the remains of which lay ignored on the floor of the courtyard. I had heard stories of the palace in its days of glory and felt like weeping when I saw what once was so beautiful so neglected.

The official stopped at the large front portal of the bastion and rapped on it with a metal knocker. Within a matter of moments a small window inside the door opened and a pair of shifty eyes peered out. Though no words were spoken, the door slowly swung open and we all stepped into a dull gray interior room. With a loud *boom* the portal closed behind us, revealing the presence of three guards in the shadows behind the door.

I could see the look of fear on the young girl's face, and I tried to give her

The Healer of Guildenwood

a look of comfort as the two of us were led through another door and down a hallway where dingy-looking chandeliers hung lifelessly above. The once-beautiful carpets lining the hall had become aged and severely worn by years of abuse, and no decorations adorned the empty walls. Having stolen so much of the people's money for his own coffers, Draigon certainly had not used the spoils for his own comfort. In fact, there was no telling what satisfaction it brought him, other than the sadistic pleasure of having strong-armed his subjects into giving him all that they had.

At the end of the hall we walked up a flight of stairs to a landing where two heavily armed guards stood. They took one look at the census official and stood aside. Apparently, he was well-known about the palace.

We walked into the interior dome of the building, a vast round room that was surrounded by windows and eight doors leading from the dome, through corridors in the inner hollows of the huge buttresses, and into the octuplet of towers that surrounded the courtyard outside. On the far end of the room was a single raised chair, a throne of sorts, but it was empty. Another chair sat several steps down from it, and on that chair sat a man with ruthless dark eyes who stared at me from behind tendrils of curly, black hair.

"I bring two prisoners for the master," the census official announced.

"He is occupied at the moment with a matter of great importance," the man commented with a husky voice, not taking his eyes off me.

"Then we'll wait," our captor murmured. Off to one side of the large chamber was an inconspicuous door with two armed guards on either side. Muffled voices came from the other side, and they sounded angry.

"Do you take me for a fool, *Galaxa*, if that be your *real* name?" Draigon's voice evoked in my mind the image of his snakelike face. "I know your game, but you will know your place!"

"Are you really so threatened by me?" It was a smooth voice that answered him. And haughty. I glanced at our captors, yet neither seemed affected by the drama taking place on the other side of the door. Perhaps they could not make out what was being said.

"Take heed! Were it not for your obvious, er . . . talents, then you could just as easily find yourself in a compromising situation that the others would not take kindly to."

"You know you need me." Whoever he was, his voice practically dripped with arrogance! "*She* does not take issue with my involvement."

She? Who was *she*?

"Then you will go to her with the latest appraisal of our scheme, but mind you, I will *not* be a cuckold!" Draigon voice rose with emotion, such that made even his lieutenants glance at one another nervously.

"And yet my services are not without charge."

"Aye, you shall get your reward, and it shall be handsome. But may it be *quite* understood . . ." There was a pause as Draigon stressed each word for emphasis. "You shall *not* share her throne!"

My eyes widened and I glanced at the floor, thinking it best had I not been privy to such a conversation. My mind was reeling. Who was this *she*, and what sinister plan was Draigon concocting? I could only imagine that it had something to do with Dar Magreth, and fear gripped my heart. What Frondamein suspected must be true—that somehow Draigon was in league with Bensor's sworn enemy, Dar Magreth.

I felt trapped, panicked, yet there was no place to hide. What I had stumbled upon felt altogether corrupt, and I immediately regretted the actions I had taken that had landed me right into the presence of such wickedness.

Suddenly from the other side of the door, there came a choking sound, and I wondered if Draigon was strangling his visitor. Yet no one else appeared the least bit alarmed that perhaps it was *Draigon* who was being strangled.

After several breathless moments, the door creaked slowly open, and I froze as the most unexpected person stepped forth. Unexpected, because from all accounts he appeared to be a decrepit old man, bent over so that his face stared straight down to the floor, a gnarled old hand clasping a walking cane as if without it he would certainly fall. He wore a cloak of green, and his head was completely concealed under a hood. To have seen his face would have required that he twist his head toward the ceiling in a painful-looking contortion.

He shuffled past me slowly, and as he did I felt a chill travel down my spine, yet my eyes were curiously drawn to him as he crossed the chamber and disappeared out the door from which we had just come.

I turned to see that the census official had entered the small room, and that the door was closed once more.

"You dare to disturb me for such a thing!"

"But sire . . . an elf . . . Baeren Ford . . . quite insolent," the census official whispered urgently.

"Baeren Ford you say?"

"Aye."

In a matter of seconds, Draigon stormed through the door, eyes glazed with fury. "You!"

I had no choice but to be deferential. My freedom and that of the girl's depended upon it. "Please, sire, I meant no offense to your officer. I only tried to protect a defenseless girl from ill-treatment . . ."

"Silence!" he screeched. "How my officers conduct their affairs is not for you to meddle with. Now"—he glared at me—"did I not warn you to never cross me again?" Suddenly there came a knock from outside the door we had entered, and a guard stepped into the room. "Sire," he said, "a witness to the event in question has come forward."

I breathed a sigh of relief, expecting either Ingmar or Kiril to appear inside the door in our defense.

"Send him in," the man with the greasy black hair replied.

In an instant, the door was pushed aside, and the person I saw standing there made me feel as though I would faint. It was not one of my friends after all, and the sight of his infuriating smirk was almost more than I could bear.

"'Ello, love," Hamloc said smugly, with a triumphant smile upon his face.

I fought to maintain my composure despite the ironic turn of events, determined to keep my emotions hidden.

"The man says 'e witnessed the 'ole event from the front door of 'is tavern," the guard said. "E'en says he knew th' elven wench back in Baeren Ford."

"'Tis true," Hamloc said. "She's a wild one, she is . . . quite the troublemaker."

Draigon fingered the hair of his goatee, his crafty eyes surveying me as Hamloc spoke. "Tell me more," he said.

"She's not to be trusted, that's for sairtain," Hamloc continued. "Associates with all manner o' strange folk, e'en sorcerers."

"Sorcerers, you say?"

"Aye, them what knows magic 'n talks t' animals."

To my surprise, Draigon's whole manner abruptly changed, and I could have sworn I detected fear in his eyes. "'From the shadow of Arnuin's Hold,'" he murmured.

Where had I heard that saying before? Why, from Eliendor himself on the day we had met! But what did it mean?

"Tell me more about this, er, sorcerer," Draigon said, turning to Hamloc.

"He is no sorcerer," I interrupted. "He is nothing more than a lonely old man who knows a few simple sleights of hand."

"And what o' you?" Hamloc said, pointing at me accusingly. "She brought a boy back from the dead. Saw it with me own eyes."

Draigon froze. Silence descended upon the chamber, and even the guards standing there appeared tense as their gaze darted to their master, whose brain was working feverishly behind eyes that had widened with fear. Slowly he turned to me and, without a word, encircled me studiously as if he were on the brink of discovering the answer to a mystery. Never had I felt more at risk as hatred oozed from his crazed eyes, and I could feel my heart pounding in my throat.

At last, Draigon stopped right in front of me, chest heaving with rage. "Who are you!" he shouted, startling everyone present as the intensity in his voice echoed loudly throughout the cavernous room. Even Hamloc appeared surprised that I had managed to elicit such wrath. "How dare you trifle with me!" he continued with the same intensity.

The harshness in his voice rang in my ears, and I fought to keep tears from welling in my eyes. "I have no idea what you mean," I whispered.

"Do you not?" he demanded. "Or do you plot even now to displace me?"

"Displace you?" I was completely bewildered. What madness was going on in his fevered mind?

"Sire." The man sitting next to the throne stood and walked toward his master. "Sire, it is not a woman you seek. The prophecy speaks clearly of a man."

The prophecy? Was that what this was all about?

"Is that what you think?" I asked, quite alarmed at the implication.

"The trouble is, prophecies are not always what they seem," Draigon said, turning his attention back to me with a fierce gleam in his eyes.

This was dangerous. I had to somehow deflect it to something else. Then I looked at Hamloc, quietly gloating.

"If it is the prophecy that concerns you, perhaps you would do well to pay mind to one who has actually threatened to challenge the Sword," I said accusingly, pointing to Hamloc.

The taverner startled, eyes wide, and he backed away guiltily as if trying to escape. All eyes were suddenly upon him. "Nay!" he said, shaking his head. "I swear it is not so!"

"He told me he meant to gather a party and travel to Emraldein," I said.

"Is this true, *boy*?" Draigon was practically seething.

By the way Hamloc was cowering, it was clear that things were not going as he had hoped.

"I . . . I didna mean it! Said it to impress this annoyin' woman who thinks she's better than the lot of us."

"'Tis true. This man is no threat," said the man with the curly, black hair, husky voice, and cruel eyes. "He is a buffoon who has nothing better to do than tell bloated tales at tavern." The look of sheer terror on Hamloc's face melted into one of indignation. "And what is the more, he no longer hails from Baeren Ford."

"Indeed," Draigon said, thoughtfully rubbing his goatee. "Yet, perhaps it has been too long since we have apprised that fair village of its men who have come of age." He then turned to the dark-haired man who appeared to be his second-in-command. "Halthrax, have one of your lieutenants gather a contingent to leave for Baeren Ford on the morrow. Tell them to be swift. And have this man tell you where you may find this so-called sorcerer," he said, gesturing to Hamloc. "I want you to question him. And for that matter, find any young man who has come of age in that village and make of him a spectacle. We want to make it quite clear what will happen should one of them take a notion to test fate."

"No!" I protested, but Draigon ignored me.

"And I want guards stationed on the road into Carona. Tell them to kill *anyone* who attempts to pass," he said, giving a glance of warning to both Hamloc and me.

"What of the elf?" said Halthrax with a gleam in his eyes. "Will you now condemn her to live out the remainder of her long, *long* life in the dungeons below?"

I gulped. Draigon turned to me and was about to speak when he stopped suddenly. His gaze trailed off as a twisted smile crossed his lips. "Nay, I am certain our friend from Baeren Ford would like a front row seat to the designs we have in store."

What? Did he mean for me to witness the cruelty and intimidation of my friends and neighbors that would come about because of this whole unfortunate situation? Or was there something even more evil at work? And what did that sinister-looking old man have to do with it?

"And yet," he continued thoughtfully, "lest you have any ideas of warning your friends, I cannot risk you having the advantage of a head start. Therefore, you and the girl shall be detained a night in Dungard."

"No!" the girl cried in terror. The guard who held her arm tightened his grip as she struggled against him.

"Please, let the girl go. It is I who has angered you. She has done no wrong," I pleaded.

"You will both go, and perhaps seeing how your disregard for authority affects others will teach you to hold your tongue," Draigon said.

"I demand to know what crime I have committed," I said.

"Your crime is that of disrespecting an officer of the law," he answered.

"What law? It is your officers who have no respect for a just law, tyrannizing the people of this land into submission," I said, forgetting any remnant of fear that I harbored within. "If this is your 'law' then it leaves much to be desired."

Incensed, Draigon walked threateningly toward me, stopping inches from me. His eyes fairly smoldered with anger and his breath was hot upon my face. "And just who is the ruler here, you or I?"

Then why is your throne not at Emraldein? I dared not say it or I would have certainly received a death sentence. As it was, I knew I had already crossed the line when all the guards present visibly tensed. Out of the corner of my eye I could even see Hamloc's eyes widen at my daring. "Why do you hate me so?" I mumbled, expecting no answer to be forthcoming. I could hardly expect such a man to harbor any amount of real introspection.

And yet, his eyes remained fixated upon mine, and in that brief moment I caught a glimpse into his soul, down, hidden far beneath layers of anger, hatred, and betrayal. There I saw the flickering image of a woman with light brown hair, a woman who had broken his heart, or perhaps only his ego. I still could find no evidence that Draigon had ever truly loved anyone or anything.

I remembered what Frondamein told me once, long ago, about the rumor that Draigon had been rejected by an elven lass. "I am not the one who scorned you," I whispered.

It seemed Draigon wavered for an instant, and then he tore his gaze from me, seething with anger. "Begone from my sight, you miserable elven wench, and pray I do not change my mind regarding your sentence," he said sharply. "But hear me now, Arwyn of Baeren Ford. If you ever cross me again, and if my guards ever find you attempting to cross the Silvendell in some misguided attempt at valor, then you *will* find your situation in Dungard a permanent one!"

Our two captors grabbed the girl and me once more, and as I was being led out, I glanced at Hamloc and could see that the smug look had returned to his face. The look on the girl's face was one of sheer terror. As we entered a dark flight of stairs, I leaned over and whispered, "Take courage, for we will be freed tomorrow!" I tried to be brave for the girl's sake, yet it sobered me to think that our freedom was altogether dependent on the wiles of a tyrant.

"'Ow kin ye be so sure?" she whimpered.

"Quiet!" one of our captors demanded.

The guards pushed us into a small courtyard and to the doorway of one of the outer domed buildings. "Look upon sunlight for what may be your last time for a while," my captor sneered.

I glanced up at the sky where a large black bird floated on the breeze and then alighted on one of the buttresses. The uncanny way Talthos had been able to keep up with my movements was more than I could fathom.

We were led through the doorway and down a flight of stairs to a sloping passageway lined with torches. The very walls seemed to close in on us the farther we walked.

Eventually the passageway opened into immense blackness, and we found ourselves standing on a precipice and gazing deep into what appeared to be the throat of a monstrous beast. And if the chasm were its throat, then we were heading directly into its dark belly.

CHAPTER 26

"I do not believe that even the Underworld itself could be a darker bastion of misery and despair than what I have found under the streets of Maldimire."

Down and down we descended into the chasm. One misstep and we would have surely fallen to our deaths. Still we descended the winding path lit sporadically with dull torchlight, passing a landing that led into a rather large guardroom and the first level of prison cells. Our descent, however, continued farther down into the darkness below. After passing the second tier of Dungard, it was clear that Draigon intended for me to be imprisoned in the bottommost level, as far below the city of Maldimire as one could get.

It was difficult to tell exactly how many minutes had passed or how many steps we had traversed when at last we reached the very bottom of the huge staircase. At the bottom of the chasm, we walked through an opening and were welcomed with a blast of foul-smelling air. As we entered, I was brushed by a guard who was most definitely a Gargaloc by his hulking manner and profusion of hair. Shocked, I shrank away as he eyed me. It was not his appearance that was most shocking but the thought that Draigon was actively employing these beasts so detested by most Bensorians. How many more were working for him?

We passed through yet another guardroom where a dozen or so guards loitered about in dilapidated wooden chairs. Discarded bones from countless meals lay in piles scattered about the room, and the stench of rotten meat and stale ale permeated the area. Such conditions, even for guards, were deplorable.

From beyond the guardroom I could detect the smell of the sea mingled with the stench of the city's sewage system, much of which emptied into the caves below, and somewhere beyond the thick dungeon walls the muffled sound of the pounding surf murmured.

Most of the guards barely looked up as we entered the room, while some lay crumpled on the bare floor in a drunken stupor. Only two guards stood at rapt attention, and there we stopped for a moment at what appeared to be some sort of inspection station.

"Check the elf's bag," a guard bellowed. In an instant, my purse was snatched from me and a rough-looking man fingered through its contents.

"Nothin' in 'ere but some packets o' dried leaves and such."

"Tea bags," I quipped. "A souvenir of Maldimire."

"Then ye'll be disappointed to know there be no tea time in Dungard," he growled.

Having found nothing more condemning, the guard shoved the purse back into my hands, at which time he spotted the ring upon my finger.

"Eh, what's this?" he said, giving my hand a jerk. "A pretty trinket, indeed." He laughed, revealing a toothless smirk, his putrid breath permeating the area.

I tried to wrestle my hand from his, but to no avail.

"Take it off!"

"No!" Panic set in. I instinctively tried to recoil my hand, an action that was met with a tightened grip that made me cry out in pain.

"I said, take it off!"

There was determination in his eyes—and there was nothing I could do but acquiesce.

I could feel a lump of anguish welling at the base of my throat, feeling as though it would strangle me as I slipped my precious ring—my only link to that other life of so long ago—off my finger, and I wondered if I was indeed giving up the one thing that would have somehow been the key to ever returning there.

I could but watch helplessly as the guard eyed the ring in the torchlight and proceeded to slip it into his pocket, when another guard who looked to be his superior, walked up and grabbed his arm. "The master gets fairst choice o' the prisoners' spoils," he said, grabbing my ring and tossing it carelessly into a crate full of belt buckles, pocket knives, ladies' ear bobs, and a pocket watch or two.

Knowing I would never see my treasured ring again, tears welled in my eyes as my captor led me away roughly. It was a terrible, unexpected blow. Oh, why had I been so foolish?

The girl and I were about to pass through a low-hanging archway when, out of the corner of my eye, I caught a glimpse of a lone dwarf standing meekly in the corner. Haggard he looked, wearing nothing but a dirty green hat, a tattered tunic, and pair of trousers held loosely on his emaciated body with a strand of twine. On his feet a ragged pair of shoes appeared as though they would fall apart at any time. The dwarf looked up as we passed by, and it seemed his dull, languid eyes brightened for a moment.

"Back to work with ye!" a guard said sharply.

The dwarf made a slight jerking motion as if he had been shaken back into reality and almost dropped the empty tray he held in his hands. Quickly he turned to retreat down a narrow passageway, yet before disappearing into the darkness he stopped and turned to look at us once more.

The girl and I were led through a doorway and down a sloping ramp to a narrow canal at the bottom. The air was heavy and damp with the musty odor of places that have never seen the light of day.

Several small rowboats sat in the water, waiting to take prisoners to their cells. A toothless boatman looked up and grinned, a gesture that was entirely incongruent with our dismal surroundings. But then I thought that being in such a dark place all the time with no exposure to the natural light of the sun was enough to make anyone go mad. Eyeing him dubiously, we climbed aboard and sat side by side on the plank in front of our escort, our backs to him.

"The old man in cell forty-seven what died this mornin', 'is body's been disposed of?"

"Aye!" The boatman cackled.

"Then take 'em there straightaway!"

"Aye! Aye!" the boatman replied as if he were accompanying us to a garden party.

Pushing away from the quay, the boat slipped into the middle of the canal and began its journey down a dark, torch-lit tunnel, fighting against the ebb and flow of the current as it surged in through the caves at the bottom of the cliff.

"Welcome to Dungard," the boatman said as he carelessly dripped water from his oar down the backs of both the girl and me. "'Tis a mighty ugly place for such a pretty lady!" Suddenly I felt this vile man touch my hair with his dirty fingers.

Instinct took over. I turned, quick as a flash, and maneuvered his arm so that he yelped in pain. "You would do well not to touch me," I warned, staring him in the eye. Still distraught over my stolen ring, I was in no mood to be trifled with.

The boatman shrank back and I let him go. "Try 'n make a pairson feel welcome," he muttered, tending once more to his rowing.

The boat emerged through the tunnel and into a watery passageway beneath a cavernous ceiling, passing miniscule cells carved into the stone on either side. Cruel iron bars stood between the canal and the prisoners, sometimes as many as three and four to a cell.

As the boat drifted by, a wave of silence spread along the channel as men, and an occasional group of women, all dressed in rags, peered at us from behind iron bars. And then there were those who sat in their dungeons unseeing; delirious victims forgotten for years by those above, victims who now lived within the solitude of their tortured minds.

I regarded the prisoners silently and respectfully, seeing in their eyes that these were not criminals at all but regular Bensorians who, like me, had fallen prey to the whims of Draigon and his henchmen.

For a while longer the boat slid through the canal into an adjoining labyrinth of underground waterways, all lined with cells. The boatman hummed a silly tune to himself, at times stopping to laugh at some twisted thought that entered his warped mind. At last he steered the skiff beside a cell that lay empty. Unsteadily the boat rocked in the water as the boatman stepped onto the stone quay and tied his skiff to one of the bars. I could have easily taken him out right there on the quay, stolen his keys, and made off with his boat . . . but then what? Become lost in the bowels of Dungard until captured and left to rot forever? No, I would take my chances on release.

"Make yerself at 'ome me dears, make yerself at 'ome," the boatman guffawed as the girl and I climbed out of the boat and into the cell. "And I wouldna take a mind to try and escape. There's bars at th' entrance to these caves and 'ungry sharks on th' other side." With that, he slammed the gate shut with a loud clank, locked it, and climbed back into his boat. He was about to row away when he stopped. "Dinner'll be served shortly. Would ye prefer the roast lamb or the quail?" He cackled.

Glad to be rid of the boatman and at last alone, I immediately sat down on the floor of the cell next to the girl, who had put her head between her knees. "Please forgive me," I said, "but I could not bear to see that guard treat you as he did."

"'Tis nothin' new, miss. They treat me as they wish." She sniveled. The girl rubbed her runny nose on the sleeve of her blouse and looked up at me with tear-filled eyes. "But no one's e'er paid me any mind, let alone stood up for me."

"What is your name?"

"Me name's Rumalia."

"And I am Arwyn. Tell me, have you a family?"

A shadow of sadness crossed her face. "Nay. The woman what raised me died a year ago. When I was but a child she found me wanderin' alone in the streets o' Maldimire. Out o' pity she took me in and let me live above 'er spice shop near the river. She provided a roof o'er me 'ead, and there were times she gave me a kind word." Rumalia stopped speaking for a moment, and I could see the tears glistening in her dark eyes.

"Yet she took too much to the bottle and would leave me to run the shop on me own for sometimes days at a time. Took sick to the bed a year ago, probably from too much drink. Left the shop to her nephew, whom I've ne'er fancied. He's a stern man who's 'ad little use for the likes o' me. Still, 'e lets me live above the shop as long as I pay rent and tend to things whilst he's away. Most o' the time I'm left to fend for meself on the streets, tryin' to earn a livin' as best I kin."

"That is no way for a girl to live," I replied, shaking my head. "And what of your real parents?"

"I've no memory of 'em. The woman who took me in said she tried in vain to find 'em. 'Tis like they disappeared—or didna want me."

"Poor, dear girl, left all alone in the world," I said thoughtfully. "No one your age should have to endure such a life."

Rumalia shrugged. "Aye, but what kin I do? 'Tis me lot . . . I suppose. But now there's this."

"Draigon will free us tomorrow—I know he will," I said, trying to sound reassuring.

Her tears had begun to flow in earnest. "Do ye really think so?"

"Yes, I do."

"I hope ye be right, for if not then I'd gladly face a dozen sharks than to live out me days in this place," she said defiantly.

The two of us grew silent for a moment. Across the waterway a fellow prisoner, a woman with long, matted hair, sat rocking back and forth feverishly, her vacant eyes staring into space. She had obviously been imprisoned for a long while. The sight of such an impoverished soul was almost more than I could bear.

Rumalia shifted her position uncomfortably to avoid looking at her. "Miss," Rumalia said hesitantly, "are ye an elf?"

"There are those who seem to think that I am," I replied, not sure how else to respond.

"When I was a child I remember seein' elves in Maldimire from time to time, but not o' late. What brings an elf such as yerself 'ere, to this forsaken place?"

"For the census, the same as everyone else."

"But I thought all th' elves 'ad moved north."

I sighed. "It is true that few, if any, now live in Guilden. I am perhaps the only one."

"Are ye not lonely, bein' so far from yer kin?"

I suddenly grew pensive. "Yes," I finally admitted. "I do long for something else at times. Yet the people I live with are very kind and have become to me like family."

"Then ye are far luckier than I," my cellmate murmured, her voice trailing off as a faint flickering coming from the tunnel caught her attention.

The light continued to grow, as did the sound of two oars splashing in the water. In a moment a tiny rowboat appeared in view, captained by the dwarf I had spotted earlier. A lantern sat on the bow of his boat, and he carried with him a large sack and several pitchers of water. The tiny boat stopped in front of our cell, and the dwarf went about the task of reaching into the sack and retrieving two small loaves of bread and one small potato, which he placed on a wooden plate. Trying as best he could to maintain his balance as a surge of water suddenly rushed into the channel, the dwarf put the plate on the ledge before the cell and unsteadily filled two wooden cups full of water. He then placed the cups beside the plate of food and proceeded to climb out of the boat and onto the ledge himself.

"Yer dinner," he said sheepishly. "The potato I stole from one o' the guards. Thought ye'd be needin' more than bread."

Rumalia wasted no time reaching through the iron bars to receive the plate. She hungrily devoured her loaf of bread but deferentially left the potato for me until I insisted she have it.

"We thank you for your kindness," I replied to the dwarf, pinching off small bites from my own stale loaf and eating them in a very deliberate manner.

"'Tis nothin', Miss," he blushed. "I always try an' do a little extra for the newcomers—takes away a little o' the horror ye feel when fairst ye arrive in the 'Dark Mouth.'"

The dwarf sat down on the narrow wharf as if he intended to stay for a while, perhaps to dispel a little of the loneliness I saw in his eyes.

"I'd like to sit for a while, if I may," he said. "'Tis better to be here in the passageways than back in the guard room, anythin' to be away from *them*."

"You are a prisoner here as well, aren't you?" I said.

"Aye," the dwarf replied. "Been here but a few months. Put me to work right away, they did, but I suppose 'tis better than rottin' away in a cell. I've the freedom to move about at least, and mostly they pay me no mind as long as I see to me duties." The dwarf glanced down the dark tunnel and then shuffled closer to the bars. "Tell me, what crime have ye committed that Draigon could justify sendin' ye to this forsaken place?"

"She did nothin' but try 'n save me from the wrath of 'is soldier," Rumalia piped in. "'Tis I who was at fault for makin' 'im mad in the fairst place."

"You cannot be blamed for the ill nature of another," I said gently.

"'Tis true. Them what work for the likes o' Draigon have little regard for anyone else, especially those whom they consider dispensable," the dwarf said with a faraway look in his eyes. "They'd not e'en stop short o' mairder."

"Tell me, what brought you to this miserable place?" I asked curiously.

A silent tear ran down the dwarf's cheek and into the dark, coarse hair of his beard. "One o' me own was killed—brutally mairdered in the Andains by one o' Draigon's guards. A fine young dwarf he was, Anglin was his name. The rest of us attempted an uprisin', but alas, most were either killed or captured and brought here to Maldimire to become slaves. Yet slaves here or slaves in th' Andains, what does it matter? 'Tis all the same."

My heart started beating faster as a curious idea formed in my mind. "What is your name?" I asked anxiously.

"Me name's Froilin."

"And I am Arwyn and this is Rumalia."

Rumalia offered a weak smile as the dwarf tipped his hat to us. "Froilin, I believe you may know two dwarves by the name of Hutto and Goodren," I whispered.

The dwarf's eyes brightened. "Ye're acquainted with those two rascals!" he said excitedly.

"That I am. Following their escape, they managed to make their way into the woods of Baeren Ford. That is where I found them, hungry and quite frightened."

"Against all hope: I feared they were dead! Was led to believe as such, I was."

"Nay, they are very much alive, but are in hiding until such a time comes when they can return to the mountains."

"Thanks be t' Omni! Such news puts me troubled heart to rest."

Eyes wide with wonder, Rumalia listened quietly while Froilin and I spoke of our mutual friends, the dwarf growing ever more excited upon hearing of their fortunate situation until a loud cawing noise from the passageway made us both startle. As it grew louder, a black thing appeared in the darkness and alighted on the landing next to the dwarf.

"Talthos!" I said.

"Ye know this bird?" asked Froilin.

"You might say he is a friend."

The clever raven then proceeded to jump through the bars of the cell and onto my index finger where he made all sorts of clicking sounds and caws. Froilin and Rumalia sat watching curiously as I listened intently to the bird. After several moments, Talthos grew silent.

"The raven entered Dungard through a secret passageway that leads north out to the river," I said in broken dwarvish, suddenly wishing I had mastered more of the dwarves' ancient language. How much more freely we could talk were we not concerned with eavesdropping ears. "It is too small for a grown man to pass through, but a dwarf . . . a dwarf could easily make it. And there are no guards anywhere around."

"A secret passageway?" Froilin whispered, scratching his head. "These caves are indeed deep, yet I dared not explore 'em too completely for fear o' what I might find . . . and for fear o' what they'd do to me if I were found snoopin' about. But a way to th' outside? What I'd not give to see trees again and the blue o' the sky."

"Perhaps you shall," I said thoughtfully.

"Why, ye're not suggestin' I . . ."

"I may suggest it, yet the path you take is for you to decide."

A broad smile crept onto the dwarf's face, and his eyes flitted about feverishly as he considered the possibilities. All about us the din of the surging sea ebbing and flowing through the passageways muffled the sound of our voices, yet we remained careful to speak as quietly as possible lest any enemy ears were about. "How I've longed for such a miracle! But do I dare t' act upon it?" he said. "And if I were to find the way out, what then? I'd be trapped by the river and me guards would eventually come and find me."

"Not if they were too asleep to notice your absence," I whispered. Froilin regarded me curiously as I rummaged through my purse. The few coins I had left were noticeably missing, no doubt now lying deep in the pocket of the guard who had searched it. "Ah, hops, lemon balm and valerian root, good for many uses, not the least of which is inducing sleep. Good for weary travelers and for making our captors fall into quite a deep slumber."

"Bless be! Ne'er would I have thought escape possible from this place!"

"And yet there are risks," I warned.

"Aye, but to risk livin' out the rest o' me days in such a place—that is a far greater risk," Froilin confided. "But what o' the river? I'm dreadful afraid o' water. I canna swim. The guards torment me about it often, threatenin' to capsize me boat and leave me for fish food should I get out o' line."

"Rumalia and I shall be released tomorrow," I said hopefully. "I will then make to the river and find a way for you to be brought across."

"And then?"

"Then we will rejoin my group and return as swiftly as possible to Baeren Ford, where you will be reunited with your friends," I suggested. "Rumalia, you may join us as well."

The young girl's eyes brightened. "Retairn with ye to Baeren Ford? Leave me home 'ere?"

"This doesn't sound like much of a home for you," I said compassionately. "You may come and stay with me until we find you a more permanent arrangement, that is, unless you would rather continue to live alone among the filth and corruption here in Maldimire."

Rumalia's response came instantly. "E'en if I have but a bed o' straw to sleep on and nothin' but bread and water the rest o' me days, I'd go with ye!"

"Very well, then. Omni willing, our plan will work, and we will all be free by tomorrow night," I said. I then turned to the raven, who had been hopping around the floor of the cell in search of any old crumbs of food. "Talthos, show Froilin to the exit and then return straightaway to your master. Tell him to be wary. Draigon has sent his henchmen to question him and to make mischief for the young men of Baeren Ford, though for what reason I do not know."

The raven gave a loud caw and then hopped through the iron bars and onto the bow of Froilin's boat.

"I'll sairch for the secret passage and retairn later to tell ye what I find," Froilin said.

Rumalia and I watched as the little boat disappeared into the dark tunnel beyond; then she turned and looked at me sidelong. "Who are ye that ye've no fear o' Draigon, ye talk to the raven, and make a habit o' comin' to the rescue o' those in need?"

I thought on it for a moment before I responded. "No one of consequence."

Suddenly we found ourselves all alone in that forbidding place, listening to the occasional sounds of tortured cries that echoed through the deep labyrinth of caves. In fissures that had been carved into the walls, candles slowly decayed to nothing but stumps, signaling the end of the day. Were it not for the waning candlelight and the changing tide in the channels, there would be no way for the prisoners to know the time of day.

Trying our best to ignore the anguished sounds that came from nearby as well as the cool drafts that now blasted through the caves, Rumalia and I, after checking for vermin, settled in as best we could on a pile of straw strewn upon the stone floor at the back of our cell. As Rumalia lay curled up on the straw, I talked for what seemed like hours about the village of Baeren Ford, describing in great detail the colors of the woodland flowers, the vastness of the windswept fields above the village, and the quaint cottages that dotted the landscape.

There was something in me that felt a strange connection to the girl. I had felt it when first I noticed Rumalia taking orders from the census officials. Yet it was more than pity that had moved me so. In the deep recesses of my mind, the girl reminded me of a past existence, an age of awkwardness and uncertainty I had once known long ago.

It was difficult to tell how much time had passed when Rumalia eventually succumbed to an uneasy sleep. Across the channel the woman in the opposite cell sat huddled in the corner, hardly aware of anything around her, and I hoped that even in her deranged state she had not overheard my earlier conversation with the dwarf.

I sat with my back against the wall, listening as a strange silence fell upon the prison. And then, faintly at first, an oddly comforting sound grew and echoed throughout Dungard. It was the sound of singing, and though it did not reach a high volume, it was strong and resolute.

> Lo! A star shines brightly, a beacon in the night,
> Brightest in the heavens, giving hope and light;
> Burning truth and beauty in the hearts of all,
> Bensor's sons and daughters, light to us befall.

> O Elwei!
> Fairest among women,
> Now fairest of all stars,
> Your heir to us, pray send.
> Shine down from heav'n afar

> O'er forest and meadow and castle by the sea,
> You look upon your Bensor and remember its glory.
> Send us now our ruler, who the Sword will wield,
> Restore to us your kingdom, truth and light to yield.

I wept silently, listening to the unlikely chorus of lost and forgotten souls, until I realized that these poor creatures, though drowning in despair around them, were not completely without hope.

Still sitting upright against the wall, I slipped in and out of a restless sleep riddled with questions raised by my encounter with Draigon. As if he and his minion, Halthrax weren't enough to give me shivers, the memory of my brief encounter with the mysterious old man on his way to some sinister errand plagued me with nightmares during my long, restless night.

And then there was Draigon's preposterous notion that I somehow had designs on the Sword of Emraldein. How could he think such a thing? I would have to be a fool to step foot anywhere near Emraldein Castle—or to even imagine that the prophecy concerning the Sword had anything to do with me.

CHAPTER 27

*"As the minutes drip by like wax oozing from a candle, I'm beginning
to wonder if perhaps we have been left to rot in this forsaken place."*

———◆———

Several hours passed before I heard the sound of a boat sloshing through the water. It was Froilin, and he stopped to replace the burned-out candle in the wall with a new one before continuing on through the channel. I waited breathlessly as he stopped in front of our cell and climbed out of his boat and onto the quay. I rose to position myself more closely to him so that we would not be obliged to speak with raised voices.

"Found the passage, I did!" Froilin announced excitedly. "E'en crawled through it and went outside where I sat on a rock beside the river for a time. Ne'er before 'ave I so enjoyed the feel of a cool breeze upon me cheek or the sight of a star-filled night."

"Could you tell where you were on the river?"

"About a half-mile upstream from the bridge, at a place where the buildin's grow sparse on th' opposite shore. There's a small cleft at the bottom o' the cliff and a small tree growin' from a crack in the rocks what shelters the openin' from eyes above."

"Then you will not be far from our camp," I whispered. "Tomorrow, after we are released, wait until the early evening and place the herbs into the guards' drinks. The hops can go directly into ale. Do they drink tea?"

"Only when there's a draft in the caves, which is often this time o' year."

"Then we will hope for a cold spell. Take the lemon balm and valerian root and tie it up in a piece of cloth and boil it in a pot of water. There is enough here to make them fall asleep quickly and for a long while. Make sure you adequately dispose of the herbs, then make your way to the river's edge under cloak of night. Take with you a lighted candle with which to signal, and we will find a way to get to you."

"There's a small cavern leadin' to the passage where the water surges in through a narrow openin', makin' entry a treacherous task. Why, I had a time in the goin' and comin'—nearly busted me skull on the ceilin'. Makes for a churnin' underground lake, and if it doesna claim me fairst, I could capsize me boat there and set me hat afloat for good measure, and they'd consider me as good as dead," Froilin said in a hushed tone.

"And by the time they discover your boat, you will hopefully be halfway to Baeren Ford."

"Aye." Froilin smiled, hardly able to contain his excitement. "But if ye dunna see me light tomorrow evenin', then ye must retairn to yer 'ome without me and send me regards to Goodren and Hutto. Until then I must tend to me duties, lest they come a-searchin' for me sooner." With that the dwarf turned and climbed back into his boat.

"Fare thee well, my friend, until we meet again on the banks of the Silvendell," I said.

Froilin took hold of his oars and started to paddle away. "Aye, 'til we meet again."

In the depths of Dungard, time stood still. How anyone could bear a week there, let alone several years, was more than I could imagine. In the hours that followed my last meeting with Froilin, I resumed a restless sleep. Only one guard patrolled the channel by night, and I was only aware of his presence on one occasion when the sound of his passing boat stirred me from my slumber.

When we could escape no longer to the blissful state of sleep, Rumalia and I nervously paced the floor, not daring to consider the possibility that we would not be released that day. With every hour that passed, I wondered if our chances for freedom were dwindling and how we could use the information regarding the secret passage to perhaps help us escape if need be. But I remembered what Draigon said about saving me for something having to do with his "plan," and even though the veiled meaning was sinister, it offered some hope of being released.

The candles set in the walls had burned down to three quarters their original size when at last a boat docked beside our cell. The same boatman who had brought us there the day before had returned. Despite his annoying manner, we were nevertheless glad to see him.

"It's yer lucky day, that it is," he said as he fumbled with his ring of keys and feigned almost dropping them into the water. "Gave ye a start, didna I?" He laughed obnoxiously. With a turn of the key, the cell door swung open, and we filed out and into the boat, relieved to be on our way. "'Tis not often Draigon'll release a prisoner so soon. 'E must've taken a fancy to ye."

"That is certainly doubtful," I muttered.

The guard continued his foolish chatter as the boat made its way through the channel. As the skiff sloshed its way along, I looked up and noticed that dozens of prisoners were lined up against the bars of their cells, watching us intently as we passed. Tears filled my eyes as I met their gaze, knowing that many would not live to see the light of day again. If only I could tell them that they would not be forgotten, that I would not forget them.

At last the boat neared the dock that led up to the guardroom. Rumalia and I disembarked and walked onto the quay.

"We 'ope ye've enjoyed yer stay at our 'umble establishment." The boatman chortled. "Do come back 'n see us again!"

Without looking back, we proceeded into the guardroom accompanied by two burly men. Out of the corner of my eye, I caught a glimpse of Froilin standing in the shadows. For a second I regarded him. With a subtle nod, he turned his head and slipped away.

Then I eyed the crate which held all the items stolen from the prisoners, and my anger flared. "I demand my ring back!"

"You *demand* it, eh?" the guard mocked. "And just who do ye think ye are, *yer majesty,* to demand anythin'?"

"You have no right to keep it!"

"We keeps what we wants!" he said as he jerked my arm roughly. "Now get movin'!"

There was no point in fighting it. My ring was lost to me forever. I could but comply and be grateful that I would at least regain my freedom.

The ascent to the surface was long and arduous. As we passed the other two levels of Dungard, I wondered how many people were imprisoned in those walls. It saddened me to consider how the city of Maldimire, so beautiful from a distance, could harbor so many foul secrets.

At last we reached the top of the chasm with only the long sloping tunnel still to go. Our hearts quickened when we saw daylight at the very end. Only a few more steps and we would be free.

In a few moments, we stepped out, blinking into the bright sunlight of late afternoon. Shading our eyes as best we could after being in darkness for the past day, the two of us were led around the northern end of the palace and across the courtyard to the front gate.

"Ye'd best be on yer way," said one of our escorts sternly. "And when ye go, heed this warnin' from Draigon himself. Cross him again and ye'll find Dungard yer permanent residence—or wairse."

I turned my head indignantly and walked away with Rumalia by my side. "'E sounded serious," Rumalia whispered.

"I've no doubt he was," I answered bitterly, "yet somehow, some way, Draigon will receive his justice in the end. Of that I am sure." I turned and smiled at the girl. "Come, let us gather your belongings. The sooner we leave this city, the better."

With that, we made our way into the crowd of censusgoers and down the main street toward the river. There we passed by a tavern that sat on the edge of the census hubbub. Inside I caught a glimpse of Hamloc, laughing and passing out mugs of ale to a throng of taverngoers who had filed in for an evening of debauchery. I turned away in disgust.

"'Ow do ye know Hamloc there?" Rumalia asked curiously.

"I'm afraid it is a long story, one that is best saved for later."

"I'm not fond of 'im meself, nor 'e o' me. Showed up a couple years ago, 'e did. I see 'im from time to time when I help out at the tavern. Flairts with all the pretty ladies but 'as no use for a plain ghel like me."

I looked at Rumalia and sighed. "Mark my word, you are much better off without his attention."

Rumalia led me away from the main thoroughfare and down a side street to the very end. There sat a small spice shop on a cliff overlooking the river. As we entered, a long, lanky man with a red face appeared from a back room.

"Where've ye been, ghel?" he demanded when he saw Rumalia. "I've been tendin' the shop alone for hours. 'Ow dare ye leave me in a lairch!"

Rumalia ignored the man and climbed up the staircase in the back of the shop.

"I'm warnin' ye! Ye'll be out on the streets for good if ye dunna watch yer step. There's plenty a young ghel who'd like yer situation."

Rumalia's head appeared at the top of the stairs. "What situation is that? I dunna call bein' worked to the bone so's I kin eat 'n 'ave a roof o'er me head an attractive situation. Not to mention the way ye speak to me as though I were a common dog on the streets."

The man turned to me apologetically. "Forgive me, miss. It's 'ard to find good 'elp these days. I'll be with ye in a minute."

With belongings tied up together in a bedsheet, Rumalia climbed back down the stairs.

"And just where do ye think ye be a-goin'?" the man said as he snatched Rumalia by the arm so hard it was likely to cause a bruise.

"The girl is with me," I said firmly, stepping toward the shopkeeper. He took one look at me and loosened his grip.

"I'm leavin'!" Rumalia announced as she pulled herself away and walked toward the door. "It seems there *are* kind people in the wairld, so I'm choosin' to no longer associate meself with the likes o' you!"

"If ye walk through that door, ye'll not be allowed back again!" he threatened.

With resolve, Rumalia walked out the front door to the shop with me following behind. Outside we could still hear the shopkeeper ranting. "Dunna ye come back a-beggin' now!" his voice raged on as we turned down an alleyway.

The Healer of Guildenwood

As we neared the main thoroughfare, Rumalia stopped abruptly in the middle of the alley. "What 'ave I done?" she cried anxiously with tears threatening to erupt.

"Come now," I said, as I put an arm around her. "Maldimire is no place for you. Let me take you to a place that's much kinder."

Rumalia looked up into my eyes and sighed. "I suppose ye're right, though nairvous I am."

"I was an orphan once, too, completely lost and alone. It was then that Frondamein found me and gave me a home," I said tenderly. "I am simply passing on that kindness."

It was not long before the two of us made our way to the main thoroughfare, where Rumalia stopped abruptly. I wondered if perhaps fear was getting the best of her.

"Come with me!" she said hurriedly, turning uphill. I followed closely behind as we wound our way through the crowd, back to the place where the slave auction had been the day before. "Stay here!" Rumalia cautioned as she handed me her belongings and rushed off to the place where the auctioneers were closing up for the day.

As she approached, the head auctioneer, a pimply faced fat man, looked up from his paperwork and scowled when he saw her. "Where've ye been, ghel? Been waitin' for ye for hours!" he bellowed. "Now get to work and clean this mess!"

"Aye." Rumalia nodded.

Scattered about the auction stand were chicken bones, overturned mugs, and crumpled-up papers. Rumalia grabbed a tray and proceeded to gather the trash on it, making me wonder what on earth she was thinking. Appearing to busy myself at a peddler's cart, I could but glance her way every now and then to try and make out her scheme.

This went on for a short while, when I suddenly looked up and saw her standing there, empty-handed, with a guilty grin across her face. "Come," she said, taking me by the arm and leading me down to the bridge that spanned the gorge.

"What was that about, pray tell?" I asked.

Rumalia glanced over her shoulder and then retrieved a crumpled piece of paper from the pocket of her frock. I could hardly believe my eyes when I saw that she held a bill of sale, officially stamped and all, for the purchase of one dwarf for forty quiddel. I gasped when I saw it and gave my devious new friend a sly smile.

We soon crossed over the bridge, glad to leave the madness of Maldimire behind, and we found ourselves walking east upon the Emraldein Road and on beyond the city gate. As we drew near to the place where the Baeren Ford delegation camped, Kiril was the first to see us.

"Miss Arwyn! Is it really you? We've been wairried sick!" he called excitedly, running to greet us.

"Yes, Kiril, it is me, and no worse for the wear I might add."

Suddenly the whole crowd from Baeren Ford gathered around us, asking all manner of questions about our ordeal.

"Kiril and I've been at the palace gates since late yesterday, requestin' yer release," Ingmar said. "We haird from one o' the guards ye'd be let out today. I dunna know what we'd 'ave done 'ad ye not been. We were about to retairn with several more in our numbers until Kiril 'ere spotted ye."

"Do forgive me," I said. "I did not mean to cause such worry. We have indeed been through a lot, but such is behind us, and I'm happy to announce that Rumalia will be returning with us to Baeren Ford."

"'Tis a good thin'," Ingmar said. "From what I've seen, Maldimire's not the place for a young ghel."

"Ye poor dears, ye must be starved!" Feyla added sympathetically. "There's some soup on the fire a-waitin' for ye."

"Feyla, would you see that Rumalia gets something to eat. I've a matter to discuss with Ingmar and Kiril," I said as the crowd dispersed.

Suddenly I could hear Avencloe neighing wildly from nearby, and I turned around to see several members of the delegation attempting to keep a firm grip on his rein, but nothing could stop him from bursting free and trotting over to place his muzzle on my shoulder.

"That's some hairse ye got there, miss," Ingmar said. "'Tis all we could do to keep 'im calm when ye didna show up back at camp. It's like 'e knew there was somethin' amiss." He then stepped closer and whispered. "I'll e'en confide there were some amongst us, whose names shall go unmentioned, who attempted to ride 'im, but 'e'd 'ave none of it. That's one loyal beast, that is."

As I stroked the white muzzle gingerly, I whispered into Avencloe's ear. "All is well, my friend, yet I must be gone again, but this time only for a short while. Now go back to the others and wait."

Obediently the majestic horse turned and trotted back to the place where the others horses stood, and I rejoined Kiril and Ingmar.

"Miss Arwyn," Kiril said apologetically, "kin ye e'er forgive us for not savin' ye from Dungard?"

"It is I who should ask your forgiveness," I said. "I know there are times when I should leave well enough alone, but in Rumalia's case I could not simply stand by and allow the guard to treat her as he did."

"Not to wairry, all's well in th' end," Ingmar said. "At least ye're back safe 'n sound. Now, all we need do is prepare to depart fairst thin' on the morrow."

"Er, there is one other matter that needs to be addressed."

"And what could that be?" Ingmar asked.

"The matter of a certain traveler who will be joining us."

"Ye mean the ghel? Why, I suppose we could spare Ansel. Most of our supplies be gone anyway, what with the extra day we'd not planned for," he said, eyeing me accusingly. "And with th' items pairchased in town, we'll make do."

"Well, not only the girl," I said coyly. "We met another in Dungard who needs our help. All we need is to see him as far as Baeren Ford and he will be on his way."

"And just who exactly . . ."

"You might say he is a worker of sorts in the prison who has grown tired of his position."

"This is no escaped prisoner . . . is it, Miss Arwyn?" Ingmar asked suspiciously.

I could feel the color growing in my cheeks, yet I remained silent, as did Kiril. He had known me long enough to understand that I would not be swayed once I had made up my mind to do something.

"Ye canna expect us to take an escaped prisoner with us, now kin ye?" Ingmar protested.

"I'm disappointed you have such little trust in me, Ingmar," I said. "The fact is, if all goes well, his absence will barely be noticed until we are halfway home. And if anyone questions us, we'll tell them we bought him in the marketplace."

"Bought a man?"

"No, a dwarf, arrested on a whim by Draigon's minions."

"Ye failed to mention 'e's a lowly dwarf. That changes the situation," Ingmar said skeptically.

"What difference should that make? Ingmar, surely a man of your stature has not bought in to the anti-Bensorian notion that not all peoples are equal in the sight of Omni," I said with passion. "The fact is, Dungard is no place for a rodent, let alone a dwarf, an elf, or any other person. Neither of you can imagine how horrid a place it is unless you've been there yourself. And if we have an opportunity to save one soul from its clutches, then I say we take that risk. If all else fails, then I will accept the blame."

Ingmar looked to Kiril for help, but none was forthcoming. For a moment he stood there looking exasperated, rubbing his chin and shaking his head until finally he spoke. "Miss Arwyn, against me better judgment I'll go along with yer plan, but I'll not 'ave me delegation put at risk."

I thought on it for a moment and realized that I would indeed be putting everyone in danger after inconveniencing them enough as it was. "I do concede your point," I admitted, glancing expectantly at Kiril. "I should leave for

Baeren Ford this night and put as much distance between us and Maldimire as possible before anyone suspects he is gone."

"Then I will go with ye," Kiril piped in. "It seems ye need someone to keep ye out o' trouble."

"And Ingmar, you'll need to tell the others that after our frightful stay in Dungard, Rumalia and I could not bear another night anywhere near this city."

"Verra well, Miss Arwyn," Ingmar said. "Now, where is this 'friend' o' yers?"

"Come, let us go down to the water."

The two men followed me down to the riverfront to the place where only two nights before we had purchased our dinner. As we went along, I explained the plan we'd concocted in Dungard.

As we neared the dock, Kiril and I found an inconspicuous place upstream from which to watch as Ingmar approached the same lone fisherman we had met previously, who sat cleaning fish on the bow of his boat.

"I say, kind fellow," he called in his booming voice.

Startled, the fisherman looked up to see Ingmar walking down toward the dock. "Eh, what is it ye want?" he replied rather gruffly.

"I wonder if I could trouble ye for a favor?"

"Aren't ye him what come by here two evenin's past?"

"Aye. 'Twas a pleasure doin' business with ye, it was. 'Tis why I've retairned, only this time with a slightly different proposition."

"Eh?" the fisherman said curiously.

"Ye see, durin' me stay in yer fine city, I found meself a lady friend who's quite fond o' the water. Thought I might trouble ye for the use o' yer boat this eve. There's nothin' romances a lady so as an evenin' upon the water under the starry skies." He winked slyly. "O' course, ye'd be paid 'andsomely for its use."

"'Ow much?"

"A shiny piece o' silver."

The old fisherman shook his head. "Two pieces o' silver and ye got yerself a deal."

"Two pieces o' silver! Why, I could buy me own boat for that!" Ingmar exclaimed. "A silver piece and a quiddel to top it off."

The fisherman eyed Ingmar greedily. "Ye've got yerself a boat, but I'll expect it back in its slip by sunup."

"Aye! 'Twill be retairned later this eve, mark me waird. Oh, and there's but one other matter," Ingmar added as he pulled yet another coin from his pocket. "I'll thank ye to keep quiet should 'er 'usband, or anyone else for that matter, come pokin' about askin' questions."

"Aye," the fisherman said as he stared sidelong at Ingmar and held out his hand for the coins. It took some time for him to gather the day's catch and climb onto the dock. "I hope yer lady friend dunna mind the smell o' fish."

"Lives down by the water, she does," Ingmar said. "'Twill make 'er feel at 'ome."

With a tip of his hat the fisherman walked away, his catch slung over his shoulder in a sack.

Face contorted at the stench of fish entrails and the sight of a bloodstained hull, Ingmar climbed into the boat and paddled upstream to the place where Kiril and I lay in wait under the cover of an overhanging willow tree.

"We've scanned the gorge for signs of any guards about and 'ave seen none," Kiril said as he tied the boat to the tree trunk. "Still, we should wait until complete darkness 'as fallen afore ye make a move."

The three of us returned to camp for a bite of soup, though the knot in my stomach made it very difficult for me to choke down anything. There were the inevitable curious questions concerning our ordeal in the "Dark Mouth." I was in no mood to think on that foul place, when in my heart I knew that I was about to embark on what could be a foolish quest that could end up rendering it my permanent residence.

CHAPTER 28

I could hear Dr. Susan's breathing, because it had become heavy, like mine. "You must be terrified," she commented.

"I feel caught in a vice that is rapidly squeezing me from the north and the south, suffocating me more with every mile that creeps by."

When the time came for us to depart, I noticed Rumalia dubiously eyeing Ansel, the packhorse Ingmar let her borrow. "You've never ridden a horse, have you?" I observed.

The girl shook her head nervously.

"Not to wairry, there's nothin' to ridin' a hairse," Kiril offered, holding out his hand to Rumalia. Hesitating slightly, she looked Kiril in the eye and then slowly took his hand. Gently he placed his other hand on Rumalia's back to steady her as she put her foot in the stirrup and then hoisted herself up into the saddle. "I'll tie yer hairse to mine, so's ye kin keep close," he said with a sympathetic smile that apparently did nothing to calm Rumalia's fears, based on her furrowed brow and wide eyes. "We've no time for a lesson on 'ow to ride, so ye'd best 'old on tight."

"Do wish Ingmar good travels for us," I said as we bid our company farewell. "Though I'd not wait up for him. It seems he's found an old friend," I added with a wink before mounting Avencloe.

The three of us slipped off into the growing darkness, doubling back to the river when safely out of sight of the delegation. When we reached an alleyway close to the riverbank, I left Kiril, Rumalia, and the horses before joining Ingmar back at the willow tree.

As the moon rose above the horizon, Ingmar and I sat patiently together under the willow, scanning the opposite bank for any sign of Froilin.

"I canna believe ye talked me into such a thin'," Ingmar lamented. "Ye've turned me into not only a liar but a philanderer and criminal as well. 'Tis 'ard for a man o' principle to swallow."

I smiled at him in the darkness. "I know you're a good man, Ingmar, and your good deed will not go unrewarded. But you must go along in order to accomplish a greater good."

"Miss Arwyn," Ingmar said, squinting toward the opposite side of the Silvendell, "me eyes kin make out a wee little light there on the far side o' the river. Just caught a glimpse of it I did."

I turned to look in the direction Ingmar faced and saw nothing but the rising moon reflecting on the water. Suddenly a tiny flickering light appeared in the darkness at about the place Froilin described.

"Come, let us make our way across," I said urgently, my heart beating faster as we untied the rope and climbed into the boat. With Ingmar at the boat's helm, the two of us finally reached a small rocky outcropping at the very bottom of the ravine. Far above, the city walls loomed menacingly as if warning us not to approach. In the darkness, I could make out a dwarfish silhouette against the shadows of the rocks below.

"Froilin," I whispered.

"Aye, 'tis me," the figure whispered back.

Ingmar drifted as close as he could to the rocks. Froilin quickly doused his candle and set it upon a rock in order to steady the wobbling vessel before he climbed in. Crouching down inside the boat's hull, his eyes flashed about wildly to the towering heights above and up and down the riverbank, scanning for any possible spies. As Ingmar rowed swiftly into the middle of the river, I suddenly remembered the candle Froilin had left on the rock.

"The candle!" I whispered urgently. "We must return lest they find it and discover that he escaped."

"Methinks it may be too late," Ingmar said as we heard voices shouting from the cliff high above. Had we been discovered? Or were those the voices of drunken revelry? We could waste no time finding out.

Desperately Ingmar fought against the current in the middle of the river until our vessel landed safely beneath the shelter of the willow's curtain of branches on the other side. Froilin and I climbed out and silently pushed the boat back into the current.

"Ye'd best be on yer way," Ingmar said with a look of caution as the boat disappeared into the murky darkness of the river.

"Could it be possible I've escaped the bowels o' Dungard?" Froilin said in a giddy whisper. "'Tis indeed a miracle!"

"We are not out of danger yet," I warned, thinking I heard the sound of dogs barking followed by three sharp blasts of a horn. Was this a warning signal? Or the product of my imagination?

"Nay, but yer potion did the trick. I left 'em all sleepin' like babes. No doubt they'll not notice me absence 'til well into the day tomorrow."

"And by then we shall be far from here. Indeed, we cannot waste a moment," I said anxiously, glancing at the cliff above.

"Oh, and miss, lest I forget or we become separated," Froilin said, stuffing his hand into the pocket of his trousers. He then placed in my hand a small round object—my ring! He had managed to pilfer it from the box of prisoner's belongings! I was so filled with joy that I bent over and gave him a kiss on the forehead.

"Thank you. From the depths of my heart, thank you," I whispered emotionally, slipping my precious ring securely back onto my finger.

We waited in the shadows for several minutes until we heard someone approach. Breathlessly, we watched until Kiril emerged from the shadows, trailing our three horses behind.

"Come, Miss Arwyn," Kiril urged. "We've not much time."

There was no time for introductions. Kiril helped Froilin to the back of his horse, where Froilin sat crouched beneath his cloak. Fortunately, the cloak covered Froilin's short stature in such a way that even I could not tell Kiril harbored a stowaway. I donned my own cloak, careful to pull the hood about my head lest I catch the attention of anyone undesirable. Together the three horses took off back through the row of buildings and across the plain toward the road to Baeren Ford, dodging the hundreds of campsites full of censusgoers along the way.

My heart pounded as we reached the main road to the north, yet before we were able to reach the edge of the woods, I looked back in time to see a host of mounted guards ride through the city gates with torches in hand. Were they on their nightly patrol? Or in search of the escaped prisoner? I was suddenly glad that out of everyone in the delegation, only Ingmar knew our secret, and he had proven that he could bluff.

In the distance I could still hear the sound of barking dogs, and it seemed to be growing louder.

"We must hurry," I urged, hoping the darkness would conceal our three horses slipping away to the north. I suddenly felt quite vulnerable without my bow and quiver, but how was I to have known I would need them on what was to have been a simple trip to the big city? And without the means to hunt, it would be a very long, hunger-filled journey, indeed, *if* we were able to escape Maldimire.

Terror gripped me, and I had to resist the urge to go tearing off to the cover of the woods. I could not leave my friends, yet it was excruciating how slow their horses were, compared to Avencloe! Panicked, I glanced behind us, but as of yet no one on horseback appeared to be in pursuit.

At last we reached the edge of the woods, where the possibility of detouring from the road if need be would be much less obvious, yet our pursuers would also have the advantage of coming upon us by surprise. We could not let down our guard.

The Healer of Guildenwood

I looked upon Maldimire one last time before we slipped away to the north. If I never laid eyes on that city again, it would be too soon!

We travelled on through the night, speaking little as we listened for movement on the road behind us. No one else was out, not even the pale half-moon that kept dodging behind clouds that raced by. Occasionally we would pass other groups of censusgoers camped out beside the road or in quiet village squares, yet they only stirred and gave us a passing glance when it was obvious we did not mean to linger.

I pulled my cloak tighter about me as a chill wind blew in from the south. The weather was changing, and I thought longingly on the warm bed and hot meal that would hopefully be waiting when at last we returned home. Yet there were still many miles to travel, and each one crept by at what seemed a snail's pace.

Under cover of darkness we trotted steadily northward, yet with the rising of the sun, I felt exposed and vulnerable. We simply *had* to get off the main thoroughfare. Fortunately, it was not long before we reached the same field where we had camped several nights before, only this time we kept to the far end behind a stand of trees that surrounded an outcropping of rock, providing at least some concealment from the road.

We arrived right as another group of censusgoers was leaving, too busy packing up their gear to pay us much mind. As it was, I kept my hood tightly about me and I crouched a bit in my seat. It would not do for word to spread to the south of an elf's presence along the way, or for me to be associated with a dwarf. But so far, Froilin had remained hidden beneath Kiril's cloak, and it was only after we were completely out of sight of the other travelers that he slid down from the back of Kiril's horse.

During the night, we had found water at the village wells along the way, but we still had precious little to eat. We consumed the last of my pumpkin bread, which amounted to half a loaf, a pound of dried beef that Kiril had thought to grab before our hasty departure, and a few apples we picked from an orchard on the side of the road. Still, it was better than nothing, and to Froilin it seemed a feast.

As the sun rose higher in the east, we settled into our hiding place behind the knoll. Kiril, who had chivalrously given his sleeping roll to Rumalia, leaned against a tree as the girl and I huddled together on the ground, with Froilin lying concealed under a pile of fallen leaves. Yet with the sun beating down on us through the ever-thinning canopy above, and with our ears constantly to the sounds coming from the road beyond, it was not until late afternoon when we all at last succumbed to a deep slumber.

"Miss Arwyn . . . Miss Arwyn." I woke with a start to find Kiril shaking me. We were in utter darkness. "We've slept too long," he said with urgency in his voice.

The moon was already directly overhead. How long had we slept? Gathering my wits about me, I jumped to my feet and helped Kiril rouse the others. We scrambled to leave, yet I feared we would not make it all the way to Baeren Ford by daybreak.

Quietly we stole past a small group of censusgoers who were sleeping soundly closer to the road and, listening carefully for movement in either direction, set out to the north. I scolded myself for having slept too long, for now we were in greater danger. As if harboring an escapee from Dungard were not enough, there was no telling what havoc the servants of Draigon had wreaked on Baeren Ford, and we were headed right into the midst of it.

The sun rose much too early to suit me, and we still had several hours before we could arrive. With my money stolen and what little Kiril and Rumalia had between them, we could not afford an inn, and none of us relished the idea of another night camped out beside the road. We decided to take our chances on the road in the daylight hours, especially as there seemed to be a number of fellow travellers heading north, making it easier for us to blend in with everyone else.

For several hours we fell in with a group of about thirty censusgoers from villages north of Baeren Ford, visibly weary like ourselves and thankfully not prone to idle chatter. The less they knew of us, the better. Only now that Rumalia had experience riding, Kiril thought it good to hand over the reins and teach her how to ride properly, if for no other reason than to pass the time. The poor girl had her share of aches and pains from her first day in the saddle, yet she showed no signs of regret for having come with us on such a daring journey to what I was still not entirely certain would be her new life.

We had yet to see any of Draigon's soldiers, but I knew they had been sent ahead to Baeren Ford to create mischief, and at some point they would return to Maldimire. The gap was rapidly closing as we neared Baeren Ford. We passed the last major village to its south, with less than twenty miles to go before we could turn off the road and travel under cover of woods to the dwarves' cave. I relaxed a bit, thinking that perhaps we would make it all the way without detection. But then my heart sank, when up ahead I could hear the thunder of hooves, followed by the sight of gray-clad soldiers on horseback, about forty in all, heading right toward us.

There was nowhere to go without being seen. Several other riders in our group had managed to come between my friends and me. Kiril looked back at me nervously, but I shot him a warning glance from beneath my hood and hoped he would remain calm. Then, to my horror, I could barely make out Froilin's ragged left shoe, sticking out below Kiril's cloak. I tried to get Kiril's attention, but to no avail. He was too far ahead, and I couldn't risk drawing more attention to us by creating a scene. All I could do was sit back and pray it would not be detected.

And then, quite unexpectedly, the entire host of soldiers veered off the road and into the woods to the west. Anxious murmurings shot through the crowd of censusgoers as the soldiers, no doubt still reveling in the spoils of their rampage through Baeren Ford, turned onto a path that had been recently cut through the woods.

"This is the place," I heard one of them say. I looked about a hundred yards off the road and saw a clearing where several trees had been recently felled. In the clearing were a half dozen tents, around which there was a flurry of activity.

"Dunna ye wairry, 'twill be fully operational by spring."

What would be fully operational? Whatever it was, it had blessedly stolen attention from our group, allowing us to slip past, ignored. That is, until several among our fellow travellers spied dark, lurching forms in the clearing, two of which were using a two-man saw to cut down a tree.

"If that dunna beat all—usin' Gargalocs to fell our forests!" a man only several lengths ahead of me yelled.

Several other angry voices followed suit, enough to catch the attention of the soldiers.

"And just who are you to tell us what we can and canna do?" one of the soldiers yelled back.

Kiril and Rumalia were about to pass the place where the path veered off the main road, the place where an altercation brewed. *Please, just get past!*

Angry words were traded back and forth, until a middle-aged woman begged her husband to mind himself and let it be before things became too heated. It was the perfect opportunity for me to slip past. And I did. No one gave me a second glance.

Kiril and Rumalia were still up ahead, and behind me the protest died down, although I could hear several around me grumbling about the presence of Gargalocs in Guilden. As for me, I felt like celebrating. Only a few more miles, and we would be home!

Then I glanced ahead, and the sight that met my gaze made me freeze with fear. Kiril and Rumalia had stopped in the middle of the road. Three soldiers who straggled behind the others stood before them. One of them was pointing to Kiril's cloak, and I am certain all the blood drained from my face as I watched a hesitant Kiril timidly lift his cloak up to reveal a very frightened-looking dwarf sitting behind him. My gaze was fixated on the unfolding scene as I rode closer.

"And what be this?" one of the guards demanded.

"Me sister and I . . . that is, sir, our da sent us to Maldimire for a slave," Kiril sputtered, glancing nervously at Rumalia. "Been needin' an extra 'and on the farm, we have."

"He's awful haggard for a slave," one of the soldiers commented, eyeing Froilin with distaste.

"Aye," Rumalia piped in. "'Twas all we could afford, but mother'll 'ave 'im fattened up in no time."

"And why's it look as though he's hidin'?" another soldier asked with a look in his eyes that I liked not at all.

"'E didna come t' us with much to wear," Kiril explained. "And 'e'll catch 'is death out in the cold."

The soldiers' gaze narrowed suspiciously. "Where be 'is papers?"

A look of utter terror clouded Kiril's face. The other travellers filed past quietly, and I was almost upon them myself when I saw Rumalia fumbling about in her pocket, from which she retrieved the crumpled-up piece of paper she pilfered from the auctioneer. Kiril's eyes grew wide with surprise and relief as she handed the paper to the soldier, who took a long look at it right as I was passing.

I resisted the urge to glance back, but after several heart-stopping moments I could hear him tell Kiril and Rumalia to move along. As I rounded a bend in the road, I slowed and the two caught up to me, wide-eyed.

"Recognized one o' the guards, I did," Rumalia lamented with a hushed tone. "'E frequents the census tables."

"Do you think he recognized you?" I asked nervously.

"With them 'tis 'ard to say. Ye think they pay ye no mind until such a time as they kin put ye to shame."

My legs went weak once more as I considered the implications. If we were indeed being pursued from the south, there was little that would keep anyone from associating Froilin with Rumalia and then Rumalia with me. It seemed only a matter of time before they would put the pieces together.

How long the road to Baeren Ford suddenly seemed! Only nineteen miles to go, yet it may as well have been a hundred and ninety. I gulped hard and urged Avencloe forward. It was the only thing we could do, but the vise that had been tightening throughout our desperate journey at last threatened to suffocate me.

CHAPTER 29

"One would suppose that such an experience should humble me, or at the very least frighten me into submission. But that is what Draigon desires, and I will not give him that satisfaction."

"It sounds like you have something up your sleeve," came the ubiquitous woman's voice.

"Yes," I replied. "It has been brewing for quite some time."

As we at last neared Baeren Ford, my three travelling companions and I slowed considerably to allow our fellow travelers to get far enough ahead so that we would have the chance to slip quietly into the woods. Once they were out of sight, we took off through the trees, relieved beyond measure to have made it that far. After a while we reached the cave where the dwarves lived, making a crunching noise through the fallen leaves that was sure to signal our approach.

As quietly as possible, I called out to the dwarves. There was no response. I dismounted from Avencloe's back and called out again, "Hutto! Goodren!"

"Miss Arwyn, is that you?" came a loud whisper. I could just make out their dwarvish outlines in the dark entrance to the cave. Each held a bow and arrow in his quivering hands.

"Put your weapons away," I answered. "And go back into your cave."

Hesitantly the two dwarves disappeared into the shadows behind them. It was not long before I followed, though entering the small passage called for a bit of contortion.

A small fire in the corner of the cave helped dispel the gloom within. A carpet of pine straw had been laid along the floor of the cave, and we had managed to collect several more household items for them, creating a rather cozy feel to their makeshift accommodations.

"Have you come to pay us a social call, or be there another reason ye come out here stompin' about, attractin' all manner of attention?" Goodren demanded.

Froilin entered the cave behind me with a big smile spread across his face. "Goodren, old man, dunna be an arse!"

For a moment, Goodren and Hutto rubbed their eyes.

"'Tis a ghost!" Goodren exclaimed as he jumped behind Hutto.

"Nay, 'tis I, yer ol' friend, Froilin!"

Hutto and Goodren stood frozen, mouths gaping and eyes wide with disbelief. With arms spread wide, Froilin walked toward his friends and embraced them both at once.

"'Tis a downright miracle!" Hutto finally exclaimed, as his shock gave way to mirth. At last all three dwarves were laughing as they tumbled in a pile to the ground.

"'Tis indeed a miracle," Goodren said. "How else kin ye explain this tairn of events?"

"'Tis quite a story indeed, one best told o'er a pint," Froilin said.

"I'm afraid we've none," Goodren replied. "But we do have some leftover rabbit stew, and it looks as though ye could stand to put some meat on yer bones."

"Aye, they dunna feed a body well in Dungard."

"So ye went to Dungard, did ye?" Hutto said.

"Aye, and lived to tell about it, all's the more. 'Tis where I met Miss Arwyn."

Goodren and Hutto's eyes grew wide at yet another astonishing revelation. "Miss Arwyn in Dungard? Perish the thought!" the latter exclaimed.

"Do sit down and tell us yer tale," Goodren gestured, indicating a pot of stew on the fire.

"As much as I would love to stay and help Froilin recount our adventure, I've more business to attend to," I said regretfully, smelling the aroma coming from the pot. "Indeed, I am not entirely certain I will not be watched closely in the coming days, so it may be that I shouldn't come 'round for a time."

With eyes glistening with moisture, Froilin extended his hands, taking mine in his. "Dear Miss Arwyn, how kin I e'er thank ye for what ye've done?" he said poignantly. "I'd have rotted away in Dungard were it not for ye."

"Rescuing my ring from those brutes was all the appreciation I needed." Relieved once more to see my ring riding upon my finger in the light of the fire, I smiled gently at my new friend. "And I am glad to have played a part in rescuing you from Dungard's clutches, though would that I could take you home," I said, glancing to all three dwarves, "take you *all* home to your mountains."

"Aye," Hutto agreed. "There are days I think we're as much in a prison as Froilin was."

"Someday, maybe all will be set right," I said hopefully. I then said the

The Healer of Guildenwood

last of my good-byes before going back outside to the place where Kiril and Rumalia waited with the horses. I was relieved to have seen Froilin safely to the dwarves' secret cave, but the time had come to turn my attention to what had happened to my friends in those past days, and my heart raced when I thought of Eliendor and the attention of Draigon that had unwittingly been drawn to the old man.

I held my breath as we neared his cottage, and the sight that met my eyes made me want to weep. There, sitting beneath the eaves of his house, was Eliendor. Before him was a charred place in the ground, a large black circle where flakes of burnt parchment stirred in the breeze.

"Eliendor, your books!" I exclaimed as I dismounted.

The old man looked up as I approached, and I could see his chest heave with relief when he saw me.

"Did they hurt you?"

"Besides the regrettable offense to my books, I am well," he said, rising from the bench and walking toward me. "Thank Omni you are safely here and not locked away forever!"

I heard a loud *caw* come from above and looked up to see Talthos on the roof. "I see Talthos told you of my ordeal."

"Aye, you certainly have a way of getting yourself into trouble with Draigon," he said sharply as relief turned to rebuke. "I thought I told you he should be avoided!"

"Yes," I conceded. I had a tongue-lashing coming to me—and I knew I deserved it. But it still stung.

"And am I to presume that you helped the dwarf escape as well?"

I nodded sheepishly. "He is now safely with Goodren and Hutto."

Eliendor stared at me intensely from under his two bushy eyebrows. "Arwyn, you must be very wary. Draigon will no doubt remember you all the more now, and he may grow suspicious should word reach him that one of his slaves in Dungard is missing. In fact, it would be good for you to disappear for a while."

Disappear? Where in the world would I go?

Kiril and Rumalia stood timidly nearby. Eliendor turned to look at them both. "Greetings, Kiril," he said, walking to the place where they stood. "And this must be the girl."

"Eliendor, I would like you to meet Rumalia."

"Pleased to make yer acquaintance," Rumalia said politely.

"It sounds as though Arwyn came along at the right time."

"Aye, saved me from a beatin', she did."

"And an honorable gesture it was," Eliendor admitted.

"My conscience would not allow me to sit by meekly when there was a wrong I could right."

"Having compassion is one thing, but having the wisdom to know the right time to act upon it, is another." Eliendor turned, staring pensively into the forest. "The time for justice has not yet come, but it will in its due course," he said quietly. "Until then you must be wary."

"But Eliendor . . . your books . . ." I moaned.

"Not to worry," he said, gesturing for us to follow, "for not all is lost." The old hermit led us into his cottage, still in a state of disarray. With a forceful push, he moved his table out of the way and then threw the rug aside to reveal the trap door down to the cellar. He creaked open the door, and we peered down to see stacks and stacks of books lying there on the earthen floor.

"When Talthos came to me with your message, I decided to take no chances on my most valued volumes, plus a few other treasured possessions," he said with a gleam in his eye, making that mysterious wooden box of his come to mind.

"But how could they have missed the door?" I asked, bewildered.

"The Gifts can change the appearance of anything, awing the pure of heart and confounding the weak-minded," Eliendor explained. "And as for me, they thought better than to trouble a silly old man who has nothing better to do than talk to himself and make houses for birds. I would imagine they felt rather foolish, having come all the way from Maldimire for nothing more than the likes of me."

"But they did not come only for the likes of you," I said with a sense of dread as I thought of what may have transpired in Baeren Ford since my departure. "Eliendor, we must be on our way. I have reason to think that Draigon has taken out his wrath upon Baeren Ford, though to what aim I know not other than to bring more despair upon me."

Eliendor's brow furrowed gravely as he slowly sat on his bench once more, eyes staring unseeing at a blade of grass on his lawn. I worried for him, but it was late in the afternoon and the time had come to see what I'd brought upon Baeren Ford, all because Draigon had taken a notion to hate me.

We hurried through the forest and down the lane that led behind Frondamein and Loralon's cottage, emerging on the main road. Even as Avencloe stepped foot onto it, I could tell that something was amiss. A solemnity hung in the air despite the blue sky of late afternoon, and those who were out hurried past with heads down, giving us no more than a quick glance. From somewhere up the road I could hear a woman crying, and closer to the village a large black plume of smoke rose above the buildings before dissipating in the breeze. My brow furrowed with concern as I led the others around to the stable, where we dismounted and tied our horses to the fencepost.

I tensed for a moment, wondering if Loralon was at home or if I should look for her in town, when the front door to our cottage flew open and she ran outside holding Amerigo securely by the hand. "Arwyn, thank goodness ye've retairned! I've been wairried sick!" she exclaimed. "Ingmar and th' others rode by a wee bit ago, a day later than expected. But when ye didna show up with 'em, I feared the wairse, and 'e wouldna tell me where ye were. Been pacin' the floor e'er since!"

"I'm so sorry to have worried you," I said with a pang of guilt.

"Oh, Arwyn, ye'll ne'er believe what Draigon's soldiers did!" Loralon wailed, pointing toward the village. "Swept in late last night, beatin' on doors, makin' us all come outside in our nightclothes whilst they sairched for all manner of 'incriminatin' material.' Incriminatin' material indeed! They took yer books, though I'd 'ardly call a few books on plants incriminatin'!" she huffed. "Gave me a terrible fright, they did. Thought they'd come for Amerigo again, and with ye gone I dunna know what I'd 'ave done, though they knew 'twas you what lived 'ere."

"How dreadful!" I said, stunned, hardly believing my ears.

"They took it all and bairned it in the village square, anythin' they deemed inappropriate, but that's not the wairst of it!" Loralon continued. "All the young men in the village, brought 'em into the square and beat 'em, they did!"

"Beat them?" I repeated, feeling weak.

"Aye, poor Taryck got the wairst beatin' of all. E'en took 'is da's swords what've been in their family for genairations." Taryck, the son of Emiloth, the town blacksmith came to mind. He was a handsome, strapping young man, barely eighteen, who had a propensity for daring that had led him to seek my healing services on several occasions when his escapades had gone awry.

"'Ad Kiril been 'ere, 'e would 'ave been beat along with the rest." Loralon added. Kiril shifted his weight uncomfortably at the thought. "Why, I've been afraid to go out all day, what with thin's bein' as they are. I've seen precious few neighbors, but when the delegation rode by a while ago, I thought for sure ye'd be with 'em . . ." Loralon had been chattering nonstop for several minutes but drew quiet as she noticed Rumalia standing there, peering out from behind Ansel's rump. "And who might ye be?"

"Me name's Rumalia."

"I'd wager there's a story there."

"Indeed there is," I said, glancing toward the road. "Though 'tis best told inside, away from prying ears. Kiril, perhaps you should go and check on Padimus and your folks," I suggested.

"Aye, Miss Arwyn, and I'll take Ansel back t' Ingmar, if ye wish."

"Yes, Kiril, thank you." I was weary but grateful for my young friend's constant willingness to lend a hand. I led Avencloe into the stable for a much-deserved rest before taking Rumalia into the cottage, where we sat down with Loralon and told her everything. That is, everything but the part about Froilin's escape from Dungard. The fewer people who knew our secret, the better, both for their protection and ours.

"Ah, the poor dear," Loralon shook her head sympathetically. "But where's she to sleep? We've not a large house 'n it seems to grow smaller by the day."

"Even if she sleeps on the floor of the parlor, it will be better than her previous arrangement."

"I suppose we'll make do for a time." Loralon sighed, smiling kindly at Rumalia.

Yes, it would do for a time, but I knew it would not provide a permanent solution for my young friend. However, I could not dwell on that at the moment. There were more pressing concerns, like seeing to the young men who had been brutalized—all because of me.

I went down into the cellar and retrieved my salves and poultices, readying to make my rounds.

"Where are ye goin'?" Rumalia asked worriedly as I prepared to leave.

"Off to see to the wounded." I sighed.

"Let me go with ye."

I was about to protest but thought better of it. I had been the girl's only security since she left Maldimire, and it wouldn't do to leave her by herself in such new surroundings.

"Not to wairry," Loralon said. "There'll be dinner a-waitin' when ye retairn."

The sun had barely set alight the treetops to the west when Rumalia and I started out toward the village, but almost immediately I realized something was definitely wrong. As we walked, I could not help but notice the way the villagers averted their eyes. Some even scowled at me, and I wondered what had happened to make them seem so hostile.

When we arrived at the village square, people were standing around the ugly, smoldering pile of ash, the black remains of what had been books and furniture and heirlooms—anything to humiliate and defeat their spirit. There was weeping and stunned looks on their faces, yet as I approached they walked away, leaving me bewildered.

I rapped on the door to the cottage next to the blacksmith shop. The door creaked open slightly and I could see the blacksmith, Emiloth, standing there. Behind him, sprawled out on the kitchen table lay poor Taryck, stripped from the waist up with bloodied gashes on his back. With tearstained face his mother was blotting his wounds with a wet cloth. But when she saw me standing there, her eyes turned cold. She had always seemed to me a stern woman, with hair pulled back tightly from her face in a bun that looked almost painful, making her look all the more disapproving.

"I . . . I've come to help Taryck," I said.

"Begone with ye now, we dunna need yer 'elp," Emiloth rebuked. "Blasted elf, all ye brought is ruin to this town e'er since ye came!"

I was stunned. Even as he slammed the door in my face, all I could do was stand there, disbelieving what I heard. I fought the tears that threatened to erupt before turning back to the road, where a dozen or so people stood, none coming to my defense.

Gathering myself, I walked past them, on to the next victim's house, but when I arrived I received the same cold greeting, only that time they did not even bother to open the door.

Disheartened, I made my way back through the village with a baffled Rumalia at my side. I did not know whether to feel angry or deeply hurt. Either way, there would be tears, but I would give no one the satisfaction of shedding them in public. How could they think I was to blame for such an atrocity?

Even though, in truth, I *was* to blame for it. But how would they have known?

After we passed the tavern, I heard footsteps running toward us. I turned to see Kiril, and he was breathless. "Miss Arwyn, ye must be warned. Draigon's soldiers told everyone 'twas all on account o' you and yer meddlin' they'd been sent to Baeren Ford."

"So that would explain it," I said quietly.

I slowed my pace as we continued on to the cottage, heartbroken that these who had been my neighbors—people I had laughed with, done business with, and healed—could so quickly turn against me. It seemed all my attempts to assimilate over those past two years or so had been for naught.

I ate little for dinner that night and spoke even less. How could I tell Loralon that, to the villagers, I had become a burden? I, whom she had taken in over two years before against her better judgment?

After making sure Rumalia was settled into her makeshift bed on the settee, I climbed wearily to my loft. Yet despite the weariness I felt, and the heartache, a flame still burned brightly from deep within my gut. I would *not* be their scapegoat! I would *not* be the one blamed for the ills in our land! That was exactly what *he* would desire. Nay, the blame lay squarely on the shoulders of one man, one whose heart had turned to darkness.

For some time that tiny flame had been growing, fueled by the outrages I had witnessed, and now that flame had caught fire, tickling an idea that had been in my head for some time, an idea that would not rest until morning. I threw off my covers and changed into my riding gown, stealing downstairs past the place where Rumalia slept and out the front door.

I walked briskly past the tavern, where only a handful of patrons mingled inside in front of the fireplace. Padimus was not one to rush paying customers out the door when the clock struck midnight, but down below in the streets of the village all was quiet.

I arrived at the mill, careful to make certain no one was around before I walked up the steps to the front door. Kiril had told me once that he often saw the glow of a candle coming from inside Ingmar's office late at night when he walked home from the tavern. Sure enough, I glanced into the window and could see Ingmar, still dressed in his traveling clothes, working away by candlelight to put papers back in order that had been strewn about by Draigon's minions. Quietly I rapped on the front door.

In a moment, the door creaked open and out peered Ingmar, holding a lantern in his hand. "Miss Arwyn," he exclaimed. "Glad I am to see ye made it back, but 'tis a strange time o' night to come pay a visit. Is anythin' the matter?"

"There is an issue I would like to discuss, and I cannot rest until I speak what is on my mind," I explained.

"Aye, then come on in out o' the chill," Ingmar said as he glanced quickly over my shoulder to the road beyond and then shut the door behind me. "Kiril returned Ansel?"

"Aye, though I doubt it's on Ansel's behalf ye've paid me a visit at such an hour."

"How are you faring?" I asked sympathetically, tiptoeing over a pile of spilled papers.

"As well as kin be expected, considerin' the saircumstances," he muttered. "I trust our, er, 'baggage' is well on 'is way to th' Andains by now."

"Why yes, I'm quite sure he is," I replied.

Ingmar eyed me suspiciously in the lamplight. "Miss Arwyn, 'tis bad enough we've a vagabond elf in the village what stirs up trouble with the powers that be. We dunna need a fugitive dwarf hidin' out, causin' e'en more trouble."

I stared at Ingmar, trying with all my might to hold back the tears that threatened to erupt. "I had no idea you thought my presence was such a liability," I said at last.

Ingmar's face lightened a bit, and for a moment I could detect an almost tender expression in his eyes, as if he did indeed regret the words that had carelessly tumbled from his mouth. Yet the imposing businessman was not one to give an outright apology. "Now, Miss Arwyn, dunna get yerself in a quiver," he said with resignation. "Everyone knows ye're the best 'ealer in the village, and p'raps in the whole o' Guildenwood, and for that reason alone ye're wairth yer weight in gold."

"Apparently I am no longer regarded with such esteem."

"Ye needn't wairry yerself. Ne'er 'ave I cared much what people think," he added. "Besides, they'll come 'round, 'specially when they hear what *really* 'appened in Maldimire, with the ghel, that is."

I smiled gratefully at Ingmar's kind words and at his attempt at an apology.

"Now, what is it ye come for?"

It was time to move on to the real reason for my visit. "A man such as yourself cannot possibly approve of the way this country is being governed," I began.

"Nay," Ingmar replied, raising an eyebrow.

"You have seen with your own eyes the atrocities of Maldimire, and now they have crept into our own peaceful village."

"Aye, but what would ye have me do?"

"Master Ingmar, you are a man of great influence, both in Baeren Ford and, I would imagine, in all Guilden. Would it not be possible to use your influence to start an uprising, to see to Draigon's downfall once and for all?"

"Miss Arwyn, ye dunna know what ye ask," Ingmar said as he brushed past me toward the window, where he cautiously peered out onto the street and then carefully drew the curtains. "Did anyone see ye come to me?"

"No, the streets were quite empty."

"All the better. Do ye not know 'ow dangerous it is to talk o' such thin's?"

"Someone must!" I protested. "If no one does, then we shall all eventually find ourselves victims of Draigon's whims, and I can assure you that he has nothing but ill will toward his subjects."

"That may indeed be true," Ingmar relented, "but such is not for ye to wairry yer pretty head o'er. Ye must leave such matters to menfolk, them what know 'ow to lead an uprisin' if there be one."

"And that is exactly what I propose. Someone must take the lead, and you are the only man in this village who could accept such a task."

"Miss Arwyn," Ingmar said, taking me by the elbow and gently leading me toward the door. "Th' hour is late and ye must be weary from our travels. Go home, get some rest, and take all notion of a rebellion out o' yer mind."

"But . . ."

I turned as Ingmar muttered a good night and closed the door behind me. Seething inside, I stood on the front doorstep to the mill for several minutes. "Leave such matters to menfolk, indeed!" I grumbled. "The country will be falling down about our ears and the 'menfolk' will still be smoking their pipes and sitting in their taverns wondering what all the commotion is about."

Feeling frustrated, I headed back up the lane toward the cottage. Surely there was someone willing to stand up against Draigon's tyranny. Surely not every man in Bensor had given in to complacency. Still, Ingmar did seem a bit nervous, as if he were hiding something. Was there some secret he was withholding, or was he simply concerned with saving his own hide?

Back at the cottage, I tiptoed through the parlor where Rumalia slept soundly, covered in blankets on the settee. It was good to see the girl finally sleeping so deeply after her ordeal those past few days. My own bed suddenly felt luxurious as I sank beneath the covers, glad to be sleeping in a real bed again, and not on the ground, or worse.

CHAPTER 30

"The ways of Omni are indeed a mystery, and I am humbled that He has used me to bring about such a miracle."

The following day I went about the cottage, trying to make up for the work I had missed those days I was gone, yet my eyes and ears were always to the road out front. In the afternoon I stole into the woods with Kiril and Rumalia to forage for what plants remained after the first biting frosts of autumn. Upon our return, I was dismayed to learn that Loralon had spied three men in gray lingering before our cottage while I was out, seeming to study it carefully before continuing on to the north.

I was beginning to realize what it meant to live under a veil of fear, and it was that night when I was certain my crimes had caught up with me. Loralon had just put Amerigo to bed, and with all my books turned to ash, Rumalia and I had settled in for a less-than-stimulating evening of watching Loralon begin work on an extra set of dwarf clothing they suddenly needed when there came a loud knock at the front door. Immediately I bolted to my feet and grabbed my bow and arrows.

Loralon crept to the window and pulled back the curtain slightly. "'Tis a man, and 'e appears to be alone," she whispered.

"Still, you'd best be careful," I cautioned.

"Who . . . who is it?"

"Me name's Fendred. A trapper I am, from east o' the village," he responded with a rough voice. "I come seekin' the healer, the woman named Arwyn."

"Ye'll 'ave to wait 'til daylight!"

"Please, I beg o' ye, me wife 'as taken ill and I mean to take a healer 'ome this eve, e'en if I must travel all the way to Peltafair to find one."

I slowly lowered my bow to the floor and nodded to Loralon. "Let him in."

Loralon unbolted the latch and both of us peered at the man standing there in the darkness. I recognized him from the village where I had seen him a time or two with a load of animal pelts draped across the back of his horse. "Do step out of the cold," I urged, throwing open the door.

The man entered the warm parlor and took off his hat. "Me name's Fendred. I live about fourteen miles from 'ere off the East Road. Me wife's Helice. Woke up this mornin' with a terrible pain in 'er belly, she did. Hasna let up since."

"And you mean to return home tonight?"

"Aye, though I hope me search for a healer is ended," he said expectantly.

"Loralon, can you get by without me a few more days?"

"Aye, go there ye must," she said.

"And could you send word with Kiril to Eliendor of my whereabouts?"

"Aye, that I'll do."

"Then yes, I'll go," I replied, "though give me a moment while I gather my herbs and pack my bag. Depending on the illness, I could be gone for several days."

"Bless ye, miss," Fendred said, relief in his eyes.

"I wish to go as well," Rumalia piped in.

The man smiled and shrugged his shoulders. "Suit yourself. I'm sure Miss Arwyn'll be glad o' the company. I'm afraid I willna be a cheerful companion, wairried as I am."

In a matter of minutes, both Rumalia and I had our belongings packed. Loralon had worked diligently since Fendred's arrival to gather whatever food for the road she could find and bade us farewell as we rode into the cold, dark night.

For a short while we traveled south, towards Maldimire, until we veered off on the main road to the east. Right as we altered course, I peered south and could see farther on down the road what I thought were moving shadows and heard what sounded like the neighing of a horse from some distance away. The road to Maldimire was being watched.

At that moment the moonlight disappeared behind a cloud and a sudden gust of wind created a small vortex of dancing leaves that muffled the sound of our horses' hoofbeats, allowing us to pass like shadows to the east—and for me to breathe a little easier.

Prior to that evening, I had been little more than a few miles down the East Road, and the ghostly light of the moon turned the bleak landscape into an eerie journey through a shadow-filled world. The miles crept by slowly, and I was glad for the thick woolen cloak that shielded my body from the chill wind. Behind me sat Rumalia, huddled against my back in an effort to stay warm. We met no one on the road and spoke little to each other. I glanced over at Fendred from time to time, whose eyes remained fixed upon the road, urged on by consuming fear.

The Healer of Guildenwood

It was well after midnight when at last he led the way off the main road to a cottage a hundred yards down a lane behind a stand of trees. Had he not led us there, the darkened dwelling would have been barely noticeable in the shadows. The moon shone from behind a passing cloud, reflecting its light on the windowpanes, yet no light came from within.

Fendred quickly dismounted and tied Avencloe and his horse to a post outside the front door. He hurried to the door and tried to open it, but to no avail. Rapping lightly, he called his wife's name as Rumalia and I joined him on the doorstep, and I could not help but notice the quizzical expression on Rumalia's face as she gazed at the cottage.

"Me poor wife, too sick t' answer the door . . . or wairse." Fendred jiggled the doorknob desperately.

"Do not despair," I said, placing a hand on his shoulder and gently pushing him aside. I stared at the doorknob several moments, all my thought focused on bending it to my will. Suddenly there came from the door the sound of a turning latch. "Try the door again," I urged.

Fendred wiped his damp eyes. He turned the handle once more and the door swung open. "Thanks be t' Omni!" He stepped into the dark parlor where a pile of dying embers glowed in the fireplace. "Helice! Helice, I've retairned!" he called out.

From the bedchamber beyond there came a faint groan. We all three filed into a room where a single candle, lit beside the bed, wavered welcome. "Thank goodness ye've retairned," the middle-aged woman in the bed said weakly as her husband sat down beside her. "I thought ye might be them rough men what come by earlier and rummaged through the barn. I locked meself in, but I'm sure we've a chicken or two what's gone a-missin'."

"Ne'er ye mind about that. I've brought a healer to tend to ye."

I stepped into the candlelight and the woman's eyes grew large when she saw me.

"Bless me soul! An elf in the Guildenwood! 'Tis a good omen indeed."

"This is Miss Arwyn," Fendred explained. "She's considered the greatest 'ealer in Baeren Ford."

"Then I'm sure to be in good 'ands."

"And this is Rumalia, her 'elper," her husband said as she edged in from behind me.

For a moment Rumalia and Helice regarded each other, and an awkward stillness fell upon the room. "What a pretty ghel ye are," Helice said, and Rumalia smiled shyly.

"Tell me, are you still in pain?" I asked as I bent down beside the bed.

"Aye, started in me back, it did, and then it moved to me groin. Been feelin' sick to me stomach as well."

I placed my hand on Helice's brow. "And you have a fever?"

"Aye," the woman replied as her face suddenly contorted in pain.

"What's wrong with me wife, Miss Arwyn?" Fendred asked nervously, wringing his hat in his hands.

"Is anything else the matter?" I asked.

"Aye, I've a great desire to pass water, and when I do there's verra little what comes out, and what does is red with blood," Helice said reluctantly. "Tell me, am I goin' to die?"

I smiled at my patient. "Not anytime soon by the looks of it. It sounds as though a stone has developed in your bladder. It causes a great deal of pain, but should pass within a day or two."

"Thanks be!" Fendred exclaimed. "I dunna know what I'd do without me Helice."

"I told ye, I'm strong as a mule, and not plannin' on leavin' this wairld anytime soon."

"That ye did, woman. I should know to listen to ye by now."

"Rumalia," I said. "I'll need you to put some water on to boil."

"Aye," replied Rumalia. "I'll go and fetch it at the well out back."

Fendred eyed the girl curiously. "And 'ow did ye know there be a well out back?"

Rumalia stopped in her tracks and thought for a moment. "I dunna know," she replied.

"No matter," Fendred shrugged. "If ye fetch the water I'll tend to the hairses and the fire."

While the other two saw to their duties, I prepared a mixture of dandelion and yarrow tea to help cleanse Helice's bladder and bring down her fever. As I waited for the water to boil, my patient cringed as another wave of pain hit. Medicine could only go so far. She would need the Gifts.

"Helice," I said gently, "will you allow me to lay my hands upon your belly for a moment?"

"Ye're the healer. If 'twill 'elp, then do as ye will."

I closed my eyes and clasped my hands together. All activity in the cottage came to a halt as two curious onlookers gathered at the door, watching to see what I would do next.

"*Ochthalia taer analon,*" I began. "*Othelmon inteleth mesonon aeronal!*" A faint glow emanated from the palms of my hands. Fendred, Helice, and Rumalia looked on in wonder as I then placed my hands on the patient's abdomen.

"Such a comfortin' warmth I've not felt afore," Helice said in amazement. "Why, the pain's all but gone!"

"Very good." I smiled. "Now try to get some rest while we wait for the water to boil."

The Healer of Guildenwood

I stood up and walked out of the room past Fendred and Rumalia, who both stared at me with astonishment.

"Er, Miss Arwyn," Fendred said, clearing his throat, "let me show you and Rumalia 'ere to yer room."

Rumalia and I gathered our belongings from the parlor floor and followed Fendred into an adjoining bedchamber. Inside was a double bed that was covered with a pretty green and white quilt. A box full of wooden toys sat in the corner and an old rag doll lay upon the bed.

"'Twas our daughter's room," Fendred explained, as he lit a lantern beside the bed. "But ye kin use it now."

I wondered if perhaps the daughter was deceased or married and moved away. He looked old enough to have a daughter of marriageable age.

Fendred left to tend to the horses. As I rummaged through my knapsack, I looked up and noticed that Rumalia stood by the side of the bed, holding the rag doll curiously in her hands. In her eyes was a faraway look, as if she were lost in a trance.

"Rumalia," I said, "are you not feeling well?"

"I'm . . . fine." Her eyes spoke of something else. Gently she placed the doll back on the bed and walked out.

Morning came much too early for the weary inhabitants of the cottage and their guests. Rumalia made breakfast while I prepared more dandelion and yarrow tea for the patient. The two of us took turns sitting by Helice's side and napping throughout the day. By midday Helice's fever had broken but the dull ache below her belly remained. I urged her to drink more water in addition to the tea, in order to help the stone pass more easily.

In the meantime, Helice seemed to enjoy our company, as female companionship in the absence of a village of any size was a rare treat. Despite her discomfort, she tried hard to maintain a pleasant demeanor, though fretting all the while about not being able to tend properly to her two guests, and enlisting her husband to make sure that no one went hungry. And Fendred was agreeable to helping out as best he could.

It was not until late morning of the next day when Helice's ordeal finally ended with the passing of the stone, much to her husband's relief. The whole event, though, left her weak and weary, and I decided Rumalia and I should stay an extra day to help her get back on her feet. As we all sat around Helice's bedside, the mood was noticeably lighter, and for the first time Fendred showed his jovial side. We discussed all manner of Baeren Ford gossip, and tears came to Helice's eyes when Rumalia told how she, an orphan, had only come to the village days before.

"Such a nice ghel ye are," Helice commented, with a sad look in her eyes. "I 'ad a daughter once."

"Please, tell us of your daughter," I said gently.

Helice's lips quivered slightly as if raw emotions still lingered close to the surface of her consciousness.

Fendred then spoke up as a solemn expression clouded his face. "'Twas o'er fourteen years ago when it 'appened," he began. "Draigon 'ad come to power 'n at the time the seizin' o' children in exchange for the payment o' taxes was a rare occurrence, but there were rumors o' such about the land. One day I was out choppin' firewood when 'e and 'is entourage were travellin' toward Baeren Ford. They stopped to collect taxes, but at the time we'd barely enough to survive ourselves, as me furrier business 'ad suffered from the migration o' pocaburs from the region. One of 'is lieutenants and I were about to come to blows when me little Imala, only three at the time, emerged from the woods where she'd been pickin' flowers. Now, what Draigon can do with a little one such as that is more than I kin understand."

"There's them what would pay a high price who canna have children o' their own," Helice added bitterly. I nodded, recalling how Frondamein once told me that wealthy foreigners often bought the kidnapped children.

"Aye, love," Fendred agreed. "We pleaded 'n fought all we could, but they rode off with me a-runnin' after 'em on me own feet, which were no match for their hairses. Me poor little one was screamin' and cryin' 'er eyes out—'tis a sight what 'aunts me to this day. 'Twas the last we e'er saw of 'er."

"Did you try to find her?" I asked.

"Aye, tried with all me might, I did. But at the time we 'ad no hairse. I 'ad to run to the nearest 'amlet, o'er two miles away, where I searched 'igh and low for someone to lend me one. By the time I found one with a sturdy constitution, precious time 'ad been lost. Travelled all through the night, I did, though ne'er did I find Draigon. Dunna know what I'd 'ave done 'ad I found 'im, but so furious I was, I probably would 'ave killed 'im," he explained, trying to control the emotion in his voice. It was obvious that the pain he felt had never fully healed.

"I rode all the way to Maldimire, where I spent a fortnight wanderin' about the streets, askin' everyone I saw if they'd seen a little ghel with dark hair and a pear-shaped birthmark at the base of 'er neck, but to no avail."

"The whole ordeal took several years off me dear 'usband's life, I'm quite sure," Helice added. "'E's not been the same since."

Suddenly I realized that Rumalia had been unusually quiet for the past several minutes. I looked over at the girl and noticed the blood had drained from my young friend's face. "Rumalia, what troubles you?" I asked.

The young woman stared straight ahead, unseeing. With trembling hand, she then reached up and slowly unbuttoned the top button of her blouse, pulling the fabric aside to reveal a red mark the size of a peanut above her collarbone. Examining the mark more closely, it did not exactly resemble a pear in my mind, yet Fendred and Helice seemed to think it was close enough, based on the stunned looks on their faces.

"Child," Fendred said with shaking voice, "where exactly were ye livin' afore ye come to Baeren Ford?"

Rumalia looked up at him with tear-filled eyes. "Maldimire," she whispered.

"'Tis true, Fendred!" Helice cried. "I knew from the moment I saw 'er eyes she was yer child."

"A miracle it is!" Fendred exclaimed as he slumped to the edge of the bed.

I thought my heart would burst as I witnessed the couple tearfully embrace the young woman for the first time in over a dozen years.

"Dear child," her father said amidst a deluge of tears, "kin ye e'er forgive us for not findin' ye and bringin' ye home all those years ago? What ye must 'ave been through is more than I kin imagine."

Rumalia looked as though she would faint. "'Tis all so sudden, I kin barely believe what's 'appened!"

For several moments tears flowed uncontrollably inside the little room, and no one said a word.

"For years I wondered where it was I come from, and who me parents were," Rumalia sniveled. "Little did I expect to e'er know the truth."

"The ways of Omni are indeed a mystery," I said pensively. "How was it that I happened upon you there in Maldimire, only to experience a chain of events that would eventually lead you to your family? 'Tis more than I can explain."

"'Owever it came about is no matter, for now I have me Imala back." Helice once again embraced her.

"Only now I'm Rumalia," she said quietly. "So much 'as changed. I'm not the wee ghel ye remember . . . Maldimire 'as its way o' changin' a pairson."

"Sadly, the years you were in Maldimire are indeed lost, never to be regained," I said. "Yet you musn't fret over that, for the past cannot be changed."

"But 'ow, if ye were there in Maldimire all along, could I 'ave missed ye?" Fendred said, his mind obviously tormented by years of guilt.

It was then that Rumalia told of her first pale memories in Maldimire, of wandering the city streets alone, the buildings towering above, seeming like mountains to a young child, who had somehow escaped, or been lost from her captors. She recalled being taken in by the spice shop owner, who gave her a place to stay and some semblance of a family, and of growing up quickly on the city streets, learning the harsh realities of life at an early age until at last she was left to fend for herself after her surrogate mother died.

Fendred had a faraway look in his eyes. "'Twas a long, long time ago, and yet I remember me search took me to a small spice shop what sat above the river," he explained. "I remember, due to the fact the woman I talked to seemed a bit skittish and kept glancin' o'er 'er shoulder toward the back o' the store. I thought it odd at the time. Walked with a cane, she did."

"Aye," Rumalia said bitterly. "She fell years ago. The leg ne'er 'ealed proper."

A silence fell in the cabin as a mixture of joys and sorrows too deep to express settled upon those inside. "Well, me darlin' ghel, ye're 'ome now," Helice said at last, placing her arm around Rumalia. "That is, if ye'll 'ave us back."

"Perhaps I should leave the three of you alone for a while," I suggested. "I could use the fresh air, and while I'm gone I could try to find some dinner."

"What a fine idea, Miss Arwyn," Fendred said. "We've much to discuss, and I'm sure 'twould be good for ye to get out for a bit."

Glad for the chance to get away from the cottage for a time, I went to the stable and saddled Avencloe, all the while amazed by the miracle I had been party to. I was not altogether convinced Rumalia was their daughter, though it seemed highly plausible. And, indeed, Rumalia had been acting strangely ever since we arrived, as if being in the cottage had resurrected memories from somewhere deep in her mind. Then again, who was I to question the ways of Omni?

Gathering my cloak about me, quietly I thanked Omni for using me to make the miraculous event come about and stole off into the woods north of the East Road. I followed a small stream and felt exhilarated to be out in the crisp air again. Yet when I thought of departing for Baeren Ford the next morning, the anticipation of returning to a life of looking over my shoulder every few minutes filled me with dread, not to mention having to work my way back into the good graces of the villagers. And, though I did not care to admit it, life in the small village had become rather monotonous.

As the sun sank through the ragged trees to the west, I made my way back toward the cottage with two rabbit carcasses thrown over Avencloe's rump. As I was almost in sight of the road, I heard the faint sound of a flute coming from a small clearing to the west, where the flicker of a fire filtered through the trees.

Curiosity getting the best of me, I altered my course to see who could possibly be making such sweet music. As I approached, I quietly dismounted so as not to disturb whoever camped there and walked stealthily up to the edge of the clearing where I paused in amazement at what I discovered.

The being sitting on the ground with his back to a tree looked almost human, and yet I was sure he was not. His fine golden hair brushed the top of his collar and the delicate features of his face had not one blemish. His thoughtful eyes were the deepest blue and almost shimmered in the light of the fire. And his ears were most definitely pointed. He wore a suit of gray upon his long figure, yet it was not the dark gray of those in Draigon's service, but the gray of a forest covered in cloudy winter's cloak of snow. Nearby stood his horse, a cream-colored creature with a shiny rich coat, saddled and reined with gear intricately decorated with tassels and runes carved into the leather. In an instant I knew that I had stumbled upon an elf, and with that realization my heart skipped a beat.

CHAPTER 31

"He is altogether the most amazing person I have ever had the privilege to meet. So luminescent are his eyes and so enchanting his smile for one who has seen over three centuries in this world. He is a wonder to me."

As if disturbed by the sound of my beating heart, the elf jumped to his feet faster than I could blink. In his hand he drew a sword and held it in the direction of my shadow.

"Show yourself to me now that I may know whether you be friend or foe," he demanded, in the common language of Bensor.

Feeling some regret for having disturbed his fair song, I slowly stepped into the firelight and removed the hood from my head. Upon seeing my face, the elf dropped his sword to the ground and fell to one knee.

"Please, forgive my intrusion," I said. "I was merely hunting in the forest when I came upon your camp. I will leave now if it pleases you."

"Nay, it is I who should beg your forgiveness." The elf picked up his sword from the ground and offered it to me. "Please, if my sword has offended you in the least, then I offer it to you that you may smite me. For I have seen the fairest of all creatures and can now die at peace," he said with a glint of playfulness in his eyes.

"There will be no such need." I laughed. "Tell me, you are an elf, are you not?"

"Yes, fair lady," he said, rising to his feet. "From the depths of Loth Gerodin I come. But we being of likeness, I would have thought you to know your own kind."

"I have lived away from my own kind for many a year, as the elves are now sparse in this region," I said in elvish, glad the wind was not blowing to reveal the all-too-human ears beneath my dark brown hair.

"Yes, pity that it is." The elf sighed. He regarded me curiously. "I am Galamir," he said, bowing low.

"And I am Arwyn."

"Arwyn," he repeated. "Your presence here intrigues me. To meet someone so unexpected is serendipitous indeed! What are you doing in the woods of Guilden? I thought we had all left."

"I came here years ago, from whence, I remember not. A kind man took me in, and I now live with his family."

"An elf living with mortals, now that is indeed an unusual arrangement."

"And what is it that brings you to Guilden?" I said in an attempt to change the subject.

"I seek an old friend of the high elf Valdir Velconium's, a lore master in Baeren Ford. I come with news from Loth Gerodin before the snows of winter."

"Eliendor?" I said, astonished.

"Aye," Galamir answered. "You know of him?"

"I know him well."

"I did not know the lore master to have any friends, so taken to anonymity he is. Why, this is indeed a fortuitous meeting!" Galamir smiled, his eyes shining with merriment. "And yet we are still far from Baeren Ford. Surely you have not come so far afield only to hunt?"

"Nay." I laughed. "I was brought to heal a sick woman, but she is now well, and on the morrow I will return to my home."

"Then perhaps I could accompany you there, seeing as we are both heading in the same direction."

"I would very much enjoy your company. But the hour grows late and although I must return to the cottage, I will invite you to go there with me as the people are kind and could perhaps provide more comfortable sleeping arrangements for a weary traveler than the cold ground."

"That I will do," Galamir replied, "although I am not averse to sleeping on the ground and have done so for more nights than I can even remember."

With that, the elf gathered what few belongings he had and turned toward the fire. *"Oluron achthalma indris!"* he said, and at his word the fire went out.

Eliendor was right—elves did have a knowledge of the Gifts. Was it any wonder that Draigon was so threatened by them?

Nimbly Galamir climbed onto his horse's back and waited patiently as I called to Avencloe. "Never before have I seen such a horse," he commented as Avencloe trotted into the clearing. "'Tis an elvish horse to be sure, and they are full of magic," he added with a note of whimsy.

"I would not doubt it," I replied.

Like wisps of smoke, my new friend and I disappeared through the forest. It was difficult for me to conceal the excitement I felt upon finally meeting one of my own supposed kind, and my heart raced a bit every time I glanced at my escort.

We arrived at the cottage soon afterward, and I entered carrying the two rabbits. Fendred, Helice, and Rumalia looked up and smiled. "We were beginnin' to fear ye'd gotten yerself lost," Fendred said.

With tears in her eyes, Rumalia ran to embrace me. "Dear Miss Arwyn, I've indeed found me home, and that means I willna be joinin' ye on yer retairn to Baeren Ford in the mornin'. Me . . . da will take ye back," she said, and Fendred gave me a broad grin.

"Not to worry," I replied. "I set out to find you a new home, and that has been accomplished, surprisingly well, I would add. And there is no need to trouble you, Fendred, as I have found a traveling companion for my return."

I motioned for Galamir to step inside the cottage. Upon seeing the tall, fair-haired elf, they all gasped. "Yet another elf in Guilden!" Helice exclaimed. "These are strange times indeed!"

"Galamir, at your service," the elf said, bowing low.

"Ye both grace our 'ome with yer presence," Helice said. "Do stay and sup with us, Lord Galamir. We've a momentous occasion to celebrate this eve and would like the company. We've already put some vegetables in the pot to boil, 'n there's bread enough for all. All we need is some fresh meat."

"And that I have. Now rest yourself, Helice, so that your strength will return," I suggested. "Rumalia and I will see to the preparations."

The evening's meal was a merry one as Fendred broke out a bottle of Elwindor wine that had been in his cupboard for ages. There was much talk about Rumalia's miraculous return to their lives and of plans for their future, but I remained intrigued with Galamir and kept glancing at him discreetly throughout the meal. He was altogether different from anyone I had ever known before, and I could not help but smile as the elf acted as though he had known the family for years, so relaxed he seemed. And yet surrounding him was an air of grace and elegance I had not seen in the mortals of Baeren Ford.

That night Rumalia and I shared the bed in her old bedroom while Galamir slept on the floor of the parlor in front of the fireplace.

"I canna believe I'm here in me own house with me own kin," Rumalia said sleepily in the dark. "Could such really be happenin'? What little I remember o' me real parents is like a dark shadow in me mind, and yet there be somethin' familiar about 'em, like wakin' from a nightmare as it were, to find everythin' both different and the same."

"Hmm, and you do have the man's eyes," I replied right before my mind slipped into unconsciousness.

I awoke to find Galamir missing from his spot on the parlor floor, and I wondered if the whole encounter had been nothing more than a dream. However, it was not long before the sound of whistling came from the front lawn, and the fair-haired elf appeared at the front door bearing two handfuls of eggs from the henhouse.

"And a good morning to you, Arwyn," he greeted cheerfully as he entered. "I thought we would need some nourishment for the road."

"A good meal to start the day is always a fine idea," I agreed.

"It looks as though the weather is in our favor, even if other travelers along the road may not be. We'll hope to avoid the less desirable kind."

At the smell of fresh eggs sizzling in a skillet over the fire, the rest of the household stirred. Fendred, Helice, and Rumalia sat down with Galamir and me for a hearty breakfast before sending us on our way.

"Our dear friend," Helice said, as she embraced me on the front lawn. "Ye've not only healed me body, but ye've 'ealed me heart."

"I am but an instrument for bringing about Omni's purpose, as are we all." I smiled, though my heart harbored a twinge of sadness at having to leave Rumalia, for in those past days I found myself growing quite fond of the girl.

"But we're nevertheless in yer debt," Fendred added. "If there e'er be anythin' ye need, anythin' at all, all ye need do is ask."

I nodded quietly and turned to Rumalia.

"How kin I e'er thank ye?" Rumalia said as we embraced. "Ye saved me from a miserable life and gave me back to me family. I've known ye but a few days, though I'll ne'er forget ye."

"Nor I you. And if for any reason you should need me, you know where I can be found."

Rumalia nodded tearfully. "'Twill take some gettin' used to. After all, I've not 'ad real parents for as long as I kin remember, nor 'ave I lived out in the middle o' nowhere, but I'm willin' to give it a try. And they seem to be goodly people."

"Indeed they do," I smiled. "I can see it in their eyes."

"Ye'll tell Kiril farewell for me?"

"That I will. And I'll ask Galamir to bring the rest of your belongings to you on his return north."

"Bless ye, me dearest friend," Rumalia sniffed as she embraced me one last time.

With tears in my eyes, I mounted my horse. Galamir, who had been observing the whole scene respectfully from his mount, nodded his head at the three mortals and turned his horse. And just like that, we were on our way.

It took most of the morning for us to reach our destination, with eyes and ears constantly to the road. Along the way, Galamir spoke tirelessly of his home in Loth Gerodin, describing in great detail the types of trees and plants that were found there, the River Triona that twisted its way under a canopy of green through many, many miles of forest, and the beautiful but hidden elven city of Isgilith, right in the very center of the forest. I was intrigued by his tales from olden times and how he would unexpectedly burst into song when I least expected it. I liked the elf and his amiable demeanor. He reminded me of someone from my long past, someone whose face flickered in my memory like a flame in the wind, someone whom I had loved very much—but lost. Likewise, Galamir treated me with the utmost respect, and it seemed he was in awe of my apparent choice to live among mortals, viewing me as more courageous than certainly I was, considering the growing threat to the south.

By midmorning, when we came to the bog that lay along the East Road, we veered onto the deerpath that eventually led past Kiril's uncle's cottage, thus avoiding whatever eyes may have been watching the main road into town. From there we made our way stealthily to the cottage of Eliendor, where we found him skillfully splitting wood in preparation for the onslaught of winter. The old man looked up as we approached, and there came a twinkle in his eyes.

"Ah, Galamir, old friend! It is good to see you," he said.

Galamir dismounted and greeted Eliendor in the typical fashion of elves, with hands clasped at the level of the chest with palms facing in.

"'Tis indeed good to see you as well!" Galamir exclaimed. "It has been a while, has it not?"

"That it has. And I'll wager there is a reason for your visit. But first, I see that you have found a friend of mine," Eliendor said, turning to me.

"Yes, but it is more the case that she found me."

"I came upon his camp in the woods while making a house call to the east of here," I explained.

"Well, Arwyn, you certainly have a talent for finding extraordinary people in the woods," commented Eliendor. "Now, please, both of you come inside where you will find a warm fire and a pot of freshly brewed tea."

It was a scene all too familiar—sitting in the warmth of Eliendor's cottage, sipping hot tea by the hearth. Yet this time was quite different from all the rest. Galamir's presence had a magical effect; it was as if the whole cottage seemed brighter and cheerier, with every note of his musical laugh and with every glimmer of his luminescent eyes. I was sure I had never met any creature like him before. So human he seemed, and yet so ethereal. For all I knew he could have been several hundred years old, yet he appeared as a youth, discovering the world beyond his forest for the first time.

Eliendor listened intently as I related the entire set of miraculous circumstances surrounding Rumalia's return to her real parents, which I hoped would vindicate my rash actions in Maldimire. And though it had always been difficult to read the lore master's thoughts, the happy ending seemed to have pleased him.

"Tell me, Galamir," Eliendor said, changing the subject as he stirred a cube of sugar into his tea, "is it ill news that brings you on this journey?"

"All is well in the heart of Loth Gerodin, at least, yet how long our peace will last only Omni knows, for the threat of Draigon and that of the unmentionable land to the north grows stronger by the day," Galamir replied. "We may be safe for now in the refuge of our forest, but Ashkar sightings are on the rise along our borders. More and more, Gargalocs and those in the service of Draigon control our major routes to the south through Grandinwolde and Stone Harbour, cutting us off from the rest of Bensor. Our spies have also spotted numerous Gargaloc camps across the border from the Greenwaithe."

"The multiplication of Gargalocs and Ashkars on Bensorian soil is of great concern," Eliendor said with a frown. "Why would he need the derelicts of another country to do his bidding?"

"If only the wall had been completed years ago, that would have provided some protection from their comings and goings," I said.

"Yes, but I am afraid it would have done nothing to protect us from the evil scourge from within our own land," Galamir continued.

"Yes, what of the Bensorian men who are in his service? What do you make of that?"

"Some, like your friend Frondamein, are in his service against their will, yet there are other Bensorians who have given themselves over to him, traitors that they are," Galamir answered. "However, by far the majority of his followers are from the lowlands of Ashkaroth, and among those alone are his most trusted lieutenants. You see, not all in that country are as foul as those who were spawned in the mountains. There are many pockets of mortals living on the plains north of the Guildenmoor Gate, though a strange lot they are—shifty and mistrustful, corrupted by many long years of living under the reign of their faceless queen."

Eliendor's expression was grave as he arose from his chair and walked to the window that looked out over his front lawn. He remained silent for several moments, appearing deep in anguished thought. "And so it is true that there is a definite link between Draigon and the north, as I had feared."

"There must be a reason, but that we have not yet determined."

Suddenly my mind returned to that conversation I had overheard in the Palace of Lords, the conversation that had chilled me to the bone in a way that no winter day could. "Before I was questioned by Draigon, before he sent me to Dungard, I chanced upon a conversation between him and a very suspicious old man," I said, piquing the interest of Galamir, who had not heard of my unintended feud with the ruler of the land. I went on to recount the whole, sordid affair for both their sakes, right up to the moments after I was arrested, and as I spoke Eliendor's brow sank deeper into a frown.

"They made reference to 'her,' whom I can only assume was Dar Magreth, and I had the feeling the old man was on his way to deliver a message to her. There was also a discussion on who would share her throne, and . . . and they both sounded very cross with one another."

"What did you see of this old man?" Galamir asked worriedly.

"Only his hand. A cloak concealed him, and he was so bent over that I did not get a look at his face."

"Whoever he was, I'd daresay he is no friend to Bensor." Eliendor sighed.

"Frondamein would know of him if he enters Ashkaroth through the Gate," I offered, "unless he enters by other ways."

"Unless he travels far out of his way through the Greenwaithe, there are no other routes into Ashkaroth."

I let out a sigh and shook my head. "I often wonder when the Bensorian people will take charge of their own destiny and take a stand against the growing threat."

"Ah, Arwyn, now you bring me to the purpose of my visit."

"You bring news of the Alliance?" Eliendor said.

My ears pricked up. "What alliance?"

Galamir took a sip of his tea and gave me a smile. "The Alliance is an underground movement of elves and men formed to address our common enemy. It started not too many years ago by a group of mortals from Lake Gildaris who have connections with the elves of Loth Gerodin, and it now thrives in safe havens throughout the land. Our purpose is to determine the exact nature of Draigon's connection to the north, his plans for Bensor, and how to overthrow his reign when the time is right."

"I always thought the Bensorian people a bit too complacent," I commented. "It is a relief to know that someone is taking charge against the tyranny we have been under for so long. Yet, how exactly is such a plan to be carried out?"

"Even as we speak, weapons are quietly being stockpiled all over Bensor for our eventual rebellion. However, it will take a coordinated effort, and much planning is yet to be done."

"And it is hoped that Draigon will not pounce first."

"What do you mean, Eliendor?" I asked.

"I cannot foretell Draigon's intent for Bensor and what secret plans he may have, but I fear something is afoot," Eliendor said.

"Indeed, he did say something foreboding to me when I was in his palace . . . something about wanting me to have a front row seat to what he has in store."

Silence descended in the small cottage as we pondered this new revelation. My mind traveled back to that unfortunate episode in the Palace of Lords. What of that phrase I had heard Draigon utter, the same one I had heard Eliendor recite long ago? "Eliendor," I said curiously, "Draigon repeated a phrase I had heard once before . . . something about the 'shadow of Arnuin's Hold.'"

Eliendor sat back in his chair, visibly surprised by my question. He remained silent for several moments, and then with a faraway look in his eyes, he said:

> "From the shadow of Arnuin's Hold
> Where river bends and reeds shine gold,
> Elwei's heir shall wake the light
> Of Veritana's stone so bright.
> The one its Sword in pureness wield,
> E'en now doth hold that light concealed
> Until the day when sound shall blast
> From Arnuin's horn of days long past.
> And he whose face for so long veiled,
> Shall relish as his words prevail,
> And there upon the vacant throne
> At last his work will be made known.
>
> Come starlight 'neath the mountains old,
> More precious than silver, rubies, gold.
> Two cities which to sight contrast,
> Below the surface, hidden fast
> The Sword their natures now reveal
> With justice, mercy, goodness heal."

"So many riddles," I mused.

"Aye, but one thing is clear," Eliendor said slowly. "It has been said that the true ruler of Bensor will emerge from beneath the fortress Elwei and Arnuin built together, a little known facet of Amiel's prophecy that has remained forgotten for years, or so I thought. I had no inkling Draigon was aware of it," he added grimly.

"And so that is why he grew suspicious when he heard of a man living in Baeren Ford who possibly possessed the Gifts." My eyes brightened with understanding. "Why, it even seemed he suspected *me* . . ."

I saw a glint of fear flash in Eliendor's eyes as his hand clasped the arm of his chair. "That is, until his chief lieutenant reminded him that the prophecy refers to a man." And then, yet another revelation came to mind. "And that is why his lieutenants come to the village from time to time, searching for men of age, who could possibly challenge the Sword."

"You are correct," Eliendor said with solemnity.

I could not help but smile as I thought of the simple, peaceable peasants who lived in the village. "Speaking strictly between the three of us, I know of no young man in the village who is up to the task! Why, they suspected poor Taryck and beat him for it, yet I know of none more reckless than he. Hardly a good ruler would he make," I said thoughtfully. "And then there is Kiril. There is none finer. He is trustworthy and brave, yet averse to much attention and with no aspiration for such acclaim."

"Such might render him all the more suitable," Eliendor added, with a rather mysterious gleam in his eyes.

"And yet that is truly ill news," Galamir said somberly. "For the days grow darker, and the land of Bensor is in need of its ruler now more than ever."

Eliendor looked deep into his cup of tea and swished around the leaves that remained puddled at the bottom. "Perhaps the true ruler will be the person you expect the very least."

I was still not entirely certain I believed in the old prophecy, yet at such a time, why would I not cling to anything that would give me hope? But what hope did it *really* offer? It seemed the only real hope Bensor had at present was this Alliance Galamir spoke of, and I wanted to hear more.

"If only there was something I could do to help with the Alliance."

At my musing, Galamir's face brightened and he smiled at me, as if the gravity of our conversation had been nothing but a passing annoyance. "An elf living among mortals in this day and age—now that is indeed a fortuitous opportunity! Among all elves, you, my dear Arwyn, have a rather unique perspective, one that could surely be useful as we seek to strengthen the ties between elves and men."

My heart beat a little faster at the suggestion. "Perhaps this is the task I have been meant for all along," I muttered, half to myself and half to Eliendor and Galamir, "to help in whatever way I can in such an important cause."

"Arwyn, would you be averse to accompanying me back to my home in Isgilith? My mother, father, and I would be honored for you to stay with us for a while." Galamir stopped to watch as the smile spread upon my face. "You say it has been ages since you have been with your own kind. It may do you well to visit with the elves of Loth Gerodin, and perhaps even come to dwell with us if you like."

I dared not look to see Eliendor's reaction. I could only guess what he would think, and I did not want to be restricted by his disapproval. Indeed, after the events of those previous days, I had begun to wonder deep in my heart if my time in the mortal village *should* soon come to an end. I liked Galamir very much, and the idea of living in a place where I could blend in was appealing. And yet, my heart grew heavy at the thought of leaving Loralon, Eliendor, and Kiril forever. Besides, how could I be of service to anyone while stuck in the depths of Loth Gerodin?

The smile upon my face disappeared, my hopes for a new adventure fading as my sense of duty nagged. "To visit the elves of Loth Gerodin and to witness the beauty of that forest would be an honor. But to dwell there permanently . . . well, that is something I cannot consider at present, at least . . . not until Amerigo is grown, or Frondamein is released from his duties, until I am no longer needed . . . or wanted here."

"It would be well for you to holiday in Loth Gerodin, and all's the better the sooner you leave!" I turned to the lore master, who had been particularly quiet those past moments and was surprised by the force of his resolve.

"Arwyn"—he stared at me gravely—"it is no longer safe for you here in Baeren Ford. With all that has transpired these past days, Draigon could still very well find cause to arrest you. And yet . . . you speak the truth when you say that your purpose here is not yet complete."

"But Loralon, Amerigo—I cannot leave them for the winter. I gave my word to Frondamein that I would look after them. I cannot simply go off gallivanting to Loth Gerodin on a whim with winter coming on!"

"I could come for you when the snows of winter have passed and the spring has come," Galamir said excitedly.

"Aye, but I fear for you, at least until this whole mess you brought upon yourself in Maldimire passes, if ever." Eliendor sighed and gave a shrug of surrender. "Though, I suppose the will of Omni will have its way, regardless of what we do to muddle things."

I was not exactly certain what Eliendor meant, but a solution did occur to me. "Fendred and Helice," I said, to which Galamir responded with a knowing nod. "Perhaps they will make good on their promise. I could stay with them until the snows hit in late autumn and it is safe to return to Baeren Ford when strangers rarely take to our roads. Loralon could let on that I have left indefinitely, and she would speak the truth."

"It could work, at that," Galamir said thoughtfully.

"Aye, that it could," Eliendor agreed.

"And you could arrive when Loth Gerodin is in its full glory, perhaps in time for the Faerenfel."

"The Faerenfel?" I asked.

"'Tis our springtime celebration, much like your Spring Festival. Only for one magical night, all the creatures of the forest come together to celebrate the rebirth of the world. 'Tis quite a spectacle to behold!"

I glanced from Eliendor to Galamir as the smile returned to my face. "Then it is settled," I announced. "I shall require one day to manage my affairs, and then the day after tomorrow I shall disappear for a time."

But there was something more, something beyond my safety or even the need to see what lay beyond Guilden that fueled my desire to go on holiday, and it had to do with my hurt pride. If I were to disappear for a while, perhaps the people of Baeren Ford would come to truly appreciate me and discover that I was not such a liability after all.

CHAPTER 32

"I canna understand!" I could see tears forming in Loralon's eyes that evening when I broke the news that I would be leaving for several weeks to stay with Fendred and Helice. "Ye needn't wairry what th' others say! There's sympathy growin' for ye, seein' as ye stepped in and saved the poor lass, and there'll always be them what willna like anyone they think a bit odd."

Loralon must have immediately realized her blunder, for she grew quiet. So it was true—they still saw me as odd.

My eyes narrowed defiantly. "The reason matters not. 'Tis better for your safety and for mine the less you know, but you must tell *anyone* who cares to ask that I have left and that you do not know when I shall return, if ever." Seeing Loralon's eyes fill with tears once more, I softened a bit. "Please, do not be dismayed, I shall be but a few miles away and will return ere winter. However . . ." I stopped, not exactly sure the best way to break my next bit of news delicately. "Galamir has asked me to go on holiday with him to Loth Gerodin come spring, and you must know that I mean to go with him . . . but only for a month, and then I shall return."

Loralon nodded and pursed her lips as understanding set in. "Verra well. 'Twill be good for ye to get out and see the wairld. We'll make do without ye if need be."

"Come," I said, giving my friend an embrace. "You are my family—how could I leave you forever?" Though the words escaped my lips, deep in my heart I was not altogether certain I could really make such a promise.

"What a dear ye are." Loralon sniffed as she put on a brave smile. "Now, about the new clothes for Goodren and Hutto—finished 'em today, I did."

"Then I'll be sure to deliver them tomorrow."

"'Tis a pity they couldna find a way 'ome ere the winter," Loralon said as she set the table. "But I suppose they'll fare as well as kin be expected, under the saircumstances."

Loralon's comment gave me an idea, an idea that tickled my mind and would not let me rest until the following morning when I went into the forest to Eliendor's cottage. There I found Galamir sitting on the bench outside with a blood-red cardinal perched on his finger. He looked up with smiling eyes as I approached. "Salutations, Arwyn!"

"And a good morning to you."

"A good morning it is indeed! There's the scent of frost in the air." He laughed and took in a deep breath, looking up into the sky beyond the nearly bare branches that hung overhead. "How exhilarating it is!"

"And where is our friend, Eliendor?"

"Our dear friend is not taking well to the cold. He chooses to stay indoors next to the fire."

"And perhaps we should join him there later, but for now a walk would do me well. Would you care to join me?"

"A splendid idea, Arwyn. I must say that after days of riding, the thought of getting around on my own two feet for a bit is a good one."

For a long while we walked in the forest speaking of many things, until I told him of the plight of my three friends, the dwarves.

"And so you would wish to see these dwarves back to their home," Galamir said pensively as he sat on a tree stump.

"That is correct," I replied, thoroughly expecting that my new friend would be opposed to my dangerous notion.

"'Twill be a rather risky proposition, to be sure," he said. "And yet it could be done. Perchance, may I meet these friends of yours?"

I could feel an excited smile light up my face. "As a matter of fact, they live not far from here."

I whistled softly three times as we approached the dwarves' cave. In a moment, a bearded face wearing a dark green hat appeared at the entrance. It was Hutto. "Come, come." He motioned, glancing around nervously. "There were hunters about earlier."

Galamir waited outside as I bent over and cautiously slipped through the low passageway. "Good day, dear friends," I greeted. "I apologize for being a bit detained these past days, though I hope Froilin is settling in comfortably."

"Aye," he responded. "'Tis a bit cramped, though I'd choose it o'er Dungard in a heartbeat."

"Perhaps this will make you even more comfortable." I held out the bundle of clothing Loralon had made, hoping Froilin was of nearly the same proportions as his friends.

"Ah, now I shall not freeze," Froilin said, taking the clothing from me, "and I shall be happy to look a bit more respectable."

"And I have brought with me someone who may be able to help you," I added as Galamir emerged from the cave's entrance. The three dwarves looked up in alarm at the tall, fair-haired elf. "Dear friends, I would like to introduce you to Galamir."

"Another elf!" Goodren wailed. "'Twill bring doom on us for sairtain!"

"Hush yerself!" Hutto warned. "Do ye not trust Miss Arwyn? She'd not bring anyone here what means us ill."

Galamir let out a loud laugh that echoed throughout the cave and the old dwarf's complexion changed to bright red. "You must be Goodren."

"That I am," the dwarf said dubiously.

The two other dwarves came forward and bowed respectfully.

"Hutto at your service."

"Froilin at your service."

"My, what a motley-looking group of fugitives you have here, Arwyn. I can see why they are so desperate to return home."

"What do ye know of us and our troubles?" said Goodren.

"Enough to know that three dwarves cannot remain hidden in Guildenwood without eventually raising suspicion. The sooner we can see you to the Andains, the better."

"Ye mean to retairn us to our home?" Hutto said excitedly.

"That I do," Galamir promised, "but I will require the help of Arwyn, and she will not be returning with me until the spring. Do you think the three of you can survive the winter in this small cave?"

The three dwarves looked at each other and nodded. "Aye," Froilin said. "We're accustomed to livin' under the ground."

"Very well, but the question of 'how' still remains." Galamir scratched his head for a moment, deep in thought. His face brightened. "Arwyn, do you think you could have two coffins made?"

"I have friends in the village who could arrange such a thing," I replied.

"Good. They will need to be of elvish size, large enough to hide three dwarves, and to latch from the inside."

"Now, wait a minute," Goodren protested. "There's no way ye'll be gettin' me int' a coffin. For all we know, 'twill end up bein' our deathbeds for real."

"Do ye want to return home or don't ye?" Froilin said. "'Tis a desperate measure to be sure, but it may be all we have."

"We'll need a cart large enough for the coffins and a small but strong horse to pull it," Galamir said, ignoring the debate. "'Twill make the going slow, perhaps lengthening our journey by a day or two. Yet I have found mortals to be rather superstitious regarding matters of death. They would likely not examine our load too closely. And should they ask, we will tell them that we are returning our kinsmen to their homeland after they met with an unfortunate accident abroad."

"It sounds as though it is your best hope, unless you would rather go it alone or take your chances by remaining here," I commented, looking directly at Goodren.

The three dwarves stared at each other for a long moment, and a wave of agreement passed between them.

"We'll go!" Hutto announced.

"It is settled then," Galamir said.

"But sir, why would you, an elf, risk your own freedom for the likes of us dwarves?" asked Froilin.

Galamir stared for a long moment at the shadows that danced on the far wall of the cave. "A great injustice has been done you and to your kind for many years, far greater even than the injustice many of my kind have faced, forced to leave our ancestral homes to the south. If I can have a part in avenging the wrong that has been done to you, then that is what I wish to do."

"We thank ye, we do," Hutto added. "And indebted to ye we'll always be."

Galamir and I returned to Eliendor's home where we enjoyed tea and sandwiches in front of his warm fire. There we revealed our plan. The lore master merely sighed and shook his head. "You'll do what you will do. It is in Omni's hands, though I do not think it wise," was all he said.

That evening Galamir and Eliendor made their way to the cottage of Frondamein as the daylight waned. Throughout our meal, it was clear that Loralon was in awe of the handsome and enchanting elf who sat at her table and played with her son with almost childlike glee. So rare it was for such people to be seen in Baeren Ford, and here both of us were, dining at her table! The merry elf seemed likewise to enjoy himself, laughing, singing, and telling tales of Emraldein in its early days.

"*You* have been to Emraldein?" I asked with amazement.

"An elven lad I was at the time," Galamir said. "My father took me there to see the beautiful artistry at the castle. I'll never forget how it felt to walk through the gardens and to smell the mingling of salt air and plumeria on the warm sea breezes. The castle was immense, with hundreds of rooms built on terraces that overlooked the blue Eleuvial. And the Eleuvial—'twas in the days before Prince Ravrik and his colony fled . . ."

"Prince Ravrik?"

"Aye, the leader of the merpeople who made their home in the shallow waters of the bay. The elves of the sea, they are, yet with the coming of the beast, even they fled to far-off waters."

Merpeople? Now that would take a while to ponder! Yet there were a thousand more questions spinning round my head.

"And the wizard? Did ye e'er see 'im?" Loralon asked, her eyes brimming with wonder.

"Amiel?" Galamir answered. "Aye, and larger than life he seemed to me at the time. Rarely did he make an appearance on the castle grounds, preferring to remain inside Emraldein's highest tower, where he gazed at the stars and immersed himself in his books. But when he presented himself, all who saw him stopped and took notice, for he had a presence about him that emanated power and wisdom."

Loralon and I listened intently, enchanted, as Galamir described what he remembered of the castle. And I wondered how the elf, with his youthful appearance, could have been alive before it was besieged by the enemy. Why, that would make him over three hundred years old!

And then I remembered what Eliendor had told me about elves, that they were *mostly* incorruptible, yet how each one harbored some sort of vice that rendered them slightly imperfect. Well, Galamir certainly seemed perfect—bright, chipper, kind-hearted, loyal. I felt safe with him, as if in him I had found someone who would do anything to protect me. But I wondered what *his* vice was.

As if reading my mind, Eliendor, who had been sitting quietly at the table, puffing away on his pipe with amused interest at Galamir's stories, leaned over to me. "Never will you find one more in love with this land than he. Aye, Galamir will see you safely to your friends' home on the morrow, and he will be true to his word and come for you in the spring."

Later, after our company had departed, Loralon collapsed upon the settee. "I daresay I ne'er dreamed I'd entertain such people me entire life. Arwyn, ye've tairned thin's topsy-turvy since ye arrived a while back," she said, adding, "and I dunna know whether to thank ye or to shake ye," to which I could only smile. It filled me with gratitude to know that to her, at least, and to my other friends, I was not a liability but one who had brought a degree of joy to them all.

As for the others, did it truly matter if they still thought me odd or looked upon me with suspicion? If being odd meant befriending the likes of Galamir or a wise old man who knew more about the mysteries of life than all the villagers combined, if it meant saving three poor souls from a ruthless dictator or bringing health to the bodies of countless hardworking neighbors, then let it be said that I was the weirdest of them all!

The next morning dawned all too early after an evening that had provided a bit of a diversion to the sadness surrounding my imminent departure. Kiril arrived before sunrise, having volunteered to help transport Rumalia's few belongings to her, after her hasty departure several evenings before, and a sack of books from Eliendor's stash that would help me bide the time until I could return to Baeren Ford.

Trying to be brave for Loralon's sake, I held back my tears as I embraced her and a sleepy Amerigo, all the while reminding her that I would only be gone until the snows set in.

Then Galamir, Kiril, and I set off across the main road, over the island bridges at the south end of the lake, and past Kiril's uncle's cottage on the deerpath that eventually led us to the East Road.

It was late morning when we arrived at Fendred and Helice's cottage, where we found Fendred outside chopping wood as we rode up.

"Miss Arwyn, Mr. Galamir, 'tis a surprise indeed to see ye so soon!" he greeted. "Helice, Ima . . . Rumalia, come see who's retairned!"

In a matter of moments, Helice and Rumalia came outside, bundled against the chill, appearing both surprised and delighted to see us. "What brings ye back so soon?" Helice asked.

"If I may, I come in search of that favor you promised," I replied.

"Aye, what is it ye need?" asked Fendred.

"A place for me to stay for a time, until the winter when it will be safe for me to return to Baeren Ford."

Fendred rubbed his chin. "As this to do with a sairtain renegade dwarf?"

I nodded. Obviously, Rumalia had apprised them of our *entire* adventure in Maldimire.

"Then what be ye waitin' for? Come on in out o' the cold!" he exclaimed.

"Aye, we've an extra mattress in the barn. We'll air it out, and it should do ye fine!" added Helice.

Relief washed over me, knowing I had found a safe refuge beyond Draigon's grasp—at least for a time.

"I didna have the chance to thank ye, nor to wish ye farewell," Rumalia said to Kiril as he handed over her sack of belongings.

Kiril's cheeks turned red, or was it simply the cold air? "Nay, nor I you." The young man cleared his throat. "Though I'm glad ye found yer folks."

Helice ushered us all inside where a pot of lentil soup simmered above the fire. After we were sufficiently full, I escorted Kiril and Galamir out to the main road. The time had come for them to go, each their separate ways.

With promises to come for me when the snows came and if the danger from Draigon's minions had passed, I gave Kiril one last embrace and sent him on his way to the west. I then turned to Galamir, who took my hands in his. "My dear friend, Arwyn, these past few days have been a pleasure."

"I cannot express what they have meant to me," I replied, tears in my eyes. His hands were so warm, as were his merry eyes. "I look forward to the day when you return to Baeren Ford."

"Spring is but a moment away, and when it arrives I shall take you to a place more wondrous than you can imagine."

I returned his smile. "I shall count the days. Until then, fare thee well on your journeys, and may you return safely when the snows thaw."

With that, Galamir turned and mounted his horse. Nodding his head and smiling at me one last time, he turned and rode away to the east.

"I stand and watch, glancing back and forth, as both my friends disappear from view, the one returning to the old, familiar life I have grown so accustomed to, a life of fragile mortality, in both its crudeness and in those moments when beautiful simplicity shine through. A life I somehow feel will soon be only a part of my past.

"Yet as I turn and watch Galamir disappear into the east, I wonder if I am peeking at my future, a future of wonder and adventure in a place I cannot yet fully imagine. I pray nothing prevents his return in the spring, for my heart quickens at the thought of journeying to his city. And I think perhaps . . . perhaps . . ."

"Perhaps what?" It had been a long while it seemed, since I had heard from Dr. Susan, the woman so near and yet so far away. How much time had passed since I had entered her presence I did not know.

"Perhaps visiting the city will at last illuminate my true nature," I replied. "But there is more."

"Oh?"

"I know now, that there are those willing to stand up to tyranny, to fight for the freedom of this fair land, and I mean to be a part of it. Though being a healer and looking after Loralon are both noble pursuits, in my heart I am certain that *this* is the reason for which I was brought to Bensor."

"You sound as though you have at last found your purpose."

"Indeed. For whatever reason Omni so deemed it, I know in my heart that I was brought to Bensor to help bring about Draigon's downfall. Though what role I shall play to that end, whether through the Alliance or by some other means, I have yet to discover. Of one thing, however, I am certain—Draigon's reign on this land must end."

—END OF BOOK ONE

Now that you have finished reading, I would appreciate a review on Amazon. Thanks!

COMING IN 2017:

THE SECRET OF ARNUIN'S HOLD,

Book Two of THE SOULTREKKER CHRONICLES

An incredible journey to the elven realm forces Arwyn to choose between the yearnings of her heart for a valiant but flawed foreigner and her pledge to aid the Alliance in the coming rebellion against Draigon—a choice that will determine the fate of Bensor.

If you would like to know more about The Soultrekker Chronicles and Mary E. Calvert, please visit www.thesoultrekker.com